Falling Up
the Stairs

R.C. Hartson

Black Rose Writing | Texas

First printing

ISBN: 978-1-68433-120-8
PUBLISHED BY BLACK ROSE WRITING
www.blackrosewriting.com

Printed in the United States of America
Suggested Retail Price (SRP) $22.95

Falling Up the Stairs is printed in Book Antiqua

For my beautiful wife, Lynie. Without her continuing encouragement, understanding and love, this book would have never been possible.

Thank you Marcia Snowden Hulce for your expertise and edits.

A special thanks to Rob Carr of *The Write Stuff* for having my back with final edits and so much more.

The author would like to acknowledge siblings, Roberta, Mitchell, Merrill, and Brian Hartson as well as Cathy Deskins and Johnny Gaines, all of whom struggled to conquer the challenging stairs.

Falling Up
the Stairs

Chapter One

I t was unusual for a car to be parked in front of the house, especially if you lived on a side street. Very few people drove by, and when they did, Joey stared until they were out of sight.

It was a special event, indeed, for a six-year-old boy whose family had no car. Most automobiles in the area were black and had an ominous look, especially the sedans. Joey was fascinated with the one parked very close to their front porch. They had company.

He spotted it from a block away after he rounded the corner on his way home from school. He moped along, taking his time, then, seeing the car, he began to run into the April wind that was colder than it should have been. It felt like the skin on his face was being stretched over his head like a mask and his heart pounded as if there were a bass drum inside his chest until he reached his front door.

Inside, the house was as quiet as an early Sunday morning. He quickly kicked off his shoes, wrestled out of his jacket, and tossed it on a chair in the living room, before rushing into the dining room.

A woman sat at the dining room table with Joey's mother, his grandma and nine-year-old sister. The woman was a stranger — at least Joey had never seen her before. Cups of coffee sat in front of the three women.

Grandma Lillian had the dining room window cracked open; the curtains fluttered with the strong breeze. The tick-tock of the pendulum on her favorite clock sounded loud in the silence of the room. They all eyed Joey when he made his, out-of-breath, entrance.

The stranger, who appeared rather short and plump, wore a blue dress with a long-sleeved yellow and green sweater draped around her shoulders. Her hair was tied back in a no-nonsense manner, accentuating the clean line and determined set of her jaw.

6

"Joey, come sit here with us," said his mother, Alice, a big-boned woman, was overweight and it was obvious that she had given up on her hair and makeup. The print dress she wore fit her like a gunnysack and was so wash-worn one could see the outline of her undergarments through the fabric.

Just for a moment, there was a brightening in her hazel eyes, a hidden thought working behind the irises like a busy insect. She feigned a smile and looked about her, as though an answer for her predicament might be found in another room. "Come and sit," she said, as she patted the seat of the chair next to her.

His sister, Beth's hands were folded in her lap and her shoulders trembled. Her head was bowed, as if she were saying grace and her face was beet red.

Joey slid onto the chair. His mother ran her fingers through his hair and stroked his head. She appeared to be in a daze as she brushed his untamed hair back off his face. Her eyes traced the movements of her hand, avoiding her son's eyes.

"Joey, I want you to meet Mrs. Kellogg. She's a very nice lady who's here to help us." There were two cocoa mugs on the table; one in front of Beth, and Alice slid one over in front of Joey.

His eyes focused on the stranger who reached out, offering her hand and a smile that was stiff and demonstrated little effort or meaning. Her face was furrowed and white, like a bleached prune; it seemed to be twisted in an expression of chronic impatience and irritability. She wore black-rimmed glasses, but removed them and pinched the red marks on the bridge of her nose. "Hello, Joseph. I am pleased to meet you. How was school today?"

Joey gave her a limp hand and managed a nod. "Hello, Ma'am."

He looked at his mother, and then back to the woman. He noticed his grandmother's wrinkled hands squeezing a hankie; her eyes wet with tears.

"What's the matter, Gram? What happened?" He shifted on his chair. There was a pause echoed by more silence as he looked at his sister.

"Sis? What's wrong?"

Beth shook her head.

Alice's face went slack. Her eyes were filled with fear and pity. She stared into space, like someone who heard sounds others did not. Her eyes glistened.

Taking a handkerchief out of her pocket, she held it in a tight ball, looked at the ceiling as though searching for the right words, and then shook her head because they weren't there.

"Joey," Alice finally blurted, "we've already explained to Beth that Gram and Gramps haven't got much money left. With the war and all, things are hard for them, you know that, don't you?" She paused and leaned in. "You see the rationing, son, and you know your daddy is still away in the war. God knows when that will end. I pray it will be soon."

"Amen," Grandma murmured.

"Indeed," said Mrs. Kellogg.

"Oh, what's the use, Joey, I might as well tell you right out," said Alice. Her voice cracked. "Gram and Gramps can't afford to keep all of us anymore." She looked to nine-year-old Beth for approval. "You kids are going to live with some nice people over in Massina until your daddy comes home and we get things straightened around."

Mrs. Kellogg feigned a smile.

Joey shoved his chair back and stood up. It scraped across the wooden floor sounding like the bark of a seal. "No! I don't want to. Why do we have to?" he screamed.

His voice sounded hoarse, and he began to cry as he looked at his sister. "Tell them, Sis. We can't leave here. You know that. Please! Tell them!"

"Joey, I . . ." Beth began.

"Kids, I'm so sorry," Alice interrupted. Tears formed in her eyes and rolled down her cheeks. She lowered her head, and Joey could no longer see the tears, but he watched her shoulders shake as his mother covered her face with both hands and sobbed.

Gram seldom wore her false teeth, and her cheeks collapsed inward on her jawbones; consequently her expression seemed to be one of anger. Her face appeared to be masked with frustration, but her eyes filled with tears. "Oh, God help me," she moaned.

Alice stood and leaned on the table. "Joey, I just told you why, son. Mommy can't do anything about it. You know I've been sick." She dabbed her eyes with the handkerchief. "I can't work, and now Gram and Gramps have run out of money. I wouldn't send you away from here if I could help it. You must know that, Son." She looked at Beth. "I'm so sorry, Beth. I don't want to do this, but it's really the best thing for both of you, right now."

"How long will we be there?" Beth asked. "You didn't tell us that."

"Oh, I wish we knew, honey. I wish we knew," said Grandma, as she patted Beth's hand. Her voice grated like a rusty gate. She wiped her eyes. "As soon as your daddy comes home, I promise, we'll bring you back home."

"No! We're not going! We can't go, Mommy." Joey buried his face in his mother's dress, his sobs, nonstop. His thin little arms wrapped around her legs, seeking shelter. He continued to scream for someone or something to change their minds: "Please, Mommy! Please let us stay here! We don't want to go! I'll be good, I promise!"

He looked to his grandmother. "Gram? Please? Please! Don't send us away." For a moment, he couldn't breathe. His windpipe tightened, starving his lungs of air. He stared at his grandmother for a beat. "Does Gramps know?"

Gram lowered her eyes and blew her nose. "Yes, Joey, Gramps knows. He had to work or he'd be here."

Joey shook his head. "Well, let's just wait until Gramps comes home — okay? Maybe he'll say no. We just can't go... let's wait, okay? I have to help him with the garden, remember?"

Alice embraced her son's head in her arms and pressed it to her body, perhaps to comfort herself more than him. Her pale face, replete with anguish, was the picture of defeat. She rubbed the top of his head as if she were washing it without water.

"What about our clothes?" Beth whispered.

"Gram and I already packed your things, honey." She pointed to a small suitcase and several grocery bags over by the cellar door.

Mrs. Kellogg scooted her chair back. She looked the way people do when they're waiting for someone to get off the phone. "I'm afraid we must be going," she said as she stood and used both hands to smooth the back of her dress.

Joey's body heaved; his hands squeezed his mother's hand, refusing to let go. "No! Let's wait for Gramps. Please, Mommy. Please?" he pleaded.

"I'll get the bags," said Alice. "Beth, come give me a hand, will you?" She pried the boy away from her. "Let me get the bags, Joey."

Joey was the last one out of the house when their things were carried to the car.

Mrs. Kellogg unlocked her trunk and helped with putting the bags inside. The Gunderson's dog began to bark from their yard next door.

Alice gave her children one last hug before she helped them into the back seat of the Packard and closed the door. Before she got in, Mrs. Kellogg waved goodbye over her shoulder with her fingers. She smiled like a little girl who didn't want to offend. When she backed her car out onto the street, the kids got on their knees and looked out the back window, taking a last look at their home on Depot Street.

The afternoon sun was beginning to dip below the trees as Gram cried and waved. She slipped her arm around Alice's waist as they turned back to the house. Alice's shoulders shook under her baggy dress.

Chapter Two

Riding in a car was a special treat for any kid in 1942. It was a nervous miracle, but there was none of the ordinary excitement attached to that first experience for Beth and Joey. They held hands and huddled shoulder to shoulder in the back seat. Folders and books were piled on the front seat, and there was a strong smell of perfume in the car.

Joey began to cry again, so Beth put her arm around his sagging shoulders and squeezed. Her insides trembled, but she managed to hold back her tears. She whispered and patted her brother's leg. "It will be all right, Joey. Don't cry."

Mrs. Kellogg ignored them as she drove through Gouvernuer. It was a town of narrow streets, a single traffic light, and very few small shops. A line of railroad tracks was grafted onto Main Street like ancient sutures.

It all seemed so odd to the youngsters. Perhaps they were getting their last look at Dilby's small grocery store with a neon Wonder Bread sign in the window. The barber shop was sandwiched in between an A- OK Chevrolet Car Dealership and the First National Bank. Woolworths five and dime was located next to the diner.

On their way out of town they passed the ancient brick firehouse, painted lead-gray, that stood on the corner of Main and highway fifty-three. City Hall was right next door, with the cannon and pyramid pile of its balls displayed out front. When they passed by the Adams Elementary School, Joey suddenly pressed his nose against the window, then fell back in the seat and whimpered.

Mrs. Kellogg eyed him in the rear-view mirror. Her face, somewhat twisted, made her appear as though she was smelling a pair of dirty socks. Tapping her fingers on the steering wheel, she said, "Joseph, it won't do any good to cry. It's best you listen to your sister, now. You don't hear her crying, do you?"

"We don't want to go away." Joey pounded his fists on his knees. "My Gramps didn't say it was okay, either. I just know he wouldn't let us go."

"Oh, my goodness, son, the Couzens are a very warm and loving family. You'll see." Her voice was without variation, a tired monotone, as if there were nothing worth saying. "Just settle down now and we'll be there before you know it." She paused as her mirrored eyes focused on him. "These folks have a boy of their own, you know. His name is Richard and he's just about your age, I believe. You two should get along just fine." Joey rubbed his eyes and looked out the window.

They passed jagged rows of trees on both sides of the road, and wide, grassy ditches appeared deep and soggy. Farmhouses, barns, forests and brown cornfields were all there was to see, except for infrequent small towns with either four-way stops or blinking caution lights. Even though it was April, splotches of stubborn snow still clung to some fields along the way.

Darkness would be closing in soon. A long stream of clouds, like curls of lavender smoke, flowed for miles and miles over the Adirondack Mountains. The sky was crimson above the trees where the sun would slowly disappear on the horizon like a flame dying on a wet match.

Mrs. Kellogg said. "If you kids count telephone poles, it will make the time go by faster. Or even houses and barns. Why not try that?"

Nearly an hour and a half later, Mrs. Kellogg pulled off the highway onto a bumpy, muddy two-tracked driveway. The setting sun behind her was red in the side mirror.

A rusty mailbox leaned toward the highway where she turned in. The kids sat up and craned their necks to see as the car bumped and swayed back and forth up the long driveway that led up a slight hill to a narrow, two-story farmhouse. The once white exterior had turned gray and was peeling. It was at least two hundred yards away from the highway and somewhat hidden by trees.

Evidently, the front yard hadn't been cared for in recent years, so clumps of dead yellow prairie grass stuck up here and there through splotches of snow. A low-slung sun porch was blinded by dead-looking saplings and shrubs. It had a sagging ridgeline and milky glass in the windows.

A large mouse-colored barn was situated well off to the right of the house and at the very rear of the yard was a small stand of withered trees with a long-dead grapevine wrapped around rusty poles and wire. An outhouse was barely visible behind the house, and a tire swing dangled from a huge elm tree between the house and the barn.

"Well, here we are," said Mrs. Kellogg. She put the car in neutral, and pulled the handle for the emergency brake, turned off the engine, then craned her head up over the front seat. "You children can just get out. We'll wait a bit before we take your things inside."

"Yes, Ma'am," said Beth. "Come on, Joey."

Just as they got out, a man appeared at the front door. His features seemed very dark with the shadow under the porch roof. As soon as he was outside, he wore a smile that hadn't been there seconds earlier. With small eyes, and a fleshy face, he had thinning gray hair that resembled cat fur... A flush in his cheeks was the color of a window-ripened peach and. his nose was pitted and red.

Lyle Couzens had narrowing shoulders which had must have curved over the years, and he walked with a slight limp, like a man whose arthritis or gout gave him no peace. He wore bib overalls and a faded flannel shirt with the sleeves rolled back over his elbows. Walking up to Mrs. Kellogg, he shook her hand and smiled.

"Hello, Judith. I see you've brought some young folks with you, eh?" He turned to acknowledge Joey and Beth just as a woman came out of the house.

"Hello, Lyle. Yes, here they are. Hi, Clara."

Clara Couzens wore laced boots, a man's oversized wool trousers and a khaki shirt. A shawl was wrapped around her head, but wisps of dark hair peeked out from the edges. She had a pale indoor face and thick black eyebrows that almost met over the bridge of her broad nose. Her eyes were unnaturally wide, the pupils shrunken to small black dots, her skin so tight that one would think perhaps someone was twisting the back of her hair in a knot.

"Hi, Judith. Good to see you." They shook hands and she bent slightly to face the kids. "Well, now, we've been expecting you two." She smiled.

"Folks, this is Beth and Joey Harrison. I've explained to the children that they will be staying with you for a bit until their family get things settled on their end. They were anxious to meet you, weren't you, kids?"

Beth nodded. "Yes, Ma'am." Joey stared at his feet.

"Well, we're certainly glad to meet you, children. We're so happy that you'll be staying with us, aren't we, Lyle?" She continued to smile.

"Sure thing," said Lyle. "Our boy, Richard, is down the road helping the neighbor, but he'll be home before long. He's a bit older than you, kids, but I'm sure you'll all get along fine."

Clara looked at Mrs. Kellogg. "Come on in, Judith, have a cup of coffee before you go." She pulled the shawl from her head and long black and gray hair spilled onto her shoulders.

"Oh, I'm sorry, I can't, Clara. Maybe next time, if you don't mind. I've got a long trip back to Watertown, and they're calling for thunder and lightning tonight. Maybe even snow, if the temperature keeps dropping. Can you believe that? Here I thought winter was over, but perhaps not." She giggled. "In any event, I want to beat the storm if I can."

Lyle asked, "Where are their things, Judith, in the trunk?"

"Yes," she said. "All they have is in there. Here let me unlock that for you."

"Thanks. I'd best get them now; so you can be on your way then."

"Yes, and I've about got supper on the table," said Clara. I hope you kids are hungry. Let's go inside, I'll show you where to wash up before we eat."

After Mrs. Kellogg left, they went inside where Joey continued to pout.

Everyone sat at a wooden kitchen table except Richard, who hadn't gotten home yet. Beth sat next to Joey and squeezed his hand. "Joey. It will be all right."

A gray and white cat crept through the kitchen and went to a yellow dish sitting by the back door. Mr. Couzens saw Joey eyeing the cat. "That there is Gussy. She's got a bunch of kittens that live out in the barn." He leaned over closer to Joey. "They keep the rats and mice down."

He pulled a pipe out of his bib pocket along with a package of Redman tobacco. "You'll be fine. A big boy like you... no need to fret. We're glad to have you here, ain't we, Missus?" His face broke into thousands of fine wrinkles when he grinned.

"Yes, of course, and we love children." She reached over and patted Joey's shoulder. "We're having spaghetti for supper. You like spaghetti, boy?"

Joey didn't answer, so Beth answered for him.

"We like spaghetti fine, Ma'am."

"Good. It will be ready shortly. Why don't I take and show you two around a bit. Least ways, show you to your room. We'll get the rest tomorrow," she said.

Lyle Couzens pointed to their bags by the door. "You can both grab your things and take them with you." He used his thumb to pack his pipe as he talked. When it was ready, he struck a match on the underside of the kitchen table and sucked on the pipe. He scratched the back of his head and blew a cloud of smoke into the air.

Beth and Joey followed Mrs. Couzens down a short hallway to a bedroom on the left. Her thin body swayed to and fro and she walked like a person with a bad back.

"Now, you'll both be sharing this room; it's a good size though, so there shouldn't be any problem, plenty of room." She spoke in rapid fire, as if she was in a hurry to finish before she forgot something. "There's the closet, but you probably won't need it. You can both put your things in there." She pointed to an old, four-drawer dresser that stood against the wall. Except for the dresser and two single beds there was no other furniture in the room. A string hung from a light bulb on the ceiling, and there was a single-paned window facing the barn. The walls were painted light yellow but they were bare — no pictures.

"And, there's a pee pot under each of your beds." She focused on Beth. "I want you to empty them at the outhouse every morning before school. In case you didn't see it before, that house is just behind us, in the back." She pointed. "Understand?"

"Yes, Ma'am," said Beth. Joey nodded.

"Okay, well, you can go ahead and put your things away. There's no need to show you anything else right now, supper's about ready, so when you finish, go wash your hands and it should be time to eat. It's past time, really. My goodness, I'll bet you're both about starved." She absently fluffed her fingers through Joey's hair. "Right, boy?"

Joey looked up, his eyes meeting hers for the first time. "Yes, Ma'am."

The back door squeaked open and slammed shut as Richard stumbled in when supper was underway. He gawked at Joey and Beth as he hung his coat on a hook by the back door.

"You're late again, Richard," said Mr. Couzens.

"I know, Pa, but Tom had extra chores and I didn't know what time it was until it was too late. I ran all the way home, I really did." His eyes darted back and forth between his father and mother. He was a tall, skinny lad with unruly red hair and uncomfortable-looking big ears. He had green piercing eyes and his face was covered with freckles and curiosity. The bib overhauls he wore had dry circles of dirt on the knees and his black boots were caked with mud.

"Well, don't come tracking in. Get them boots off and wash your hands," said his mother.

Richard sat on the floor and unlaced his boots as he studied the newcomers.

"You should say hello to the new kids, Richard. This is Beth and Joey."

"Hi," said Richard, as he drifted over to the kitchen sink.

"Hello," Beth and Joey responded at the same time. When Richard finished washing his hands, he pulled out a chair and sat next to Beth.

There was awkward silence for a moment or so while everyone ate their food. Joey thought he felt Mrs. Couzens eyes boring into him...

"You're liking the spaghetti, ain'tcha, boy?" She tapped her fingers up and down on the table next to her plate.

"Yes, ma'am." The quiet that followed was deafening.

"Seeing as how tomorrow is Saturday, you kids will have more time to look around and get acquainted before we sign you up at school Monday morning," said Mrs. Couzens. "We'll have to go through your clothes, make sure you've got something to wear."

"Are they gonna be riding the same bus as me, Ma?" Richard asked.

"Yes, of course, Richard." She looked at Beth. "Have you got plenty of school clothes, Missy?"

"Yes, Ma'am. I think so. All my clothes are in the bags."

"Of course. And how about you, boy? Hey! Whoa! You'd best slow down there a tad. That spaghetti ain't going nowhere. There's plenty."

Richard giggled and Joey lay his fork on his plate and dropped his hands into his lap.

"Yes, ma'am, he's got good clothes," said Beth. "They're new from Christmas."

There was a beat of silence. "Doesn't he talk?" said Richard.

Joey's ears turned red around the rim.

"Richard, be quiet!" said Mrs. Couzens. She stood and took her plate to the sink and came back to the table. "Ordinarily, it will be one of your chores to clean up and do the dishes after we eat, Beth. But, since this is your first night here, we'll let it go. I'll do it. I think you'd best turn in right away. I'm sure this has been a long day for both of you." She zeroed in on her son again... "You can skip the radio tonight, too, Richard. Get to bed early, it'll teach you to get home on time."

"Awww, Ma. Why should I have to just because they do?"

She slapped the table with her hand. "What did I say, young man? Don't argue with me."

Lyle Couzens slid his chair back away from the table. Crossing his legs, he lit his pipe again and said, "Serves you right, son."

•   •   •   •   •

Joey was frightened. A sliver of light from the kitchen sliced through the scary darkness of the hallway just outside the door to their room. He heard the muffled sounds of Mr. and Mrs. Couzens voices. They were probably in the living room, because he heard the radio, too. He knew that tonight it would be Fibber Magee and Molly, but it wasn't loud enough to hear their words. He could only make out the sounds of audience laughter.

He was propped up on one arm, with his hand supporting his head and whispered, "Sis?"

"What, Joey?"

"I don't like them, do you?"

"I don't know, Joey. Let's wait and see."

"I especially don't like Richard. I don't like it here, I want to go home."

"Shhhh, Joey. We can't go home right now. Just go to sleep now, okay?"

She heard her brother sniffling and whispered, "Don't cry. Everything will be all right. You'll see. Goodnight, Joey."

Joey lay with the covers pulled up to his chin feeling like his head would explode from so much crying.

"Sis?" Getting no response, Joey sat up.

"Sis?"

"What, Joey?"

"Do you think Gramps will come and get us when he finds out we went away?"

"I don't think so, Joey."

"Why? He didn't even know we were going away. I'll bet he'll get Uncle Glenn to drive here and take us home."

"I don't think so, Joey. Shhhh, now. Please go to sleep, okay?"

Joey lay back. He was almost asleep when he heard the sound of a train.

"Wooooooo! Wooooooo! Wooooooooooooooo!"

Richard had told him about the trains before they went to bed. He said they ran on tracks way out past their corn fields. Yet, to Joey, the train seemed so close. He liked the sound the train made. But, that night, it just made him miss home. He thought about Gramps who worked for the New York Central Railroad. It was hard to hold back the tears.

He missed his mother's hugs... and eating Grams' chocolate cookies with big glasses of cherry Kool Aid, before bedtime. They always tucked him in at night with their soft, wet kisses. Joey saw their faces so clearly before sleep took him away and set his mind free.

Chapter Three

T he following night as the sound of the train faded into the distance, Joey once again lay awake and thought about home. He thought about his hero, Gramps and how much he missed him more than anything.

Carl Powet was "the best Grandpa in the entire world" according to Joey. At fifty-one, he boasted a full head of hair that he wore slicked back, showing ruler-straight teeth marks from the comb. His face had peerless character that was tanned and scored with time lines. His soft dark eyes were reassuring. Gray hair peeked out of his nose and ears, and broad smiles cracked his entire face.

Gramps worked as a switchman at the railroad for nearly twenty years. His job entailed sitting in a little green shack alongside the tracks in Gouvernuer, where he waited monitored trains. He had paperwork that told him when trains were coming and going, but he knew their schedules by heart. During his shift, he stepped outside the shack, from time to time, in order to pull a lever that switched the tracks for certain trains, which in turn sent them in a different direction going forward from Gouvernuer.

Gramps was like a father, as well as a best friend. With Joey's father stationed somewhere in the Pacific, fighting the war against Japan, Joey didn't have many real friends, but Gramps made him feel like he was special. Sometimes, even more than his mother, Alice. But, as Joey told her one day, "It's not your fault, Mommy. It's just because you're a girl."

Living with Gramps was almost like having his father to talk to. Joey often said, "If my daddy was home, it would be so great, because then I'd have two best friends and a daddy, too."

Gramps was steady. He always appeared as calm as a summer

sunset. He was a slow-talking man with a booming baritone voice who spoke very little. Sometimes, when Gram talked to him, he didn't answer until much later. Gram lovingly called him "Silent Sam."

He was a roly-poly man who liked to eat. With reddened skin, the color of the rind on a smoked ham, he had a big hard belly and a wide neck. His fingernails were the thickness and color of mottled tortoise. Over six-foot-two, Gramps found it necessary to duck from time to time in their flat-roofed house where the ceilings were so low that the dangling flypaper in the kitchen could be a troublesome obstacle. His big belly pre-ceded him when he walked, but he was very sturdy and strong. Even the wide girth of his middle carried the promise of exceptional power. When he rolled up his sleeves, he revealed forearms that were enormous, like thick fence posts.

Joey's mother told him that his grandfather was a hero in World War I. She said he had medals, but Gramps never showed them to anyone. He walked well with both legs before the war, but, after he was shot two times in the left leg, he lived with arthritis and a limp. When Joey asked to see the medals, Gramps just smiled and said: "Not important, Sonny." Joey never knew why Gramps called him Sonny... he just did.

Tears welled up in his eyes as he lay there picturing his grandfather's' face. He thought he heard that deep voice saying, "Where are the kids, Alice? Where is Joey? Where's Beth? We have to get them back here right now." It brought a smile to Joey's face, momentarily, but he knew the voice wasn't real and it brought tears to his eyes.

Before he fell asleep, his thoughts drifted back to a special day when Gramps took him to work with him. It had been one of the best days of his life.

The New York Central tracks were less then a hundred yards from their house, and every day he and Beth could hear the trains coming. Joey knew when to be out in the front of the house so he could watch them pass. Beth joined him if she wasn't helping Gram in the house.

At first, the trains always sounded so far away, but as they moved closer and closer, the house began to shake. It was louder than thunder and the windows rattled. They stood in the front yard and waved at the men riding inside the big, black engines as they rumbled by. The men always waved and smiled. Sometimes, they even tooted the horn. The kids watched and listened to the musical clickity-clacking of the wheels, over and over and over again, until the caboose slowly disappeared in the distance.

When he closed his eyes, Joey was sure he could smell his grandfather's pipe. He'd be lying on the living room floor with Beth, listening to *Gangbusters* on the radio while Gramps sat in his rocking chair, puffing on that pipe. Every so often the kids heard the *tink – tink – tink sound* when Gramps tapped the ashtray to empty the pipe.

Gramps wore his spectacles down low on his nose when he read the newspaper, and most nights they listened to shows like *Fibber Magee and Molly, Boston Blackie* and *The Shadow* on the radio while Gram and Alice played Rummy on the dining room table.

"Well, we could listen to *Amos n' Andy*," Gramps had said. Joey and Beth both liked *Amos n' Andy*. Gramps knew that; so did he.

"Sure thing, Gramps, that would be swell," said Joey. Beth nodded, but then Gramps raised one hand like a traffic cop.

"Course now, Sonny, if you're going to work with me tomorrow, you'd best get to bed early...like right now, I imagine."

Joey didn't know if he heard Gramps right or not and he jumped up. "You mean, you would take me with you? I really *can* go, just me and you? I get to go to the railroad shack with you?"

Gramps nodded. "Yup "And that was that. He leaned up in his rocker, looked at Joey, and smiled. "Five o'clock comes awful early though . . .you think you can do that?"

"Yes, Sir. You bet I can!" said Joey, as he hugged him.

"Easy now, lad, you'll knock these durn specs right off my face." He glanced down at Beth. "Sorry, Sissy, I think it's best you just let us two men go this time. Okay?"

Beth was disappointed because she wasn't going, but she smiled. "Oh, that's okay, Gramps."

"Maybe your Grandma can find something for you to do tomorrow," said Gramps.

Joey remembered how awful early it was when Gram shook him awake that next morning. She smiled and put her finger up to her lips.

"Shhhhh. Quiet, don't wake your sister up," she whispered.

Joey sat up and rubbed his eyes. He smelled fried bacon and heard the coffee pot bubbling on the stove. He heard that sound lots of other mornings, too, before he got up, but that morning was different. The bubbling told him to hurry and get downstairs.

Gramps sat on the edge of his rocker near the bottom of the stairs. He wore his brown work pants and one of his white undershirts—like always. Grunting and breathing loud, he pulled on his black, railroad work boots. Looking up at Joey, he grinned as he laced the rawhide strings around shiny brass hooks.

"Morning, Sonny." He looked Joey over and chuckled. "You've got your shirt on backwards and inside out."

"Oh, good morning, Gramps." He yanked his shirt up over his head, and was still fixing it right side out when he got to the kitchen and saw Gram standing at the stove. The bacon smelled sweet, and it made wonderful crackling noises in the frying pan. She was slicing potatoes into another pan with bacon grease.

Without turning around, she said, "Joey, go on out and use the pot before your Grandpa gets out here." Her gray hair tumbled all the way down the middle of her back like a horse's tail. It looked odd to Joey because during the day she had it tied up on top of her head. She always seemed to look older than Gramps. Her face was badly wrinkled, and some of her teeth were missing, Consequently when she talked, spit oozed out of the corners of her mouth; she had to wipe her face before it dripped down her chin. Most of the time, she wore a blue dress covered with little red flowers, but that morning, Joey remembered, she was wearing a pink bathrobe.

It was still dark at five in the morning and when he ran to the outhouse, it was cold and the moon dangled in the sky like a loose earring. A strong breeze slapped the outhouse door closed behind him, sounding like a pistol shot. Joey had to climb up and sit down on the hole in order to pee because he wasn't tall enough to get his pee to go in the hole without getting the seat wet. Gramps missed the hole sometimes too though, and it upset the women

Joey came back inside and sidled up beside Gram to smell the frying food. He watched as she sprinkled a lot of pepper on the potatoes.

"Go sit down at the table, Joey; breakfast will be ready soon enough."

Joey sat down, and before long he heard Gramps coming. His footfalls were loud, and then there was that silly thing he did sometimes. He made tooting noises while he walked and, after each toot, he'd say "Wooop!" It made Joey giggle, but Gram didn't think it was funny, so Joey covered his mouth as Gramps tooted with almost every step from the stairs all the way through to the kitchen. "Whoop! Whoop! Whoop!"

"Carl, I swear! Stop that! You're a fine example for the boy. You sound like a pig. And, don't you laugh at your grandpa, either, Joey. He's not funny, he just thinks he is."

Gramps winked at Joey and began humming as he limped across the creaky linoleum floor of the kitchen with his suspenders draped down around his hips. The screen door's spring stretched when he shoved the door open, and when it swung shut behind him, it made a loud slapping noise...

Gram always made a big breakfast for Gramps before he went to work, but that morning Joey was going to work, too, so he also ate his grandfather's kind of breakfast instead of his usual bowl of oatmeal.

"A man's breakfast," Gramps announced when he came back in. He smiled at Joey.

That morning they had a half-dozen eggs, sliced bacon, potatoes with onions and pancakes covered with melted oleo and real maple syrup. Gram made toast with the bread she baked the day before. She loaded their plates while Gramps finished washing up at the kitchen sink; she told Joey to wait until he sat down before he started eating.

With his sleeves still rolled up, Gramps pulled out his chair, grunted and sat down. He immediately poured some of his coffee out of his cup, onto the saucer and slurped. His lips made a sucking sound when he did that. Alice had told Joey it was bad manners, but Gram didn't care; she drank her coffee the same way.

There wasn't any talking once they started eating. Joey thought he was going to drink a glass of milk as usual, but Gram surprised him that day. She smiled and said, "Joey, how would you like to have a cup of coffee with your Grandpa this morning?"

"Can I? Wow! That would be swell!" Joey felt wide awake and so much like a big man, just like Gramps. A big railroad guy. He was afraid he would spill the coffee, so he didn't sip it from the saucer like they did. He wished Beth could have been up to see him drinking coffee, but she was still sleeping and so was his mother.

While Gramps and Joey finished eating, Gram packed lunches and filled Gramps' tall thermos bottle with coffee. She made three bologna sandwiches on bread with mustard-two for Gramps and one for Joey. She wrapped some fresh peanut butter cookies and let Joey take a shiny red apple. Gramps didn't care for apples; he said they bothered his teeth.

He slurped the rest of the coffee from his saucer and stood to grab his railroad coat that hung on the back of the kitchen door. The coat was blue with tiny, white stripes. His cap was the same color, only it lay atop the icebox, where he tossed it every day after work.

"You be sure and keep a special eye out for him, old man, hear?" Gram warned. "And Joey, you mind your P's and Q's and listen to your Grandpa." She kissed Gramps on the cheek, then bent down and hugged Joey and gave him a kiss on his forehead.

"We'll be just fine, Lillian. He's a big boy," Gramps said as he packed his pipe.

"Your mommy's not up this early, but she said to tell you she loves you and be a good boy," said Gram.

When they left, faint traces of light crept over the tops of the houses. Birds were chirping and Gramps said they were talking because they just woke up, and they were hungry. Joey scooted a little bit ahead of him and ran towards the tracks.

"Whoa, Buster Brown! Don't get your britches in an uproar," Gramps called out. "We'll get there soon enough. You wait for me, okay?"

Joey held up and waited, the entire time his eyes searched the length of shiny tracks. They seemed a lot bigger than he imagined for some reason. He had never been allowed to get that close to them before, and he wanted to bend down and touch them. See what they felt like.

Gramps limped closer, his pipe dangled from the corner of his mouth. They crossed over the tracks, and Gramps stopped, scratched a match on his pants, and lit his pipe. He wasn't in a hurry. Joey had been trying to mimic the way Gramps swung his black lunch pail to and fro as he walked, but he didn't follow too close behind him, just in case his grandfather was to toot and whoop.

Gramps began to sing. "Oh... deeee-oat dote dote do-dee oat dote-dote . . ."

Joey waggled his head back and forth to the rhythm of the tune until he spotted the little green shack up ahead. In his anxiety to get there, he strayed off the path, through the tall grass, and passed Gramps.

"Wait for me, Sonny," Gramps yelled. They were just a little ways away from their destination, but Joey stopped and stared at the shack while he waited for his grandfather to catch up.

"Wrong place to run, Sonny. You could fall real easy around here. We don't want you getting hurt. Your grandma will whack me with a stick."

Joey giggled. "Okay, Gramps."

A padlock was on the door, but Gramps had a key and opened it. Everything seemed too quiet for Joey. "How come there ain't no trains yet, Gramps?"

"There will be, Sonny — there will be."

The shack had a cement floor and lots of small windows on three sides. A big, red and white checkered Purina dog chow calendar hung on one of the walls, and a clipboard hung next to it. A tall, wooden stool sat by one larger window facing the tracks and a blue cushion covering the top had white stuffing peeking out of it. Situated in a corner, was a pot-bellied stove with black piping leading up to a hole in the roof. A bucket of coal sat next to the stove.

Gramps sat his lunch pail and thermos on a ledge next to a can of Prince Albert pipe tobacco, then grabbed the clipboard and slid himself onto the stool and put on his glasses. He unscrewed the top off of his thermos, poured some coffee in the top, and thumbed through the papers on the clipboard. When he was finished he took off his glasses, smiled at Joey and said, "Well now, we'll be needing a chair for you, young man." He stepped outside, and when he came back, he had an empty milk crate.

"Here you go, Mr. Engineer. This should do. Have a seat."

Joey grinned. "Gee, thanks, Gramps."

"I don't get company very often," he said, as he shoveled some coal and started a fire in the stove. Taking his glasses out of his bib pocket, he reached for the clipboard again, checked his watch, and looked down at Joey.

"Yup. The 451 heading for Syracuse should roll through here in less than an hour. You just keep listening. You'll hear her. When I tell you, get down there." He pointed to the floor. "You put your ear to the floor and I'll bet you can hear her coming. You'll feel it too."

"Gee, really?"

"Yessiree-bob."

The sun had just come up when Gramps said, "It won't be long now. Go ahead, get down there and listen."

Joey got down on his hands and knees and closed his eyes. He put his ear to the floor and heard the rumbling that got louder and louder, and not long after that, the "woo woo wooing" of the train as it rumbled closer and closer.

Jumping to his feet, he nearly backed into the stove.

"Careful there," said Gramps. "Now, when Old 451 comes rolling by, I want you to just stay put. Don't come running outside. I have to be out there, but you stay in here — Okay?"

"Okay, Gramps. Can I sit on the stool and watch, though?"

"Yup. That'll be good. Just don't come outside."

Joey stayed, but he wanted so much to be out there with his grandfather. He wanted to see the train up close-closer than he ever had from their front yard.

He watched as Gramps limped down the track a little ways until he stopped and bent down to do something to the track. Joey saw what looked like a handle in his Gramps' hand. The early morning sunshine made the thing sparkle. When Gramps finished, he walked back down the track and stood out in front of the shack. The "woo woo wooing" got much louder, as he looked through the window at Joey and smiled. He waved, beaconing Joey.

"You can come on out here now, Sonny," he yelled.

The train was still a long distance down the track, but Joey could see the engine's smoke and hear the thunder of it rolling towards them. The ground shook under their feet and he squeezed Gramps hand.

Gramps put his arm around Joey's shoulders and puffed on his pipe. Joey grinned as he remembered the thrill of having his hero standing next to him that day. He wished so much the special day had never come to an end. Two railroad guys, doing their job, and he had been one of them.

He remembered Gramps leaned down to make sure he could hear him: "Now, this train is going on to Syracuse, Sonny, but if I didn't do my job it would have gone right on to Buffalo. That's why I had to switch the tracks over. See?"

The rumble of the train was much louder as it passed them, the engineer blew the horn. "*Wonnk! Wonnk! Wonnk!*" Joey put his hands over his ears. The engineer waved and Gramps waved back. Hot air gushed at their faces, and Joey's hair blew every which way...

There were lots of cars in the train, and it took a long time to pass. So many cars, all different colors, shapes and sizes. The huge iron wheels made a "clickity-clack, clickity-clack" sound, over, and over, and over again and the horn kept honking until the entire train had passed. The very last car was called the caboose, and they watched it until it turned into a tiny dot moving farther and farther away.

Joey remembered feeling sad after it was gone; it was like a good friend was never coming back again. When they went back inside the shack, Gramps said, "Sonny, there isn't another train for almost an hour. After we have some a sandwich you can walk on the tracks for awhile before it comes if you promise to be careful and don't fall."

"Really, Gramps? Can I? Wow! I'll be careful, honest, I will."

He gobbled up his sandwich long before Gramps had one of his sandwiches finished. He chewed on his apple until Gramps finished drinking his coffee. After he put the top back on the thermos he ruffled his fingers through Joey's hair.

"We're not in a big durn hurry are we, Sonny?" His face had cracked into that wonderful Gramps' smile. He paused for a moment then said, "Okay, go ahead then. But, listen... let me show you something first." He walked outside with Joey and pointed. "You see that yellow boxcar sitting to the side down there?"

"Yes, I see it."

"Well, I don't want you going any further than that. You see where I'm talking about?"

"Yes, Gramps, I see it. I won't go past it —promise."

"Okay, then, go along, and have fun, but don't run."

It was scary at first, walking down the middle of those tracks. Joey wondered if trains ever came by that Gramps didn't know about. The tracks looked like long silver ribbons that stretched as far as he could see. He jumped from one tie to the other, then one track to the other. The smell of tar was strong and black stones were scattered everywhere.

The yellow boxcar looked so lonely sitting there all by itself. Joey wondered where it came from. Did it have a home? Maybe something was broke on it. He stood and stared at it for a long time before he started back to the shack. He asked Gramps why it was just sitting there all by itself.

"Got to sit somewhere, Sonny. They don't need it right now, I guess."

Three more trains rumbled by that afternoon. Gramps had to switch one of them. Number 329 was going straight through to Buffalo, but another was destined for Utica. He let Joey walk down the tracks over and over again; and, by the third time, Joey was talking to the yellow boxcar as if it was a new friend. He asked it where it had been and where it wanted to go?

Gramps had locked up when the late afternoon sun was like a yellow flame in the trees and they walked home.

Joey stirred. He suddenly realized where he was... a strange bed in a strange house. People he didn't know. He had to pee but was afraid to get up. He remembered Mrs. Couzens had said there was a pot under the bed, but he didn't know exactly where it was, and he was afraid to look under there. He decided to hold it and wait until morning.

It was dark and still less than an hour later when he was jarred awake with the warm and wet feeling a seven-year-old child feels when they wet the bed.

Chapter Four

J oey woke up shivering; he was soaking wet and cold. He had not been a bed-wetter at home, and worried that he would probably be in trouble for his infraction here at the Couzen's place. When he heard Mrs. Couzens' shoes banging clomping on the hallway floor, he closed his eyes and wondered what she would do about it. Her footfalls sounded closer and closer until she was standing between their beds. The ceiling light scalded his face when she pulled the string.

"Time to get up, you two." There was a somewhat musical sound to her voice. "Get dressed and do your business, then come to the table for breakfast."

Joey squinted his eyes as she turned and clomped out of the room, leaving the light on. He smelled coffee and it reminded him of his grandmother's kitchen in the morning.

He lay there a moment, wondering what to do about his wet pajamas. Beth stirred in her bed and he hurried over to her. "Sis? It was obvious to her that her brother was stifling tears.

"What is it, Joey? What's wrong?"

"I don't know what to do. I was afraid to get up—I peed in my bed last night."

Beth slowly sat up, rubbed her eyes, and yawned. "It'll be alright, don't cry, okay? Go in the closet, take your wet stuff off and get dressed. You look cold and you're shivering, so hurry up."

"I know, but where should I put my pajamas? What about the sheets?"

Beth glanced at his bed, then studied her brother's face a moment. "I don't know, Joey. I guess you shouldn't make your bed, let it dry out first."

"But then she'll know, Sis." He squeezed his hands together to fight the waves of panic.

"Yes, she will, but she's going to find out anyway, so you might as well not hide it," she whispered. "I have to dress, too, so let me go in the closet and get my clothes out, then you hurry up and get those wet pajamas off.

Joey always listened to his sister, but he counted on her now, more than ever, because she was all he had. He no longer had Gramps to be his friend, or the caring love of his mother and grandmother.

Once he was dressed, Joey came out of the closet and wadded his pajamas up in a ball. He bent down and shoved them under his bed, then stood, with his hands in his pockets and waited while Beth brushed her hair. He paced back and forth, then peeked out the window where it was still dark and whispered, "Why should I tell her, Sis? Maybe she won't ever know if I don't say anything."

"Because, Joey, you will really get into trouble if you . . ."

"Come on you two," Mrs. Couzens called. "If you want to eat, get a move on. Don't be lollygagging in there. Richaaaaaard! Come and wash up for breakfast."

"Geez! There's no school today. I wonder why we had to get up when it's still dark," Joey grumbled.

Beth eyed her brother's bed. "Wait until after breakfast. We have to take the pots out to the back, remember? I think you should tell her then. Come on, I smell toast." They moved quickly down the hallway that led to the kitchen.

Mr. Couzens was bringing in fresh milk. He carried a two-gallon pail in each hand and set them on the drain board by the sink. Steam rose like small clouds from each pail.

The kitchen was much warmer than the hallway and bedroom. A big, black Franklin stove stood against the wall. It was a lot bigger than Gram's. A few chunks of wood were piled in a wood box next to the stove.

"Mornin' kids," said Mr. Couzens.

"Good morning, sir," they said in harmony. Mrs. Couzens was stirring a pan of oatmeal on the stove and didn't speak. With no bathroom, Beth and Joey waited until Mr. Couzens was finished at the sink, then washed their face and hands at the kitchen sink. They dried themselves on a towel that hung on the cabinet. Mr. Couzens went back outside while Mrs. Couzens poured his coffee. The kids watched as she smeared Oleo on a pile of toasted homemade bread.

When Mr. Couzens returned, the porch door banged shut behind him as he brought in an armload of firewood and dumped it into the wood box. The door on the stove squeaked as he opened it and shoved pieces of wood inside. Sparks flew up in the air as he jabbed at the wood with a long, black poker. He closed the door, but fire could be seen through the cracks around the door. The stove's damper screeched when he adjusted it in the stovepipe. Sweat trickled out of his gray hair as he pulled off his checkered jacket, sighed heavily, and took a seat at the head of the table. Mrs. Couzens sat at the other end, opposite her husband.

Mrs. Couzens stared at the kids for a moment then pointed to the chairs.

"Missy, you sit there—and Joey, you sit next to her —right there. Just like last night."

Beth's chair was next to Mr. Couzens', and Joey's was next to hers. Richard's place was on the other side of the table by Mrs. Couzens, but he wasn't at the table, yet. The stack of toast sat in the middle of the table next to a mason jar of real maple syrup.

Mrs. Couzens crossed her arms and sat back, her lips a tight little pucker. "Those will be your regular seats from now on. Please see to it that you sit there when you come to the table. It does away with a lot of confusion when it's time to eat." She scooped out ladles of oatmeal in each of their bowls just as Richard got to the table.

"Mrs. Couzens scowled. "It's about time, mister." Richard appeared to ignore her and reached for the toast.

Mrs. Couzens got up and used a dipper to scoop milk from one of the pails into a glass pitcher. She sat it on the table in front of her husband who had stopped thumbing through a Montgomery Wards catalog for a moment in order to pour milk on his oatmeal. When he was done, he passed it to Beth and reached for the syrup. Mrs.

Couzens waited until he was finished then took the syrup from him and poured a small amount on each of the kids' servings.

Mrs. Couzens looked at Beth and Joey. "The mister makes this syrup himself. He taps the maple trees in February; you just missed seeing how he does it."

Mr. Couzens looked up and smiled, then went back to perusing his catalog. He ran his finger down a page and then used both hands to slap the catalog shut. He sipped his coffee and wiped his lips with the back of his hand. Pulling a rumpled handkerchief out of his back pocket, he dabbed at his sweaty forehead.

Beth studied him for a moment, out of the corner of her eye. She hadn't noticed before, but he had a spray of brown moles on his unshaven face and one eyebrow twitched. Mrs. Couzens seemed to ignore her husband when he took his teeth out, wiped them on his shirt, and put them back in his mouth. She didn't serve herself any oatmeal, but pulled out her chair and wiped her hands on her apron before sitting. She sipped her coffee and stared at the ceiling. All was quiet, except for the tapping sound of her fingers on the table.

"Are you gonna' show them their chores today, Pa?" Richard asked.

"Yes, we are, son. That doesn't mean you get out of doing yours though."

"Yeah, but I won't have so much to do now, right?"

Mrs. Couzens glared. "Just finish your breakfast, Richard. Let your pa worry about all that. She looked at Mr. Couzens. "Would you please find time to fix that leak around the water pump today, Lyle?"

Joey ate his oatmeal and toast, but he continued to fret about his wet bed and pajamas. He hesitated to look at any of the Couzens family. When he did, but Mrs. Couzens blinked and stared when she felt his eyes on her.

Mr. Couzens gulped the rest of his coffee, and farted as he stood up. "Ooooops! Got to get back out there, getting that plow ready, and I think I'm gonna need a new front tire for the tractor, by the way, Clara — so figure on it."

She stared at her husband for what seemed like a long time, her nostrils swelling with air, her small mouth was a tight seam of anger. It was as though she had been talking to either a deaf or stupid and a pig as well... Her eyes peeled the skin off his face. "That wasn't necessary, Lyle. And, we'll see how the money goes this month. A tire would be the last thing." She stood and said, "We can't always have what we want. You above all people should know that."

Mr. Couzens stared blankly at her. He was clearly disappointed. "You're probably right," he said.

She turned to Beth. "Missy, you can help me here in the house. Do these dishes up, first thing, while the mister takes the boys out to the barn." She gathered up the empty bowls and turned to the sink.

Richard looked at Joey with an idiot's grin on his face. He made a farting sound with his mouth, and his mother whirled around.

"Richard! That will be enough. Now, go and get your pot emptied before you go out to the barn with your father, and take the boy with you. Missy, you go empty yours, too."

The smile never left Richard's face. He stuck his tongue out at Joey and moved over to the stove where he warmed first one side of his body, then the other. Joey, not sure of what to do, simply stood there with his head lowered.

"Come on, boys. Let's leave the women alone," said Mr. Couzens. "We've got plenty to do this weekend. Richard, be sure to bring my thermos of coffee, I'm going out. You hurry along."

Mrs. Couzens had her hand on her hip and sighed. "Beth, come to think of it, it's probably best you go along with them for just a bit so you get to see the farm. You'll be gathering eggs and such, so go ahead—just come back in right away. Don't forget to empty your pots before you go."

"Yes, Ma'am."

She and Joey scurried down the hall to their bedroom to get their chamber pots.

Joey whispered, "I know you said to tell them now, Sis, but I just can't." They looked at the bed sheets thrown back on the bed, right where he had left them. "Maybe they'll get dry and I won't even have to tell her."

He yanked the covers up to the top of the bed and smoothed everything out with his hands before he reached under the bed and picked up the chamber pot.

Beth covered her mouth with her hands for a moment, then said, "Gee, I don't know, Joey. What about your pajamas?"

"She won't look under the bed, will she?"

"I hope not, but if she does, it might make her mad"

They both stood there for a moment.

"Come on, Joey. Let's go before she comes in here. I have to pee, too, so let's hurry."

The porch was cold and dark when they passed through to the outside. Stacks of newspapers were piled on top of old furniture that nearly blocked the back door. Dozens of brown paper sacks full of clothes, were piled so high, they nearly touched the sloped ceiling.

Beth looked at the sky. There was a beautiful day on the horizon. The first streaks of dawn lit up a orange and crimson sky. The east was pink-tinted on the edges and immediately adjacent to an expanse of sky that was still robin's-egg blue. A clan of crows flapped overhead looking much like little specks of India ink thrown against the sky.

At nine years old, Beth already appreciated nature, when the gardens burst into bloom, wild with roses and laurel, yellow forsythia, and multi-colored azaleas. On days like this at Gram's house, the sun shone brightly through her parlor window, the thin material of the curtains splashed with thousands of tiny points of light as they puffed in the breeze.

She longed to hear the buzzing of bees, attracted by the trilliums and lilacs growing at the end of their grandmother's yard. And there were the pink buds of the wild apple tree in the front of the house.

Joey pointed to an iron bell that dangled from a wooden post to the right of the door. "What's that for?"

Richard was waiting by the door and took the opportunity to inject himself in the answer. "That's what my mother uses to call Pa if she needs him right away. You can hear it all the way out in the barn and corn fields. Ma rings it for me, too, sometimes. Don't touch it though, she'll get mad."

The barn was about three hundred feet from the back porch steps, beyond the chicken coop, water pump, clotheslines, and tool-shed. Lyle was already out in the barn, and when all the chamber pots were emptied at the outhouse. Richard led them toward the barn. They also passed a huge woodpile and a hen house. Beth and Joey took their time in order to watch the chickens peck at the ground. The kids were fascinated with a big red-and-black rooster that sat on the fence, twitching his head this way and that.

"You better keep up," Richard yelled. "Haven't you ever seen a chicken before? Geez." The kids ran to catch up.

A brown horse grazed in the pasture to the left of the barn. Hot air poured from its nostrils in the chilly morning air.

"His name is Ned," said Richard. "We had another horse; it was a mare. Her name was Callie, but she died last year. We've got four cows though. C'mon, I'll show you."

"We've never been close up to a horse or a cow before," said Beth.

"Not chickens, neither," said Joey. They skirted past a John Deere tractor sitting by the barn door. Richard slid the big barn door back and they went inside.

"Come on in, and slide that door closed behind you, son. It's cold enough in here," Lyle. Couzens yelled. "Just stay in that middle aisle, kids, and you'll be fine."

The barn smelled of cow manure and hay.

"P—-yoo. What stinks?" Joey asked.

Richard giggled. "Are you kiddin'? That's cow poop, stupid, see?" He pointed to the gutters. "That's going to be one of your jobs—shoveling it out." He laughed again. Beth stood as if frozen, her fingers laced together behind her back. She stared at the cows.

"We've still got to milk two of these cows," said Mr. Couzens. "Gert, she's the brown Guernsey there—and Annie, the black and white one. I already milked Suzie and Ruthie over there." He pointed at two more Holsteins. "You might as well learn how to milk them, first thing. Show them, Richard" His eyes met Beth's. "You can just watch and learn, girl."

"Come on," said Richard. He grabbed a bucket and the stool, then got situated under Gert. He said, "Now, the first thing is . . ."

Claaaaang! Claaaang! Claaaang! A bell was ringing. Richard got up and scrambled to the door. "That's the bell. He slid it open, stepped outside and waved at the house. After cupping his hand to his ear, he ran back inside. "Joey—Ma wants you. You better hurry." Beth stood with her mouth agape while

Joey ran for the house. He knew he was in trouble, but he had to go in. A shiver slid like a bony fingertip down the back of his neck. She must have found my pajamas, he thought.

Mrs. Couzens met him at the back door, her hands were on her hips and she looked mad.

"Come on in here, boy."

Joey hesitated and stood still for a beat. His face turned red and his chest heaved. He felt the urge to pee.

"Come in-no sense standing out there." Her voice was laced with obvious anger.

Joey edged past her and saw his pajamas lying in a pile on the kitchen floor.

She pointed. "Sit in that chair."

"Now then, young man, I don't know what's worse—you peeing the bed or your trying to hide it from me." Her arms were folded across her chest as she paused and stared at him.

"Did you honestly think I wouldn't find out you wet the bed last night? Hmmm?"

"No, Ma'am."

"No? Then why did you try to hide your pajamas? Your sheets, too. You had them covered up in there. Real sneaky, if you ask me. They'd never dry that way, boy." Her eyes widened as she stood over him.

"I was going to tell you," Joey murmured.

"You were gonna tell me? When? Tomorrow?" She paused, waiting for an answer. "No, you thought I wouldn't find them, that *was* what you *really* thought, wasn't it?"

Joey had no answer.

"Well?"

"I don't know, Ma'am." Tears streamed down his cheeks. "I want to go home to my Gram and Gramps house. I want my mommy."

Mrs. Couzens was silent for a moment.

"Well, that's just not any kind of answer." She waited again. "What do you think they would say? They certainly wouldn't want you to behave like this either, now would they?"

"No Ma'am." He wiped his nose on the sleeve of his jacket, but the tears continued to come.

"No, Ma'am, is right. You know they wouldn't. Now, then, I'll show you where the washtub is — you can wash your sheets and pajamas and hang them on the line to dry. Is that understood?"

"Ye... yes, Ma'am."

"And dry up that blubbering right now-you hear me?" Her lip trembled as she said, "You're too old to be crying like a baby on any account. Now, you'll need to remember not to sneak and lie again, so you'll be going to bed without supper. Understand?"

"Ye... yes, ma'am." Joey wiped his eyes with the back of his hand and started to get up.

"Whoa, there." She held up her hand to stop him. One more thing, boy. See to it that you don't cause this mess again. I cannot abide with a child your age wetting the bed in the first place." She picked up the pajamas and threw them at him. "There you are. Now, follow me."

Chapter Five

T he young have aspirations that never come to pass; the old have reminiscences of what never happened.

Alice Powet and Joe Harrison were barely twenty years old when they met in 1933. She was a beauty, with wavy, chestnut hair that she wore shoulder length, soft, big, brown eyes, a perky nose, and lush lips that now and then flashed a radiant smile.

Alice was living with her parents, Carl and Lillian Powet, in Gouvernuer, New York at the time. She had worked hard, stayed at home for the most part, and seldom dated prior to her involvement with Joe. She was employed as a checker on a factory assembly line where he was a supervisor.

A tall, sturdy man, Joe was ruggedly handsome, with curly black hair and a square jaw, a brilliant individual who was very opinionated. He was an intellectual. He felt as though he was wasting his time supervising for Watertown Textiles, but jobs were hard to find during the depression and he was making a decent wage.

Joe was an only child whose parents had been killed in a car crash when he was twelve. He had very few family ties and lived in an apartment in nearby Black River. He enjoyed his single life, but confessed to himself that he needed to meet that special someone and settle down.

Alice admired Joe; she liked the way he treated people, and was attracted to his good looks, intelligence, and sense of humor. They chatted now and again at break time, and Alice was both surprised and thrilled when he asked her to go dancing one Saturday night.

They had driven down to what was considered lover's lane and parked along the rim of Butterfield Lake. Yellow slicks of moonlight, like patches of oil paint floated on the lake's surface, and it was dark except for occasional headlights passing by out on Highway 451. Crickets, frogs, locusts and other nocturnal inhabitants made weird sounds while they cuddled and talked. Joe eventually kissed her that night and took her home with stars in her eyes and dreams on her mind.

Their third date evolved into a very special night. They went to dinner at the local best, Huff's Steakhouse, and dined by candlelight. Alice's eyes shone bright with the wine, and when Joe's knee rubbed hers under the table, they both felt the same spark and expectation of what was to follow.

Parked outside his apartment, they exchanged a quick kiss, and then a longer one. Their movements were so easy. No choreography. Their heads turned at just the right angle, they embraced each other with no wasted motion, like pieces in a puzzle fate was sliding together.

Was it possible that one could know another person for so short a period of time and feel like it was several lifetimes? Joe nuzzled his face into her hair, absorbing every particle of her scent. Alice couldn't resist when he suggested going to his place, and they spent the rest of the night falling in love.

Alice wasn't sure what true love was, but she knew acceptance was part of it and she sensed that from Joe. It was a quality that had been rare in her young life, and she found its nearness thrilling and disquieting at the same time. However, Alice's folks weren't impressed with Joe. They felt he was a know-it-all who would ultimately hurt their daughter. Nevertheless, Alice and Joe had mountains they wanted to climb together, and they eloped by the year's end. They settled into a small house on Bronson Street in Watertown where Alice became pregnant and quit work at the factory. The next three years blessed them with two children, Beth, then Joey.

With rationing stamps and job layoffs, post-Depression times were hard for the middle class and even more so for the inherent poor. Yet, for the most part, the Harrisons were a happy family, just getting by like everyone else.

By 1941, America was swept into a blazing war in Europe, where Adolph Hitler was determined to take over the world. And then there had been the attack on the United States naval fleet in Honolulu by the Japanese which brought war in the Pacific. The entire world was in chaos.

Two weeks after the attack on Pearl Harbor, Joe told Alice, "Honey, I went and signed up today. I'm going in the Army."

Alice was shocked of course. Her mind was in a whirl questioning why Joe would do such a thing. "Why not let them draft you... why volunteer? You have a family to care for."

Joe chose his words very carefully. It took him a long time before he finally said, "Those sneaky bastards attacked our boys while they were sleeping. We can't let them get away with that, Alice. Hell, no! Hitler's taking over one side of the world, and now the Japs are after the rest. I've got to go and do my share — all the guys are going to help — not just me."

Alice was dazed. She couldn't believe what he said. Joe watched as her face paled. "Honey, are you alright?" He reached to pull her into his arms. She hedged away from him.

"What do you want me to say, Joe? Why? Why are you doing this?"

"I told you why, I just have to."

"No!" Alice pulled away. "You don't *have* to," she cried. "This isn't your deal, Joe. What have you done? She wheeled around. "Let the single guys do the fighting," she pleaded. "You're married, for God's sake. You've got kids, doesn't that matter?"

"Yes, of course you all matter, Alice, you and the kids, but this is something I just have to do. Can't you see that?" He wrapped her in his arms. "Now, listen, you can live with your mother and father until I get back. I'll talk to your dad- he's a vet — he'll understand. He most likely wants me to go, since he's too old. Besides, I'll send you most of my pay every month, honey. You and the kids will be fine."

"Joe, . . ." She started to say something, and then stopped and looked down, suddenly wary. Tears filled her eyes and she felt as though the ground was sinking under her.

Joe tilted her head with his fingertips and looked into her eyes. Her bottom lip quivered.

"Oh, Joe. What will I do without you? What does this all mean? What about the kids? I'm so afraid. This is like a nightmare." She looked into his eyes and sobbed, then lay her head on his chest. Joe rubbed her back in small aimless circles with his hand.

"Hopefully the war will be over soon, and I'll be back before you know it," he murmured. But Alice knew it was useless to hope. She knew that hope was nothing more than deferred despair.

"I love you," he murmured.

"No! If you really loved me and the kids, you wouldn't go," she cried.

There was nothing more to say. Neither of them realized Alice was pregnant with their third child when Joe left.

Chapter Six

C lara Couzens had the heart of a scorpion and spent thirty-six years perfecting the art of assigning blame. Her personal credo — *Everything bad that happens is someone else's fault* — could be stretched to fit any circumstance. The world owed Clara and always would. The Child Welfare Program in New York was not aware of that when they authorized her and her husband Lyle to be foster parents.

Raised by a Dutch father on a farm in rural Pennsylvania, she had never known the love and nurturing of a mother. She harbored a life-long grudge, never forgiving the woman who had given birth to her. Blanche Van Wyck left home in the dark of night when Clara was just four years old. Her father, Ezekiel Van Wyck, was a righteous, difficult man, who treated her like the son he never had. Clara subsequently learned early on that nothing was easy, and her sex wouldn't discount her from performing the hard labor of a man.

Clara was allowed one dress for church on Sundays; she'd get a new one only when she outgrew the one she wore. The rest of her wardrobe consisted of bib overalls and flannel shirts. Ezekiel made it clear she was far better suited to milking cows, scraping gutters, and slaughtering pigs and chickens, than braiding her hair or picking flowers.

She failed to learn to be grateful for small favors and was impetuous and careless with favor's use, subsequently she had very few friends. Two older ladies at the First Baptist church gave her some books when she was eleven years old. Among them were first editions of *Heidi* and *Little Women*. As she walked home from church that day, Clara tossed them in the lake and waited with nonchalance to be sure they floated downstream before she left.

Running away from home when she was sixteen, Clara met Lyle Couzens, and married before she turned eighteen. Lyle wanted children, but Clara did not, and it was purely an accident when she became pregnant with Richard at twenty-seven.

Taking in foster children was a ruse. Clara didn't love children — she tolerated them enough to impress the powers that be. Figuring it was easy money, she applied with the State of New York and was promptly given a license. Since it was well established as to who was in charge of such important decisions in the marriage, Lyle had agreed just as he went along with everything Clara wanted. The farming was not prospering and the extra money would be a good thing.

Clara disguised her nasty personality very well — certainly well enough to fool the authorities at the Welfare Department, who saw her as very efficient and caring.

Clara developed health issues over the years, including a bad back and ulcers. The intestinal unrest that troubled her from time to time was the result of tolerating her husband's accelerating penchant for hard liquor. Further, she was fed up with "scraping the bottom of the barrel" as she put it, to make ends meet. She blamed the shortage of money on the war and the inadequate pay she got for providing foster care to children. She was good at confrontation; in fact, she seemed to relish and thrive on it.

Beth and Joey soon learned their foster mother had a lack of patience to go with her cold reserve and laser-like glare.

A big issue circled around Joey's lack of bladder control. He didn't know how to stop wetting his bed or his pants. Mrs. Couzens made him nervous when she screamed. Sometimes, just the way the woman looked at him or Beth would frighten him enough to make him lose control. In the beginning, his punishment for such an infraction was to stand in a corner of his bedroom with the wet pants pulled down over his head, arms extended straight up in the air.

"And don't you let them arms down either, boy," Mrs. Couzens yelled.

Beth felt sorry for her brother, but helpless. She tried to console

Joey when she could. She had to be careful though, because Mrs. Couzens didn't allow any talking when she doled out punishment. At bedtime, Joey cried and they spoke in whispers.

"I can't help it, Sis. She makes me do it when she yells. Why is she so mean? I want to tell Gram and Mommy. Gramps will come and get us. I just know he will."

"Shhhh! I know, Joey. Just try to use the pot more times, that's all. Even if you don't have to go — try to do it anyway. That way you probably won't wet your pants, I'll bet. Please don't cry. Please?"

When there was an incident, Richard always seemed to be close by to laugh and poke fun. Mr. Couzens, on the other hand, rarely remarked on his wife's disciplinary measures and the kids grew to realize that he was just as fearful of his wife as they were. Beth was her brother's only ally and they both missed home and the loving arms of their mother and grandparents.

Joey's tears were always coupled with pleas to Beth about leaving. "I'll run away, that's what. Sis, I want you to come with me. Please, let's just get up at night and leave. We can go back home and tell Gramps how mean she is."

"Joey, we just can't do that. They'll find us somehow and bring us back. Think about what will happen then."

Over time, Mrs. Couzens' punishments became more severe, and when Joey had an accident, she ridiculed him and took away meals. Bread and water for meals became commonplace.

The kids had been at the Couzen's for nearly six months, and one particular cold morning in the fall, Mrs. Couzens was on a rampage with Lyle about something. They were in their room arguing, and the kids could tell she was upset with Mr. Couzens because she was doing the shouting while her husband's voice was nothing more than muffled mumbling.

The kids were sitting at the breakfast table with Richard. Hearing the racket, Joey's heart thumped like a baby sparrow's. He got a panicky look on his face and felt a trickle of warm pee running down his leg — even though he had just come in from the outhouse moments before.

The tirade in the bedroom was at its zenith, with Mrs. Couzens screaming: "Well, I won't put up with it anymore, Lyle. Maybe you'd like to do it all, mister. I'll leave and let you figure out what to do with these brats and the State, too."

When they finally came out of their room, and Mrs. Couzens discovered Joey had wet his pants, she was furious. At that point, it was like gasoline had been poured on a raging fire.

"Again? You have done this again?" She shook her head and waved her finger in his face. "You're a bad boy, Joseph! Get out of my sight, you little pig. Go out on the porch, and don't come back in here until I tell you to! Go on, get out!" She pointed to the back door.

Mr. Couzens scratched his head and shuffled out the door ahead of him. It was nearly freezing on the porch that morning, and Joey stood out there shivering for over an hour before Mr. Couzens came in from the barn with milk. He saw Joey's teeth chattering. When he went inside it was one of the few times he spoke up.

"Clara, I just wonder... I mean... the lad has been out there long enough, don't you think you should let him come in?" Beth was on her knees scrubbing the floor, and she was surprised as she watched Mrs. Couzens, hoping she would listen to her husband.

"Why don't you mind your own business, Lyle! I'll decide when it's time, thank you! I don't need your two cents. The boy has to learn a lesson. I won't put up with it any longer, I tell you."

Mr. Couzens put the milk on the counter. He stared at his wife for a a moment, then tossed his hat on the table and poured himself a cup of coffee.

By the time she told Joey to come in, his corduroy pants were stiff, and he could barely walk. He cried and struggled to run to his room while Richard giggled.

Mr. Couzens stared at Richard with wide eyes and touched his finger to his lips, signaling silence, while his wife followed Joey down the hallway. Beth had stopped scrubbing the floor and listened with tears forming in her eyes.

"How would you like to sit in the cellar, sonny boy? Huh? You just pull anymore of those nasty shenanigans and that's where you'll go." She punctuated that with another threat. "We've got rats down there, too. Big ones! You don't want me to put you down there, do you?"

Joey's insides quivered. "No, Ma'am," he cried.

"Well then... stop this peeing nonsense, you're too old for it, I tell you."

Joey lay awake many nights and stared at the ceiling. He worried that if he fell asleep he would pee the bed. Sluggish doing his chores the next day, he also frequently nodded off on the bus or in school.

The kids were never able to figure out what it would take to make Mrs. Couzens happy. Her emotional explosions always targeted them for something perceived to be real in her mind, or simply contrived.

Beth was a good girl, but she could never please Mrs. Couzens performing her house cleaning chores.

"If you put one of these plates away with egg on it again, you'll eat bread and water for a day, maybe you'll learn to be more careful. When I was your age I did all the housework and scooped cow poop besides. If you do something, do it right the first time, Missy."

Richard, for one reason or another, was generally spared her wrath and Lyle simply avoided his wife's tantrums altogether, whenever possible. He preferred to spend most of his time in the barn or thereabouts "attending chores."

Clara's voice had the tense quality of a woman who had bought seriously into a secret place of unhappiness. When agitated, she sounded like a tortured witch: "All right. I want to know who stole the banana from the pantry!" she screamed one snowy Saturday afternoon. Their chores finished, Joey and Beth were in their room playing with the only game they had- *Tiddly-Winks*. They had brought it with them from home. Hearing Mrs. Couzens yell, they stopped playing, looked into each other's eyes and waited.

"Richard! Get out here!" Her anxiety caused the light to go out of her face and leave her lips parted, with her eyes wide, as though she had been slapped. A nervous tick caused her head to jerk repeatedly to the right when she was excited, and it served to make her more threatening. Richard was in the parlor, listening to *Let's Pretend* on the radio, but flew out to the kitchen when his mother called.

"What, Ma?"

She stood with her hands on her hips and pointed. "Son, I had six bananas left here in the cupboard, one's missing. Did you take it—that's all I want to know?"

Richard shook his head from side to side. "No, Ma. Not me, I'd have to ask you first."

She glared at him a moment and searched for a lie. "Go on out of here then." Richard ran and his mother turned and peered down the hallway. "Elizabeth! Joseph! Get out here!"

The kids ran to the kitchen where they found her poised in the doorway with her arms folded across her chest. "I'm missing a banana from the pantry. Now, I know one of you took it, only question is which one?" Her dark eyes were scary pinpoints burning right through them. Her rigid jaw and twitching head was scary. "Which one of you did it? I don't want any lying either, who did it?"

Beth and Joey stared at each other while she stood inches away with a challenging smugness on her face. She tapped her foot and waited.

Joey shrugged. His legs were shaking. He thought it must have been Richard, but he said, "I didn't do it."

"Not me, either," said Beth. She looked to her brother. "We wouldn't take any bananas, would we, Joey?"

"No! We didn't take no bananas, Ma'am."

Mrs. Couzens pulled at her lip as though she was wrestling with a tough decision. She glared at them for a few seconds but said nothing. Her neck turned crimson and she swallowed hard, working her jaw.

"You little snots! You think I don't know better? I count everything around here. There were six bananas here yesterday, now there's only five. You expect me to believe they just grew feet and walked out of here? No! I think not. So,I'll ask you once more... which one of you took it? Tell the truth and shame the devil."

Beth backed up just a bit. "I don't know, but I didn't take anything, honest, Ma'am, and I don't think Joey did either."

"You, be quiet, young lady. Let him answer for himself."

Joey shook his head from side to side. "No. I didn't" He began to pee and couldn't stop, even though Mrs. Couzens could certainly see the wet stain spreading in his corduroys. She pointed.

"Look what you're doing, boy! How dare you, after all I've warned you! Well, you will have to learn the hard way." She turned her head and called out, Richard!"

Richard, who had been watching everything from just beyond the parlor door, ran to his mother's side.

"Yeah, Ma."

"Go fill the dishpan with snow and bring it here, right now."

Richard looked dumbfounded. "What do you need that for?"

"Richard, just do as you're told, please. Go fill the pan and bring the flashlight too, and hurry up!" she snapped.

Richard ran for the back door with the big, silver-colored dishpan in his hands. Mrs. Couzens suddenly grabbed a fistful of Joey's hair and yanked. At the same time, she reached out like a striking rattler and snatched Beth's arm. She dragged them both over to the cellar door. Her nails dug into Beth's young flesh, causing the girl's face to twist in pain. She screamed so loud her face turned red, and her hair came loose from its tie and flew every which way on her head. Joey felt like his hair was being pulled out of his head. The more he tried to pull away, the more it hurt.

"Owww! Owww!" he yelped.

Mrs. Couzens wobbled his head back and forth. "You're going to tell me the truth or you'll both sit in the cellar?"

"Owww! You're hurting me!" Beth cried.

Joey felt like he had to do something; he couldn't watch this woman hurt his sister any more. He suddenly yelled, "Ma'am, It was me—I took..."

"No, Joey!" Beth screamed.

"What?" Mrs. Couzens yelled. "What did you say, boy?" She let go of his hair and studied his face. "What were you saying? Go on, tell me."

"Nuh... nothing, Ma'am."

Clara Couzens eyes were huge and her breathing came in rapid-fire bursts. Joey slowly backed away from her and banged into the china cabinet. The glasses inside jiggled and tinkled and he looked back over his shoulder just as Richard came running back with the pan full of snow and a flashlight.

"Take the dishpan downstairs, Richard." She let go of Beth's arm and flipped the hook on the cellar door. "Joseph, you get those pants off, right now. You're going learn to stop wetting yourself, young man."

Joey didn't like to undress in front of anybody, but it wasn't the first time Mrs. Couzens had made him take his wet pants off in front of people. He quickly unbuttoned the pants and dropped them. Fumbling, he finally used his feet to shove them off his ankles.

"Now get down there, both of you little liars." She held the flashlight and followed them down the creaky wooden steps. At the bottom she flashed the light onto the dirt floor.

"Put that pan right there, Richard." He did as he was told, then stood and watched.

"Now you sit down on that pan, boy."

Joey slowly sat on the snow-filled pan and immediately started crying. She shone the light in his eyes, blinding him. "Don't you dare get up either. This will teach you to stop peeing everywhere. I'm sick of it, you hear."

Joey whined. "But, I can't stay here, it's too cold."

Beth said, "No, he can't do that, Mrs. Couzens. Please don't make him."

Mrs. Couzens ignored them and flipped the light into Beth's eyes.

"You shut up. You're going to keep him company, Missy. Since neither one of you wants to tell the truth about the banana, some time down here might change your tune." She turned to Richard and shoved him. "Get back upstairs, Son."

When they reached the top of the stairs Mrs. Couzens yelled back down. "If you don't move a lot, the rats shouldn't bother you." With that, she slammed the cellar door. Beth and Joey screamed in the dark.

Chapter Seven

C lara Couzens always put on her nice face when Judith Kellogg was coming to visit. Notified four days ahead of time, on a Friday, her demeanor changed for the few days before and after Kellogg came and left. Kellogg said she would be coming out the following Tuesday afternoon when the kids would be home from school.

It was in the waning days of May and school would soon be out for the summer. Tuesday morning was warm and promising hot.

Beth, Joey and Richard had been up an hour and a half. They made their beds and emptied their slop pails, then washed up and went to the breakfast table. The bus would be there to pick them up for school in less than an hour, and they still had chores to accomplish before they left.

Joey was hungry. He had been sent to bed without supper for forgetting to empty his chamber pot, the previous day.

"Can I have some more toast, Ma'am?" Joey asked.

"No. You've had plenty, Joseph. I have to bake again today. Seems like that's all I do since you children came here. I've only got enough bread for the mister's breakfast." She sat at the table sipping a cup of coffee. "Only so many hours in the day," she mumbled. Her back was stiff and her hair was tied back in a bun. "You go out and do your chores. That goes for you, too, Richard. Elizabeth, you'd best get about doing up these dishes." She poured herself another cup of coffee and cleared her throat.

"Now, as I told you both, Judith Kellogg will be here when you get home from school, so I don't want your good clothes getting messed up. That means be careful at recess, too." Glaring at Joey, she added, "There's no need to crawl around on the ground like an animal during recess, right, Joseph?"

"No, Ma'am."

"You can wear that flannel shirt of yours to do your chores, then change before the bus comes. Missy, you wear my apron until you're done.

"Yes, Ma'am."

It was Beth's job to gather eggs from the henhouse and wash and dry the breakfast dishes. She was also responsible for making both beds in Mr. and Mrs. Couzens' room. Joey was to slop the pigs and milk two of the cows. Richard had to feed the chickens and the cows and Ned, the horse.

Mrs. Couzens tapped her fingers on the table and stared out the kitchen window, as if in deep thought. She looked at Beth. "And when you two get home, I want you to leave your good clothes on and wait until Mrs. Kellogg is gone before you change and do your evening chores. Understand?"

"Yes, Ma'am," they both answered.

"Now, hurry along, and finish up, then get your clothes changed for school—both of you. Hurry, you don't want to miss that bus. That means no lollygagging, Richard."

Beth wore a faded, green-print jumper with her brown- and-white saddle shoes. She brushed her long brown hair without the aid of a mirror. There was no mirror in their room, and she desperately wanted to see how it looked, but the only way to do that was to check in Mrs. Couzen's mirror while she was making their beds.

Joey wore his blue pants, the only pair without holes in the knees. The corduroys were faded. but clean. His favorite red-and blue-striped pullover shirt was dirty, so he grabbed the yellow-and-green-striped one.

When Mrs. Kellogg visited, he wore his best pants with his favorite shirt and clean socks, the ones with no holes. He wasn't allowed to wear them any other time. He said he wished he could show them off at school. One of his classmates, Timmy Pullman, wore different clothes every day and all of his stuff looked brand new. In fact, most of his classmates were always dressed well.

He whispered to Beth before they ran out to the bus. "I'm still hungry, Sis. Gee, I just wanted one more piece of toast."

"I know, Joey, I'm still hungry, too, but you heard what she said."

"Yeah, I know. Please, Sis, let's just run away, like we talked about before."

"Shhhh. Don't talk so loud. Joey. I told you- don't say that anymore. We can't run away; there's no place to go. They would find us, don't you see? Then we would really be in trouble."

"Why can't we just go back to Gram and Gramps house?" Joey pulled the polo shirt over his head as he spoke. "Gramps would be real mad at Mrs. Couzens if he knew how mean she was. I'll bet he would punch her right in the nose."

"No, he wouldn't. Nobody's going to punch anybody, Joey. Hurry up now and get your shoes on before she starts yelling," said Beth. She brushed her hair again and again while she waited.

"I hate it when kids tease me about my shoes and socks."

His dress shoes were brown and shiny, but the pair he wore to do chores were the same ones he wore to school. They had small openings around the soles, and the laces had broken two times. Mrs. Couzens refused to buy new laces.

In gym class, when they played dodge ball, and were required to take off their shoes, Joey tried to hide the holes in his socks by squeezing his toes together.

Beth was a third-grader and she also took a lot of teasing because her school dresses were stained from rusty wash water. Her hair was never fixed real fancy with bows like a lot of the other girls. Both of the children tried to avoid harassment, but it was difficult because more kids jumped on the bandwagon all the time. They nicknamed Joey "Little Hobo" and Beth was "Little Orphan Annie."

"Alright then, will you tell Mrs. Kellogg when she comes this time? Tell her about the cellar. We can even show it to her, and I'll show her the dishpan, too. Mrs. Couzens will get into trouble, I bet." Joey watched Beth's face for a positive sign, but there was none.

"Please, Sis? You're older, she'll listen to you—just tell her about that."

"Shhhh . Please don't talk anymore, Joey, Come on, we're gonna miss the bus- Richard is already out there."

Mrs. Couzens stood, holding the back door open for them. "Remember, you two, Mrs. Kellogg will be coming. She might even be here when you get home, so wash up as soon as you get in the door. I don't want to have to remind either of you."

"Yes, Ma'am," said Beth.

"Here, take this." Mrs. Couzens reached into her apron pocket and pulled out a little, black change purse. The kids were rarely given money for lunch. But, she always gave it to them on the day of Judith Kellogg's visits. The rest of the time, they took peanut butter sandwiches, and sometimes an extra penny for milk.

She handed Beth a nickel. "Now, don't lose this, you hear? Put that in your pocket, Elizabeth." She tied Joey's nickel in the corner of a checkered handkerchief and stuffed it in his pants pocket. "And you hang on to yours, too, Joseph. Now, you'd better hurry."

They ran. The morning had a chill to it; they could see their breath. The sun was up and there was a fresh smell in the air that comes after a spring rain. Beth loved those early-morning hours, when there was a cold cut to the air, yet one could sense the heat coming over the horizon to warm the day.

They ran halfway down the muddy driveway until Beth suddenly held up. "Wait, Joey. There's the bus, way down there." She pointed. "I can see the red lights. We don't have to run, just walk fast, okay?"

"Okay, but, Sis . . ."

"What?"

"Promise me something, okay? Please don't tell Mrs. Kellogg I peed my pants or my bed, okay?"

"No... I won't tell her, but I think Mrs. Couzens will, or maybe she already did."

"You'll tell her about the cellar though, okay?"

"I'll try, Joey, that's all I can do. It's not that easy. Mrs. Couzens scares me too, you know. I want to ask about Mommy and Gram and Gramps, too, but I just have to wait until the right time. I don't really think I should talk about the cellar."

Joey stopped walking and studied his sister's face. "Why not?"

"Because" said Beth. What if Mrs. Kellogg doesn't believe me? Kids do lie, you know. What do you think will happen to us then? Stop talking about it now, or Richard will hear you. There's the bus anyway, come on."

Chapter Eight

Mrs. Kellogg hadn't arrived by the time the kids got home from school. Richard's uncle Jim was waiting for him which was to be expected. It was routine when Mrs. Kellogg visited. There was always appeared to be a reason for Richard to be away from the house. After Jim left with Richard, Mrs. Couzens turned her attention to preparing for the caseworker's visit.

"Beth, after you get washed up, I want you to make sure your brother's hair is combed. Don't leave it sticking up like it is. Jumpin' Jehosephat!" She handed a jar to Beth. "Here, use some of Richard's Brylcreem." She clomped back down the hall, and yelled back. "Young man, make sure you go out to the pot before she comes, too, you hear me?"

"Yes, Ma'am," Joey answered.

When they were done, Beth and Joey ran to the window in the front room to watch for Mrs. Kellogg's black car. A few minutes passed when he saw her pull in down by the highway. Both he and Beth ran to the door, intent on going outside to meet her.

"Uuuh uh," said Mrs. Couzens, as she breezed around the corner. "Don't go out there. You know the rules, go to your room until you are called."

The kids scooted back to their bedroom and jumped on Beth's bed under the window. They watched as Mrs. Kellogg got out and opened the back door of the sedan. A tall, young girl got out and followed her to the door.

"Who's that?"

"I don't know, Joey. Here, you messed up your hair." She ran her fingertips across the top of his head as they heard the knock on the door and sat down on the bed.

"I don't care who she, Joey whispered. "All I know is when Mrs. Kellogg is here, I feel like Mrs. Couzens can't hurt me."

"I know, Joey, me too."

They watched as the short, stout woman, with heavy, dimpled arms and legs waddled to the door. Her black shoes had little dotty holes in the sides, and appeared too small for her feet. It was obvious that her wardrobe was limited, as she a jacket over what appeared to be the same dark blue dress she had worn on the previous visit. She had her glasses on, and her brown hair was done up in a slightly lopsided bun.

The girl was taller than Beth — in fact, taller than Mrs. Kellogg. A bit on the thin side, her silky red hair hung in her eyes, like a little boy's, and most likely always needed combing. She had lots of freckles on a milky-white face. She carried a small brown suitcase.

"Hello, Judith," Mrs. Couzens smiled and the two women shook hands.

"Good afternoon, Clara." She turned to the girl. "Mrs. Couzens, this young lady is Ginny... or Regina, actually — but she likes to be called Ginny. She just turned sixteen three weeks ago. Say hello to Mrs. Couzens, Ginny."

Ginny had a small voice and appeared shy as she said, "Hello, Ma'am."

"Hello, Ginny. Have a seat, won't you? Judith, can I get you a cup of coffee."

"Yes, I could use that, for sure. It's unusually cold out there today, isn't it? Where in the deuce is spring, anyway?" She set her purse on the floor by her feet and twisted out of her coat. Hanging it on the back of the chair, she sat next to Ginny on a wooden kitchen chair. Mrs. Couzens smiled and began to fuss over pouring the coffee and gave a cup to Mrs. Kellogg.

"Yes, the days have been unseasonably cold I think. I hate to say it, but it like snow. The radio didn't call for any, did it?"

"Not that I heard," said Kellogg.

Mrs. Couzens sipped her coffee and smiled. "So, Ginny — I guess you'll be staying with us for awhile."

Ginny nodded. Her hands were in her lap and twisted around as if she was playing cat's cradle, and her eyes were busy searching her new surroundings. Gussy, the cat, rubbed the entire length of her body against her leg, and Ginny cautiously reached down to pet her.

Several long minutes passed before Mrs. Couzens called: "Elizabeth! Joseph! You children come on out here now. Mrs. Kellogg is here, and she has a surprise for us."

Joey's stomach lurched as he thought about the earlier conversation with Beth. He was sure she wouldn't tell Mrs. Kellogg about the cellar, but he knew somebody should. *I wish I could do it myself.*

They walked up the hallway to the front room and stood in the doorway, scrunched together, shoulder to shoulder.

"Here they are!" said Mrs. Kellogg. "Ginny, look here, you have two new friends." She reached out with arms open wide. "Come over here, you two dears. My, it's wonderful to see you children. You're looking very well, I must say."

She circled an arm around each of their waists. "How are you?" She hugged them before they could respond. Joey smelled her perfume—the same perfume she wore the day she brought them to the Couzens farm. When she hugged him, Joey felt like he was going to cry. He wished Mrs. Kellogg would keep her arms around him and take him with her.

"Beth, Joey —meet Ginny. Ginny is going to be staying with you and the Couzens for a bit. Isn't that nice?"

"Yes, Ma'am, but when are we going to go back home?" He felt his heart thumping, his mouth went dry and he felt his face turn red.

Complete silence hung in the air and a hard, embarrassed smile passed quickly over Mrs. Couzens's lips, Mrs. Kellogg cleared her throat. She gave Joey a pitiful smile.

"Well, now, that's a good question, young man." She twisted in the chair and leaned one fat elbow on the table. "It seems your Gramps hasn't been feeling himself lately, and I am afraid your Mommy has been quite ill, also. So, you see, right now is a real bad time for us to make any changes."

"Mommy's sick?" Beth's eyes widened.

"Yes, but musn't worry, Beth. She has been to the doctor and she'll be fine. It will just take awhile for her to get better. You'll be fine here with the Couzens until then. Okay?"

Beth looked down at her feet. "Yes, Ma'am."

"Maybe before Christmas, we'll have to see."

Mrs. Couzens fidgeted on her chair. "My goodness, Joseph, don't act like that now-Mrs. Kellogg will think you're not happy here, silly boy." She giggled. Her voice was so different, Joey thought. It was like two different people could talk out of one face.

"Well now, Beth, why don't you and your brother take Ginny and show her to her room while Mrs. Kellogg and I take care of some paperwork. She pointed. "Take her to the bedroom upstairs..."

Joey spoke again: "Well, how about our Daddy? Can we go stay with him?"

"No, I'm afraid not; he's still away, overseas, fighting for Uncle Sam, Joey"

"Who's Uncle Sam?"

She laughed and took his hand in hers. "Our country, Joey, The United States. Hopefully, the war will be all over soon. Lord, I do pray it will."

"Amen," said Mrs. Couzens. "We've all had enough of this war."

"Come on, Joey, let's help Ginny," said Beth. She pulled him by the arm. Ginny picked up her suitcase.

"Oh! Wait a minute, Joey. Come here, just a sec."

Joey slowly edged his way back to Mrs. Kellogg. She was staring at a black and blue spot on his neck. She lifted his chin, leaned in to study the bruise. Mrs. Couzens got up and crowded in for a better look.

"What's this nasty bruise on your neck? What in the world?" She caressed the bruise with her fingertips. "Were you playing rough at recess today?"

Beth shook her head slightly indicating "no" and Joey panicked. He surprised himself with his answer. "No, Uhhhh, the wind blew the gate and it hit me when I wasn't looking."

"The gate?"

Mrs. Couzens said, "He means the gate that closes off our pasture to the barn, don't you, Joseph?

Joey kept the lie going and said, "Yes, I was out at the barn, doing my chores and the lock thing... you know... the thing that keeps the cows from getting out." He formed his hands in a circle. "That handle on the gate, it hit me right there when the wind blew it hard." He rubbed the bruise.

"I see. Yes, well, it has been windy lately, hasn't it? "She took off her glasses to look closer. "You'll have to be more careful, won't you, Joseph?"

"Yes, Ma'am."

"The darn thing looked a lot worse right after it happened a few days ago," injected Mrs. Couzens. "You know boys—they don't watch things like they should."

"Come on, Joey. Let's go." Beth pulled on his hand and they took Ginny to her room upstairs where she heaved the suitcase onto the bed with a heavy sigh.

"How old are you, really?" Beth asked.

"Sixteen," Ginny said, but a strange look crept over her face. "Are these people nice?" Her voice squeezed out sharp and flat like sheet metal.

Beth and Joey looked at each other.

"Do they give you lots to eat?" she asked. An uncomfortable quiet still hung in the air.

"We get enough to eat, usually," Beth finally answered.

"Where's the outhouse?"

"Out back behind the house. I'll show you. There's a pot under your bed, you have to empty it every morning."

"Yes," said Joey. "Mrs. Couzens will get real mad if you don't do that."

Ginny sat on the bed and bounced slightly, checking the firmness. She ran her fingers across the bed covers. "Do they ever beat you?" She stared at Joey but he didn't answer.

"I mean, did you really get that mark from a gate?" She waited and smirked. "They *do* beat you, don't they?"

Beth tried to fight back the tears. She finally decided to just let them pour down her cheeks as she hugged her brother to her chest. "Please don't ask us anymore stuff right now, okay?" she said.

Chapter Nine

Lyle Couzens huddled just inside the barn doors and took a long swig off the pint of Old Crow whiskey. He licked his lower lip nervously. The nip in the Adirondack air was a perfect excuse. All of Lyle's drinking was done in the barn, and usually in the very same spot, where he could watch all the comings and goings at the house. He was particularly careful to not let the kids see him, lest they tell his wife.

Lyle struggled from day to day dodging the harsh reality of his lot in life with Clara. When they married, he thought Clara was a sweetheart. In truth, of course, she was mean-spirited and hard. Talking to her about most anything could be like walking through cobwebs or accidentally raking your hand across a hornet's nest. Love was absent in their relationship and sex was never discussed, much less acted upon, particularly after Richard was born.

Bobbing through life's turbulence like driftwood, Lyle no longer looked at calendars or watched the faces of clocks. With each of Clara's tantrums, he became more emboldened to make his move. It was all mapped out—in his head at least. He would take whatever money he had squirreled away along with very few clothes. With nothing to lose and everything to gain, he'd sneak off in the middle of the night. He'd drive the old Dodge pickup as far as it would hold up and hitchhike if need be, but he would leave. The idea of spending the rest of his days in the rich Sonoma Valley of California enticed him. He read about the place in both *The Saturday Evening Post* and *Look* magazines. The allure of grape farming had him convinced to make his move as soon as possible.

That was before Clara corralled them into the foster parent thing. Although he wasn't that keen on raising youngsters, the extra money swayed his thinking and he temporarily gave up on his California dreaming. The years had come and gone since he seriously considered leaving.

Lyle figured Clara would loosen up a bit and be so much easier to live with if she had more money coming in. But it just wasn't so, and yet he couldn't just walk away. Nothing had changed except Lyle's taste for alcohol had increased ten-fold. Clara was all too familiar with the smell on his breath, but tended to ignore such things as long as Lyle let her have her way about everything else without interfering. Of course, if she was having a very bad day, his drinking was the butt of a vicious attack regardless.

Sometimes, it was Joey's job to feed the cows and the horse, Ned. It was the boy's favorite thing to do. Ned had tiny spots of white on his front legs, and Lyle allowed Joey to climb up on the fence and pet the horse's pink and black nose before he fed him. Joey also carried new straw to the stalls and eventually grew to like the smell of the barn.

Richard was supposed to help, too, but Mr. Couzens usually had to yell at him, to get the most menial job completed. He liked swinging from the barn's rafters and tried to coax Joey into playing in the hay with him.

Mrs. Couzens often sent one or both of the girls to the barn to help Lyle when they were caught up on chores inside the house. As far as she was concerned no work was too hard for a girl anymore than a boy.

"Go on out and see what the mister has got for you to do, Ginny. She glared at Beth. "There's no sense in you two being in here tripping over one another."

As the months passed, Ginny changed. She never did talk much, but she also seemed listless, and withdrawn—even with Beth, with whom she had begun to bond. The girl rarely, if ever, smiled and went upstairs to her room, more often than not, as soon as her chores were done. She skipped meals despite Mrs. Couzen's nagging that she should eat. When she did attend the dinner table, she was extremely quiet and sulky.

"I don't know why you bother to come to the table, Regina. You pick at your food and make everyone else uncomfortable with your pouting,"

"I'm just not hungry, Ma'am. I never did eat too much, even at the other place."

"Well, maybe the other place didn't have good food like you get here. No matter. Go to your room if you want to sulk."

Friday was the last day of school, and, as usual, Beth waited for Ginny by her classroom door. The buses were ready to leave and Beth was afraid they were going to miss theirs if Ginny didn't hurry. Then she spotted her coming down the hall from the opposite direction. Beth noticed she had come out of the principal's office and was walking very slowly.

"Hurry!" Beth called, and Ginny walked faster. "Gosh, what were you doing in there? We have to run now; the bus is going to leave without us."

The driver was ready to pull away and had to reopen the doors for the two girls. When they were seated, Beth studied Ginny's somber expression. "What's the matter? Why were you in the principal's office, anyway?"

Ginny moved her head slowly from side to side. "Nothing." Her voice sounded small; she was blinking her eyes as if she were about to cry, or at least fighting the urge.

"What do you mean, nothing?" Beth leaned in and lowered her voice. "What's wrong?" Ginny didn't answer. She stared straight ahead all the way home. Tears began to form in the corners of her eyes.

•　　•　　•　　•　　•

Saturday morning, the sky was cloudy and it was sprinkling. Richard had been picked up by his uncle Jim, and Ginny was upstairs in her room. With their chores done, Beth and Joey were in their room playing War with cards Ginny had brought when she came. The telephone rang. After four long rings and one short one, Mrs.

Couzens answered it. The telephone didn't ring that often, and the kids were curious; they huddled near their door to listen. At the same time they heard the back door slam. Mr. Couzens had just come in from the barn.

Mrs. Couzens sounded nervous on the telephone. "Yes. Oh, I thought you were going to wait until Monday. At least that was my understanding."

There followed a long pause before she spoke again. "Yes. Very well, then. She'll be ready of course. . . Yes. Oh, Judith, I am so terribly sorry. I don't know what to say. I just don't."

After another long pause, she said, "Yes, alright. We'll see you in a little while then. Yes. Goodbye."

Beth decided to see what was going on and went to the kitchen. "I'm just getting a drink of water, Ma'am."

"Yes, very well," said Mrs. Couzens. Her face was gray and her mouth was slack. She covered her mouth and began to sob uncontrollably. Lyle backed against a chair and sat down. He suddenly looked as though he'd been diagnosed with a terminal illness.

"Lyle, in here, right now." They headed for their bedroom and closed the door.

Joey joined Beth in the kitchen. The kids had never seen nor heard Mrs. Couzens cry. But now, when she spoke to Lyle, she was crying. At first she spoke in a low, deliberate voice that seemed somewhat muffled. But, it wasn't long before it became obvious that she was very angry with her husband about something. Her words were much louder and then she was shouting. .

"Stop this, Clara. It's not true, I told you."

"Oh, stop! Do you think I'm blind or born yesterday, Lyle? For God's sake, why? How could you do this to me-to us? You're a dirty, evil man, Lyle Couzens.

A goddamned liar, too. Think of what this is going to mean. You're just no good. You never have been. If you weren't so lazy, we wouldn't need their money. Good God in heaven, what am I going to do now?"

Mr. Couzens spoke in a much lower voice. "It's not true, Clara, and who are you siding with, anyway? Why can't you believe me about this? Haven't I been there for you through thick and thin? It was your idea bringing those kids in here in the first place, you know."

Their voices got louder, especially Mrs. Couzens'.

"I just knew your drinking would get us in trouble someday. Now you've dragged me down with you. It's your gutter, not mine. I can't side with that. Are you crazy? I don't deserve this and you know it. Does Richard deserve this? I hope they hang you for this, mister."

Lyle came out of the bedroom and paced round and round the kitchen, then threw on a jacket and went outside. The back door slammed once again as he left.

Beth covered her mouth with both hands and hiked her eyebrows. She backed away from the door. Joey gawked at her and followed her back to their own room.

Joey whispered, "Wow! What do you think she's mad at him for, Sis? "I'll bet Mr. Couzens broke his tractor again."

"Shhhh, Joey. No, it's not that, but... I'm not sure, Joey."

Mrs. Couzens cried for a long time before she finally came down the hallway. She dabbed her nose with tissue as she spoke.

"Mrs. Kellogg is coming to visit, children." She sniffled. "I'll not be making supper tonight. Beth, you needn't peel any potatoes. You can both come out and have a peanut butter and jelly sandwich. Then I want you to change into your good clothes and wait back in here until she comes." She turned and abruptly left them standing there. They looked at each other and Beth covered her mouth with both hands.

"Wow! Mrs. Kellogg is on her way? Boy, I wonder how come we didn't know yesterday?" said Joey. He bounced onto his bed. "Good. I'm gonna ask her about going home, Sis."

"You can if you want to, Joey. I hope she says yes this time. I really do."

•   •   •   •   •

Nearly two hours later, Joey stood on his sister's bed, staring out the window. The wind had picked up, and the rain was splashing against the windowpane when he saw Mrs. Kellogg's car pull in. It splashed through puddle after puddle in the driveway then stopped by the porch. Another car pulled in right behind her and parked off to the side. Mrs. Kellogg popped open an umbrella and raced for the front of the house, water splashing on her calves and the bottom of her skirt.

A tall man in a cowboy hat got out of the other car and followed her to the door. His face was red and splotchy, and his stomach hung over his belt like a sack of grain. His black moustache was thick. The kids scurried to their door and listened.

"Hello, Judith."

"Hello, Clara. I apologize for coming out on Saturday, however, under the circumstances, we thought it best."

"Yes, I know."

The man stood right behind Mrs. Kellogg. "This gentleman is Frank Densby. Frank, I'd like you to meet Clara Couzens. Frank is a constable for St. Lawrence County, Clara."

"Hello, Ma'am." His voice matched his bulk. It was deep, and the words were half swallowed by a heavy chest. His tan shirt was getting soaked with rain as he stepped inside the door.

"Hello, Mr. Densby. Can I get either of you some coffee?" said Clara. Densby raised his hand to signal no and pulled out his pipe which he lit with a wooden match that he snapped into flame with his thumbnail. "We'll have to be moving along. Long drive back, you know."

"As I told you on the phone, I'll be back tomorrow afternoon to get the other two, said Mrs. Kellogg. She stared right past Clara, as if she were in the way, then turned to the man. "Frank, why don't you go find Lyle; I need to talk to Mrs. Couzens alone."

"Yeah, sure," he said, as he drifted over to the door.

Mrs. Kellogg paused a moment until he was gone. "Clara, would you mind making sure the kids' door is closed."

"Yes, of course." When Mrs. Couzens went to the hallway, she saw the children scrambling back to their room. "Elizabeth, you and Joseph stay there in your room and close the door until I call you, please."

"Yes, Ma'am," Beth answered.

Nearly a half-hour passed until Mrs. Couzens came back. "Come on out, children. Mrs. Kellogg wants to see you."

"Well, hello there, kids." Mrs. Kellogg smiled and hugged them one at a time. Ginny sat next to her. She had obviously been crying. Her face was flushed and her eyes looked glassy. Sadness drifted from her like a morning fog, a sadness that you could almost touch. Her suitcase sat next to the door. Beth and Joey stared.

"How are we doing?" said Mrs. Kellogg.

"Fine, Ma'am," said Beth.

"Okay," said Joey.

"Good. Well, I have a surprise for you. I'll be here again in the morning to take you with me."

Joey clapped his hands. "You mean we're going back to house, or Gram and Gramps' house? Mrs. Kellogg winced and shook her head.

"No. I'm afraid we can't do that just yet. I really wish we could, but you'll like the people you're going to live with until your Mommy and Daddy are ready, I assure you."

"Okay, Ma'am." Joey glanced back and forth from his sister to Ginny and back to Mrs. Couzens. He wanted to scream. Ginny stared at her shoes; she said nothing.

"Alright." said Beth.

"Good." Mrs. Kellogg ran her fingers through Joey's hair and wobbled his head back and forth. "Well now, we're in a bit of a rush today, so we'll be going, but I'll be seeing you two in the morning."

"Go ahead, children, wait in your room," said Mrs. Couzens. "Mrs. Kellogg and I still need to talk."

The kids ran back to their room and kneeled on Beth's bed to see if Ginny was really leaving. The rain had let up. They saw Lyle Couzens standing by the back of the constable's car. His hands were behind his back, while he vacantly stared at the barn.

The constable's arms were folded across his barrel chest the entire time he was talking to him. After a while, he opened the back door of his car and helped Lyle get in. Then, the kids kept watching as the man slid into the driver's seat, turned the car around and drove off, taking Mr. Couzens with him. Soon they saw Ginny carry her suitcase as she followed Mrs. Kellogg to her car. She lifted the suitcase into the back seat; then got in the front with Mrs. Kellogg.

Joey looked at his sister who was still staring out the window. "I wonder where Mr. Couzens is going."

"I don't really know," said Beth.

Joey looked out the window again. "Ginny really is going, too?"

"Yes. It looks that way, Joey. I wonder why?"

That evening, Mrs. Couzens was in her room crying when the kids went outdoors. The rain had stopped earlier and the sky was crimson above the trees and the rooftops, It appeared to turn lavender, and finally a deep purple, as the sun burned itself out in a crack of brilliant fire on the horizon. The air was damp and cold, fireflies traced their blinking glow patterns in the shadows. Beth and Joey stood in the thickening darkness, silent but for the oscillating hum of insects.

"She didn't even say goodbye to us, or anything," said Joey.

"That's okay, she probably had a good reason," said Beth. "You know the way Ginny is. Just think, Joey—this is *our* last night in this house, too."

Chapter Ten

A lice woke up just before the alarm went off. Moving to the edge of the bed, she sat up and rubbed her face. Her head throbbed and she was sweating, in addition to feeling fog-headed and emotionally drained.

Fred Simms slept with his back to her and continued to snore. Not wanting to wake him, Alice stood and quietly stripped to the waist. Tip-toeing to the sink, she ran the faucet and splashed water on her face. She continued massaging her face with the cold water until her senses cleared. Drying herself with a towel, she studied herself in the mirror. Her face was dull with sleep and revealed a tremendous hangover. She slowly ran a comb through her hair, eased back into the bedroom and grabbed her robe. She was dreading the fact that the twins would be awake soon.

Tears rolled down her cheeks as she thought about Joe, and wondered if today would be the day he came home. Japan had surrendered and the war was over. *What in God's name will he say? What can I tell him? I still don't have any answers.* "God, help me," she whispered.

She shuffled to the window where the morning sun shone brightly. The sky was blue and filled with an abundance of wispy clouds. The thin material of the curtains reflected thousands of tiny crystals of light as they puffed in the breeze. Standing at the open window, she looked down, allowing the gentle breeze to wash over her while she smelled air that held the fragrance of cut grass. From her second storey apartment she could see the blooming tulips and the big old maple, fully leafed and fluttering in the soft breeze. Birds sang and bees zipped around pollinating flowers, while butterflies alighted in the most unusual places.

Alice massaged her temples with her fingertips and moved back to the bed to sit and ponder the day ahead. The same scenario unfolded the first thing every morning, and it was the last thing on her mind before she fell asleep each night. *What am I going to tell Joe? He's not going to understand and then what will I do?* Her mother's words haunted her: *"Just what do you think Joe will say when he finds out about you and your gigolo friend? And what about these babies, Alice? What's going to become of them?"*

Alice fiddled with her hair and looked behind her at the sleeping man... the father of her twin boys. *Can I really depend on him for anything — least of all to be a loving father to those boys? I'm so tired of this small place- both babies in one crib. And, what about Beth, Joey and Brian? My God. What have I done? I hate myself for living.*

His name was Fred Simms, a frequent patron of the Shoo-Inn Bar in Watertown where Alice waited on tables. She met him a little over a year after Joe left for the Army and he remained nothing more than a customer acquaintance at first. There was no romantic magic involved. Fred was a die-hard regular who simply offered to buy Alice a drink after work one night. That was that. Alice found him fun to be with. He was quick with his wit and smooth with his charm. A generous tipper, Fred was always good for a couple of free drinks, too.

Fred had curly dark hair and sharp brown eyes that gave nothing away. He often looked amused, but seldom smiled around strangers. He had odd eyebrows. Tangled and ratty, they grew at an angle that gave his rugged face the look of perpetual anger. His fixed, furrowed expression was that of a drunk trying to wobble his way through a roadside sobriety test. Yet, Fred, who worked as a machinist's helper at Hammner's Textile Mill, considered himself a first class gentleman. He kept his shoes shined, always wore a tie, and usually kept a brown fedora displayed in the back window of his 1942 Chevy coupe.

To his cronies at the bar, Fred was not only an easy-going guy but smart too — an expert at picking winners at the track. Because of his success with the ponies he garnered the nickname — "Mister Lucky."

When he first started paying attention to her, Alice figured Fred was destined to be at most, a very short paragraph in her future autobiography. After all, she was still a married woman. Joe was her husband and always would be. How strange the way things turned out, she thought. But, as with many women during the war, who missed their husbands, Alice desperately needed company—a strong shoulder to cry on. She was lonely and severely lacking in self-esteem.

There was so much to talk about and nobody to tell it to— certainly not her mother and father. They simply didn't understand. Alice constantly felt guilty about her kids living in foster care, but then there was the way Joe had left to join the Army. He lied, telling the Army he was single with no dependents in order to enlist.

So, Fred soon became Alice's closest confidant and drinking buddy. After work, she and Fred went bar-hopping and more often than not, Alice ended up spending her nights with him instead of going home. Before long, staying over became the norm despite her parents' protests. They were disgusted when she became pregnant, and after the twins were born, Alice decided to stay with Fred. That way she wasn't putting a burden on her folks, she reasoned.

"You belong here at home, Alice. Don't you care what people are saying?" Lillian harped.

"Have you no pride left at all, daughter?" said Carl. "I don't care what you say about Joe joining up, you're still his wife. You're a married woman, dammit!"

Fred rented the upper floor of a ramshackle place off Harbor Avenue. Located south of downtown, Carthage, the house hadn't been painted in thirty years, A worn-out lawn that had been driven on repeatedly had dandelions growing from patches of oily grass.

At thirty-eight, Fred had never been married and lived pretty much for himself. Life seemed to betray him again and again, tricking him into thinking he wanted one thing when he needed something else. His hunger never stopped, it just changed its guise.

Fred was a perfect drinking companion for Alice but over time, she would discover Fred was also impatient, irascible, and darkly obsessive. He was hardly father material. Many of his friends didn't know the real Fred like Alice did. He had contempt for Roosevelt, taxes, homosexuals, immigrants, Germans, Japs, bossy women and honest work. Alice certainly hadn't counted on getting pregnant by Fred, but there they were — twins.

There was an abrupt halt to the snoring as Fred stirred and turned over on his side. He blinked his eyes awake and ran his fingers through his dark hair.

"I didn't hear the kids — are they awake?"

"No," Alice whispered. "Not yet."

"Good. Why don't you lay back down here with me, then?" He patted her spot.

She gave him an acid glare. "Not this morning, Fred. I've got a terrible headache."

"You're getting a lot of headaches lately, aren't you?" He raised up on an elbow and watched her brush her hair.

"It's just a hangover. I had quite a bit last night, in case you didn't notice."

Fred sat up and reached for the pack of Camels on the nightstand. Sliding one from the pack he lit up and studied Alice's face. "You still figuring on taking the boys to your mother's place?"

Alice stared out the window and hesitated. "Well... she did ask me again. I don't know, though. I hate to leave them there. God, I feel like such a failure, Fred." She reached for a Kleenex,, her eyes shining like crystal, tears poised to spill down her cheeks.

Fred scooted down and leaned into her. "Not this again, honey... Please. It'll be alright." The cigarette dangled from his lips and it bobbed up and down as he spoke. He rubbed his hand in slow circles on her back. "There's no sense getting yourself upset all over again. We can keep the boys here just like we have been as far as I'm concerned, but you know yourself they're a handful. Especially when we want to go out at night and all. Just think you won't have to keep worrying about babysitters if your ma takes them."

"Shhhh!" Alice squeezed his hand and looked towards the small bedroom off to the side. One of the babies cooed and gurgled.

"One of them is awake," she whispered.

Fred sucked his teeth and nodded. "Well, anyway, I think we've given it one hell of a good try for nearly a year now, don't you? I mean things would be a lot easier if your old man was to send some money home once in awhile, ya' know?"

Alice stared at him. "They're our kids, Fred, not my Ma and Pa's. Can't you see that?" She clenched the tissue in her hands. "My folks aren't well, either, dammit! That's part of the reason I had to give up the other kids. You know that!"

Fred took the cigarette out of his mouth and wiped his lips on the sleeve of his T-shirt. His voice dropped to a growl. "Okay! Alright then, quit bawling. Just tell me once and for all, what you want to do, will you?"

"Waaaah! Waaaah! Waaaah!"

"Damn. There's one of them now. That means the other one will be wailing too," said Fred. He slid off the bed and headed to the sink, his face plastered with disgust.

"It's Merrill," said Alice. She dried her eyes, tightened the belt to her robe and went to get them.

"Waaaah! Waaaah!"

Fred called after her. "I swear, I don't know how you can tell which one's bawling without seeing them," A few moments later Alice came back with both of the boys- one in each arm.

"A mother just knows. Merrill sounds different from Mitchell, to me, somehow."

"Well, hold on, I'll give you a hand." Fred stood and took Mitchell from her. "But, like I said, you'd best make up your mind what you want to do."

•   •   •   •   •

The twins lived with Alice's mother and father for two months after that day, and she seldom spent much time with them when she did drop by. One day when she came home for one of her sporadic visits, Fred drove his coupe with a rumble seat and a hand-cranked engine. It was old, but he enjoyed showing it off. Gas-ration stamps were pasted to the side window. He was clean-shaven, his pin-striped white shirt neatly pressed, the crease in his gray slacks sharp.

He parked well over fifty yards down from her parents' house on Depot Street. "I think this is close enough, honey. I don't need your old man to get on me for nothing. Know what I mean?"

Alice nodded. It was nearly noon and she was on her way to work. Before she got out, she opened her purse and looked in her compact mirror. When she checked her face and hair, she grimaced and did the best she could with lipstick and a small hairbrush. The July heat made her sweaty and sticky. Her waitress uniform clung to her body, and her hair was beyond salvation thanks to the humidity. She got out and leaned through the window. "I won't be too long," she said. "Please be patient, okay?" Fred winked and nodded.

"Sure thing, baby."

A few clouds moved across the sun and made brief shadows over the freshly-mowed lawn. Her mother's flower beds bloomed with azaleas, lilies, hibiscus and philodendron. Four-o -clocks and wild rosebushes thrived along two sides of the house.

Alice walked fast across the front lawn, into the shade of the big elm and around the side of the house where Carl was hoeing the garden. Her pink waitress uniform was cute enough, white trim on the collar and sleeves, but because of her thick body it looked much too small on her. She worried, so much raced through her head: *Is Pa going to harp on me for being away so long again? What about Ma? The twins are colicky babies, just like Brian was. I hope they've been sleeping at night.* She was sure her mother didn't appreciate being up all night with one, much less two babies.

She stopped at the end of the garden, right next to the tomato plants. Her back was turned away from the road when she spoke:

"Good morning, Pa."

Carl didn't look up at first. He continued to chop dirt with a hoe, slowly and methodically, his pipe clenched between his teeth. "Morning," he murmured.

Alice, figuring an explanation of some sort was in order, began by saying she was sorry. "I've been working some long hours, Pa."

"Saloon business must be good, eh?" The old man lifted his head but he wasn't looking at her. His wrinkled face darkened as he listened, but his eyes traveled up the road to where the coupe was parked.

Fred had his door open to let in more air. Still unsatisfied, he got out of the car, walked on the street and lit a cigarette. He didn't look in Carl's direction, but they could see each other well enough. There was a smirk on Fred's face and a gust of wind made a comical nest of his hair. He smoothed it down, hesitated, then flipped his cigarette away in the ditch and slid back behind the steering wheel. Wearing two-tone brown and white shoes, he wiped the dust off their shine with a rag from under the front seat.

"God, it's so humid," Alice groaned. "The garden's looking good, Pa."

"Umm huh."

Alice hesitated, then said, "How you feeling, Pa?"

"I'm alright. Better question is what about you?" said Carl.

"I'm okay. I hope the babies aren't keeping you up at night."

"Nope, not me." Carl paused. "I can't say the same for your ma, though." He stopped working, laced his wrinkled hands over the handle of the hoe, and rested his chin on top. Squinting from the sun, he studied her face. He'd never seen his daughter looking so worn out and gloomy.

"You really belong home here, Alice. The little ones are your responsibility, you know." He flicked his hand in disgust.

Alice lowered her head. "I know Pa... I know." Her voice was hushed and her eyes watered as she turned slowly and moved toward the house. The sound of a crying baby echoed across the lawn.

Joe Harrison's *Greyhound* bus pulled into Gouvernuer at 12:20 the same afternoon. He'd lost some weight, but was strikingly handsome in his tan Army uniform with sergeant stripes. He also had a single hash mark on his sleeve, signifying four years of service.

He was anxious to see Alice and the kids. They had been on his mind a lot while he was overseas. He had written to Alice a few times, but getting no answer in return, he quit... for awhile at least—then last year he began writing again. Still, getting no response, Joe wondered if she was getting her mail okay. He'd tried calling, a month ago to tell her he was coming home soon.

The day he left San Francisco, he figured he'd surprise everybody. Now that the war was over, maybe they'd all be able to rebuild the life they had before he left. He knew Beth would be nine now — Joey, seven. He wondered if Alice would forgive him for stranding her with them. It was most likely the guilt that had him tuck twenty dollars inside each of his letters.

Joe grabbed his sea bag as the bus driver unloaded. Then, hiking the duffle up over his shoulder, he walked to the platform where he sat the bag down and fished a pack of Luckies out of his shirt pocket. He lit up and snapped the Zippo closed, then slid it back in his pants pocket. He shaded his eyes and looked around. The place sure hadn't changed much at all, he thought. It was good to be home.

He was anxious, but decided to save the cab fare and walk over to Depot Street. It wasn't far after all, and that way he could look around and enjoy the sights he'd missed for so long. The banging and thumping of machinery from Hammner's Textile Mill could still be heard from the bus depot. Woolworth's across the street was as busy as ever. Picking up the duffle he began to walk.

He took in the disintegrating boundaries of his former life: dilapidated homes with peeling paint and crumbling porches, sagging wire fences, and dirt front yards running down to narrow, cracked streets where twin streams of ancient, battered Fords and Chevys docked. Lots of old people sat on their sagging front porches. A smile crept over his face again. Some things never change, he thought.

Carl saw a soldier crossing the lawn alongside the house. *By God, it's Joe!* Carl waved. "Hello, stranger!"

"Hi, Carl! Long time, no see." Joe dropped his duffle and hugged his father-in-law, shaking his hand at the same time.

"Welcome home, Joe. It's darned good to see you, son." Carl beamed.

"Yes, it's good to be back. I see you've got the old garden jumping again. Won't be long before we have some of them tomatoes. I missed all of your vegetables, that's for sure." He paused a moment. "Where's Alice and the kids, inside? I wasn't sure where she would be staying, but I figured you folks would know if anybody did."

Carl nodded wanly. "Yes, Joe. She's in the house." The old man pointed.

"Well, I'd best get in there then, right?" He smiled and turned to go in, then suddenly stopped- glanced down the road, then back at Carl.

"Oh, Carl, did you notice that guy in the car just down the road." He pointed. "See... right over there?"

Carl shielded his eyes and looked. "Nope. I hadn't noticed. Been busy with the garden, actually."

"Hmmmm," said Joe as he kept walking toward the house. He dropped his duffle, jumped the three steps leading to the screen door and knocked on the rickety screen door.

"Hello! Anybody home?" He stood there a moment when he heard a baby cry. "Hello?"

Lillian came to the door and pushed it open. "Oh, mercy me. Hello, Joe."

"Hi, Ma! I'm home." They hugged and kissed and Joe stepped inside.

"I'm so glad to see you home safe, Joe," said Lillian.

"Yeah, I'm glad to be back. Say, Is that a baby I hear? Don't tell me Glenn and Betty surprised you with another grandchild, you lucky lady you? Hey, where's Alice?"

Alice drifted in from the dining room. She held the twins in her arms. Lillian took Merrill and moved to the kitchen while Alice stood, staring at her husband. Tears welled up in her eyes.

"Hello, Joe." Her voice had a plain, flat how-do-you-do sound to it.

"Alice! Hi, sweetheart. I'm home, baby!" He glided over and leaned in past Mitchell in order to kiss her. Alice reddened and backed up one step. Merrill started crying again.

"Hey, Come on," said Joe. "Is that any way to greet your old man after all this time?" His throat turned into sawdust. When he tried to speak he sounded like a busted violin. "I know you're probably still mad at me. You didn't write and all, but hey... we can work this out... you'll see. I'm home! Home for good, Alice."

Alice stood silent.

"Hey!" Joe shrugged. "What gives?"

"Joe... I . . ." Alice hesitated, unable to find words.

"What?" He glanced at the baby in her arms. There was frozen calm in his eyes. "Hey! Who's babies are these, anyway?" He turned and looked briefly at Lillian. "Lillian?" He waited a moment before he spoke again. "Well, my instincts are pretty damned good." He pointed an accusing finger at Alice. "Yours, aren't they?"

Alice said nothing as she hugged the twins closer and kissed them on their foreheads.

"Really?... These kids are yours?"

Alice broke down, sobbing uncontrollably as she handed Merrill off to her mother and rushed out of the room. Both babies were crying.

"Lillian. What is this? Are these two her kids, or not?"

Lillian bounced Merrill up and down on her hip to stop his crying. She nodded, putting on a game expression, but it appeared a bit crooked, letting her worry seep through. "Yes, Joe. The twins are Alice's."

"Jesus! What? Where's the kids? I mean, where's *our* kids? Beth and Joey?" Joe's face was flaming red now, as he called... Alice?" He leaned around the corner and saw her sitting in her father's rocker. "Jesus! Come on out here, right now."

Alice hugged Mitchell. She refused to move or look at her husband. Joe turned and squinted suspiciously at Lillian. "Where are *my* kids, Lillian?"

"Joe... they... they're living out on a farm, in foster care. I'm sorry." She started crying just as Carl came in. Joe stared at him and sneered in contempt.

"And you knew about this all along, didn't you, Carl?" He turned back to Lillian. "What farm, Lillian? Where, for God's sake?" He looked shaken and confused and paused a moment before waving a finger in both of their faces.

"Okay... I see how it is." Joe grabbed his duffle, then threw open the screen door so hard it smacked against the wall. "Thanks, all of you," he yelled as he marched off the property and headed back towards the bus depot.

Alice sobbed as she ran to the door and called after him.

"Joe! Wait, please!" When he didn't stop she yelled again. "There's another one, Joe. You have another son. I was pregnant when you left, Joe.

Joe dropped his duffle and stopped, but didn't turn around.

"He's yours, Joe! A boy! His name is Brian! Your son, Joe . . ."

Joe picked up his duffle, hesitated briefly and kept walking. Alice stood sobbing and watching until he was a mere speck in the sweltering afternoon sun.

Chapter Eleven

M rs. Kellogg drove through New York's summer countryside of green and tan that boasted tall corn and plentiful green beans. Blue oat fields fell in front of slow-moving John Deere tractors along the way and weeping willows hung over the banks of isolated ponds. Wild coneflowers spotted the sides of the road. It was a perfect July day, with a few fair-weather clouds in a light blue sky—when the temperature after dark hovered at eighty and the humidity felt as though it was one hundred percent. Mrs. Kellogg's window was the only one rolled down.

Beth and Joey sat in the back seat, with Joey craning his neck to see over the top of the front seat. His stomach was cramped with frenzied butterflies, but he was somewhat relieved that they had left leaving the Couzen's farm.

"Can I roll my window down, Ma'am? It's so hot."

"No," she spoke over her shoulder. "We have mine open and that will be adequate. It's all we need."

.　　.　　.　　.　　.

A lengthy pause of silence followed before Beth said, "Where are we going?"

Mrs. Kellogg looked at her in the rearview mirror. "I'm taking you children to the Bushkin's farm, Elizabeth. You'll like it there. It's much bigger than the Couzen's place, not too far from here, actually."

Joey ached with dread. He scooted up in his seat and leaned forward. His lip began to quiver. "Why can't we just go back to Gram and Gramps' house?"

Mrs. Kellogg's eyes narrowed, and her eyebrows pushed together.

"Now, Joseph, your grandparents aren't well, you know that." She fidgeted, twisted sideways, and used a hankie to wipe sweat from her forehead. "And, as I've told you before, we must wait until your father comes home, and then you'll be able to live in your own house with your father *and* your mother. Won't that be nice?"

"Yes, Ma'am." Joey began to slide back with disappointment on his face. "How long will that be?" he mumbled.

"Oh, it shouldn't be too long now—I would say before Christmas. The war will be over soon—at least they say it will. We must pray it is, children—yes... pray it is."

Joey thought about that. He desperately wanted the war to be over, so his father could come home and rescue them. To him, It seemed like nobody else's father was away because of the war.

"I don't hear many kids in school say their daddies are still gone for the war, and so what if they are? All those kids still get to stay with their own mommies anyway."

"Yes, well-everyone's situation isn't the same, Joseph. Now sit back please. I must keep my eyes on the road."

Traffic rolled down the two-lane Highway 126 with the sun reflecting on their windshields, their tires whined on the pavement as they sped by headed west, towards Watertown. Humped green shapes of oaks lined the road for miles and the heat waves looked like pools of water on the road.

When they approached Carthage, Mrs. Kellogg slowed down for the town's only traffic signal, a blinking caution light. A small grocery sat on one corner with Gerber baby food and Chesterfield cigarette posters displayed in the window. A bright red *Coca Cola* cooler sat next to the door.

Bill's Timberlane bar was on the opposite corner, and farther down 126, there was Betty's Diner with a picture of a huge hamburger and all the trimmings painted on the front. A gas station was located at the far end of town where Mrs. Kellogg pulled in alongside a solitary gas pump. A glass globe on the top of it read *Esso* in red letters. A bright red *Coca Cola* cooler sat next to the door.

Mrs. Kellogg squirmed around in her seat to better see her

passengers.

"Okay, children, do you need to go potty?"

Both Beth and Joey shook their heads to indicate no.

"That's fine. Then you both sit tight. I'm just going to stretch my legs a bit here and buy some gas. I'll just be a minute. The Bushkin farm is just a mile or so down the road, so we're almost there."

"I'm thirsty," said Joey. He had been eyeing the Coke machine.

Mrs. Kellogg's smile suddenly disappeared. Long wrinkles squeezed together across her forehead, and she took a somewhat stern tone.

"Child, I said we'll be there shortly. You can wait, just sit back."

"Do as she says, Joey," said Beth.

As they approached the farm, a white cross could be seen, standing like a religious sentinel at the entrance of the Bushkin's driveway. Standing next to the mailbox, its unusual location appeared more like a warning than a religious decoration. Road salt had severely chipped away at the paint and the cross leaned to one side.

A large gray house stood quite a distance from the road, and a faded red barn was about two-hundred yards off to the side. As Mrs. Kellogg pulled in the bumpy driveway, roaming chickens scurried away from the front of the car. She drove slowly and tooted her horn. The kids watched through their side windows as the birds scattered, squawked and fluttered their wings.

A rusty, old pick-up truck with a holly bush sprouting from its dashboard sat in a field on the far side the house. Despite the tall grass, a license could be seen revealing that the car had a 1938 plate. A red Farmall tractor was parked halfway between the house and the barn.

As they got closer and could see behind the house, a line of thick oaks appeared. They seemed to mimic the movements of the tall grass as they swayed back and forth. The latticework by the side door was thick and dark with vines of some sort.

A dog, with gnarly black hair and bushy tail bounded up to the car. It barked incessantly. The kids hadn't seen many dogs except in books and magazines, but they knew it was a big one. When it jumped at the car door, Joey jerked back in his seat. His eyes bulged and his mouth opened in complete and total surprise. He stared at the dog's big teeth, worried it would bite him when he got out.

"This is it, children. The Bushkin farm," Mrs. Kellogg announced, as if it were a treat they had been looking forward to. She saw Joey shrink to the corner and laughed. "Oh, don't mind the dog, Joseph. Daisy won't hurt you. She just gets excited by the car. You'll all get used to each other real quick, I'm sure."

"Yes, Ma'am," said Beth.

Margaret Bushkin came out and slowly sidled up to the car. She was a short and heavy hatchet-faced woman in her mid — thirties. Her brown hair was pulled back tight in a bun and her lips appeared as dry as ash. Her eyebrows were stitched in one dark, uninterrupted line. She wore no make-up, and the only thing that decorated her face was several dark moles. One in particular, located on the left side of her nose, was disquieting to look at.

Her husband, Elmer, stood six three, weighed roughly 310 pounds and had a head shaped like a cinder block. He wore blue bib overalls that strained to contain his girth. His upper body was matted so heavily with hair that he perspired copiously; a sweat-drenched red and black checked shirt appeared skin-tight on his frame. He kept his hands shoved deep in the pockets of his overalls as he followed his wife over to the car, where he squatted to look inside. He waved to Mrs. Kellogg and smiled.

"Hello, Judith!" His dark eyes scanned the back seat. Mrs. Bushkin stood at his side rather suddenly, with her arms folded across her bosom. She barely smiled.

"Hello, Elmer... Margaret, I've brought you two more little folks."

"Hello, there, children!" Mister Bushkin said. His voice matched his bulk. It was deep, and the words seemed to be half swallowed by a heavy chest. Neither Beth nor Joey answered.

•   •   •   •   •

"Children, aren't we going to say hello?" said Mrs. Kellogg. They stared at her until Bushkin finally shrugged and stood up.

"These children have been through a lot lately, folks. They are understandably, a bit shy, but they will be fine, won't you, kids?

A long hollow pause followed.

"Well, then, go ahead and hop out, children. We'll get your things out of the back," said Mrs. Kellogg. Daisy sniffed around Beth's legs and feet after Mr. Bushkin opened the back door and she got out. Keeping a constant eye on the dog, she said,

"Come on, Joey." She tugged at his hand before Mr. Bushkin began to lean inside the car.

"Hello, Beth, nice to meet you," he said. "Hello, lad. Climb on out of there, now —let's have a look at you." He rolled the tip of his tongue around the inside of his cheeks, as if he were probing for a lost wad of Redman. "Don't you mind Daisy now," he said. "She just don't know who you are, is all. She won't bite, I promise." He laughed as Joey eased out of the car.

Mrs. Kellogg unlocked the trunk, handed them their bags, and they all followed Mrs. Bushkin through a side porch into the kitchen. The screen door hummed with flies and the place smelled of grease, fried meat and sweat.

Daisy sniffed Joey's legs all the way to the door. Joey glanced down but kept moving. *Look* magazines and soiled newspapers sat on top of an old Maytag washing machine and a bunch of car tires were stacked to the right of the door. Firewood was stacked in a pile on the other side of the porch.

Mrs. Bushkin opened another door that led to the living room. A clock as tall as Mr. Bushkin stood against one wall. It looked like the one in the dining room at Gram's house, Beth thought. A big brass pendulum swayed back and forth with a soft snick.

Daisy scooted past everyone and Joey jumped out of the way. She was headed to the dining room right next door. A waist-high table could be seen at the far end of the dining room, just beyond a huge dinner table. A Bible lay open on its top.

A small boy sat on a dusty and uneven couch. Two cushioned armchairs were situated directly across from where he sat. His hands were folded in his lap. He didn't appear to be as tall as Joey, with blonde hair, startling blue eyes, and a wide smile. Suddenly, the boy jumped up and covered both ears with his hands. He ran to Mrs. Kellogg and wrapped his arms around her skirted legs.

"Owwww! Owwww!" he shouted.

Mrs. Kellogg bent down and hugged him. "Awwww. Hello there, Timmy! Mercy me, what in the world? What are you trying to say, young man?" She glanced at Mrs. Bushkin. "Margaret?" He acts as though he is hurting in some way. What on earth . . ."

"Oh, I can't imagine. He hasn't complained in any way." Mrs. Bushkin shrugged. "I think he's just excited to see you, Judith. That's all." She reached across and rubbed her hand on top of Timmy's head "All excited, are you, Timmy?" She grasped him by the shoulders and turned him to face Beth and Joey.

"This young man is Timmy, children. Timmy's been part of our family for over a year now. Unfortunately, he doesn't speak. You see, he was born deaf. He understands things as well as we all do though. Smart as a whip, this boy is." She tilted Timmy's head up and looked into his eyes. "Timmy, these are your new friends, Joey and his sister, Beth. We told you they would be coming, remember? They're going to live here with us for awhile." She stretched her mouth to better form her words and help the boy comprehend.

Timmy shook his head back and forth and looked up at Mrs. Kellogg with pleading eyes. His hands covered his ears again. "Owwww! Owwww!"

"How about that? He really *is* excited. Mr. Bushkin said, as he eyed Timmy. "Well, you'll have plenty of time to become friends."

Timmy turned and stared at Joey. A thin smile of understanding came to his lips as he nodded. "Nuuuuh. Nuuuuh," he said.

"Well, Margaret—Elmer, while the children get acquainted, what say let's go in the dining room and handle the paperwork," said Mrs. Kellogg.

"Certainly," said Mrs. Bushkin "How about a cup of coffee, Judith? It's fresh-I just made it as a matter of fact."

"That would be most appreciated, Margaret. Thank you."

Beth and Joey sat on the couch with Timmy sitting between them. Joey didn't know what to say to the boy. It felt strange talking to somebody who couldn't hear anything.

"You like it here, Timmy?" Joey asked. Timmy shook his head back and forth, indicating no, but he continued to smile as if he wanted to make friends.

Joey looked at his sister. "Does he know what I said, Sis?"

"I think he does, she said; "he probably reads lips."

"Reads lips? What? What do you mean?"

"We learned about it in my class. You have to be looking at him, or he can't do it, though. He watches how you move your lips and can tell what your words are."

"Gee. He shook his head, Sis — he said no?"

"I know; I saw that. Don't worry though, Joey. It will be all right. I'm sure. He's probably scared of a lot of things because he can't hear."

When Mrs. Kellogg was leaving, Beth and Joey ran to the windows on the porch. It was starting to get dark outside. They watched the red lights on the back of her car as they moved down the driveway until they couldn't be seen anymore.

While Mr. Bushkin was doing evening chores, his wife showed the kids around the house Timmy tried to help. He pulled on Joey's hand in an attempt to guide him.

The kitchen, right next to the dining room, was larger than all of the other rooms. They had much more room than the Couzens, Beth thought. All the floors were dark wood and creaked most everywhere anybody walked. A Bible was in every room, except the bathroom and the porch. No pictures adorned any of the walls, except for the framed one in the dining room showing Jesus in prayer.

Mrs. Bushkin spoke as they walked. "Beth, you will have your own room, however, Joseph, you will share yours with Timmy.

Joey balked. "Ma'am. Would it be all right if me and my sister have the same room, together?"

Mrs. Bushkin's eyes were suddenly turned hard and a row of wrinkles pinched tightly around her mouth.

"What? No! My Lord, of course not, young man. Why everyone knows that boys share rooms with boys, and girls share with girls. That's ridiculous, Joseph. And it's certainly not God's way. Mercy!" She rubbed her long, white fingers over the Bible that sat on the dresser and closed her eyes. "No—not God's way at all. Now, then, you can have the two top drawers of this dresser. Tim has the bottom ones. You, being taller than he is, it should be best all way round."

She quickly showed the children through the other rooms. "More rooms are upstairs," she said, "but we don't need to go up there, tonight. The door at the top of the stairs stays locked, by the way. She led them to the bathroom. Timmy had let go of Joey, but still tagged along.

"As you can see, we do have a tub and a sink, but you still have to use the outhouse. And you each have a chamber pot; they must be emptied every morning." She paused and squeezing her hands together, added, "Please don't make me have to remind you."

"No, Ma'am," said Beth.

"Nuuuuuh! Nuuuuuh!" said Timmy.

"Is there a cellar?" Joey asked.

"No. Not a cellar here, lad. Why?"

"I just wondered," Joey murmured.

Mrs. Bushkin left the boys in their room and led Beth down a short hallway to her room. Joey and Timmy sat on their beds, looking at each other. Joey felt strange. Timmy never stopped smiling, and he watched every move Joey made.

"Nuuuuunh." Timmy made the same grunting sound when he wanted to communicate. "Nuuuuuuh."

Joey didn't know what to do. He couldn't tell if Timmy meant yes or no, or what he was trying to say. Joey shrugged his shoulders. "Sorry, Timmy. I don't understand. I just want to go home to my Gramps house."

Before supper, Beth learned where things were and set the table. While Joey and Timmy were taking turns washing their hands in the bathroom, Mr. Bushkin returned from the barn. He strode to the kitchen sink, rolled up his sleeves and pumped the water to splash over his face and hands. Mrs. Bushkin put the food on the table and showed the kids where their chairs would be. She stood erect behind her chair and waited.

"We never sit until the mister is ready," she said.

A Bible lay open on the table in front of Mr. Bushkin's place. A bright red piece of linen dangled from where the book was separated

Joey and Beth eyed the food on the table. There were pork chops and bowls of mashed potatoes, beets and green beans. A stack of homemade bread as well as a pitcher of fresh milk sat in the middle of the table.

Mr. Bushkin finally strolled to the table, and after he took his seat, everyone else did. He glared at Joey. "Arms off the table, boy. Let's bow our heads." He placed his hands on the pages of the Bible, closed his eyes and spoke.

"Oh, Lord, we thank thee for the gifts you've chosen to bless us with this day. Bless all these youngsters you have delivered unto our hands. May they grow with us and find your everlasting love in the days ahead. Bless this food we are about to receive. We ask in Jesus name, Lord. Amen."

"Amen," said Mrs. Bushkin. She had watched Beth and Joey. "Children, you might as well learn, we say Amen when the Mister finishes the prayer from now on."

"Yes, Ma'am. Amen," said Beth

Mr. Bushkin closed the Bible and placed it back on the small table behind him.

"Not now... at the end of the prayers, when Mr. Bushkin says Amen, then repeat it. Understand?"

"Yes, Ma'am."

"You, too, lad?"

"Yes, Ma'am."

"Nuuuuuh, nuuuuuh," Timmy uttered.

"Now, after Mr. Bushkin is through serving himself, I will put food on your plates. We will always do this at mealtime. This is the way it's done." Timmy smiled. His hands were in his lap. He seemed to understand very well.

"Yes, Ma'am." Beth and Joey both answered in harmony.

Mr. Bushkin slapped a big pile of everything on his plate. He took three pork chops, still leaving enough for everyone else. The food tasted good and Joey and Beth would later agree, there was a lot more of it than they had gotten at the Couzens' place.

Nobody was allowed to talk at the table besides Mr. and Mrs. Bushkin. When he was done eating and picking his teeth, Mr. Bushkin slowly pushed his chair back, stood, stretched his arms and legs, and strolled along the table to the end, where he stopped and turned.

"Now is a good time to let you youngsters know a bit about living here, I suppose. Might as well set things straight, right from the get go. There has to be rules in this world. There's God's rules- we call them the Ten Commandments, of course-and then there's my commandments called Mr. Bushkin's rules. You will obey all of them. Do that... and we will get along just fine." He hesitated a moment and then addressed Timmy. "Right, Timmy?"

"Nuuuuuh, nnuuuuuh." Timmy's lip suddenly quivered and his eyes filled with tears.

Chapter Twelve

A fter supper, Mrs. Bushkin ordered everyone into the living room to hear the rules mentioned earlier by her husband. Mr. Bushkin's jaw was puffed out with a gob of Redman chew and his hand coddled a silver spit cup. A Bible lay open on the small table in front of him. Pacing the room, he ran his fingers through his hair and scratched his chin. His eyes narrowed as he surveyed everyone in the room, including his wife.

"Bedtime is eight o'clock most nights. School nights, it's seven, immediately after I finish reading the Scriptures. Baths are every Saturday night. There will be no nonsense when you go to bed — no talking or other silliness. You will get down on your knees and say your prayers — then it's to sleep." His bushy eyebrows wiggled up and down while he spoke, and he stopped briefly to spit in the cup before he continued.

"You will get up when the Missus wakes you, and you will take your slop pots to the outhouse before breakfast." He focused on Joey. "Lad, you and the other boy use the same pot. You take it out, not him. I don't need him slopping that mess all over creation. This is to be done as soon as you rise at six in the morning. When school begins again, you will get your chores done and eat before the bus comes at seven-thirty. Regardless of school, it's six o'clock; rise and shine in this house. Sunday morning, you will have your chores done before Bible school. That's held right here in this room. Nine sharp — no excuses for being late." He paused once again to spit. "If you do not accept Jesus and live a Christian life, you will simply go to hell."

Mrs. Bushkin's head was bowed. She nodded after everything her husband said, and at times, appeared to be praying, whispering amen repeatedly. With the tips of her fingers, she rubbed both of her temples in a slow circular motion. Beth watched her out of the corner of her eye, her own hands balled with tension.

"There will be absolutely no arguing or fussing in this house. You will get along and talk in whispers when I'm inside. I don't want to hear any bellyaching about this or that, either. You will do exactly what my wife tells you, when you are told to do it." His eyes met Joey's again.

"Son, I'm going to teach you about farming. Maybe you'll grow up to be a farmer, who knows? Pay attention and you'll learn."

"I know how to be a farmer already, sir."

"Tut-tut-tut. Quiet, boy! You don't never, ever interrupt me when I'm talking. Let's make that clear right now."

"Yes, Sir." Joey's cheeks turned crimson. Timmy sat on the end of the couch, smiling, his hands cupped over his ears. He was jittery, swinging his legs back and forth, his eyes danced, and his head jerked more than usual.

"Now, I don't know what farm you been on boy, but you will learn things my way here. We're going to put some muscle in those scrawny arms of yours." His eyes then focused on Beth. "And you, sister—you will learn how to take care of a home. Help Missus around the house in every way she tells you. She will let me know if you fail her. Understood?"

Beth nodded. "Yes, Sir."

"Good." Mr. Bushkin spat in his cup and patted his belly. "Then we'll have no problems. We understand each other. I shan't speak of the penalties to be paid if these rules are broken. Just know that punishments are given for those who need reminders. The good Lord guides me as he shall you. Think of me as your shepherd. Any questions?"

"Yes, Sir." Joey raised his hand.

"What is it?" His irritation lay just under the surface.

"Can we listen to the radio if there's time before we have to be in bed?"

Mr. Bushkin reared back and laughed. "Radio? Radio? There's no radio in this house, boy. God didn't mean for us to addle our brains because sinners broadcast their evil. We do just fine around here without a radio." He chuckled. "You have been spoiled, haven't you? Now then—it's been a long day for all of us, so I'll now read from the Gospel of John, and then you can get to bed." He cleared his throat, spit in the cup, and began. His voice boomed.

"In the beginning was the Word, and the Word was with God, and the Word was God. He was with God in the beginning. Through him all things were made; without him nothing was made that has been made. In him was life, and that life was the light of men. The light shines in the darkness, but the darkness has not understood it.'

Mr. Bushkin rambled for a fifteen minutes before his recitation was finished.

•   •   •   •   •

The boys were in their room changing into pajamas when Joey saw the black and blue marks on Timmy's back. He held him by the shoulders, looked him in the eye and mouthed the words just above a whisper.

"What happened to your back? Who did this, Timmy?" He turned him around and gently rubbed his fingers over the bruises.

"Nuuuuh, nuuuuh," he said much too loud.

"Shhhh!" Again, Joey mouthed the words. "How did this happen? Did he hit you here?"

Timmy patted the top of his head and quickly nodded. His eyes were full of fear as they shifted to the bedroom door.

"Okay. It's okay, Timmy." He squeezed his hand. "Let's get in bed," he whispered. "I'm sorry and I understand, okay? Just nod."

Timmy nodded.

"Goodnight, Timmy," whispered Joey.

Joey lay in bed thinking about everything. Especially about what Mr. Bushkin said about punishment. He kept seeing the marks on little Timmy's back. He thought about the cellar at the Couzens' farm too and wondered if things would be worse living at Bushkins' place.

It was hot and humid. Joey kicked the sheets off so he could breathe. Their window was open, and he heard the sounds of the night. Bullfrogs croaked and crickets sang their screeching chorus, calling to each other across the fields. It was a serenade he would hear every night unless it rained. He felt a slight draft pass over his body as a rare summer breeze was pulled toward the living room.

He knew nothing could be as frightening as getting left in the cellar, but Mr. Bushkin was so big and scary. He wondered if the man might hurt him or his sister if they made him mad. He couldn't sleep.

He hit Timmy. Wow! A ray of light from the kitchen slanted into his room and he was glad for that. His shoulders twitched and his eyes rolled up and fixed on the ceiling. He tried to think about something good like fishing with Gramps, but it was impossible.

Everything keeps changing. We keep moving, and things feel so mixed up. Where is Mommy and Daddy? Don't they care about us? I'm afraid of the dark, too, but I'm not really alone, because Timmy is right over there in the other bed. I wish Sis was in that other bed, so we could whisper before we go to sleep. We got to do that at Couzens' and that made me feel better before I went to sleep. I miss doing that. I wish Timmy could talk. Mommy and Daddy, please come.

He felt the covers twist away from his body as Timmy crawled in bed with him. He sat up.

"Timmy, what are you doing?" he whispered. Then he remembered Timmy couldn't hear. *He's scared. Even if he does smile all the time, he's scared of Mr. Bushkin. I just know it. I'll get into trouble if Mrs. Bushkin finds him in my bed in the morning though.*

"Timmy," he whispered again. "Timmy—you have to get back in your bed." Timmy groaned and curled, snuggling up against Joey. When Joey was sure Timmy was asleep, he would use the pot and then put him back in his bed. He would be too heavy, but he'd do it somehow. He had to.

It was still dark when Mrs. Bushkin came into the room and shook them awake. Opening his eyes, Joey was so glad that he hadn't wet the bed.

"Time to get up, lads, it's Saturday. Mister will be wanting you in the barn, Joseph." She walked over and slid the curtains open. Timmy sat up and smiled at Joey. He didn't remember that Joey had dragged him back over to his own bed.

"Nuuuuuh. Nuuuuuh." Mrs. Bushkin ignored him.

"Joseph, get dressed and take that slop pail out, then get washed up for breakfast, and don't dilly dally, either."

"Yes, Ma'am." Joey was in a daze, eyes half open and downcast, dreading a day in the barn with Mr. Bushkin.

"Ma'am?"

"What is it?" She posed with her hands on her hips.

"Ummmm, why does Timmy smile so much?"

"Well, certainly, he smiles; he's happy. Better to be smiling then frowning. Aren't you happy, lad?"

"Yes, Ma'am."

Joey carefully carried the chamber pot outside, but nearly bumped into Mr. Bushkin, who was coming down the path after using the outhouse.

"Here! Here! Watch where you're going, lad. No need to slop any of that out here, is there?" He grunted and spat into the weeds.

"No, Sir." He emptied the pot then headed back inside. Beth stood by the porch steps waiting.

"Hurry, Joey. We don't want to be late to the table. Go wash your hands."

"Gee! Okay. But, I just got up, Sis."

"I know, me, too. Just hurry."

Joey smelled coffee and bacon and remembered those smells from Gram's house. He was hungry, and after taking the pot back, hurried to the kitchen sink, where he pumped water and washed his hands and face. Mr. Bushkin came in; the screen door slammed behind him. Everyone waited behind their chairs until Mr. Bushkin was ready.

Thick, brown pancakes were stacked on a platter in the middle of the table, and a pile of bacon was on another. There was fresh, warm milk from the barn and Mrs. Bushkin splashed some in each of the glasses. After saying grace, Mr. Bushkin stabbed four of the pancakes with his fork and flipped them onto his plate. He used his fingers to take most of the bacon, then slathered butter on the pancakes and drenched them in maple syrup while everyone else waited.

Mrs. Bushkin put one pancake on the kids' plates as well as her own. There were two pieces of bacon left for her. Joey helped Timmy with the butter and syrup.

Mr. Bushkin made loud, slopping noises while he ate. He ignored the thin, brown trail of syrup that dribbled into his beard. Leaning forward, he lifted another heavy fork to his mouth, then paused once to belch before devouring the rest of his breakfast.

It was deathly quiet except for Daisy barking outside. Nobody was allowed to talk at the table. Mrs. Bushkin ate with one hand in her lap and she instructed the kids to do the same.

"You two must learn some good manners," she said.

"Soon as we're done here, boy, I want you to come out to the barn," said Mr. Bushkin. "Don't bring him with you, neither." He jerked his head towards Timmy. "He ain't allowed near the barn. Understand?" He talked with his mouth full and exposed the mess inside.

"Yes, Sir," said Joey.

Mrs. Bushkin settled back into her chair and ran her fingers back and forth across the green-and white-checkered oilcloth as she sipped her coffee.

"And, you'll do your Saturday chores in here, Elizabeth," she said. "Today, you'll learn how to scrub floors and wash clothes. I want you to keep the boy out from under foot, too. He's good at getting in the way. He likes to watch everything up close, so see to it that he stays in his room while we're working. Give him his soldiers to play with. They're in that oatmeal box on top of the ice box. See, there?" she pointed. Beth noticed her hand trembled slightly.

"Yes, Ma'am."

Mr. Bushkin cleaned his plate, then polished his glasses with the tail of his shirt before perusing the Farmer's Almanac with a third cup of coffee. He was in the habit of doing so every morning before going to work. "Still no rain," he grumbled and slapped the book shut. Shoving his chair back, he strolled to the kitchen window. The sun was undaunted by clouds, the sky coming to life with streaks of orange and yellow reflecting off the wet grass.

"Well, I'm going out to the barn," he said as he grabbed his thermos and the egg basket. "Come on, boy, time to go." Joey drained his milk glass and followed.

As they walked Joey saw the morning mist rise from the field and pasture near the barn. The early sunlight dappled through the maple branches overhead slid back and forth across his body like a myriad of yellow dimes. Mr. Bushkin led the way to the chicken coop and filled the basket with eggs. With the chickens roused, the rooster began to crow. Mr. Bushkin handed the basket to Joey.

"Take these eggs back to the house and then come out to the barn, hear me?"

"Yes, Sir."

When he got back, Mr. Bushkin continued to show Joey around. There were five cows, three Guernseys and two Holsteins. He said the cows all had Bible names, but Joey couldn't remember them because Mr. Bushkin said them too fast. He did remember the last one in the end stanchion was called Jezebel.

Mr. Bushkin showed him the brown workhorse as he lifted a wooden bar and let him out to pasture. "Name's Charley," Mr. Bushkin mumbled.

A sow and six baby piglets were in a pen at the rear of the barn, and a bunch of chickens scurried this way and that, some white, some brown and black.

"I'll show you how we clean out the gutters in a while, but right now we'll feed the animals." As he fed the animals, Mr. Bushkin was adamant. "Don't you give them anymore than what I just showed you — understand? Watch you don't spill the oats, neither."

"Yes, Sir."

"I know how much feed I got, and I don't want it wasted."

Joey had learned how to milk a cow at Couzen's farm, but he listened while Mr. Bushkin showed him his way. He explained the cow's tits and how to work them in order to get milk, then he left Joey alone to milk Jezebel and Ruth.

Joey sat on a small, wooden stool and set a bucket under Jezebel.

R.C. Hartson

He squeezed and squeezed but no milk came. He kept trying, but suddenly, the cow swung her tail and it smacked him in the face. Joey jerked back and fell off the stool. Falling over, his feet flew up in the air and he landed in the gutter.

"Oooooh!" He yelled. Wet manure splashed all over him. "Oh, no! Oooooh!" He struggled to get up and wiped his hands up and down on his shirt and pants, and at the same time, he began to cry.

Mr. Bushkin saw him fall. He slapped his knee and laughed so hard, he had to sit down on a railing and hold his belly with his arms.

"Ha! Ha! Ha!" He pointed at Joey. "Look at you, boy! Ha! Ha! Ha!"

Joey's throat was dry, and his lower lip quivered. He was both hurt and embarrassed and didn't know what to say. The manure covered his clothes. Some splattered his face. He ran for the house with Mr. Buskin's laughter echoing in his ears.

On her hands and knees in the kitchen, Beth was scrubbing the floor with her back to the door when Joey stumbled in. He didn't see Mrs. Bushkin, but Timmy was standing right behind Beth. Throwing his arms in circles with a toy airplane; he looked at Joey and dropped the toy. He covered both ears, and his eyes opened wide.

"Nuuunuuuh. Nuuuuuuh." He pointed at Joey. Beth turned around.

"Where's Mrs. Bushkin?" Joey groaned.

Beth quickly jumped up, her mouth agape. "Joey! What happened?"

"I was milking the cow, and... and, I fell in cow poop." He sobbed uncontrollably.

"Oh, no, Joe! Here, let me help you get that shirt off. Gee, it's all over you." Somehow her words made things worse and he wailed louder.

Mrs. Bushkin heard the racket and rushed into the kitchen. She folded her arms across her chest and glared. "What is that all over you, lad? What in the blazes have you gotten into? It smells like cow dung."

"I fell in the cow poop, Ma'am."

"You fell into... what? Here now, you get out of my house!" She screamed and chased Joey out through the porch... "Get outside and take those clothes off — all of them! Elizabeth, look there — he's tracked it onto my floor. Get it cleaned up immediately!" Beth was still in shock and gawking at Joey...

"Well! Don't just stand there, get busy!" Mrs. Bushkin yelled.

She called out after Joey: "You need to scrub yourself all over, mister. Fell into the cow poop, indeed," she stammered. "I never! How in the world? Oh, never mind. Hurry up, both of you. Good Lord!" Her jaws waggled so hard, her false teeth popped loose. She quickly grabbed them and shoved them back into her mouth.

The tub, hardly wide enough for Joey's small body, was in a remote corner of the back porch, shielded from view by an old bed sheet. He hauled buckets of water from the pump to the back porch, where he filled the tub about a third of the way. He pulled the bed sheet across the porch and stripped naked with remarkable speed. With a bar of Lava and a washcloth, he scrubbed everywhere he could touch. He avoided using the soap on his hair for fear of getting it in his eyes.

The water smelled like the barn and was the color of mud when he finished. Pulling the plug, he got dressed and watched the water seep through the cracks in the floor of the porch.

Mr. Bushkin came in while Joey was getting clean clothes on.

"I need more coffee, Margaret. And I want that boy right back out there soon as he's done here." He worked a blade of grass that dangled from the corner of his mouth and Both thumbs hung in his overall pockets as he glared at Joey.

"What am I gonna do with you boy? You don't clean the gutter that way." With his tongue he moved the blade of grass to the other side of his mouth. Joey hung his head.

"Elmer, I need to talk to you before you go back out," said Mrs. Bushkin.

"Can't it wait?" He spat in the sink then turned around. "Or should I drop everything and listen to your prattle the rest of the day? You know full well how busy I am, Margaret. I'm sure whatever you have can wait."

"Oh, yes, it can wait. I just wanted to tell you that Judith Kellogg called. She's coming back out on Monday."

"Oh, I see... okay. So, did she say whether she'd be bringing the others with her?"

"Yes. She said that's why she's coming. She'll have them with her be with her."

"Fine. You'd best be sure the extra rooms are ready then, I'd imagine."

"I took care of that last week. I'll have the girl help me tidy them up a bit, though... dust and what not."

"Good, well, come on boy. Let's see if you can do something useful out there. Time to clean the gutters." His laughter trailed him out the door.

•　　　•　　　•　　　•　　　•

Mrs. Kellogg arrived late Monday afternoon.

Beth and Joey waited inside the back door with Timmy. The Bushkins went outside to meet her. Mrs. Kellogg waved and smiled from the inside of her car. Another woman sat in the front passenger seat and got out at the same time as Mrs. Kellogg. A boy was in the back seat. Joey ran up to Mrs. Kellogg and she bent down to hug him. Beth and Timmy were right behind Joey, and she sort of hugged them as well.

"Well, Joey. We are certainly excited today, aren't we? Glad to see me, are you, kids?" She smiled at the Bushkins then she focused on the kids. "Hello there, Beth—Timmy. How are you? Everybody looks healthy."

A curly-headed boy eased out of the back seat of the car and stood next to the other woman. He was almost as tall as Joey and freckles sprinkled his face. He was biting the back of his hand and stared at all the kids.

"Margaret—Elmer, how are you?" said Mrs. Kellogg.

"Hello again, Judith," Mrs. Bushkin smiled. "Seems like you just left here, doesn't it?"

"Yes. It certainly does," said Mrs. Kellogg. "Mr. and Mrs. Bushkin, I'd like you to meet my new assistant, Shirley Gunderson."

"How do you do," said Mrs. Bushkin. She gave the woman a faint smile as if they were hard to come by.

"Hello, glad to meet you," said Shirley.

Mr. Bushkin stood with his hands shoved deep in his pockets. "Howdy, he said, "And who do we have here?" he asked as he lay his hand on the new boy's shoulder.

"This young man is Brian, folks. Say hello to everyone, Brian."

Brian didn't move. He appeared to be frozen to one spot. "Hello," he murmured and continued to gnaw on his spit-covered hand.

"Well, that's not all," said Shirley with a big smile. She turned and opened the back door of the car and leaned inside. One by one she brought out two more small children. They got out and she helped them get down. Both of them had blonde hair and looked to be about one year old. Both wore matching light green shorts with green-striped shirts. One of them began to cry.

"Everyone... this is Mitchell and Merrill. They're twins. See how they look so much alike, children. Isn't that nice?"

Mrs. Kellogg lifted the crying boy up into her arms. "Shhhh! Shhhh! It's okay now. Elmer, would you be a dear?" said Mrs. Kellogg. "Bring their things out of the trunk?" She turned to Beth and Joey with a broad smile on her chubby face. "Now then, children, I'm pleased to tell you all three of these boys are your brothers and they'll be staying here with you."

The kids stared at one another. It was as if they had forgotten how to speak. After a long pause of silence, Mrs. Kellogg cleared her throat and spoke.

"Well now, Margaret, as I told you, Timmy will be leaving here today."

"What? Timmy is leaving?" said Joey.

"Why?" Beth asked.

"Yeah, why?" said Joey.

"It's all for the best, kids," said Mrs. Kellogg. "Some nice people over in Messina are adopting him."

"What's that mean . . .adopt him?" asked Joey.

"Well, unfortunately, Timmy's folks died in an accident when he was a baby, and he doesn't really have anyone else, so the folks over there agreed to be his mommy and daddy. Isn't that wonderful?"

Timmy held on to Joey's arm. "Nuuuuuh! Nuuuuuh!" He repeatedly tugged and shook his head trying to say no.

Joey sniffled as he looked down at Timmy's begging eyes. "Ma'am, he doesn't want to go." Then, looking at Beth, "Sis tell her... Please! We want to leave here, too. We want to go back to Gram and Gramps."

"Now, Joseph, I've told you, that's just not possible right now."

Joey sobbed. "Why does everybody else get to have a mommy and daddy but us?"

Chapter Thirteen

Mrs. Kellogg and Ms. Gunderson were ready to leave. The fact that Timmy was leaving the Bushkin farm both surprised and shocked the kids. Joey wanted to go with Timmy, but Beth seemed to resign herself to the fact that they were stuck on the farm; Timmy was lucky in her mind.

Brother Brian stood absolutely silent; his eyes boring into the ground. Beth and Joey stared at the newcomers; they were amazed they had three more brothers.

The heat was stifling. The late summer breeze afforded no relief of the humidity for everyone standing around by Mrs. Kellogg's car.

"Can I hold one of the babies?" Beth asked.

"Why, yes, of course you can, my dear," said Mrs. Kellogg. "Here, careful now. Put your arm around this way. That's it. This one is Mitchell." Beth smiled as she held the baby and slowly walked back over to where Joey stood.

"They're just about eighteen months old, Elizabeth. I'm counting on you to be a big girl and help Mrs. Bushkin with them, won't you?" she said with a smile.

"Yes, Ma'am. How is our mom? And Gram and Gramps. How is everybody? Are there any more? I mean do we have any more brothers or sisters?"

"Your folks are all doing well. There's just the five of you." She clasped her hands together in a gesture of finality and sighed. "Now you're all together. Isn't that nice?"

"No, we're not. We don't live with Mommy and Daddy yet. Not even Gram and Gramps," said Joey.

Mrs. Kellogg looked at him without responding and instead looked at Mrs. Bushkin. "The department always likes to place the siblings in one household, as you know. And thank goodness for gracious people like you and Elmer, to shoulder such responsibility, Margaret."

"Where's Mommy and Daddy?" Joey asked. His voice was small and flat, and they all stood silent for a moment.

Mrs. Kellogg cleared her throat. "Ummmm... well, he's uuuuh... the war is over now, Joey, so your daddy should be coming home soon. Any day now, really and I believe your mommy's still working at the restaurant, so together, they should get things straightened around shortly, I expect."

Beth paid little attention to what Mrs. Kellogg was saying. She was content smiling and making faces at the baby in her arms. "How do we tell them apart, Ma'am?" she asked.

"My, my — that's a good question, Beth," said Mrs. Kellogg. "Here, I'll show you. You are holding Mitchell, and Mrs. Gunderson is holding Merrill. I believe I have that right, don't I Shirley?" She walked over to the other woman and pointed to Merrill. "See, here — Merrill has this tiny red mark under his chin." She tilted his head in order to show her. "Mitchell doesn't have that mark. For now at least, that's how you can tell them apart, okay? Lord knows they do look alike, don't they?" She turned to face Brian.

"Brian, say hello to your brother, Joseph; you can call him Joey, of course. Joey — this is your brother, Brian." She waited while the two boys stared at one another,

"Go ahead, Joseph- tell him you are glad to meet him, and shake hands, please." Joey moved in closer, but Brian stumbled back, trying to hide behind Shirley Gunderson. He continued to stare at the ground, but had finally stopped gnawing on his hand.

Brian finally said, "Hello."

"Hello," said Joey.

"This whole thing is new to them, that's all," said Shirley. "Brian will be fine, once he's settled in."

"Yes, of course he will," added Mr. Bushkin. He took the bags from the car and carried them to the porch. When he came back he had Timmy's bags in his arms and put them in the trunk.

Timmy clung to Joey's arm—trying to hide behind him. Mrs. Bushkin feigned a smile. "Those two have gotten real close. Ain't a day goes by when that boy isn't traipsing around behind Joseph. Say, won't you come in and have some lemonade? It'll cool you ladies off a bit before you start back."

"Thank you, but no, Margaret. It's a long trip back to Watertown and this humidity is so very pressing, you know." She fanned herself with a brown envelope she was holding.

"So, Judith, how was the trip over—I imagine you had your hands full," said Mr. Bushkin.

"Actually, the trip was rather uneventful, thank you, Elmer. The children were fine. Thank goodness I had Shirley along today to help out."

"Amen to that," Mr. Bushkin chuckled.

Mitchell began to fuss, so Beth bounced him up and down on her hip while touching his nose with her finger. "Kitchy-kitchy-coo," she teased.

Mr. Bushkin attempted to shake Brian's hand. "How are you, young man? Brian pulled away and shrank back, behind Shirley.

Mrs. Kellogg looked at Ms. Gunderson. "Well, Shirley, I know this has been rather brief, but we've got a long trip back, and we still have to deliver Timmy to Messina." She looked back at the bushkins. "If there's anything you folks need, you know where to call." She handed Mrs. Bushkin the brown envelope. "The usual papers are in here. You can fill them out, sign and send them back or I'll just pick them up on my next trip out."

Mr. Bushkin took Timmy's hand. "Come on, Timmy, time to go bye-bye."

Timmy began to cry. "Naaaaah! Naaaaah! Naaaaah! Naaa . . ." He worked himself into a frenzy, getting so excited, his breath came in ragged, choppy spurts and he reached for Joey,

Joey circled his arm around Timmy's neck and thought, *I don't care where Timmy's going; they won't like him and understand him the way I do. I bet he won't even smile for those people. I wonder what Mrs. Kellogg would do if she saw the black and blue marks on his back. She just comes here and leaves so fast.*

Timmy screamed as Mr. Bushkin grabbed him by the arm. "Baa, Baa, Baa." Mr. Bushkin continued to drag him to Mrs. Kellogg's car.

"You children go inside now," said Mrs. Gunderson. "Beth, you take Mitchell inside-would you please?"

"Yes, and I'll bring Merrill," said Mrs. Bushkin. "Bye bye, ladies. See you soon, I imagine."

Joey stood inside the porch, and even after the inside door was closed he still heard Timmy's screams until the car drove away. Beth was crying when Joey finally wandered to the living room.

Brian wouldn't look at either of them. His hands were shoved deep in his pockets, while he stared at his feet. He wasn't as tall as Joey. His unruly brown hair covered his forehead, and freckles spotted his face.

Mitchell crawled around on the floor. Mrs. Bushkin put Merrill down next to him. He scooted around and began to crawl towards the kitchen.

Joey watched. "Where did these brothers come from, Sis?" He spoke in a half whisper.

"I'm not sure, Joey. I don't know a lot of things, same as you."

Joey knelt down by the twins. He extended his hand to Brian. "It's okay, Brian. I'm your brother." He waited for a response, but got none.

"How many years old are you?"

Brian held up four fingers, then folded one down, then raised it again.

"Four?" Beth asked.

Brian nodded.

Beth picked up one of the twins, still not sure which one was which. "Joey, watch him," she pointed to the other baby. "He's going too far that way."

Joey picked up the baby and sat him down by Beth's legs. He started to cry. "Shhhh, shhhh," Joey said. He looked at Beth. "I didn't want Timmy to go."

"I know, Joey, me neither."

"Why does stuff have to be like this, Sis? I think Mrs. Kellogg is lying. Daddy will never come home. We will never, ever, get to leave this place." He began to cry.

"Please don't cry again, Joey. You'll make me cry and I am so tired of crying, aren't you?"

"Yes, but I can't help it. Why can't we just go back to Gram and Gramps' house? I want Mommy to hug me like Mrs. Kellogg hugs us. Nobody nice wants to take us home with them like those people who adopted Timmy. I wish I could talk to Gramps right now. He would help. He would know what to do. Gramps knows everything."

Chapter Fourteen

The heat broke in the first few days of September. The nights became cool, and the trips to the barn in the morning were chilly. The stifling humidity was gone, and the sun lost its glare. By noon, it was hot again, but not August hot, and by twilight the air was light.

The seasons were changing, the days grew shorter. The trees along the edge of the property were changing colors to yellow and crimson, and leaves were falling.

Joey was nine and Beth was eleven, both definitely old enough to care for their baby brothers according to Mr. and Mrs. Bushkin. New rules were put in place almost immediately after the three boys arrived on the farm. As the days passed, Mr. Bushkin made it clear that he didn't want the twins bothering him. He had very little to do with them. Beth overheard him talking to his wife one morning before breakfast.

"I don't care, Margaret, I won't stand for that infernal bawling during scriptures, nor while I'm trying to eat. I had no idea they would be so much aggravation or I wouldn't have said yes to Kellogg."

•　　•　　•　　•　　•

At the dinner table one night, he stared at Beth with angry eyes. His eyebrows jumped up and down like tiny, black snakes when he he spoke.

"Girl, you get up there and get that squawkin' taken care of, right now." Beth shoved back her chair and raced upstairs. She and the twins would always be fed before everyone else from that day forward. Beth was made to stay upstairs with the twins until bedtime. If they cried or fussed, it was her responsibility to get them calmed down.

Mrs. Bushkin reminded her, "Elizabeth, you told Mrs. Kellogg you would be helping with the twins, and that's only right. That's the way it should be, as far as we're concerned. From now on, I'll expect you to get up with them during the night, to change them and what not. Especially when they bawl, you must get right to it, calming them down. The Mister can't be woke up; he works too hard to put up with that nonsense. I'll do the changing when I have time and you're in school, but when you get home I'll expect you to handle it. Is that understood?"

"Yes, Ma'am."

"And you'll take care of washing those diapers too, of course."

"Yes, Ma'am.

Joey felt sorry for his sister; he hardly got to do things with her after the three brothers arrived. But, Brian and Joey soon became best friends. Brian followed Joey around, just as Timmy had.

Going to school was a reprieve from the Bushkins, the kids thought. Brian was still too young for kindergarten and stayed home, but Beth and Joey were happy to go to school, and in fact, dreaded coming home in the afternoon to chores. They felt somewhat safe when they were away from the farm if only for those few hours. The kids learned a lot from their classmates. Being without a radio in the house, kept the kids shut away from the rest of the world.

Chores had to be finished each school day before the bus came. Beth fed Mitchell and Merrill before she left. The rest of the day, Mrs. Bushkin kept them in their crib or a playpen upstairs.

Many times, Beth found the twins in nasty diapers, even though Mrs. Bushkin had said she would take care of it during Beth's absence. Both babies had developed severe cases of diaper rash and cried incessantly. Although Beth gave them a bath two times a week, the rash never seemed to heal. When they cried during the night, she was expected to get up and give them bottles or do whatever it took to stop the noise. Mrs. Bushkin instructed Beth to use *Vicks* on their behinds to clear up the rashes.

Two weeks before Thanksgiving of 1948, a cold rain had stopped but the sky was still dark, and thunder could be heard in the distance. The wind was blowing hard, the limbs of trees whipped back and forth. The sky was bursting with branches of lightning. The sun had popped out earlier, but it was gone.

All chores were done and Joey and Brian were playing in their room that Saturday in November. They didn't have many toys. Brian liked to play with the rubber Superman doll that Timmy had left under his bed along with some soldiers and an airplane. He started carrying Superman with him everywhere. Other than that, there was a Tiddly-Winks game, a deck of Old Maid cards, some Jacks and each of them had a box of crayons together with Peter Rabbit coloring books Mrs. Kellogg brought them. But, it wasn't long before most of the crayons were short or broken in pieces.

Joey was patient with his brother, many times showing Brian how to stay inside the lines when he colored and continually told him things to keep him out of trouble. That afternoon, Joey hadn't noticed Brian using a blue crayon to draw four squiggly lines on the wall of their room. Brian still held the stubby piece of blue crayon in his hand when Mrs. Bushkin came in to check on them. When she saw the marks on the wall she was irate and grabbed Brian by the arm.

"What do you call this?" She pointed to the marks. Brian shrunk back, with his head down, saying nothing.

"Well? I'm talking to you, mister! Answer me!" She placed her hands on her hips, and glared at Brian. There was a moment of deathly silence before Brian began to cry.

"It was you, wasn't it? Answer me!" she yelled. Everything happened so fast after that.

Smaaaaack! She slapped Brian in the head,

"Owwww, ye... yes." She grabbed him by the ear and yanked.

"Owwww," Brian screamed.

Joey backed into a corner and rubbed the side of his head; it was as if he felt the slap, too.

Mrs. Bushkin snatched the piece of crayon out of Brian's hand while he was rubbing his face and wailing.

"Here!" She waved the crayon in front of his face. "You like this color do you? Well, you can eat it then, young man!" She smeared the crayon back and forth over Brian's lips. "I said eat it!"

Brian tried to spit it out and duck at the same time.

Smaaaaack! She slapped him in the head again. Brian didn't have a chance to put up his hands and deflect the blow.

Joey wished Beth was there. Where was she? He wanted to help but didn't know what to do. He was terrified. His mouth turned dry and he couldn't speak. His knees shook.

"I said eat it!" Mrs. Bushkin yelled. She pushed the crayon past his lips, and into his mouth. Her hands shook like an old man with Palsy.

"I will! I will!" Brian screamed. His hand shook while he stuck the crayon in his mouth.

"Now, chew!" Mrs. Bushkin snarled. With a scrunched-up face, Brian chewed, but he spit pieces out onto the floor, some landing on Mrs. Bushkin's dress.

"How dare you!" She dug her fingers into his arm and yanked him close enough to shove more crayon in his mouth. "You young heathen!" She had a wild animal look in her eyes.

Brian choked and then, something snapped inside Joey's head. He kicked Mrs. Bushkin in the leg as hard as he could.

"What the. . ." She wheeled around and grabbed a fistful of Joey's hair. "Who in the hell do you think *you* are, boy?" She slapped him across the face, hard, again — again — and again. Smaaaaaack! Smaaaaack! Smaaaaack!

Snot trickled down onto Joey's lips and his nose started to bleed. He felt the warmth of the blood and cupped his nose, but the blood oozed between his fingers and he fell back onto Brian's bed. The top of his head smarted from the hair-pulling.

"That's it, boy! That's the last straw! Dare to kick me, will you? We'll let the Mister deal with your smart, little self." She stomped out of the room and left both boys, crying and shaking.

Brian was still choking on the crayon when Beth came running into the room.

"Joey! What happened? You're bleeding! What happened?" She used the dishtowel in her hand and held it against his nose. Joey cried as he tried to explain. He pointed to Brian.

"She... she was... was making him eat the crayon!"

"What? No! No... spit it out, Brian. Here." She grabbed Joey's hand. "Hold this towel on your nose, Joey." She had tears in her eyes as she patted Brian's back repeatedly. "Come on, Brian. Spit it out!" She had her hand under his chin when he suddenly threw up all over her dress. She quickly grabbed a shirt out of a drawer and wiped the vomit off him and herself. Brian cried uncontrollably while she hugged him.

"It will be all right now, Brian. Shhhhh! Shhhhh," she said. "It's okay now." Patting his back. "Shhhhh! What happened in here, Joey? How did you get a bloody nose?" She took a closer look at his nose and sat on the bed. "Mrs. Bushkin almost knocked me down on the way out the back door. She looked awful mad and she was going to the barn." She touched Joey's eyebrow. "And your eye — what happened to your eye? It's all swollen up." She winced. "Oh, my goodness, this is terrible. She did this, didn't she?"

"Ye... yes."

"But why, Joey? What do you mean she was making Brian eat a crayon?" Her eyes darted in all directions.

"She was, Sis. She was mad because Brian colored on the wall." He pointed to the wall. "So, I kicked her."

"Joey! Oh, no! You kicked her? Why? Why did you kick her?"

Joey cried harder. "I got scared, Sis. And I told you, because she was making him eat the crayon! He was choking, and she still kept making him do it." Beth put her arm around his shoulders as he said. And... and, she slapped him in the face, too."

"Oh, no, Joey — no! I'm scared. I'm afraid of that man and her too."

"She hit me too, Sis. I kicked her in the leg, but I couldn't help it. She was hurting Brian, and I didn't know what else to do. I'm sorry." Beth reached over and held Brian in her arms. "Shuush. Shuush. It'll be all right now, Brian. Shuush." She looked at Joey. "Joey, stop crying, now."

The rain came down harder, and the sky blackened. From the west came a roll of thunder that shook the leaves. The back door slammed.

Mr. and Mrs. Bushkin stood in the doorway. They were soaked from the rain, their hair matted to their heads... Mrs. Bushkin's arms were folded across her chest and Mr. Bushkin surveyed the room very slowly. There was a mean look about him. With his right hand, he scratched the back of his neck, something he always seemed to do when wrestling with a difficult decision. His thumbs were hooked on the sides of his britches and he stared at Joey with his scary dark eyes.

"Well now, looks like we have a lesson to learn here, eh, boy?"

Beth begged. "Please, Sir, Joey didn't mean it. He really didn't. He won't do it again; I promise he won't."

"You're right, little girl. He sure won't," Bushkin growled.

Joey felt warm pee running down his leg. The floor was spinning under his feet.

"Come on, boy." Mr. Bushkin snatched Joey by the arm and yanked.

"Owwww!" Joey yelped.

Mr. Bushkin sauntered toward the back door, pulling Joey behind him like a stubborn mule. The boy tried to pull away, but Mr. Bushkin jerked, making Joey trip and fall on his side. He yanked him back up on his feet.

Beth was right behind them. "Please, Sir. Don't hurt my brother, please."

"You get back in the house, girl — mind your brothers."

When he got to the barn, Mr. Bushkin threw Joey onto a pile of straw, and slammed the barn door shut.

"You've got the devil in you, boy! You need to put your mind to the scriptures more; I see that. You haven't listened have you? Just who do you think you are? You're a sinner, is what you are."

Mr. Bushkin unbuckled his black belt and slid it through the loops, drawing out the action with deliberate ease. He turned his head slightly to the side and spat a gob of tobacco juice.

"No! No! Please, Sir. I didn't mean to. I won't do it again. I'm sorry. Please! I don't want that. Please!"

"I warned you, didn't I, lad? God's rules, my rules, remember?"

"Yes, Sir! Please. I'll be good! I promise I will. Please don't hurt me!"

Bushkin growled. "Get them pants down, now!" His eyes appeared to bulge out of his head, his nostrils flared.

Joey trembled and shook all over; his hands couldn't open the buttons on his pants fast enough. His fingers wouldn't work right. He cried so hard, he couldn't see what he was doing.

"Hurry up, boy!" He spat again.

Joey shoved his wet pants almost all the way down, then peed again. Struggling with his pants, he tripped and fell in the wet straw. He kept kicking until his pants were almost all the way past his shoes.

"Good enough, now stand up," He gave the order through clenched teeth.

Joey sobbed, "Please, Sir. I can't! Please don't! Please!"

"I won't say it again, boy! Stand up and turn around."

Joey continued to sob as he slowly pushed himself up, but almost fell over again.

"Now bend over and grab them ankles," Mr. Bushkin hissed.

Joey continued to beg. "I'm sorry Sir. Please don't hit me. Please, don't."

Bushkin ignored Joey and swung the belt.

Smaaaaack! Joey screamed. "No, no, no — please, nooooo…"

"Sinner take thy punishment."

Smaaaaaack! One blow knocked Joey down into the straw. He held his hands over his butt and tried to scoot away, sobbing hysterically, but Mr. Bushkin was still there above him.

Smaaaaaack! He repeatedly swung, not caring where the blows landed. The belt struck Joey's back, his arms and his legs. Joey raised his arms to cover his head and the rest of his body was wide open to further assault. He heard his own screams and wanted them to stop, but they wouldn't. He felt dizzy.

Mr. Bushkin finally stopped. His breathing was ragged and heavy, his shirt, stained with sweat, stuck to his chest. Wrapping the belt around his hand he said, "Now, get up!"

Joey jumped up. He continued to cry as he rubbed his butt. His pants were still clustered around his ankles.

"You sinned, boy. This was all your doing. Your actions made me beat that devil's poison right out of you. You'll be lost in this world if you don't take the Lord as your Savior and live by God's word understand?" Joey was still sobbing.

"Yes... yes, Sir."

"I don't want to have you out here again, Joseph. Next time, I fear I won't go so easy on you. Now get them pants up, and get back to the house. You tell the Missus you're sorry, and get cleaned up."

"Yes, Sir." He quickly managed to get his pants up and ran to the house. When he got inside, Mrs. Bushkin stood waiting by the door. With hands on her hips, she smirked. Joey couldn't stand to look at her face. Beth stood at the kitchen sink and cried softly when she saw him.

"Well, Joseph, you've got something to say to me, do you?"

Keeping his head down, he said, "Yes, Ma'am. I'm... I'm sorry."

"Well, you should be. Don't you ever touch me again. You hear? Now, you get washed up, then, I want you and your brother to scrub that wall, from top to bottom before supper. That little snot is waiting for you in your room... if it had been up to me, he'd a got a taste of that belt, too." She handed Joey a blue and yellow can of *Old Dutch Cleanser* and two wet rags.

"Yes, Ma'am."

Joey went to the sink and splashed cold water on his face. The skin around his eye burned and his nose felt like it was full. He finished and ran to his room with the cleanser and rags. Brian sat on his bed, his face was blotchy and red from the ordeal. He still cried softly. Blue pieces of crayon clung to the skin around his lips. His tongue was blue. He sat up, and they hugged each other.

"She hurt me," Brian moaned.

"Mr. Bushkin hit me with the belt, too. She wants us to scrub the marks off the wall. You just sit still, okay? I'll do it."

A few minutes later, they heard the clomp, clomp, clomping of Mrs. Bushkin's shoes coming down the hall, and Joey continued to scrub the wall. He tried to pull Brian up on his feet, but it was too late by the time she came through the door.

Chapter Fifteen

Joey's ached all over. The skin around his eye stung where the tip of Mr. Bushkin's belt had struck him. As he scrubbed at the crayon off the wall, he wondered if there would be any further punishment coming. For some reason he felt the hardest part was over and he never wanted to feel Mr. Bushkin's belt again.

Margaret Bushkin came into the boy's room and saw Brian sitting on his bed while Joey was doing the scrubbing. Brian sat on his bed watching his brother.

"And why aren't you helping your brother with the cleaning, Mister?"

"I told him I would do it, Ma'am. He is feeling sick to his stomach"

"Well, that's awfully nice of you considering that your brother is the one who instigated all of the trouble this afternoon." She glared at Brian. "Just let me catch you using crayons on the wall again, young man. We will see to it that you get a taste of the Mister's belt. I want all of the crayons, right now."

Brian gathered up all twelve of the crayons and pieces of crayons they had and put them in her outstretched hand. "We'll see how you do without them for a month."

She started to leave when she noticed that the front of Brian's pants were wet. She shook a finger in his face. "Going to start doing that too, are we? Well, you can just take them off and bring them to me—understand?" She glared at him for a moment before stomping out of the room. Brian fell on his bed, crying. There was little Joey could do to console him.

Mrs. Bushkin and Beth just finished preparing supper when Mr. Bushkin came in from the barn. He lumbered over and tousled Joey's hair as he rolled up his sleeves and headed for the sink. Everything seemed fine with him. Joey couldn't understand. Mr. Bushkin acted as if there had been no whipping at all. Nothing.

He washed up at the sink and eyed Brian who still stood in the corner with his wet underpants draped over his head. His small cries only subsided when Mr. Bushkin sat down at the table. After he said a longer than usual grace, Mr. Bushkinc glanced at Joey, then Brian, before he said, "Oh, Lord, give us the strength to prevail over our sins. Amen."

Brian sniffled during the entire meal. At one point, his knees weakened and he leaned on the wall. It hurt Joey to see his brother humiliated like that, but he was glad Brian didn't get a whipping like he had. Beth's eyes watered; she felt so helpless. The tears flowed almost to her chin before she wiped them with her fingers.

Supper was liver and onions with mashed potatoes and gravy-one of Mr. Bushkin's favorites. Joey hated liver but he wasn't really hungry anyway. He picked at his potatoes and peas and drank his glass of milk. Everyone ate in near silence, the only sounds being Brian's sniffling.

Mrs. Bushkin was aware the disgusted look on her husband's face and tired of Brian's interruption, she pushed her plate aside and cradled her cup of coffee with both hands before she spoke:

"Brian, you'd best go on to bed now. We don't need to hear anymore. Get going! You'll have no supper this night."

Brian cried as he ran from the room. Beth and Joey glanced at each other briefly and waited to be excused.

From upstairs, one of the twins could be heard crying. Mr. Bushkin cleared his throat, and his wife looked to Beth

"You'd best get up there," said Mrs. Bushkin. "They are your brothers, you know. Probably need changing again. And that reminds me, you'll need to wash diapers before you go to bed."

"Yes, Ma'am."

Mr. Bushkin continued to stuff mashed potatoes into his mouth, all the while seeming to be oblivious of Joey's swollen eye.

Brian was still awake and shivering when Joey and Beth finished the dishes and went to bed. His skimpy blanket didn't keep him warm enough and his teeth chattered... "I'm so cold, Joey. Can I just come over there and sleep with you?" he whispered.

"Gee, you'd better not, Brian; if we get caught, it could be worse for both of us. I don't ever want the belt again. I am hurt all over, too."

Joey wanted to tell him to get up and change clothes, but Mrs. Bushkin was still in the living room. He knew she could hear everything and besides, she might come in to check on them before she went to bed.

"I'm sorry. Maybe after she goes to bed I can help you get warm, somehow. He lay in his bed listening to his brother crying softly. He couldn't lay on his back. Crossing his arms over his chest he curled up in a fetal position and closed his eyes. He waited for the living room lights to go out and thought about home. He wondered why nobody had come to see them.

Where was Gramps? What was he doing? Soon, he fell into a deep sleep.

•   •   •   •   •

Beth woke the twins at six-thirty and quickly had them dressed and fed. Mrs. Bushkin turned the overhead light on in the boys room, but Joey was already awake. For the last hour he had been staring blankly at the ceiling without moving an inch. No matter which way he moved it seemed, his body hurt. He was glad that Brian was sleeping. He slowly swung his feet from the bed and sat on the edge of it. He reflected on yesterday's whipping and his Brian's cries for help.

I hate these people. I hate this place.

He didn't want to go to school with his ugly black eye. The swelling had gone down somewhat during the night, but it throbbed more than it had yesterday. Shame burned his face when he looked in the mirror. What will all the kids at school say? What can I tell them? They are gonna laugh at me, anyway. He thought about running away but just as quickly dismissed the idea.

When he got to the breakfast table, Mrs. Bushkin waited until Mr. Bushkin had left for the barn before she bothered to talk to Joey. They ate their bowls of oatmeal, and Joey was on his second piece of toast when Mrs. Bushkin suddenly tapped Joey's arm.

"Now listen to me, Joseph, and listen good. You and your brother were rough-housing yesterday, and he accidentally kicked you in the eye." She stopped talking and simply glared at him. Joey didn't understand and said nothing as he looked into her dark eyes... "Understand me, boy?" She watched him intently as she announced her plan.

Joey was unsure of what she meant and glanced at Beth for a second... then back to Mrs. Bushkin. "I don't know what...?"

"You heard me, Joseph" she went on... "I'm saying, if anyone asks how you got that black eye, you tell them your brother kicked you, and nothing else. There will be no speaking of your trip to the barn with the Mister. What happens in our house goes no further. Is that clear?"

Joey hung his head while he ran his spoon round and round in his bowl and contemplated her words. *So, she wants me to lie.* He paused before he looked up and answered her. "Yes, Ma'am."

"Good." Mrs. Bushkin looked at Beth. "Same goes for you, Elizabeth. If anybody asks about your brother's eye… you understand me?"

Beth nodded. "Yes, Ma'am."

They barely managed to finish their chores before the bus came. Joey hurt more than ever as he milked cows. His lower back and buttocks still smarted. As bad as he felt, he wished he could change clothes. It might make him feel better somehow. But it wasn't allowed. He knew he smelled like the barn, but Mrs. Bushkin only allowed them to change clothes when Mrs. Kellogg was coming. Grabbing his books, he and Beth began to run when they saw the red lights of the bus coming down the road.

Mrs. Bushkin yelled after them. "Here, you two. You liked to forget your lunch bags and milk money." She quickly handed them the sacks and three pennies apiece before they ran to catch the bus.

"I hope Brian will be okay, alone with her today. She hates him," said Joey. "I wish he was old enough for school."

"I don't know," said Beth. "I think he will be alright though because she's afraid that Mr. Bushkin hit you too hard with the belt." She studied the black and blue area forming around Joey's eye when they got to the road. "She might even be afraid you'll tell. Do what she said, Joey. We can talk after school."

"But, what if she tells Mr. Bushkin to beat Brian with the belt?"

"She won't, don't worry."

"I hope not. She scares Brian so bad, he might wet his pants again," said Joey. "Then, what? I know how he feels. I bet he'll be hungry, too. Do you think she'll let him eat?"

"I think so. Stop talking about it now, Joey. Here comes the bus."

Joey felt all eyes on him when he got on the bus, but nobody questioned him. He sat next to Beth and stared out the window for the entire ride. Since he hadn't eaten much for supper the night before, the oatmeal and toast at breakfast was not enough. He decided not to wait and bent down in his seat where he quickly devoured the peanut butter sandwich that was supposed to be his lunch. There was nothing else in the sack. . He swallowed the last of the sandwich, wadded up the bag and shoved it in his pocket. Beth watched him and shook her head in disapproval.

"Now you won't have anything for lunch," she whispered.

"I know, but I'm hungry," he mumbled.

As soon as he stepped inside the school, the questions began... and so did the teasing. The kids rushed through the door where Mr. Schnure, the janitor, stood. He grabbed Joey by the shoulder.

"Where'd you get the mouse, kid? Run into a doorknob?" he chuckled. Joey pulled away and headed to his locker.

The art teacher, Mr. Campbell, was strolling through the hall and stopped him. He held Joey's chin steady while he studied the eye. "Hey! What happened, Joey, somebody told you to sit down, and you stood up? Ha! Ha! Ha!"

"No, sir." Joey felt his face get hot; he couldn't wait to get to his classroom. His teacher, Mrs. Beatty, checked his face as he made his way to his desk. She stopped him and caressed his forehead as she studied the eye. "What in the world? Joey, what happened to your eye?"

There was a slight hesitation before he answered. "Ummm, nothing, Ma'am. My brother, Brian, kicked me while we were playing is all." He answered in a hollow, hoarse voice.

"Kicked you? Oh, my, I'm so sorry, but it looks terrible, son. Your mom put ice on it, right away, did she?"

Joey answered without hesitation. "No, Ma' am." He started to pull away. He wanted to go sit down; all the kids began to gather around. Mrs. Beatty, however, stared at him a bit longer. "I'm sorry. It just looks so bad. Well... go take your seat. Do you want me to have the nurse, Mrs. Dempster, take a look at it? Maybe she can help take that swelling down somewhat."

Joey felt the embarrassment that goes with the lying. "No, Ma'am. It will be all right, I promise."

By eleven o'clock Joey was hungry again. He looked at the big white face of the clock on the wall behind Mrs. Beatty's desk and saw that lunchtime was only fifteen minutes away. He would have nothing to eat unless he could share something with somebody. He would feel stupid asking; besides he just couldn't. There was one thing... something he had done one time before when Mrs. Bushkin didn't give him a sandwich to bring. He raised his hand.

"Yes, Joey?" said Mrs. Beatty.

"May I use the bathroom, Ma'am?"

She checked her watch. "Well... yes, I suppose so. Lunch is just a few minutes away, but if you can't wait, just go ahead, but hurry back, Joseph."

Joey left by the classroom door. He closed it quietly behind him and stopped a few steps away at the cloakroom door. Quickly looking both ways, he went in and grabbed the first lunch bag he saw from the hat shelf just above where the coats were hanging. He didn't care who the bag belonged to or what was in it. There had to be food that was all that mattered. His hands shook, and his breathing labored as he quickly ripped the bag open. A bologna sandwich and a chocolate cookie were inside.

He crammed the sandwich in his mouth in big chunks as his heart pounded. It was hard to breathe. He was still swallowing as he shoved the crumbling cookie into one pocket, the empty sack in the other, then rushed to the boys room. His heart pounded furiously, but at least he was breathing right again. His shoulders were suddenly lighter. He even managed a very small smile as he scrunched the sack into the garbage can before hurrying back to the classroom.

After school, Joey sat with his sister on the bus. He whispered in her ear, "I've been thinking, Beth. Let's run away."

"Oh, no, Joey—no." Her eyes widened as she glanced behind them where other kids were busy talking. She was suddenly nervous and searched her brother's eyes.

"Well, I have to Sis, I'm scared. You come with me, okay? We'll run back to Gram and Gramps house. They'll let us stay after we tell on the Bushkins. I just know they will."

Beth leaned in close. "No!" she whispered. "Don't you see, we just can't do that."

"Well, I'm going. I mean it." His eyes roamed around to be sure nobody was listening. "I just can't live there anymore. I'm afraid of Mr. Bushkin and his belt, Mrs. Bushkin's screams and everything. You don't know, Beth, because he didn't hit you, yet. I think he's a crazy man. So is she. I just want to leave there. I want to go find Mommy and Daddy."

She rolled her eyes at her brother, but he ignored her. "Shhhhh. Don't you see, I can't go, Joey. What about Brian and the twins? Who will take care of them? How do we know what they'll do to them if we go? I can't just leave them like that. You shouldn't either."

Beth had tears in her eyes when they got off the bus. They walked very slowly up the driveway. She kept trying to wipe away the tears, wanting them gone before they got to the house. "Joey, please don't run away. I want to be with Mommy and Daddy, too, but if you leave, I will feel so scared and alone. At least we have always been together, haven't we? I try to look out for you, but now I have to watch out for Brian and Mitchell and Merrill, too."

"I know Sis, but I . . ."

"Please—please just promise me you won't leave me here alone with these people, okay? I know what I'll do. Next time Mrs. Kellogg comes, I promise I will tell her we want to go somewhere else to live, okay? I'll tell her how mean they are to us and how he beat you—I'll tell her everything."

Joey suddenly felt there was some hope. "You will, you promise?"

"Yes, Joey. I promise,"

"Well, when is she coming again?"

"I don't know, but I will try to find out, okay?"

They got close to the side door and Joey stopped walking. "Okay, but remember, you promised. Mrs. Kellogg will believe you cuz you're older."

Beth flushed with relief. "Yes, I promise."

Mr. and Mrs. Bushkin were both in the kitchen when they got home. The kids both knew something was wrong. Mrs. Bushkin had her hands on her hips, and her face was a mask of anger.

"Sit down here; we're gonna have a talk, you two," she said. "Go ahead—sit."

Beth set her books on the table; Joey held his and they both pulled out chairs. Mr. Bushkin sat looking down at his Bible. His lips were moving as though he was praying to himself. His meaty hands were folded, and he was unusually quiet.

"Now, then," said Mrs. Bushkin. "Which one of you two told them at school that Joseph got a whipping?" The kids looked at each other, then back to her.

"Not me," said Beth.

"Not me; I didn't, either," Joey added.

Mrs. Bushkin jumped to her feet and jabbed a finger in Joey's face. "Oh, so I suppose it's just some whammy-kazam magical thing that made Principal Grimes call here asking questions, eh? You think he just decided to call here out of the blue? Is that what you really expect us to believe?"

"No, Ma'am, but I don't know; really, I don't. Nobody even asked me about my eye, honest they didn't."

Beth suddenly closed her eyes and covered her mouth with a hand. Her shoulders trembled. She bit her lip and fought back tears.

"Are you lying, Joseph? Don't lie to me. Did your homeroom teacher, Mrs. Beatty, ask you where you got the black eye? Yes or no."

Mr. Bushkin remained silent. He rose up slow, and strolled over to the kitchen sink. Using his fingers, he pulled a wad of tobacco out of his mouth and then spat in the sink. He leaned against the sink and listened.

Joey's eyes followed every move he made. He was afraid of a surprise smack in the head, or worse. "Oh... yes, Ma'am, she did. I forgot."

"And you told her what, exactly? Don't lie to me, Mister."

"Well... uh, I told her that Brian kicked me while we were playing around, just like you said."

"Then, pray tell, why did Grimes call here, telling me that your eye needs medical attention? I'll tell you why, because you told your teacher that I didn't even put ice on it? I suppose he made that up, huh?"

Joey felt sick to his stomach; the floor felt like it was spinning like the merry-go-round at school.

"I don't know, Ma'am, really I don't." He felt as though his voice was far away when he talked. It seemed like he was watching everything from across the room. Mr. Bushkin moved close to Joey's chair and spoke. His voice was much lower than usual—like the growl of a bear.

"You're lying, boy." He breathed slowly. "I won't abide with lying. You need another trip to the barn, do you?" He bent over Joey with his face so close that his whiskers nearly touched the boy's face. His breath smelled like rotting meat.

"The Lord doesn't cotton to liars. Tell the truth, boy—shame the devil."

Both kids began to cry.

"Sir, I did tell Mrs. Beatty that Mrs. Bushkin didn't put ice on it, but that was because she asked me," Joey wailed. "And, I told her that Brian did it—just like I was supposed to. I didn't know what I was supposed to say when she asked me about the ice thing."

"That's what I mean, you went bellyaching to her, and now the whole damned school wants to know about it. You see, boy? See the aggravation you caused everybody?"

Beth jumped up. "He didn't mean to, Sir, I swear he didn't," she said. You can tell he's not lying, can't you?"

"You'll swear nothing! You just sit down and shut up!" Mrs. Bushkin yelled. "If we want your two cents, we'll ask for it."

Brian peeked around the corner; he was obviously afraid to walk into the kitchen. Then, as if on cue, both twins began to cry. They were still in the playpen in the living room where Mrs. Bushkin kept them during school hours. Her eyes darted toward the crying, then back to Beth.

"You just go tend to those two; don't worry about sticking your nose in this."

"Yes, Ma'am." Brian ran up behind Beth when she walked in the living room. She clenched her fists and tried to listen while he clutched her dress and leaned against her legs.

"Well, it appears, we just need to keep you home from school until that eye heals up proper, Joseph," said Mrs. Bushkin. "Get them busy-bodies at school to stop asking questions."

"Yes, ma'am."

"Meanwhile, for opening that mouth of yours, you can go without eating for awhile. Stay hungry; maybe then you'll learn to do as you're told."

Joey was not allowed to go to school. He was kept home both Thursday and Friday, staying in his room all day except when it was time to do chores. He was given two slices of bread with water for each meal. No milk.

Brian kept him company, and Beth managed to sneak him half of her peanut butter sandwich on Friday. Joey still had some pieces of the cookie in his pocket from school. But, he was still hungry — so hungry his stomach ached. He remembered all the good things his Gram used to cook.

Lying in his bed most of the day, he thought about Gramps and how much he missed him. That smile. He could smell his pipe and hear his laugh. He closed his eyes and remembered his mother's hugs and kisses... heard his Gram call his name.

He decided he wouldn't wait for Mrs. Kellogg to come; he would run away as soon as he could.

Maybe I can find Gramps' house; it couldn't be that far to Gouvernuer. I could leave from school on Monday. Beth doesn't understand and she doesn't have to know. When I get to Gramp's and tell Mommy about these people, they'll come and get Beth and my brothers. I know they will. Then Beth will be glad.

Sunday morning, Joey was allowed to eat again. After breakfast, Mr. Bushkin taught Sunday school in the living room just as he always did. He was telling them about King David when Daisy began to bark. It sounded as if someone had pulled in the driveway. Hardly anyone ever stopped at the Bushkin's farm, especially on a Sunday morning.

Mr. Bushkin slowly took off his glasses and closed the Bible, then crossed into the kitchen to spit in the sink. Daisy barked incessantly.

There was a knock at the porch door, and Mr. Bushkin pulled his suspenders up over his shoulders. He used the back of his hand to wipe the brown juice off his chin as he went to the door. Mrs. Bushkin wiped her hands on her apron and prodded the back of her hair with her fingers.

Beth held Mitchell on her lap while Merrill was still crawling in the playpen. Joey got up and started for the door but Mrs. Bushkin put her hand up like a traffic cop, showing him she wanted him to stay back. She put her finger up to her lips and shushed him. Brian didn't move off his chair. Other voices could be heard and everybody felt the draft as Mr. Bushkin closed the door. He was talking to somebody and even seemed to be laughing a bit.

"Well, come on in, folks," everybody heard him say. "Welcome."

Joey immediately jumped to his feet. It seemed impossible, but there they were- their very own Uncle Glenn, and Aunt Betty.

Chapter Sixteen

A t first, neither Beth nor Joey moved. Their eyes widened, and then it was as if a fire had been lit under Joey's feet, as he was propelled into the waiting arms of his Uncle Glenn.

"Uncle Glenn! Uncle Glenn! he shouted, as tears of joy streamed down his cheeks and he clung to his mother's only brother. "Gee, Uncle Glenn, I didn't know you would come here," said Joey. He looked past them in search of more. "Wow! Where's Mommy and Daddy?"

Glenn ignored the question as he wrapped his big arms tight around the boy. "Hi there, Sport!" he said.

To Joey, it felt so unbelievably right to hear Uncle Glenn call him "Sport" again. It had been so awfully long since he'd heard that name and he was so overjoyed, he wanted to laugh, but he felt like crying at the same time. Everything was unfolding so quickly.

Beth yelled, "Uncle Glenn! Aunt Betty! Oh, thank goodness you're here. She still had Mitchell in her arms, as she moved forward to hug Aunt Betty.

Betty planted quick kisses on Beth's cheeks, "Hello, Honey. She quickly took Mitchell and after briefly looking him over hugged him to her ample bosom. "I can't believe how this baby has grown." She paused and stared at Beth. "And you... just look at you, Elizabeth. My, but, you've all gotten so big since the last time we saw you. And Joey... my goodness, Joey." She continued to hug and kiss Mitchell and asked Beth, "Where's Merrill, Honey?

Beth's eyes were full of tears. Brian had left his chair and stood behind her, gnawing the back of his hand. He didn't recognize the visitors. Nearly two years had passed since he'd been put in foster care, and he was simply too young to remember the adult relatives.

Mrs. Bushkin sidled over to stand next to her husband. They both exhibited artificial smiles as they absorbed the Sunday morning interruption by unexpected visitors.

"Won't you folks have a seat, said Mr. Bushkin. Margaret will get some coffee, if you'd like."

"Yes, that would be just fine Sir, said Uncle Glenn. Right betty?"

"Yes, I'd like that too, if you don't mind. Heaven knows there's a lot of commotion going on here alright."

"No. No trouble at all. You folks just make yourselves comfortable with the kids."

Beth noticed that Uncle Glenn looked tired. He showed signs of battle fatigue from the war. His black hair, which was cut close, revealed touches of premature gray.

"Well, hello, Brian!" said Uncle Glenn. "Come on over here and see your Uncle Glenn."

The wrinkles around his eyes made him appear much older than his thirty years, and although his face bore the ravages of teenage acne, he was still a very handsome man. There was his slight belly, but he appeared solid through his chest and forearms as he always had.

Aunt Betty had tears in her eyes, but she looked exactly as the kids remembered her. A wide, squatty woman with frizzy, brown hair and a perpetual loud voice that begged attention. Her heavy smoking accounted in part for her raspy breath and gravelly voice, and probably contributed to the countless wrinkles clustered around her eyes. Nearing thirty-five, she had dark skin and a small black mole on her chin. She rarely used any makeup, but today she wore a fresh touch of lipstick, mascara and rouge with the slightest hint of an elusive perfume.

"Oh, honey" Aunt Betty could no longer contain herself and burst into tears. She dabbed her nose with a hanky, her mascara smeared as she hugged Beth. "Oh," she said as she watched Brian's hesitation. "Poor boy. He doesn't remember us, does he, Glenn? Oh, I feel terrible."

Mr. Bushkin cleared his throat. He sounded phlegmy when he

said, "These youngsters are sure glad to see you folks... He leaned on the counter, turned slightly and spat tobacco juice in the sink.

"Indeed, what a nice surprise for the children," said his wife.

Joey stood there wanting to scream with joy.

Aunt Betty dried her eyes, crouched down to reach for Brian. "Butchie! Come here, darlin'." She looked up at the Bushkin's. "We have always called Brian, Butchie." She smiled and laid her hand on Brian's shoulder. "How are you, sweetheart?" She slowly drew him into her and wrapped her fleshy arms around him. "You don't remember Aunt Betts, do you?"

Meanwhile, Merrill began to fuss in the other room. He was standing up in the playpen and crying.

"That must be Merrill," said an excited Aunt Betty. She looked at Mrs. Bushkin. "Do you mind if I go get him? Maybe he needs a bottle."

"No, that's alright," said Mrs. Bushkin. "You stay with the kids. I'll go get the baby; I'm sorry, we didn't know you were coming. The caseworker, Judith Kellogg, hadn't mentioned it the last time I spoke with her — last week, as a matter of fact."

"Oh, I know," said Aunt Betty. "We had nothing to do after church today and knew the kids were out here, and — well, we have missed them so much. Glenn has only been back from Germany a few months. We've been wanting to come out, but there has always been one thing and another, you know."

"Yes, I can imagine," said Mrs. Bushkin. She went to get Merrill and Uncle Glenn looked at Mr. Bushkin.

"Yes, we figured we'd just drop in. There's been so many problems in our family. Mercy. The kid's grandfather hasn't been doing well for quite some time. And there's still so much going on for their mother. It's been so long since we've seen them — poor kids. I do hope we're not intruding. We certainly didn't intend to cause a fuss."

Mrs. Bushkin came back with Merrill, and overhearing the conversation, was quick to respond. "Why, no. Your visit will be good for the children, won't it, Elmer? I'm sorry, we haven't introduced ourselves. I'm Margaret, and this here's my husband, Elmer Bushkin.

And you folks are... ?"

"Powet. Glenn Powet. Sorry. And, this is my wife, Betty. We're from their mother's side of the family. I'm Alice's brother." They all shook hands. Uncle Glenn bent down to Brian's level.

"It sure has been a long time since we laid eyes on you, Butch," He picked Brian up and hugged him. "Jumpin' Jiminy! You're a big boy, aren't you?"

Brian nodded. He stopped gnawing on his hand and smiled.

"You were in diapers when Aunt Betty saw you last." She laughed. "Of course you don't remember, Butch, but it was at your Aunt Mainie's house for Thanksgiving. You've grown so big since then."

Brian now had both arms wrapped around his Uncle's neck. "Whether he does remember or not, he sure is warming up to me now," said Uncle Glenn.

There was a lull in the conversation, a clumsy moment for all, it seemed.

"Big place you folks got here," said Aunt Betty.

"Yes, it is. Twenty-six acres—great place for kids to grow up, we figure," said Mr. Bushkin. He tucked both gnarly-looking hands inside his bib overalls. "Course now, all kids can be a handful sometimes, you know, no matter how much room they've got to run." He laughed. "That coffee should be ready pretty quick, I'd say."

Mrs. Bushkin had prepared the coffee, and opened and closed cupboard doors as if she'd forgotten where the cups were; she acted very nervous.

Joey wanted to tell Uncle Glenn everything, right away. He wanted to reveal how much Mr. Bushkin's belt hurt and how mean Mrs. Bushkin was. He wanted to tell about the crayons, too. Joey had lots of secrets and no way to unload them... until now.

I will tell on them, just as soon as I get the chance. I'll tell him everything. Oh boy! They'll be in big trouble, I bet. His hands were growing sweaty, and his heart banged in his eardrums as he got ready. He felt like he would explode.

"Hey, Butchie,—you sure are glad to see your Uncle Glenn, aren't you?" said Aunt Betty.

Brian nodded his head, but he didn't move his face away from where it was buried in Uncle Glenn's chest.

"Yes. I see that. It's amazing," said Uncle Glenn.

Mrs. Bushkin set coffee cups and spoons on the table. "You folks take cream and sugar?"

"No, thanks. We both take it black," said Uncle Glenn. "It certainly will go good right about now. It's a bit chilly out there, isn't it?"

"Yes," Mrs. Bushkin countered. "It was awful cold when the Mister came in from milking. I'll be glad when winter is done and gone, myself."

Aunt Betty gazed at Beth who sat in her regular chair holding Mitchell who was crying. "Awwww, poor baby seems upset," said Aunt Betty. She paused as she looked at the baby. "So-Beth, you sure have turned into a young lady, haven't you? Mrs. Kellogg told Gram and Gramps that you're a big help with the twins; is that right?"

"Yes... I try anyway." Beth looked at Aunt Betty, and tried to ignore Mrs. Bushkin's eyes while she had Mitchell on her lap and was attempting to get him to stop crying by jiggling him up and down on her knee.

"Big responsibility for a girl your age, Honey," said Betty.

Joey stood back a bit, listening and watching—preparing to tell about tell everything as fast as he could.

"Sport, what are you doing over there?" said Uncle Glenn. "Come on over here." He sipped his coffee, then put it down and drew Joey into himself. They hugged each other for a long time.

"You rascal." He tickled Joey in the ribs but stopped smiling when he noticed Joey's eye. "Hey, what happened here?" he pointed. Although there was no more swelling, the black and blue with a hint of green was still obvious. Uncle Glenn's brow creased as he studied the bruising.

This is it! Right now! Now is the time. I have to tell him Mr. Bushkin whipped me with his belt. Uncle Glenn will get mad and beat him up, I'll bet. . He knows how; he was in the Army. But I . . .

Yet, Joey couldn't say the words. He didn't know why... he just couldn't. Not with both of the Bushkins sitting right there staring at him.

"Oh, ummm... me and Brian were wrestling and he kicked me. But, it was by accident—he didn't mean to." While Joey told the lie, Brian shook his head. Uncle Glenn and Aunt Betty took that as a denial of guilt and questioned no further...

"That's okay, Butch. Accidents happen," said Glenn. He sipped his coffee again and paused as he gazed at Mr. and Mrs. Bushkin.

"We were sort of hoping we could take the kids into town and get them some ice cream—if that's okay with you two, of course. We'd have them back before dark—won't be gone long."

Joey's heart sang. He felt as though he was going to stop breathing. Going to burst! It was as if he hadn't actually heard his uncle's words. Beth rolled her eyes at Joey and smiled. Brian was still hugging Uncle Glenn and murmured, "Yes, please."

Mr. Bushkin stood and stretched... He scratched the back of his neck and scrunched his eyebrows, as if trying to remember something.

"Well... I don't know about that, now. I imagine the State would have to give their permission for something like that, Mr. Powet?" He looked at his wife rather than Uncle Glenn as he spoke. "How about that, Margaret, what do you think?"

Merrill squirmed on Mrs. Bushkin's lap. "Yes. I think we'd better wait on Judy Kellogg to give the okay before we do that, folks. I mean, we could be liable, you know, that is, if anything, God forbid, was to happen."

"By accident, of course, you understand. Not that you folks wouldn't watch out for them, proper," Mr. Bushkin added.

"Yes. We were concerned about that part Friday morning, too, so we called Mrs. Kellogg to check. I'm surprised, quite frankly, that she didn't contact you," said Aunt Betty.

"Oh, I see, and what did she say?" Mr. Bushkin asked.

"Well, as a matter of fact, she said if we decided to come out, and there was any question on your part, you could call her at home. We weren't sure if we could make it at the time, you see. I have her number right here in my pocketbook, if you want to call, of course." She started to go inside her pocketbook.

"No! No! That won't be necessary. We have her number. Uh... how long would you be gone?"

"Oh, I don't know. What do you think, Glenn—two or three hours, maybe?"

"Yeah. Something like that, I suppose. We have to head back to Gouverneur before dark. We can't be long." He had a reassuring smile on his face as he drained his coffee cup.

"Would you folks like to take a minute to look around?" Mr. Bushkin said. He turned and spat in the sink again. "Show you my stock and so on. It's a big spread—lots to keep up with. Of course, Joey is such a big help. Beth too. We darn near couldn't do it all without them." He grinned at Joey. "Things can get a bit sticky once in a while, if you know what I mean."

"Yes, I can imagine there is a lot to do," said Uncle Glenn. "But no, thanks, Elmer, maybe next time. We'd better scoot if we're going to get back here on time. Right, Betts?"

"Yes, so is it okay that we take the kids, then?" Aunt Betty asked.

"Why, yes, I suppose. I don't see any harm, long as Judith told you it was all right. What do you think, Elmer?"

"No! That's fine." Mr. Bushkin waved his hand dismissively and cleared his throat as though he was ready to spit again

Joey ran to get his coat. "Come on, Sis! Get your coat, so we can go. I'll get Brian's

"Hold on there, Joey, we have to get the twins ready. I think Mitchell is wet," said Aunt Betty. She looked at Mrs. Bushkin. "Where's the diapers?"

"No, I'll change him, Aunt Betty. Give him to me," said Beth. "I'm used to doing it all the time."

"Well now,, that's not exactly true, Elizabeth." said Mrs. Bushkin. She gave a saccharine smile. "I do my part, too, of course. She couldn't possibly handle those babies by herself, you understand. For goodness sakes." She laughed, but it was the sort of nervous laugh that leads you to believe that whatever was supposed to be humorous was really not.

Beth checked both babies then went off into Joey's room to change them.

.   .   .   .   .

Daisy barked and ran alongside the car when Uncle Glenn drove down the driveway. It was fully light outside, although the sky was still gray and gloomy. Beth caught a glimpse of Mrs. Bushkin peeking from behind the curtains in the boy's room. She saw her suddenly jerk her head away and disappear. Joey felt a new twinge of excitement as they pulled out onto the highway. They were leaving the Bushkins and the nightmare behind them.

They passed through long stretches of farm country where corn fields had been harvested and silos were filled. Some parts of the road were straight, and narrow, a back slash between towering pines and rambling hills.

Aunt Betty held Merrill on her lap in the front seat, while Mitchell sat next to Beth in the back. Brian was sandwiched between Joey and Mitchell and seemed quite content. Beth kept Mitchell occupied with a baby rattle as the miles flew by, while Joey stared out the window anticipating his chance to tell all.

"Our bus goes the other way," said Joey.

Aunt Betty turned in her seat and looked back. "Oh-and do you like your school, Joey?" she asked...

"No, we like our old school in Gouvernuer," Beth injected. "Right, Joey?"

"Yeah, I don't like anything away from Gram and Gramps. We want to go back there. How much farther do we have to go?" he asked.

Uncle Glenn was looking in his rearview mirror. "Oh... It's quite a ways yet, but it won't be *that* long." He paused. "Everybody in favor of getting an ice cream, say I."

The kids screamed "I" in near unison and giggled. Aunt Betty chimed in late with her approving "I".

"It sure looks like the ayes have it, then. Ice cream it is, everybody," said Uncle Glenn.

"So, tell us kids. How is it there at the Bushkins'? They seem like nice enough folks. Do they feed you enough?" asked Uncle Glenn.

"Yes, how about that?" said Aunt Betty as she turned in her seat again. "You kids look plenty skinny if you ask me."

"No... well... sometimes," said Joey. He gazed out the window, and Aunt Betty, unable to meet his eyes, slowly turned back around.

"What do you mean, sometimes?"

"Well, this week, I only got bread and water."

"What?" said Uncle Glenn. His eyes went from the road to the mirror and back again.

"Oh, Joey. That's not a nice thing to say, honey," said Aunt Betty. A beat of absolute silence engulfed the inside of the car.

"He's telling you the truth," said Beth.

The obvious quiet returned for a moment. The hum of the car's engine the only sound other than an occasional whimper or grunt by one of the twins. The countryside continued to whiz by as the kids stared out their windows.

Uncle Glenn studied Joey in his rearview mirror again, and saw the serious look covering his face.

"You mean it, don't you, Joey? Are you telling us the truth? Don't lie. This is too serious, son."

"No, Sir. I'm not lying."

"Well, why in the world would they only give you bread and water?" Aunt Betty asked.

"Yes... explain that. Why couldn't you have any more to eat?" said Uncle Glenn.

"Joey is bad," said Brian. It was practically his first words all day up to that point.

"No. That wasn't it at all, Brian," Beth said, "Be quiet, I'll tell. See, Mrs. Bushkin hit Joey hard in the face, so, he got a black eye and went to school like that. The principal called Mrs. Bushkin and she thought Joey told on her. So, Joey couldn't have anything else to eat for three whole days, because she was mad at him."

"And, besides that," said Joey, "Mr. Bushkin took me out to the barn and whipped me with his belt. His belt hit me in the eye that time."

"Yes, Joey, but that wasn't what gave you the black eye," said Beth. "Mrs. Bushkin did that when she hit you with her hand."

Aunt Betty and Uncle Glenn glanced back and forth at each other. Glenn's eyebrows arched in disbelief, his head shook slowly in bewilderment. Aunt Betty's face turned beet red. She started to say something else, then suddenly wary, stopped and looked down at her feet. "Oh, my God!" she murmured.

"Now take it easy, Betts," said Uncle Glenn. "We don't know anything for sure, yet." Aunt Betty reached inside her pocketbook and got a handkerchief. She dabbed at her eyes. "Oh my, oh my."

Joey scooted forward and put his hands on the top of the front seat. "You believe me, don't you, Uncle Glenn?"

Glenn cleared his throat and answered, "Yes. Now sit back, Sport. It's only about eight more miles to Watertown. Right now we're going for ice cream. So, what's your favorite?"

"Mine's chocolate," said Joey.

"Mine is vanilla," said Beth.

Brian shook his head. "Mine too, I think."

"But, can we go to see Mommy and Gram and Gramps first?" Joey pleaded.

Uncle Glenn hesitated for a moment. "Your Mommy and Gram and Gramps aren't home right now, they went to visit Aunt Evelyn. Besides we haven't got enough time to do everything and still get you back on time, Joey. I'm sorry."

"We don't want to go back to the farm," said Beth. "Those people are awful mean."

"No! We don't ever want to go back there," Joey added. "How come Mommy couldn't stay home to see us?" He paused. "Gosh. Don't they want to see us? We want to see them real bad."

Aunt Betty turned and looked over the top of the seat. "Yes, of course your mother wants to see you kids. My Goodness sakes! It's just not possible today, that's all." She glanced at Glenn. "I have a feeling you'll see her soon though."

Uncle Glenn caught her eye and nodded, then glanced back over the seat.

"So, tell me, Sport... why did you get a whipping?"

"He kicked her," said Brian.

"What?" Aunt Betty and Uncle Glenn practically harmonized their reaction.

"No!" said Beth. "Brian—let me talk, okay? Yes, Joey did kick Mrs. Bushkin in the leg, but it was because she was shoving the crayons in Brian's mouth and he didn't know how else to make her stop."

Uncle Glenn pulled off to the side of the road by a farmer's driveway. He and Aunt Betty gave each other furtive looks. Glenn sat rigidly, gripping the steering wheel so hard his fingers turned white.

"Hold on here, now." He yanked on the emergency brake and turned to face the kids. "What is all this? You tell me right from the beginning, Beth. You other two, hush now, and let your sister talk, okay?"

Beth sat forward and gripped the top of the front seat. "Okay. Well, see, they were playing in the coloring book, and Brian drew some marks on the wall with a purple crayon. I wasn't there, I was changing the twins diapers, upstairs. Mrs. Bushkin went in their room and saw the marks on the wall and got real mad. So, she stuffed the crayons in Brian's mouth. Joey saw him crying and choking and begged her to stop. He was scared. Mrs. Bushkin wouldn't stop doing it, so Joey kicked her in the leg. Then, she smacked him in the face and went and told Mr. Bushkin everything. He took Joey to the barn and whipped him with the belt. And, that's what happened. That's how Joey really got the black eye... and that's the truth."

Nobody talked. Aunt Betty's hands were clenched. Her eyes were closed tightly and tears ebbed from the corners of them.

Mitchell broke the momentary silence when he wailed and began to squirm and slide off the back seat. Merrill was still asleep on Aunt Betty's lap.

Uncle Glenn and Aunt Betty stared back and forth at one another before he finally released the brake and pulled back onto the highway.

"Let's go get that ice cream, Betty. I think everybody is ready and they certainly deserve a treat," said Uncle Glenn.

"Yes... they are as ready as they're ever gonna be."

Uncle Glenn appeared to be in a daze of sorts. "What?" He acted startled. "Yeah. Okay. Sure." he said.

"I'll bet they have strawberry, too, Uncle Glenn?" said Joey.

"Yes, Sport, I'm sure they do."

Aunt Betty gave her husband a sidelong glance. "Of course, they have strawberry, Joey. All good ice cream shops have strawberry. It's my favorite, too," she said.

When Uncle Glenn parked the car next to the ice cream shop, the kids crawled out. Beth held Mitchell and Aunt Betty lay Merrill on the front seat. She turned to Joey and circled her arms around him and hugged. Joey looked up at her knowingly and bit his lip. He squinted through tears as they stared at each other. Tears formed in his aunt's eyes. She couldn't stop them, nor did she want to. She held him closer.

"Shuush, it's going to be alright now. Joey, please don't cry."

But, Joey sobbed loudly- with no attempt to hold back. Aunt Betty felt her own tears slide down her cheeks; she hugged Joey as tight as she possibly could while his thin body shook in her arms.

Chapter Seventeen

Gouvernuer was not a prosperous place, but picturesque with its tiny gas station, sagging pine houses, and mom-and-pop stores. It was a region rich in farming and poor in living conditions.

The Oswegatchie River wound like a snake on the outskirts of town. Main Street had one stop light and a tired stretch of old buildings. Two small business clusters contained a supermarket, drugstore, bar, diner, a women's clothing boutique, and an insurance company. Windy's was the only ice cream parlor.

Aunt Betty stood on the sidewalk holding Joey for what seemed like forever that day, letting him cry, letting him shake, but telling him everything was going to be okay.

Uncle Glenn held Mitchell, and Beth had Merrill. Beth wiped tears from her cheek and held Brian's hand. Seeing Joey upset instantly brought on thoughts of his pain at the hands of Mr. Bushkin, and she hoped they would never go back to the farm.

The sky was the color of gunmetal and it was beginning to snow. Just a few fuzzy flakes at first, drifting down but gone in an instant when they touched the ground.

Uncle Glenn had parked their 1945 Chevrolet on an angle in front of Windy's Ice Cream Emporium. He gently squeezed his wife's shoulder.

"Come on, Betts, let's go inside and get the kids their ice cream." He bent down and looked in Joey's eyes. "Let's go, Sport," he murmured and patted his head. "Things will work out... you'll see." He fluffed Joey's hair with his hand.

Clouds of mist boiled and hissed behind each passing car along Main Street as they all went inside.

Chattanooga Choo Choo by the Andrews Sisters was playing on a

Wurlitzer jukebox situated in the back. The floor was checkered black and white squares, and a long counter stretched from one end of the parlor to the other. Shiny nickel trimmed all of its edges, and matching chrome-colored stools were mounted on the floor topped with bright red leatherette seats and backs. A tall, young man stood behind the counter wiping a glass with a towel. He had a round white hat on his head and smiled at his new customers.

Various large pictures of Gouvernuer's yesteryears hung on the walls. They were surrounded by much smaller ones depicting smiling customers enjoying Windy's ice cream treats.

A few customers sat here and there, but plenty of tables and booths were available. Uncle Glenn picked a booth by the front windows and everybody sat down. Joey sat with Uncle Glenn along with Brian. Aunt Betty and Beth each held one of the twins on the other side.

"This feels so funny," said Joey.

"What's that, Sport?"

"Being here makes me feel like I'm doing something wrong. Like, I'm not allowed to do this for some reason, but I am."

Aunt Betty patted his hand. "You're just not used to being away from the farm, Joey." She smiled and paused. "But, you are here now, so enjoy yourself, young man. That's an order! Right, Uncle Glenn?"

"Yes. Your Aunt Betty's right. Just relax, Sport."

"Where's that music coming from, Uncle Glenn? I don't see a radio anywhere," said Brian. Glenn laughed.

"It's coming from that Wurlitzer jukebox over there. See all the lights flashing on it? It's called a juke box. I forgot, you kids probably have never seen one before, have you?"

"No, sir," Beth answered.

"This place is where your Uncle Glenn used to bring me on some of our dates, kids. He sure spent a lot of nickels in that thing, too." She pointed to the jukebox. "Didn't you, Honey?" She absent-mindedly covered her mouth with her fingers. The tears started to gather in her eyes, and her lips started trembling. Was it the melancholy or the strain of all she'd seen and heard that day or both?

"Yup. Sure did," Glenn smiled. "Remember the last time we came here? I was home on leave."

Aunt Betty smiled and reached across the table to squeeze his hand. "In fact the song that's playing was one of our favorites." She softly began to sing along with the music:

"You keep me waiting 'till it's gettin' aggrivatin' You're a slowpoke. Why should I worry when you never seem to hurry, you're a slowpoke. Time... means nothing to you. I wait... and then... Late... again. Eight O'clock... Nine O'clock... quarter to ten."

She stopped singing. "It's called *Slowpoke*. They've sure got some old ones on there, haven't they, Glenn? That used to be one of our favorites. The singer's name was Pee Wee King. He was just a short little guy, so they called him Pee Wee."

Joey held his breath for a moment, but then busted out laughing. "Pee Wee?"

Beth giggled, and then she started laughing too, then chanted,

"Pee wee? Pee Wee. Pee Wee." Suddenly, Brian began to laugh. It was obviously contagious. Joey repeated it again and everyone was laughing. Then, the kids all said it together and giggled. "Pee Wee."

"Shuuush." Aunt Betty had been laughing a little bit, too, but then she felt they were attracting too much attention and wanted them to stop. Brian kept giggling.

Outside, the air was thick with heavy snowflakes. They were falling gently but relentlessly. There was no wind. Each one of the billions of flakes came parachuting straight down, sometimes spiraling... and they were accumulating. Aunt Betty paused to examine pedestrians who were strolling along the sidewalk.

The man from behind the counter walked over to their table. Dressed in a white from top to bottom with silver buttons down the front, he wore that little white cap on his head. A red-and- white-checkered towel was draped over his shoulder and he had a friendly face- straw-blond hair, and caramel freckles from his forehead to his fingertips.

He carefully laid out napkins and shiny silver spoons with long handles in front of each of them.

"Howdy, folks. I see it's beginning to snow out there. Well, that's winter for you, eh?" He looked at Uncle Glenn. "What's it gonna be today?" He had a pencil and a pad at the ready.

"Betty, you start off," said Uncle Glenn.

"No, no. Today is the kids' day. Beth, you go first. Tell him what you want."

"Okay. I'll have one of them vanilla ice cream things, with whipped cream and a cherry on top." She designed it with her hands as she talked. "I forgot what you call them."

"I think you mean an ice cream sundae, don't you, Honey?" said Aunt Betty.

"Me, too, just like hers, only chocolate," said Joey.

"Me, too," said Brian. "Like his."

"Gee, kids, give the poor man a chance to write," said Aunt Betty.

"Oh yes, that's pretty easy." The guy kept writing. "Three sundaes." He pointed his pencil at Merrill and smiled. "How about the little ones?"

"Oh, they'll be okay," said Aunt Betty. "I'll just let them have some of mine. I think I'll get what the kids are having, and make mine chocolate."

"Same here," said Uncle Glenn. "Make mine vanilla though, and sprinkle it with some nuts, please."

"That definitely makes it easy. I'll be right back with your order, folks."

"He's got a keen job," said Joey. "I bet he eats a lot of ice cream working here. I like his white suit, too."

Uncle Glenn smiled and rolled his eyes. "Yes, I'll bet he gets his share alright." He paused for a moment, then turned to Joey and nudged him in the ribs with his elbow.

"Peeeeeeee Weeeeeee," he mumbled. Everybody laughed again.

A few strained moments of silence followed while they waited for their ice cream. "Uncle Glenn, where's Mommy?" Joey asked.

Uncle Glenn looked at Betty as if wanting to get permission to answer. He made a noise like a truck tire going flat.

"Joey... uuuuh, well, your Mommy's been real sick. See—she's got sugar Diabetes. Now, I know you don't know what that is, but it's a bad disease. Don't worry though, she'll be okay. She just can't travel a lot right now. She does have a job writing for the newspaper in Watertown and she sees Gram and Gramps every so often."

"Well, when is she coming to get us? When can we see her?" Beth asked.

"Your Mommy had to work today, Joey, but she will see you real soon. She said to tell you she loves you, kids." A long pause of silence followed.

"Where is Daddy?" Joey asked.

"Hold on, you kids. Hold on. I'm not sure about your daddy. I don't want you to get your hopes up, but I think he just got out of the army and he's working on getting you away from the Bushkins, as a matter of fact—right Aunt Betty?"

"Yes, that's right, kids." Her lips pursed at the taste of the lie in her mouth.

The waiter came with the ice cream; he carried them on a red tray that said Coca Cola. "Here ya' go, folks... five of our most popular sundaes." He passed them out. "The gentleman gets this vanilla with the nuts, right?"

"Right," said Uncle Glenn. The waiter placed the others where they belonged without any reminders as to who got what.

"There. I think that's right?"

"Yes, everything's fine, thank you," said Uncle Glenn.

The boys wasted no time digging in. Beth and Aunt Betty fed some to the twins as they ate theirs. The ice cream was eaten in near silence while *Because of You* by Tony Bennett played on the juke box.

Brian had chocolate all over his fingers and his face; he looked like someone had pushed his face into the dish.

"When can we leave the Bushkins' for good, then, Uncle Glenn?" Beth asked. "We don't want to live there. You don't want us to, do you?"

"Yeah, how about if we go back and live with Gram and Gramps... or come and live with you and Aunt Betty until Mommy and Daddy come back?" said Joey.

Uncle Glenn put down his spoon and leaned back in his seat. He let out another slow breath. "Listen, kids. We'd like to do just that, but it's not that easy. See, Gramps had a stroke. That means he's not working, and he needs a lot of help getting around. That's wearing your Gramma out, as it is. So, the Social Services people know that, and they won't let you live there, even if Gram and Gramps wanted you to. And they have asked, believe me." He rolled his eyes toward the ceiling. He paused and wiped his lips with a napkin.

"And as for our place — well — do you remember how small our house trailer is, Beth? There are only two bedrooms... and one of them is real tiny, where Eric sleeps. We just don't have the room, and that's most of the reason why they won't let you stay with us, either. It's called improper living conditions, or something like that."

Joey said nothing. His face went blank.

"But, he whips me, Uncle Glenn. He's a crazy man, and Mrs. Bushkin made Brian eat crayons, too. That shows how crazy they are, doesn't it? We hate them. We want to go away from there."

Mitchell started fussing. "I think the twins need changing, Glenn," said Aunt Betty. "Beth — is Merrill dry?"

"I think so," said Beth.

"Check and see would you?" She smiled knowingly. "We'll change them both before we head back if need be. I have diapers in my pocketbook."

"Yes, and we'd better be heading back, too," said Uncle Glenn. "We told them three hours and now there's snow to drive in." Apprehensively, he checked his watch.

Leaving a quarter for the waiter, he went to pay the bill while Aunt Betty and Beth went out to change the twins on the front seat of the car. The boys followed them and tried to scoop snow off the sidewalk with their bare hands while they waited.

The snow was starting to stick and Uncle Glenn had to wipe his windows off before he drove again. Traffic crept down snow-covered Main Street with drivers getting accustomed to the first significant snow-fall of the season.

"Go ahead and get in boys," said Aunt Betty. "With no boots, I don't want your feet to get wet."

"I've got to get something out of the trunk," said Uncle Glenn.

Joey and Brian jumped on their knees in the back seat and craned their necks to see what Uncle Glenn was doing back there.

He slammed the trunk, came back around and opened his door. He carried a big sack in his arms.

"Aunt Betty and I bought a few things for you kids," he said as he got in. He began to hand out some gifts that were wrapped up in red and green Christmas paper. It was cold in the car, but when he passed the presents to each one of them, everybody forgot about the temperature. They laughed and giggled as they tore into the unexpected presents.

Joey got a Red Ryder jig-saw puzzle and some crayons, while Beth got a diary with its own key. Brian finally got his open, and it was a Tonto Indian doll. Aunt Betty opened the twins' presents for them. Aunt Betty handed each one of them a little red fire truck.

The kids took turns scrambling around in order to give their aunt and uncle hugs.

"Thank you, Uncle Glenn. Thank you, Aunt Betty," said Beth and Joey. Brian said thank you, but he was busy showing his new doll to Merrill.

"You're welcome kids," said Aunt Betty.

"Christmas is coming too, kids, and don't worry Santa Claus won't forget any of you," said Uncle Glenn.

The twins played with the wrapping paper. Merrill tried to put some in his mouth, but Aunt Betty grabbed it away from him.

"Well, I suppose we'd best get back, kids," said Uncle Glenn. "We did tell those folks we would only be a couple of hours." He got out and used his coat sleeve to wipe the snow off the windows again.

"Whew! It's really coming down, too," he said.

A terrible silence hung like a thick fog inside the car. Darkness was closing in and some stretches of road were getting slick. Uncle Glenn looked up ahead nervously as he drove. His wipers struggled to maintain visibility in the face of the increasing snowfall.

"Looks like it's time to put the chains on the car, honey." said

Uncle Glenn.

"That's for sure," said Aunt Betty. She tried to encourage the kids to sing.

"Row, row, row your boat, gently down the stream. Merrily, merrily, merrily, merrily... life is but a dream." Joey was silent. Beth tried to sing awhile, but she soon stopped. Brian tried to sing by himself, but he couldn't get the words straight. Merrill was on Aunt Betty's lap and he began to cry. She tried to comfort him with his new fire truck and it seemed to work.

"Maybe he's hungry," said Uncle Glenn. The windshield wipers slapped back and forth, and the sound was like some kind of rhythmic tune harmonizing with the humming of the car's engine. It was hypnotic and before long, Joey's head lay on his sister's shoulder and Brian had fallen asleep on Joey's lap. Uncle Glenn and Aunt Betty spoke in hushed tones as the miles clicked by ever so slowly because of the snow-covered road.

When Joey woke up, they were passing the Carthage school, and his stomach turned. He knew they were almost back to the Bushkin farm. Uncle Glenn saw him moving around in his rear-view mirror. Beth sat up too, then Brian.

"Ahh, you're awake, sleepy-heads. We were getting lonely up here." He paused and turned his head slightly. "Kids, don't think we don't know what's going on, and we know it's hard for you right now. But, I promise you, Mrs. Kellogg will hear from us about everything you told us, first thing in the morning."

"What will she do?" Beth asked.

"I'm not sure, honey, but they better do something, or I'll know the reason why not. Maybe they'll move you, at least that much, until your mommy and daddy get things together. But I will make sure something is done... and I mean right away."

"Promise?" asked Joey."

"We both promise," said Aunt Betty.

"You bet, Joey. Something will be done."

"Yay," said Beth. "That will be a good thing. Then at least we will get away from those people, huh?"

"I would certainly think so," said Aunt Betty.

It was library-quiet again until the twins stirred. Joey's stomach lurched when he saw Uncle Glenn pull into Bushkin's driveway.

"Listen, kids... I don't want you letting on that we know anything. Do you understand what I mean by that, Joey? It's very, very important. Just tell these people that you had a real nice time, and in case they ask you, we never talked about any of the bad things at all. If they ask you if we know, just tell them 'no'. Understand?"

"Yes, Uncle Glenn," said Joey.

"Yes, we understand, Uncle Glenn," Beth added.

"And how about you, Butchie," said Aunt Betty. "You understand what Uncle Glenn is telling you?"

Brian nodded. Uncle Glenn pointed a finger at him and pulled an imaginary trigger with his thumb and made a clicking sound with his mouth. At the same time, he winked. "Good boy."

Joey's knees were like putty, but he managed to walk to the porch; his heart pounding with dread.

Uncle Glenn and Aunt Betty smiled but said nothing to the Bushkins about what they had learned. Joey felt his cheeks burning from embarrassment and fear.

Uncle Glenn hesitated. He approached Mr. Bushkin as if he were staring at a loaded gun. "We want to thank you folks. We really appreciate your letting us have the kids for a few hours. Sorry if we're a bit late. The roads are a mess as you can imagine."

"Yes, we saw it's getting bad out there," said Mr. Bushkin. He locked his arms across his chest, spat in the sink and gave the appearance that all was fine.

"Be careful driving home," said Mrs. Bushkin.

Brian had his head pushed up against Uncle Glenn's leg, and he wouldn't turn around. He began to cry. Uncle Glenn and Aunt Betty hugged and kissed all of them and said goodbye. Aunt Betty had tears in her eyes on the way to the car.

Joey was tired of crying.

Brian screamed when Uncle Glenn and Aunt Betty walked out the door. He and Joey both ran to their bedroom window to watch as the red tail lights of the Chevy drifted farther and farther away. When they couldn't be seen anymore, Brian bounced down onto the bed and sobbed.

Mrs. Bushkin sat in her bedroom, reading her Bible. After Beth finished getting the twins fed and ready for bed, she told her to come to her room. "Did you have a good time, Elizabeth?" This came out more like a hurled piece of spit than a question formed with words. Her attempt at smiling came across as no more than a smirk.

Beth couldn't meet her gaze, but answered, "Yes, Ma'am."

"Joseph!" she called. "Joseph... come in here."

Joey ran to her room. "What about you? Did you have fun today?"

"Yes, Ma'am." He felt his cheeks burning from embarrassment and the fear that she possibly knew something.

"And of course, neither of you happened to mention the punishment Joseph got from the mister, did you?" Again, Mrs. Bushkin spoke with a sneer on her face- a scary tone in her voice.

"No, Ma'am," they both answered.

She glared at both of them for what seemed to be forever.

"I think you're both lying, so there. Go to bed."

Snuggled in his bed, Joey lay wake thinking about all the nice things that happened that day. Even though they were back at the Bushkins', he felt that Uncle Glenn meant what he promised. They would be leaving the farm soon.

Chapter Eighteen

A lice's face had aged in recent months, with a network of deep wrinkles that looked like cracked house paint. Her soft blue eyes were red and worried, and her thoughts were as organized as a puzzle box that someone had shaken violently.

Her entire situation was a nightmare. She constantly beat herself up over the loss of her children. Especially the twins. She wanted to get them back, at the very least she needed to go visit them... hug and squeeze them—-feel their warm little arms wrapped around her neck. She had to assure them somehow that she did indeed love them.

They should be with her, but she had no means financially and Joe was gone for good. A rumor had it that he was living in New York City, but no one knew for sure. And, Fred Simms, the man Alice was living with—father of the twins—wanted no part of raising them. He had made that clear more than once.

It was November 1948, and Fred and Alice sat in their apartment talking about everything and anything. Alice had just got home from her waitress job at Ranger's Family Restaurant and Tavern. Fred always got home two hours before Alice; he worked the early shift at the textile mill.

Alice lit a Chesterfield and watched the smoke billow toward the stained plaster ceiling, where it upset an existing cloud and swirled around a hanging light. She coughed a hacking, irritating cough, which reddened her face.

Fred sat back on their sagging sofa that had no arms. Two straight-backed chairs stood against the wall in the unlikely event company materialized. To the left was a kitchen area with a small table and three miss-matched chairs. The bedroom was on the right with an unmade bed and clothes on the floor. The rug was stained and threadbare, and the windows were covered with dark, drab curtains.

Alice puffed on her Chesterfield. Fred, who smoked cigars, couldn't stand cigarette smoke and waved his hands to clear the rancid smoke.

"This damned apartment is starting to smell like dead mice," he said. The bourbon had already found its way to his brain and was loosening his tongue.

Alice poured a glass of *Gallo* wine and slowly rolled it back and forth on her forehead. She gazed out the living room window and admired the orange and violet clouds that clung to the western horizon. She thought about how nice it would be to have a car of her own. She was tired of having to beg Fred to take her everywhere.

Fred looked at her moist eyes and asked, "What's the matter, Alice?"

"Nothing... but I want to stop by my Ma's house, if you don't mind. She wants to see me about something or other, besides, it's been awhile, and I need to see Dad, too. He's not getting any better, you know."

Fred wilted. "Mmm-hmm, I'd rather not, myself. You know me and your mother don't get along. This is the same discussion we've had too damned many times."

Alice looked shocked at first; then there was a glint of hope in her eyes. "Please, Fred. I haven't asked you in weeks. Ma called me at work and told me she has to talk to me. It's important, she said. It won't take us that long to go to Gouvernuer. You don't have to go inside... you know that. You'll take me over there though... won't you?"

Alice was used to begging but she still hated it. She despised Fred because he made her do it. He loved to have control.

Fred slowly stood and gave her a peck on the cheek. He looked at her closely. He saw the quality of damaged beauty about her. He dreaded facing her mother and father again, but he would keep the peace if he did. "Oh, I suppose I'll have to," he said. "You won't let me breathe easy until I do."

Alice was elated and grim at the same time, like a burned survivor of a plane crash. "Thanks so much, Fred. See... you can be so nice when you want to, can't you, honey?" She kissed him on the forehead.

"Yeah, what the hell. But don't expect me to go in—-I'm waiting in the car as usual."

.   .   .   .   .

Alice got out of the car and braced herself, ready to make another foray into the cauldron of boiling family blood. There was a slight hesitation in her step as she went to the back door of her mother and father's house on Depot Street. She didn't bother to knock.

Carl sat in his rocker with the Watertown Times on his lap. He puffed his pipe and stared at his daughter when she came through the door.

"Well, glad to see you, honey. Did you forget where we live?"

He turned his cool gaze on her, saw her sudden nervousness. He smiled and moved slowly, just a slight shifting of his weight to one side and tapped his pipe on the ashtray standing next to his chair.

Alice drifted over. "How are you, Pa? Feeling any better?" She leaned over and kissed his forehead.

"Oh, I'm doing about as well as can be expected, I guess," said Carl. "How about you? Still working at the beer garden, are you?"

"Yes. Jobs are hard to find right now, Pa. Lot of people coming back from the war are scooping them up right and left. I have to keep what I've got or I'll have nothing at all. I do have an interview scheduled with the Times, though."

"Well, that's good to hear. When is that?"

"Next week. But a car is the big thing. I'll have to get there four or five days a week for a while, then I may be able to write at home and drop off my columns once a week. If I had transportation, I would be a lot better off, you know?"

"Wouldn't we all," said Carl.

Lillian entered from the kitchen where she was finishing up the dishes. She dried her hands on her apron and threw her arms around Alice.

"Good to see you, sweetheart. How about a glass of Gallo?"

"Oh—I don't know, Ma. I can't stay very long... Fred's waiting outside for me and you know how he is. But, I guess I will have just a smidge of that wine if you have enough."

"Oh, the old woman has plenty, honey. Never fear about that," said Carl. "Not a bit worried about your sugar diabetes, eh? That wine won't help it, that's for durn sure."

"Hush, old man," said Lillian. "Sit down for a minute, Alice." She reached over, pulled back the curtain and looked out front. "That selfish scoundrel in the car can just cool his heels."

Lillian got another glass and sat it next to her own, then filled them both to the brim. "I've got some news about the kids," she said, just above a whisper.

Alice pulled out a dining room chair and sat down. "Really? What sort of news? Did somebody call you?" She could barely contain her excitement.

"Easy now," said Carl. "You won't like what she's going to tell you, honey. Pretty upsetting stuff. Go ahead and tell her, Lillian."

"Well, I'm going to, old man, if you'll just give me a chance. My goodness. Well, Glenn and Betty stopped out at the Bushkin's farm to see the kids last weekend."

"What?" Alice studied Lillian's face for a moment. Alice leaned in. "Really? Why? I mean why did they do that and not tell me they were going?"

"Well, I tried to call you at Fred's and the phone's disconnected. I left word with Bev at the bar to have you call me, too, but I guess you didn't get the message. I'm sorry, sweetheart."

"I didn't get any message."

"Well, anyway, Glenn and Betty got the kids away for the day, somehow, and took them to Windy's Ice Cream parlor in town."

"They're starving those kids out there," said Carl.

"Carl, stop!" said Lillian.

Alice jumped to her feet. "What does he mean? Oh, no!"

Lillian took a long sip of her wine and lit a cigarette. She handed one to Alice, then struck a match and lit it. "Your Pa is right though. Joey told Glenn and Betty and Beth agreed, it was true."

"Oh, my God! I don't understand. Glenn could have told me they were going out there, you know. That's just Betty's doings, you can bank on that."

Alice took another drink, stood up and took a long drag on her cigarette. "That's not fair."

"Well, honey — that's not all. Sit back down." said Lillian.

"Oh, no! What else for heaven's sake?"

Carl spoke from the other room. "Just listen for a minute, honey. Let your mother finish."

"I guess that fella out there, Mr. Bushkin, has been whipping Joey something terrible, and . . ."

Alice jumped up and threw her hands over her face. "No! No! Oh, my God, no!"

". . . and," Lillian continued. "His wife shoved crayons down Brian's throat, if you can believe that."

Alice covered her mouth with her fingertips, and then stood motionless. Her stomach churned and her knees quivered. She tried to speak, but nothing came forth at first.

"Oh, my God! Are you sure?" Tears formed in her eyes and she sat back down and sobbed.

Lillian put her hand on Alice's back and rubbed. "We don't think the kids were lying, Honey. Glenn called Mrs. Kellogg right away."

"Why... why didn't Glenn just bring them home with him? What's wrong with him?"

"Because he could have gotten in a lot of trouble, Alice, that's why. Like kidnapping and God knows what. No, that would have been the wrong way to go about it. Glenn did right. The state will handle those people. The kids will be out of there soon enough. I'm sorry. I just had to tell you."

Alice stared at her mother with desperation in her eyes. She picked up her glass and gulped down the rest of the wine. "Ma, we have to do something. Did Glenn get a hold of Kellogg? What are they doing? I have to see the kids for myself."

Chapter Nineteen

C hristmas was only weeks away and Mrs. Kellogg hadn't visited the Bushkin farm since early November. Five days had passed since the kids had gone out with their Uncle Glenn and Aunt Betty, and Kellogg still hadn't come out to the farm. Mrs. Bushkin believed the kids hadn't said anything, because there wasn't so much as a phone call from the caseworker.

Joey constantly reminded Beth of the promise made by Uncle Glenn and Aunt Betty. The kids were both careful not to talk about it in the house where they might be heard. When they did talk about things, they were on the way out to empty their pots.

"They said they would get us away from here, Sis. You heard them. But, Mrs. Kellogg hasn't been here in an awful long time. Aunt Betty and Uncle Glenn promised. Do you think they really told somebody?"

"She'll come, Joey. Any day now, I'll bet. Just hold on, things are going to get better, wait and see," said Beth. "I promise I'll tell Mrs. Kellogg everything, but I can't until she comes. I don't know her telephone number, or I would call."

"Well, she better come pretty soon or I'll just run away... I promise that," said Joey, as they stood by the outhouse.

"No, no, Joey. Please don't even talk like that now. What will I do if you leave?" Beth felt the tears slide down her cheeks as she hugged her brother. "We have to believe Aunt Betty and Uncle Glenn. Something must have gone wrong, that's all. It is probably taking longer than they thought. They would never lie to us, Joey." Her body shook and she squeezed his arm. "Please, please, listen to me." They stared into each other's eyes.

"Okay, Sis. I'll wait a little longer, but somebody better hurry up."

Beth set her chamber pot down and hugged her brother. "Thank you, Joey. Thank you."

·　　·　　·　　·　　·

Joey was punished and sent to bed with no supper that night. Extremely hungry, he decided to take a chance and find something to eat. He waited until he thought everyone was asleep before he slid out of bed and tip-toed down the hallway to the pantry. He stopped and listened, but heard nothing other than the thunderous beating of his own heart. Nobody had heard him.

There was no light, but he remembered where things were and felt around until he found a box of crackers. He tried to open the package of saltines, but his hands shook; the paper wouldn't open. His shaking got worse and he couldn't stop it. When the paper finally ripped open the crackers flew out and scattered all over the floor. He froze while his body tingled with fear, his breath was loud and irregular.

Suddenly he heard footsteps behind him and turned to face Mr. Bushkin.

"Thought I heard something, you little thief!" he growled. "You think you're so clever, eh? Shame on you! You know what the Bible says about stealing?" He abruptly backhanded Joey, then snatched him up by the back of the neck and shoved him into the kitchen.

Mrs. Bushkin appeared and stood behind her husband with her arms folded over her chest, her hair in disarray. "Hmmmmph! Caught him, eh?"

Joey cowered in the corner, trying to shrink into himself; he wrapped his arms around his legs. His entire body shook. His lip was bleeding; he tasted the blood. He was sure Mr. Bushkin would get his belt and beat him.

"Get up! Get up right now and get back to bed," snarled Mr. Bushkin. "I'll deal with you in the morning, boy."

"Yes, sir, I won't do it again... I promise."

"Oh, I know you won't, boy... I know you won't." He raised a threatening hand as if to slap Joey again before Joey ducked and ran to bed.

Lying in bed, crying, Joey brushed his fingers over his swollen lip. This was it. Now, he had to run away. He couldn't face the morning and get another whipping from Mr. Bushkin.

I'm going. I know Beth will be mad at me, but I just can't wait. I'll go and keep going until I find Gramps' house. Gramps will come over here and then Mr. Bushkin and his wife will be in lots of trouble. I'll bet he'll take Beth and Brian and the twins away from here, too. I hate the Bushkins.

Darkness had brought a cold wind, and four inches of accumulated snow covered the rural landscape that night. Joey had to decide what to bring with him. Bringing a bunch of clothes would mean too much to carry. He'd wear his school clothes, his winter coat and black boots. He didn't have any gloves since he'd lost them at school and Mrs. Bushkin wouldn't buy another pair.

He thought about food. Now he wouldn't dare go back to the pantry. He was afraid he'd get caught again and decided to worry about eating later. Gram and Gramps would have food for him anyway. Still, it might be a long time before he'd get to Gramps' house, and he didn't even know for sure how far it was.

He was very quiet as he dressed in the dark, careful not to wake Brian. He slipped on his coat, sat on the edge of his bed and waited a moment.

I hope Daisy doesn't bark. She could ruin everything if she does. I'll just run if she does bark. I want to say goodbye to Beth and Brian, but I can't. I just can't. Brian would want to go with me, and Sis would just try to change my mind again. But, after I tell Gramps and Mommy what these people are like, they'll come and get them anyway.

He heard Mr. Bushkin snoring from their bedroom down the hall. The snoring was always loud. He hoped Mrs. Bushkin was asleep, too.

He was ready to go. It was difficult to see in the dark, and he wisely stood still for a moment—too afraid to move. His poor brain was choked with fear and he felt dizzy. He closed his eyes and squinted fiercely in a vain effort to push himself forward.

As he crept through the kitchen and headed to the back porch, it was so quiet he could hear the drip, drip, dripping of the kitchen faucet. It seemed loud but he knew it really wasn't. He felt the hair stand up on the back of his neck as he took each deliberate step.

Fire burned in the wood stove; he saw it through the cracks around the stove's door. He stopped moving in order to listen again. His own breathing was loud in his ears and his heart pounded as he twisted the handle for the door to the back porch. It squeaked ever so softly when he pulled the door open. He stopped. *Oh, no! I bet somebody heard that!* He waited, but hearing nothing he tugged the door open just far enough to slide his body through, then left it. He carefully turned the knob on the outside door and edged out into the cold night air.

Daisy had been lying under the porch. When she suddenly appeared, it startled Joey and he jumped back. The dog licked his hand and sniffed his pant legs.

"Shhhhh," good dog," Joey whispered. He hoped she wouldn't bark.

The cold wind slammed his face. The trees were skeletal and scary, and smoke from the kitchen stove hung in their moonlit branches.

Joey's slow deliberate walk turned into a run. He ran fast, with both arms stiff and straight down by his side, leaning forward at the waist. He tripped one time, but didn't fall.

Lights from cars passing on Highway Eleven illuminated the snow banks straight ahead. The night was very still and quiet, except for the snow, crunching under his feet.

He'd only gone three hundred yards or so, when a doe wandered into a car's headlights. It stopped directly in front of the car, then bounded off toward the other side of the road. It startled Joey. The car passed and he waited, then watched as another doe, and then a third, crossed in front of him, like ladies on their way to market.

Wow! Look at all the deers, right here on this road the bus takes to school. If I follow this road I can probably find Gramps' house. Maybe I'll find some place to get warm and eat before I get there though. Gee, I never saw deers that close before.

Joey stayed a good distance from the road as he walked. Each step took him farther and farther away from the farmhouse he hated, and he continually looked over his shoulder, fearing that Mr. Bushkin was right behind him. From time to time, a car or truck alarmed him as they whizzed by. Occasionally they slowed to a near stop. Their brake lights, flashed on then off as they sped away.

Joey decided to move farther away from the highway and skirted along a stand of pine trees. He trudged a long distance before the land finally opened up into open pasture. Drifting snow made it difficult to walk and he was tiring fast.

Far ahead, in the distance, Joey saw an eerie brightness surrounding a town; it seemed to paint an electric glow against the night sky.

That must be Antwerp — where my school is, but it's still so far away. It's going to take me a long-long time to get there — maybe all night.

Freezing wind bit his face and with no gloves, he had to shove his hands deep inside his coat pockets. He moved as fast as his legs would let him, but they ached more and more from plodding through the snow. Straining his eyes, he saw that he wasn't too far away from a billboard that stood like a shadowy monster waiting in the field in front of him.

Maybe I can hide behind that sign and rest. It might be warmer there too. I better hurry.

He picked up the pace, practically running. Once there, he circled the billboard until he spotted a wooden brace to sit on. The huge frame of the billboard blocked some of the wind and he instantly felt warmer. It was a good place to rest. He wrapped his arms across his chest and blew hot breath into his hands. Then, listening to the hum of the traffic passing by on the highway, he gradually nodded off.

When he awoke, twenty minutes later, he was colder than before. Remembering what he learned in school, he realized he had to keep moving. He shook his arms and legs and jumped up and down, then ran back out towards the road, using the same path he made going in.

I wish I had a watch. I know how to tell time now, and, if I had a watch,

I'd be able to tell how long I've been gone. I wonder if Mr. Bushkin has started milking the cows yet. He will be looking for me to do my chores pretty soon. I bet he'll be awful mad.

Daylight began to unfold ever so slightly as Joey neared the outskirts of the town. A green dinosaur on the Sinclair gas station sign was a familiar sight. His bus passed it each day on the way to Carver Elementary School. It was closed but a big clock hung in the window; the face was accented with green neon. The time was twenty minutes after six.

Three blocks down the road was Jesse's Diner. The entire town was still fairly dark, but the diner glowed like a promise. A boxlike building that had been there for over fifteen years, a flashing red sign in the window boasted: BREAKFAST SERVED ALL DAY.

With its cozy atmosphere and home-made daily specials, Jesse's was very popular with the locals. There were plenty of padded booths, a dozen tables, and a long counter faced the grill, where everything was cooked in the open. Jesse Evans never saw the need for printed menus in his diner. Years before when he first opened, he couldn't afford menus, and now that he could, he didn't need them because most folks knew what he served.

As he got closer, Joey smelled bacon. Even when he wasn't hungry, he liked the smell of frying bacon and he hadn't smelled it for so awful long. He crossed the road to the diner. A swoosh of warm air gushed in his face as soon as he stepped inside. It felt so good; he wished it would keep blowing on him. He stopped and looked up at a little bell jingling above the door.

Jesse stood over the grill cooking. He heard the bell, and turned to face Joey. Nodding, he smiled at the boy, as he wiped his hands on a soiled apron.

A rather short individual, Jesse carried the heft of a man who liked his food rich and often. He had a horseshoe of graying hair around his broad head and a large nose with a bump at the end. His voice was low and croaky.

"Well, what have we here? Good morning, Sonny!"

I don't know him. Why is he calling me 'Sonny'? Uncle Glenn and

Gramps are the only ones who call me that — nobody else. Does he know where I'm from? Does he know Mr. Bushkin? Is he going to call him?

Another man was sitting at the counter, sipping coffee while he read a newspaper. Turning around on his stool, he stared at Joey, then grinned and went back to his paper.

Joey was afraid to sit down. "Good morning, Sir," he said to Jesse. He wondered if he could see his knees shaking.

"Hey, there. Up kinda early, ain'tcha, boy?" Jesse kept his eye on Joey as he stirred pancake mix in a bowl, then he reached for his coffee cup on the counter. Taking a sip, he smacked his lips as if he'd been in the desert for a month and continued stirring.

"Yes, sir. I'm on my way to school — I'm a little early is all."

"Early? I'll say you are." Jesse did a poor job of masking his doubt, checking his watch without actually looking at it. "What did you do... pee the bed?" The man at the counter lowered his paper and chuckled.

Joey blushed. *I didn't pee in my bed. Why did he say that?*

"No, Sir. I didn't pee in my bed."

Both men laughed out loud.

"I would hope not. Not hungry are ya?" asked Jesse. He turned to face the grill and work the bacon.

"Ummmm, yes, sir — a little bit," said Joey. He was finally able to exhale; his heart seemed to calm a bit, and he moved towards the counter. Yet something told him he should leave now and run. Jesse turned to face Joey. "You got any money, son?"

Joey hung his head. "No, sir — I don't."

Jesse studied Joey for a moment. Something shifted in his face. "How come you didn't eat before you left home? Hey, you ain't runnin' away, are ya?"

Joey wanted to run, but his legs wouldn't move. *How did he guess? I think I should go right now, but I'm so hungry and that bacon smells so good.*

"No, Sir. I just wasn't hungry when I got up, but I smelled your bacon, and I am now."

"You are, eh?" He paused to scoop pancakes onto the grill. "Well, grab a stool." He looked over his shoulder. "Pete, what do ya' think? Should we treat this young fella' to some of my famous pancakes n' bacon?"

Pete looked Joey up and down and stared. He made Joey nervous. "Yeah. He's a bit scrawny, if you ask me. I say give him some eats." He chuckled. "Put it on my ticket if you like, Jess."

"Naw, I'll get it. A man has to have breakfast." He turned back to Joey. "You on your way to school, are you, Sonny?"

There... he called me Sonny again.

"Thank you, Sir. Yes, my mother dropped me off in town on her way to work.

"Oh, and where does she work?"

"In town someplace, I'm not sure, exactly."

Why is he asking me all this stuff? I'll have to eat fast and get out of here. He might call the police or something. Maybe he knows Mr. Bushkin.

"Well. No mind. Sit down right here. Pancakes coming up." He smiled. "Coupla' slices of bacon, too, how's that?"

"Thank you, sir."

Joey started eating as soon as Jesse put the plate in front of him. There were two big pancakes and several strips of bacon, which Joey hadn't seen since he lived at Gramps. Joey started thinking as he gobbled it all down.

I wonder if Beth is up with the twins. Does anybody know I am gone yet? I bet Beth will cry. I wish she wouldn't. Maybe I shouldn't have left her, but when I think of the whippings and stuff, I know I had to. I won't go back. I'd better hurry up, too.

Pete kept staring at Joey—making him feel uncomfortable. Joey felt his eyes, and finally stared back. Pete went back to reading his paper and continued to eat. Early-morning sunlight spilled through the front windows when Joey was almost done.

"Jess, give me some of that pancake syrup back there, would ya? The real stuff, if you don't mind," said Pete.

"Sure thing," said Jessie. He took the bottle of maple syrup to Pete and then stopped in front of Joey.

"You want somethin' to drink, boy?"

"Yes, sir. Could I have some milk?"

"Oh, I think we got some of that around here," Jesse said with a smile. "What's your name, anyway?" He went to the icebox.

"Uuuuh, my name is Billy," said Joey.

"Uuu- huh, well, here's your milk, Billy," said Jesse as he sat the glass down.

A blonde woman wearing thick black-rimmed glasses came in the front door and stomped the snow off of her boots. She removed the scarf from her head and looked at Joey as she stuffed it in her coat pocket. She wore a waitress's uniform under her coat. It was white with pink trim around the collar and pockets.

"Mornin', Jess, mornin', Pete." She stuck a pencil in her hair and took a pad out of her pocket. She studied Joey for a moment, then picked up part of Pete's newspaper.

"Morning, Marcie," the two men answered.

Marcie sat at the counter. She took off her glasses and cleaned them with a handkerchief, put them back on and continued to peruse the paper.

"Seems like things are lookin' up, since the Japs surrendered, eh?" she said as she tossed the paper back on the counter by Pete.

"Yeah, and I see where our hero, Eisenhower, might make a bid for the White House," said Jesse. "By God, they'll sure miss old Harry Truman when he leaves."

Joey finished his milk and eased out the door while they were talking. He waved, but Jesse didn't see him. Looking both ways, he quickly crossed back to the other side of the road, where there were more stores.

I can duck in someplace and get warm when the stores open. But I have to keep watching for Mr. Bushkin's truck. I'll hide between the buildings if I do see him coming, that's all. Gramps house can't be much farther.

Town Circle Park was just a few blocks away. The bus passed it everyday on the way to school and sometimes teachers walked their classes there in the spring. Joey decided to get away from the main road. That would be the place to go — the park. He jogged there as fast as possible. The park was covered in snow, the gleaming winter sun made everything look pristine.

Sitting on a bench, he wrapped his arms around himself and watched while the town came to life and the sun became brighter. A few cars parked in front of the stores. He needed to get some gloves somehow. His hands were already freezing again.

The red and gold colors of the Woolworth store could be seen from where he was sitting. It would probably be a good place to find gloves, he thought. A school bus rolled down the street; it was empty. After it passed by, Joey got up and ran across the street.

He entered Woolworths and found it was spooky-quiet inside; the wooden floor creaked as he slowly walked to the back of the store. The smells of new leather, pine trees and hot chocolate permeated the air. The warm air felt wonderful on his chilled body.

A tired-looking lady with gray hair appeared out of the back room. "Can I help you, young man?" She startled Joey, and he jumped.

Wearing glasses that were situated on the tip of her nose, she reminded Joey of a grandmother. She wore a green and yellow polka-dotted apron, with a small pad edging out of the pocket, and a big smile spread over her wrinkled face.

"No, ma'am. I'm just looking around, is all."

Joey saw disbelief in her eyes.

"Shouldn't you be in school?" She checked her watch. "My goodness, it's late... way past nine, did you know that?"

"No, ma'am. I'm not late. I don't have any school today. We're moving, so I don't go to school until next week at my new school in Gouvernuer."

"Oh, I see." She studied his face for a moment. "Well, let me know if you find anything I can help you with. I'll be right over here by the sheets and pilla' cases." She indicated with a nod of her head.

Joey walked up and down the aisles, taking his time to look for gloves. He passed the plates and silverware, and saw butcher knives. Big knives. He made up his mind he would need a knife to protect himself from anybody who tried to hurt him.

The lady was two aisles away and had her back turned. While she was reaching for something up high, Joey grabbed a butcher knife, stuck it under his coat and walked out without gloves.

"Oh... bye, young man," the woman yelled over her shoulder. "Good luck!"

"Bye, Ma'am, Joey mumbled.

He rushed up and down side streets for a while to avoid more people asking questions he'd have to lie in order to answer. He knew he had to stay off of the main street, but he still needed gloves.

Crossing some railroad tracks, he stopped as he noticed a green storage shed sitting a few feet from the tracks. Faded lettering was stenciled on the side said: New York Central R R.

Trains must come here, or else there wouldn't be any tracks and that shed wouldn't be here. If I follow the tracks, I bet they'll take me right to Gramps house in Gouvernuer.

In the distance, a man was walking alongside the tracks; he was coming toward him. Joey noticed that the man walked slow and easy just like his Gramps and became anxious to see who it was. As the man got closer, Joey waved, and the man waved back.

Wow! I wonder if it really is Gramps. The man must work for the railroad, because he's walking along by the tracks like that. Only railroad guys do that.

When the man was close enough, Joey was disappointed to see that it wasn't Gramps at all. Gray hair stuck out from the sides of his blue and white striped cap and he had a pipe in his mouth. A lantern swung to and fro in his hand.

"Morning, young man."

"Good morning, Sir."

"You've been watching me for quite a spell, aint'cha?"

"Yes, sir."

"No school today, eh?"

"No, Sir, not me. No school today. Our family is moving to Watertown. I 'm just wasting some time until this afternoon when we leave. I thought I'd come and wait for the trains to go by. I like trains.".

The man puffed on his pipe and looked Joey over. "Nothing wrong with that, lad. I like trains, too—have for almost twenty years now." He took off his hat and held it for Joey to see.

"Gee, that's a long time. Can you tell me when another train will come by here?"

"Well, that all depends," said the man. He took the pipe out of his mouth and used his coat sleeve to wipe away some spit that rolled down his chin. "Which way you want to go? The northbound gets in here in about... let's see . . ."

He pulled a pocket watch from his pants. It dangled and glittered in the morning sun. "Northbound gets here about 45 minutes from now—ten fifteen. If you want the southbound—it won't pass here until twelve-twenty. You haven't got a watch, I suppose."

"No, sir."

"I see." He bent over and took a closer look at Joey's face. "Say— where'd you get the shiner?"

Joey slowly rubbed it with his fingertips and told the lie he was used to telling once more. "Me and my little brother were playing, and he accidentally kicked me in the eye."

The old man studied the eye for a moment. "Boy, it's a beauty." He laughed. "Well, I've got to work, so good luck over there in Watertown. Like I said, Old 46 should be coming by here in a little bit —the northbound. You'll like her. She's one of them new diesel jobs. Good luck to you, lad."

"Thank you, Sir." Joey watched as the man opened the shed, took something out, locked it up again and waved as he walked away.

Joey stared at the shiny tracks remembering that special day when he went to work with Gramps. He wondered if he could ever do that again. *Maybe I should just walk along the tracks until I find Gramps shack, but I have to find out which way first. I should have asked that man.* He looked back and saw the man fading in the distance.

Two benches sat alongside the shed, and Joey sat down to wait. He was tired from walking most of the night. His eyes kept trying to close, so he lay down to rest.

Cars and trucks swished by on the wet road and he closed his eyes. He had no idea how long he had been sleeping when a man's voice jarred him awake. He sat up and the butcher knife tumbled to the ground. Joey rubbed his eyes and reached for it, then looked into the angry eyes of Mr. Bushkin.

"Stand up, Boy!"

Chapter Twenty

Joey jumped up and tried to run, but Mr. Bushkin grabbed the collar of his coat. "Oh, no you don't. You're done runnin', boy!" He slowly bent down and picked up the knife. "What have we got here?" Joey's legs shook. He whimpered and peed his pants.

Holding the knife up to Joey's face, Mr. Bushkin snarled, and glared like a rabid dog. "Where did you get this, huh? Stole it, didn't you? What in the name of heaven did you plan on doing with a knife?"

Joey looked away, but he felt Mr. Bushkin's caustic eyes boring into him.

"Answer me!" Mr. Bushkin was breathing fast, as if he had just run up two flights of stairs. The tip of his tongue ran back and forth across his lower lip, and his voice sounded hoarse. He dragged Joey to his truck, threw the door open, and shoved him inside.

As he closed the door, Joey screamed, "Please don't hurt me again!"

"Quiet, boy. Don't you move. Just sit right there; you're in enough trouble, better not make it worse." He tossed the knife in the back of the truck and climbed in. Rubbing his hands together, he stared at Joey for a moment. Taking off his hat, he ran his fingers through his dirty gray hair and coughed.

Joey considered running. He wiped tears from his face with his dirty fingers as the thoughts ran through his head. *I could open the door and run. He couldn't catch me, and somebody might help me if I run fast and yell real loud. No... I better not try.* He clamped his hands between his knees in an effort to stop shaking.

"I thought we took care of that devil's poison in you, lad." He shook a finger in Joey's face. "It appears you need another whipping to get him gone again, eh? You are a thief. How much do you figure the good Lord and me can stand, anyway? It don't do no good to run away from the truth, boy."

Joey's heart raced. He was breathing as if he'd just run a race. He still wanted to jump out, but his hands trembled and his knees wouldn't stop shaking.

Mr. Bushkin drove fast through town. The early morning sky had been a canvas with the sun splashing its awesome array of colors with bold strokes. But by the time Mr. Bushkin had found him, the sunshine disappeared, and gray, low clouds blanketed the region. A squall churned out of the south like smoke twisting inside a bottle. Solitary snowflakes spiraled down and hit the windshield. Joey's mind was filled with fear of the whipping he would get.

They passed Jesse's Diner, and the abandoned feed mill that sat near the railroad tracks half-way down the Main Street in Antwerp. Mr. Bushkin rolled down his window and spat, then rolled it back up and swiped his lips with the sleeve of his coat. "I got better things to do than hunt you down, lad. Running away will only bring you pain." He paused and stuffed a new wad of tobacco in his jaw.

"Did you really think you could get away with leaving like that? Where did you think you would go? Your family don't want you and you're damned lucky me and the missus keep a roof over all your orphaned heads." He glanced sideways at Joey as he spoke. "Answer me, Boy."

"No," said Joey. He wouldn't look at him.

"No? No what?"

"No, sir—I'm sorry I did it."

"Sorry, huh? Well, I don't believe you. You're a liar, and a thief! Did you really think you would get very far? People ain't stupid. Tim Sastick has been with the railroad for as long as I can remember, and he knows a troublemaker when he sees one. He figured who you were and he knew you were lying." He chuckled. "I got friends all over town, boy. I've lived here all my life. You ain't a very good liar. But, just you wait, we'll take that lying streak out of you yet."

A feeling of dread washed over Joey like bathwater. He wanted to cry, but couldn't. They drove in silence the rest of the way back to the farm, and Joey's fear mounted as he realized they would soon be there.

When they turned in the driveway, Mrs. Kellogg's black sedan was parked by the back porch. After Mr. Bushkin rolled to a stop, Joey jumped out and ran into the house.

Mr. Bushkin got out of the truck and froze in his tracks to consider the situation. He couldn't figure out why Judith Kellogg's car was there. She had always let them know when she would be out. And, there was no phone call, was there? It was awful early, too.

Joey found everybody in the living room: Mrs. Bushkin, Mrs. Kellogg, Beth, and Brian were all gathered in a circle. The twins played with Tinker Toys on the floor. Brown grocery bags full of clothes sat on the couch.

Beth ran to Joey and hugged him tight. "Oh, Joey!" Her smile was as welcome and bright as a sunrise.

Mr. Bushkin sauntered into the room carefully, as if he was entering a dark cave. He wasn't far behind Joey, and he wore a half-smile to show that he had nothing to worry about. He wanted to communicate with his wife somehow, but couldn't under the circumstances. Squinting his eyes, he frowned. Three huge wrinkles creased neatly across his mammoth forehead.

Mrs. Kellogg sat on the sofa, next to the bags. "Well, good morning, Joey," she chirped. The pitch of her voice dropped however, when she greeted Mr. Bushkin. "Good morning, Elmer." She quickly looked away, purposely avoiding his eyes.

"Morning, Judith," Mr. Bushkin said as he removed his hat and took a seat.

"Judith just arrived a few minutes ago, dear," said Mrs. Bushkin. She emphasized "dear," as she eyed Joey. "For goodness sakes, Joseph, you gave everyone such a scare."

She smiled and faced Mrs. Kellogg. "Joey was running around out there, God knows where, doing his chores, we thought. Elmer has been off looking for him. He really is so good about doing those chores, isn't he, Elmer?"

"Uuuh, Yep. Can't find him half the time out there. That boy stays busy." He slowly drifted out to the kitchen, spat in the sink and came back.

Mrs. Kellogg started to speak then leaned forward and rubbed her temples as she spoke. "Is that right, Elmer."

"Yes, of course." He rolled his eyes and looked at the ceiling. Shaking his head slowly, he kneaded the folds of his neck, pulled a handkerchief out of his pocket and blew his nose.

It seemed to be silent for an eternity until Mrs. Kellogg decided to speak. "Well, I... uuuh." Her smile widened, but she was pensive as she put her hands together and touched the center of her upper lip with her steepled forefingers. Her face squeezed up and her cheeks reddened a little. She seemed to be thinking of how to say whatever it was she wanted to say. Her lip started to quiver, and her eyes watered.

"I was just telling Margaret, Elmer—I've come out today to pick up Beth." Her voice was calm, yet controlled and firm.

"Oh." Mr. Bushkin sat down. His neck turned red, and he said no more. He rubbed his chin, and crossed his arms.

"Come over here, Joseph." Mrs. Kellogg reached for Joey. She studied his black eye for a moment, then saw his wet pants. "I believe Joseph has had an accident." She pointed. "You'd best go change, son—before you catch your death of a pneumonia." She paused. "Wait! What on earth happened to your eye?"

"Go ahead and answer Mrs. Kellogg, lad," said Mrs. Bushkin. She smiled at Mrs. Kellogg and proceeded to give her own version of the incident. "It's really not as bad as it looks, Judith. Joseph and Brian were playing outside and things got a bit rough. You know how boys are. I guess Brian accidentally kicked the poor dear in the face."

Mrs. Kellogg looked into Joey's eyes, searching for a different answer. A "she's lying" response would have been ideal at that point. Joey didn't respond and Brian quickly ran out of the room, nearly stepping on Mitchell at the same time.

"Ooooops! Careful there now, Brian. You almost stepped on your brother's hand," said Mrs. Bushkin.

Mrs. Kellogg squeezed Joey's hands between hers and felt them tremble. "What on earth...? She glared at Mr. Bushkin. "Why in the world?" He gazed at her the way people do when you say something they didn't think you knew.

"Well, no matter," said Mrs. Kellogg, as she warmed Joey's hands in her own. "The important thing is you're here now, and I have something to tell you — a surprise, if you will." She patted the top of his head. "Tomorrow, I'm coming back, and when I do, I'll be taking you with me, young man. Your brothers, too. What do you think of that?"

"Really! You are?" Joey's eyes lit up. "We're going to leave here?"

"Yes, we're leaving for good, Joey," said Beth. She moved in and hugged him again.

"Well, yes, your sister is right," said Mrs. Kellogg. "Your grandfather is feeling better and they have decided to let Elizabeth live with them in Gouvernuer. As a matter of fact, as I said, I'm taking her with me today. Isn't that nice?"

Joey swallowed hard. He felt dizzy — as though he was going to fall on his face. He couldn't believe what he was hearing.

Mrs. Bushkin gazed out the parlor window, while her husband continued to stare at the floor. They were both silent.

"Really? Is this for real? Now? Today?"

"Yes, Joseph, your grandparents are taking Beth back to live at their home today."

"Me, too... all of us, right?"

"No, No, Joseph, I'm afraid not," said Mrs. Kellogg. "They don't have enough room for all of you. I will be back for you and your brothers tomorrow."

Joey began to cry and Beth quickly wrapped her arms around him. Tears rolled down their cheeks.

"Why, Sis? How come just you? Why can't I come, too? What about Brian — and like you said before, what about Mitchell and Merrill? You can't leave them here. Remember — you said that? Where will we all live?"

"Oh, my. I knew this wouldn't be easy for them," Mrs. Kellogg murmured.

Joey stomped a foot on the floor and glared at Mrs. Kellogg. "I don't want my sister to leave us here." He could barely see as the tears continued to fill his eyes and stream down his face. He grabbed Mrs. Kellogg's coat sleeve. "Please, let me go with her?"

"I'm sorry, Joseph, but really, I can't . . ."

"Why? Why can't you take us too? Don't take her without me! Please!"

There was a tremor in her voice as Mrs. Kellogg slowly buttoned her coat and picked up her pocketbook. "Now, you'll be all right, Joseph. Sssssh!" She combed her fingers through his hair. "It won't be too awful long before your mommy and daddy find a place and arrange things. Then you'll all be together."

Joey pulled away. "No! I don't believe you! You always say that stuff to us! It's not fair! You said that last time."

Mrs. Kellogg slowly moved toward the door. There were tears in her eyes, yet she seemed to be in a hurry to leave. She turned at the last moment and looked at Elmer and Margaret Bushkin.

"You folks understand, I am entrusting these boys to your care until I get back here tomorrow. I would certainly pray there will be no more *accidents*... of any kind, before then." She glared at Mr. Bushkin. "Am I I'm making myself perfectly clear here, Mr. and Mrs. Bushkin?"

They nodded.

"Do not concern yourself, Judith. They will be fine, I assure you," said Mrs. Bushkin.

"But, I am concerned. Very much so," said Mrs. Kellogg.

Joey couldn't stop sobbing. Brian ran up and hugged his arm and started crying too. Beth circled her arms around both of them, and they all hugged each other and cried. Beth picked up Mitchell and Merrill one by one and kissed and hugged them. "Bye, bye, Mitchell. Bye, Merrill." She turned and went to Mrs. Kellogg's car.

Joey rubbed his eyes and looked to Mrs. Kellogg as she was leaving. "We get to leave here tomorrow, though, right? But, where will we go? Will it be close to Gram and Gramps house, so we can see them and Beth?"

Mrs. Kellogg brushed the damp hair out of Joey's eyes. "Well, Joseph, you, Mitchell, Merrill, and Brian will be going to live with some other fine families... just until things get settled, you understand. We'll talk about it tomorrow."

Joey looked at Mr. Bushkin sitting there, looking like nothing bothered him... like he couldn't wait to whip him.

"No! Please! Please don't leave me here!" he screamed.

Mrs. Kellogg seemed to ignore him. She dabbed her eyes with a handkerchief and turned to the Bushkins. I'll most likely be by around the same time in late morning.

"We'll have them ready to go, won't we Elmer?"

Mr. Bushkin nodded. "Yes, of course."

"Good," said Mrs. Kellogg. She picked up one of the bags and walked out the door. Mr. Bushkin grabbed the other two bags and Mrs. Bushkin followed them out to the car.

Joey was still crying when Mrs. Bushkin said, "Joseph — go change your pants, right now. You should have done that right away... my heavens. Hurry up before you catch your death of pneumonia."

After Mrs. Kellogg drove away, Joey ran to his room. He fell onto his bed and slammed his head into the pillow. He cried harder than he ever had before about anything. Brian was still standing out in the living room, crying. The twins were crawling on the floor, whining.

Suddenly, Joey felt he had to see Beth one last time before she left. He ran to the living room window and nearly stepped on the twins, but the black car was already at the end of the driveway.

Sis is gone.

Mrs. Bushkin sat on her chair in the kitchen, face in hands, elbows on knees, sobbing pitifully. Her husband said nothing; he slammed the kitchen door on the way out to the barn.

Chapter Twenty-One

T he Bushkins hadn't said a word to Joey about running away. It was just as if it never happened. The mood of the house was funereal after Mrs. Kellogg left with Beth. With her gone, Joey felt all alone, even though his brothers were still there with him... even though they would all be leaving in the morning.

That entire evening, the Bushkins' tone of voice and general demeanor towards them changed dramatically — so much so, that Joey felt that both of them were probably in big trouble, and he was glad.

Mrs. Bushkin seemed like a completely different woman, taking everything in stride. Joey watched her carefully. She sat in her chair across the table and folded her hands in a little steeple in front of her chin. She appeared to be in very deep thought. She didn't even get upset when Merrill smeared mashed potatoes in his hair. Her face was instantly red, but that was all.

"Oh, my... it looks like we'll have some cleaning to do." She barely looked up and seemed to be talking to her coffee cup.

Mr. Bushkin said grace two times before they ate. Everything was very quiet, as if someone had died. The sound of his munching food managed to break the silence. He sat stiff and straight in his chair with no expression on his hairy face. He ate carelessly, slopping streams of melted butter onto his beard.

Mrs. Bushkin silently observed, as her husband swooshed it off with one hand and wiped it on the front of his shirt. She wrangled her fingers together until finally Mr. Bushkin shoved his plate away like a displeased king and burped. For a moment, he buried his rubbery chin in his hands, before he got up and did a turn around the kitchen, the palms of his hands pressed tight against his temples. He said nothing.

Joey breathed deeply and tried to appear calm. He was so grateful that he escaped the whipping with Mr. Bushkin's belt and hoped the man hadn't changed his mind.

After supper, Mrs. Bushkin got up, pushed her chair in and announced: "We have a surprise for you boys." She jerked her head in a signal to her husband to go get it. "We bought a family Christmas present."

Mr. Bushkin went into their bedroom and came back out with a radio. It was a new Crosley console model. He sat it on the floor in the living room, plugged it in and smiled at the boys. He stood so proud with hands on his hips.

"A new radio. Ain't that the cat's whiskers?" He poked Joey with one finger and pointed to the radio. "We figured it was about time." He grinned as he pulled out a Prince Albert tobacco pouch and stuck a pinch behind his lip.

Joey nodded but did not speak. Brian stared at the radio.

"Well now, go wash up, and get your pajamas on — then you can listen to it for a while," said Mrs. Bushkin. She stood behind her husband. "Me and the mister will get these dishes tonight, seeing as how it's your last night here. Right, Elmer?"

"Uuuuh, yeah... I'm just gonna get it tuned in for them first." He was on his knees fiddling with the knobs. "You go ahead and get started, Margaret."

Joey was mystified. He and Brain searched each other's eyes for some sort of answer for this unexpected treat.

These people didn't even have a radio when we got here. Wow! I remember Mr. Bushkin said it was against God's rules to have a radio. I thought he was teasing, saying we could listen to a radio tonight — but he wasn't. There it is. I wish Beth could be here for this.

It felt strange to be huddled on the living room floor, listening to *Charley McCarthy* and *Fibber Magee and Molly,* and for just a little while, Joey's mind was at ease. He fidgeted nervously, but attempted to forget everything else except the voices coming out of the brown console. Hearing them made Joey feel like he was right there by Magee's closet when Molly opened the door and all that junk came tumbling out.

Mrs. Bushkin took Mitchell and Merrill upstairs to bed. They were still fussing just as they were near the end of supper. They just miss Beth, thought Joey. He wished Mrs. Bushkin would let them listen to the radio or else go and hold them — do something to make them quiet somehow.

After Fibber Magee was over, Mr. Bushkin surprised the boys again when he sat in his chair and joined them while they listened to *The Great Gildersleeve* until bedtime.

In his room that night, Joey's brain jumped recklessly, from one thing to the other; so much on his mind. Thinking about home caused tears to come to his eyes. He wished he could hear his grandfather's voice, filled with warmth and understanding.

During the night, he heard Mrs. Bushkin stomp upstairs where the twins werel crying. She said something loud, but it was muffled. Joey couldn't tell what was said, but when she slammed their bedroom door, the boys cried even louder while she tromped back downstairs to her room, and slammed the door.

Joey worried about his brothers. *Beth should be here to hold them and make them stop crying.* His eyes closed because he was exhausted, yet he kept opening them. He hadn't slept the night before, except very briefly, behind that billboard, on Highway Eleven.

Sitting on the bed in the dark, he watched the door, worried that Mr.Bushkin would still come after him. Sometime after midnight, he tried to sleep by laying curled up with his knees not far from his chin.

He thought about Beth and how he missed her already. She was probably very happy now at Gram and Gramps' house. She was so lucky, and in a way, he was glad for her, but missing her made him cry hard into his pillow.

I wish I knew where I'm going tomorrow. What about Brian, and Mitchell and Merrill? Will we all be going to live at the same place? Will we be close to Gramps house? Where are Mommy and Daddy right now? I'm all mixed up, even worse than when I was at the Couzens' farm. Why can't we have just one place to live at like other kids? I don't know any kids that don't live with their real family. It's not fair.

When the Bushkins talked in their room, Joey could often hear their soft, low sounds creeping down the narrow hallway. He couldn't understand a word, because, he was sure, they tried their best to make sure no one heard them. Brian was asleep very soon, but Joey lay like a stone and listened.

"Rinnnnnnnng! Rinnnnnnnng! Rinnnnnnnn! Rinnng!" The telephone sounded three long rings and a short one and at first the sound jarred Joey. It was unusual for this time of day, but the rings meant the telephone call was for the Bushkin's house. Mrs. Bushkin came out of her room and hurried to the living room to answer it.

Throwing the covers off, Joey tiptoed over to the door and put his ear up to the crack. His legs were rubbery and his mouth felt dry.

"Hello? Yes. Oh, hi there, Judith. No. That's quite all right. We were just listening to the radio with the boys. Yes. Uuuh huh. Oh, it's not really that late." She paused. "No, Judith, you go right ahead."

It seemed like a long time before Mrs. Bushkin spoke again. "Yes, well... is there some reason? Because, as I told you, they're perfectly fine here with us until you get things in order. No, of course not. That will be fine. Yes, I'm sure. Of course, I understand. She paused again. "Nine then. Uuuh huh. Okay, I will. Uhhh huh. Yes. Yes. Well, goodnight, Judith."

When she hung up, Joey ran back to bed, but got right back up, when he heard her talking to Mr. Bushkin. She was obviously upset and evidently forgot about keeping her voice down.

"Well, it's a sure thing now... they're leaving here tomorrow."

"Fine- good riddance as far as I'm concerned," Mr. Bushkin groused. "We should have never taken them on; you know that as well as I do, Margaret. Hard enough with three, let alone five. I swear, I'd brain those two upstairs before I'd put up with another day of their bawling. Just listen to them. It's been going on since we finished eating—and they've been going at it all night."

"Listen to me, Elmer? I want you to listen to me for a change. Put down that damned Bible and talk to me, please!"

"Oh, I'm hearing you, Margaret. I'm hearing you. You'd better keep it down too. Go on. Get it out. Just please, finish up so's I can get some sleep, would you do that for me?"

"Is that all you're worried about, your precious Bible and your sleep? You know she's not stupid, Elmer, when she saw the boy's face... well, you could see it in her eyes, I tell you. She knows. And, did you see the boy? He was just about ready to spill the beans about the whippings."

Joey heard it all. They were talking loud, and he smiled in the dark. They were really in trouble. When Mrs. Bushkin finished talking, Joey had to hold his hand over his mouth, so he wouldn't giggle out loud. There was a long pause before she spoke again.

"Judith even sneaked the boy's sleeve back to peek at his arm. Did you catch that? I did. Your belt caught him there, too, Elmer. What does that tell you? We'll be lucky if we even get our check this month. Does that part matter to you?"

"Margaret, for God's sake, calm down. What would you have me do about it? Huh? Answer that for me, woman. What do I do?"

Mrs. Bushkin didn't answer for a moment.

"I don't rightly know. I only know she's talking like we're done. Like there's going to be an investigation of us. It seems that principal Grimes called the office in Watertown about those bruises a while back. Judith said she has been instructed by her supervisor to remove all of the children as soon as possible.

"What? You mean right this minute? Tonight?"

"No, of course not. She'll be here tomorrow morning at nine. That's why she took the girl today. Only reason she didn't take the boys is they're going different places and she was pressed for time. Oh, we're done for, alright. I feel it in my bones."

Joey continued to press his ear to the crack. His breathing was heavy. He couldn't hear everything anymore, but enough. The twins were both whining and crying, but Mrs. Bushkin wasn't concerned.

"How are you going to explain, Elmer? You know the boy is going to tell her everything."

"What if he does? The lad needed discipline—still does. Did you forget why I thrashed him? Get a hold of yourself, woman—no need in all this."

"No. You don't worry. Let me do all of that, isn't that right?"

"No. Shhhh. You'd best keep it down," said Mr. Bushkin. "For all you know, those boys are listening to every word."

With that, Joey scooted back to his bed and turned on his side facing away from the door. He yanked the blanket over his head just in time. Mrs. Bushkin's footfalls softened as she approached their room. There was a slight hesitation in her step. Joey squeezed his eyes closed; he felt her standing in the doorway. She stood there, breathing loudly, until she finally pulled the door closed. She didn't close it all the way before she quietly walked back up the hallway.

"Well, they're asleep... I thought as much," she said.

Joey waited a moment before he slid out of bed once more and tiptoed back to the door.

"I worry about losing our license, Elmer. Remember, that close call is on our record already from that mess eight years ago with those McCalley brats."

"Yes, and they never proved a thing, did they? If they had, we would have lost the license way back then. Don't be talking so drastic now, Margaret. Everything will be alright. We'll manage. You should be glad she's taking this bunch. It'll be a darn sight easier on you — both of us. It'll be okay. Trust in the Lord. Now, please — just go do something about that infernal caterwauling upstairs," he snapped.

"Well, I suppose you're right. But, for God's sake, I can't help but worry."

Mrs. Bushkin clumped her way back upstairs, and Joey quickly ran back to bed. She didn't come back downstairs for a long time, and when she did Mitchell and Merrill had stopped crying.

Joey heard the Bushkin's bedroom door close, and finally he succumbed to much-needed sleep.

Chapter Twenty-Two

The sunrise beamed through his window, while Joey sat round-shouldered on the edge of the bed, rubbing sleep from his eyes. The winter sky was pink and blue just like a painting on the wall in art class, he thought. This would be a good day. They were leaving the Bushkins. He anxiously got dressed putting on his favorite blue-striped shirt and brown pants.

Brian's hair stuck out from under the covers; he moaned when Joey flicked the light on and shook his shoulder.

"Brian! Hey! You've got to get up, Brian." It was a loud whisper. "We get to leave here today. We don't want to be late for when Mrs. Kellogg comes."

Brian moaned, then crawled up to a sitting position and rubbed his eyes. "Are we really going?"

"Yes. Go ahead—wake up. We have to eat and get ready before she gets here. I'll be right back. I'm taking my slop pot outside. You'd better hurry."

Joey pulled his coat on and headed for the outhouse. It was nearly seven-thirty and Mr. Bushkin was returning from milking. On his way to the house, he carried a full bucket of milk in each hand.

"Morning, Joseph. No chores today, lad. Just get ready to leave, that's it." He looked up at the sky. "Good day for travel, I reckon."

"Yes, sir." Joey walked slowly and gingerly as if counting his steps. He emptied the pot and went back to the house where he slid the empty pot back under the bed. He waited for Brian to finish dressing and take his pot out before they both washed their hands and went to the table for breakfast.

"Come on, hurry up, Brian."

"Okay, I am—I am."

Mrs. Bushkin had finished frying her husband's eggs and buttered toast. She stirred the oatmeal, served it in bowls for the boys, and then she sat down and carefully sipped her coffee. Tinkling of silverware on plates was the only sound heard during the meal.

Mrs. Bushkin, helping the twins eat, said, "Can I get you boys some cocoa this morning?"

"Yeah, I want some cocoa," said Brian. Joey kicked his brother's foot under the table as Mrs. Bushkin set about making the cocoa.

Mr. Bushkin groaned and shoved his plate away. He stared at Joey, and then leaned in close. "Boy, I just want you to take something with you today. Hear me good now." He cleared his throat. "Every bit of what I did was for your own good. Understand me? I never liked whipping you; I was only trying to teach you right from wrong—respect for people, and an unselfish love for Jesus and God Almighty. You think on that and you'll understand, won't you boy?"

"Yes, sir. I guess so."

"You guess so?" He grunted in disbelief. "Why, of course you will. No guesses to it. How could you not?" He leaned back on his chair and stuck a wad of chew behind his lip. "You'll thank me someday down the road, wait and see."

Mrs. Bushkin glared at her husband as she wiped the oatmeal off the faces of the twins. She left the table and busied herself gathering up grocery sacks full of clothes and setting them by the back door.

"Joseph, be a good boy and go get the other two bags sitting by your dresser." When she talked her eyes darted quickly around the room. "I believe that will be everything. I've got to finish getting your brothers cleaned up before Mrs. Kellogg gets here. Brian, go wash your face and hands, if you're done—you need to be ready."

Joey wasn't sure, but he thought he saw tears in her eyes.

"Yes, ma'am," said Joey and Brian at the same time.

As it neared nine o'clock, Joey kept watch at their bedroom window. When he saw the black sedan turn in the driveway, he turned to Brian, who was kneeling next to him. "She's here—come on, let's go!"

When Mrs. Kellogg's car pulled up, Joey grabbed Mitchell's hand,

and Brian took Merrill's. They scrambled to get outside and nearly ran into Mrs. Kellogg at the door. Mrs. Bushkin was yelling for them to wait, but to no avail . . .

"Whoa! My, my. Good morning, boys," said Mrs. Kellogg. She had her hands up like a school-crossing guard. She wore a heavy wool coat and a matching turban-like hat covered her head. She slipped her gloves off. She reached out and patted the cheeks of both Mitchell and Merrill.

"Anxious to get going, aren't we, boys?" she said, as she looked at the door. "Well, you go ahead and help your brothers into the car, Joseph. I'm sure we have some things to put in the trunk, don't we?"

"Yes, ma'am," said Joey. Mrs. Kellogg glanced at Mr. and Mrs. Bushkin.

"Well, you can take charge of that, Joseph. I'll be right out. I have some business with Mr. and Mrs. Bushkin before we go."

Joey and Brian raced out the door and Brian slid into the back seat with the twins.

"I'm gonna go back in and get our bags, Brian. You stay here with the boys," said Joey.

"Okay, just please hurry up, okay?"

When he got back inside, Joey saw Mrs. Bushkin's hands fluttering in front of her, like she was tossing a garden salad. The three adults stood in the kitchen, and Mr. Bushkin was talking. He stopped when Joey entered. Mrs. Kellogg jingled her keys in her hand and stared down at them as if they were her last possession in the world. A fake smile covered her face, and Joey felt he should grab the bags and go. He gathered up two of them and started back outside.

"Just leave the others, Joey," Mrs. Kellogg said. "We'll get them in a minute. You go stay in the car with your brothers. I'll be there shortly."

"Yes, ma'am."

Mrs. Kellogg was inside for a long time. Joey sat in the front where he had the bags on the floor between his feet. The twins were already beginning to get squirmy. After a while, Joey began to worry that something might stop them from leaving. "*I* don't want Mrs.

Kellogg to change her mind because Mr. Bushkin lies. I want to go," he told Brian. "I wonder if she's telling him he's in trouble for whipping me. Does she know Mrs. Bushkin stuck those crayons in your mouth. Oh, please, please... come on, let's go."

Joey decided he just had to sit back and wait. Still, he worried. Looking out at the barn where he got the whippings, he realized that he would never have to look at it again. The early morning sun reflected off the roof, and it looked like a giant mirror had been put up there. He saw Dan, the horse, walking along the fence on the other side of the pasture. That horse was one thing he would miss at the Bushkin farm.

He craned his neck to look out the back window and saw the Cars whizzing by out on the road. It was the same road he'd followed when he ran away two days earlier. He wondered who told Mr. Bushkin he was in town. Who told Mrs. Kellogg about the whippings? Probably Uncle Glenn and Aunt Betty. There were so many questions, but they were leaving and that's all that mattered.

Mitchell was using his finger to draw lines on the window. He turned and smiled at Joey. "Bye-bye?" He pressed his nose against the glass.

"Yes, Mitchell — bye-bye, soon," said Joey.

"Bye-bye, too," said Merrill.

"What's taking her so long?" Brian whined. "It's getting awful cold."

Mitchell fell over onto Merrill's lap and giggled. They were all giggling when Mrs. Kellogg finally came out to the car. She loaded the bags in the trunk, then walked back around to her door and climbed in. She surveyed her passengers.

"Well, looks like I have one happy bunch here this morning, huh?" She started the car, and drove over icy bumps and slushy holes on her way down the driveway. They were about a mile down the road when she spoke again:

"So, Joseph... tell me now — where did you *really* get that black eye?" A long moment of silence followed.

"It's okay, you can tell me. I believe I know, but I'd like to hear your side of it. The Bushkins and I have had our talk. You can tell me the truth."

Joey hesitated at first then said, "Mr. Bushkin took me to the barn and whipped me with his belt, and he hit me in the face. I got a cut on my butt, too." Joey pointed to his eye. "But this time he gave me a black eye when he hit me in the face with his hand."

"And, why in the world did he do that? What did you do, not that it matters, but I need to know the truth for a change."

Brian had leaned forward. "He hit Joey hard with the belt."

"Yes, I know, but please let Joey tell me now, Brian... sit back, okay?" Joey turned sideways and looked at her face when he answered.

"I was just so hungry," said Joey. "Mr. Bushkin told me I was a thief, like in the Bible because I took some crackers without permission. He didn't get a chance to whip me but he hit me with his hand, real hard, when he caught me eating crackers. Honest, Ma'am, that's what happened, and I ran away. Will he get in trouble for doing that to me?" Joey paused for a moment. "He should get in lots of trouble, right?"

"Indeed, he will be dealt with, I can promise you that."

The twins were climbing around, and stood up, trying to look out the back window.

"You boys sit down now!. Would you help me with them, Joseph? Make them sit down, please."

"Yes, Ma'am. Okay, Mitchell! Merrill, you heard Mrs. Kellogg... sit down on the seat before you get into trouble." He pulled Mitchell down, and Brian pushed on Merrill until he sat down, too. Mrs. Kellogg watched through her rear-view mirror.

"Thank you, children. Now, Joseph, go on, tell me what happened. Why did Mr. Bushkin punish you in the first place?"

"Ma'am, I was hungry. They wouldn't let me eat supper, so I thought everybody was asleep and I went in the pantry and took some crackers."

"I see. Well, I'm glad you've finally told me. You should've told me long ago about the barn, Joseph. I understand you were punished with the belt other times too. Your principal, Mr. Grimes, called and said he thought that something was going wrong at your house when he saw your eye the last time."

"Yes, ma'am."

"Well, we'll take care of the Bushkins. Now, the home I'm taking you to today is entirely safe. I'm very sure that the people won't whip you or treat you badly. You can depend on that, okay? So, don't be afraid."

Joey felt himself choking up. His heart pounded like a drum. "Okay, but, I thought you said we could go live with Mommy and Daddy, next time we had to move."

"I'm sorry, Joseph... I truly am." She put her hand on his arm and rubbed. "It's just not possible right now. Please try to understand. Don't cry; you'll get your brothers going. Listen, I'm taking you to the Matthews. Herb and Myrtle Matthews are very nice people."

"But, you told us that about the Bushkins too, Ma'am... remember?"

"Well, we didn't know, now did we, Joseph? The Matthews can't have children of their own, but they love kids. They're new foster parents; never done it before. You get to be their first ones. They'll take good care of you kids. And, if anything ever happens... like what just happened to you at the Bushkins',you must, by all means, tell me. Understand? You don't wait."

Joey felt tears coming on. "But, you promised!" His body shook as he squeezed her arm. Mrs. Kellogg gritted her teeth and sighed a heavy sigh.

"No, Joseph, I did not promise any such thing." She protested with a wet cough. "I told you that I would take you to your mommy and daddy as soon as possible. When they got things together again, is what I said. I wouldn't be changing homes for you right now if it wasn't for the... well... these things I've learned about."

As they got closer to Ellisburg, the woods became more dense and the terrain started to roll, the roads seemed more snow-covered and serpentine. One small lake, off to the left, glistened like glass behind the screens of trees. Mrs. Kellogg waited for a long time before she spoke again.

"I chatted with Beth on the way to your grandmother's. I know a lot of things now that I wasn't aware of before, and I'm sorry. I just didn't see. We trust these people, and then they... they just... "

Joey leaned forward and tried to look into her eyes as she drove.

"Did Sis tell you about the cellar?"

"The cellar? What cellar?"

"The cellar at the Couzens farm?"

The twins began to sock each other. Mrs. Kellogg shook her head and glanced over her shoulder.

"Oh, Please, Joseph, would you be a dear and make them stop that?" He turned to tell the twins to behave, but they had already stopped. They stared at him wondering why their big brother was crying.

Mrs. Kellogg retraced the conversation. "At the Couzens'? My... that was some time ago, wasn't it?" Her face suddenly appeared empty. A moment of silence passed before she said, "Nobody mentioned a cellar to me." She clicked her tongue regretfully. "I'm sure it can wait... perhaps you can tell me about it next time I visit, okay?"

Joey continued to cry. He had a thick knot in his stomach.

I wish I didn't get caught yesterday, I would have kept on going, even if I didn't find Gramps' house. I'm gonna run away from this new place too. She doesn't care about us, and I bet these new people won't either — just like the Bushkins and Couzens. She always says people are good, but she doesn't know like we do. I don't ever want to see her again, either.

The twins fell asleep. They were lying against each other like tent poles — their heads touching when Mrs. Kellogg spoke quietly in an effort to keep the twins sleeping.

"Just a few more miles, boys. The Matthews' place is just on the other side of town," said Mrs. Kellogg. She glanced in the rear-view mirror. "I see we've lost Mitchell and Merrill. God love them. So cute, aren't they, Joseph? It's good that they are tuckered out, though. They'll sleep well tonight."

"Yes, Ma'am. We're all staying here, right?" Brian had scooted up closer to the front seat, in order to hear the conversation.

She paused for a moment and smiled at Joey. "No, as a matter of fact, I will be dropping Brian off at another location, Joseph. You won't all fit at the Matthews. Brian is going to the Vanderbarg farm. That's quite a ways from here—over near Messina."

Brian slumped back in the seat and wailed. "No! No! I want to stay with Joey. I have to stay with all of them."

Mrs. Kellogg glanced in her rear-view mirror. "Oh, my, please don't cry now, Brian. The Vanderbargs are absolutely wonderful people. They're looking forward to meeting you so much. You'll like them, I'm sure."

"You always say that. You don't care about anything, Ma'am." Joey glared at her through his tearing eyes. "He's scared, Ma'am. My brother is real, real scared. Don't you know that?"

"Now, Joseph, don't talk like that please. I certainly do care about all of you children. Yes, I know Brian is scared. We all are, but, there is nothing to be worried about, boys... you'll see."

Chapter Twenty-Three

T he fringes of Ellisburg were basically three unpainted cinder-block buildings and a red light. A few clapboard houses, some with paint, dwindled away from the cinder block. Downtown consisted of the Purina feed and seed store, The First Bank, a few shops around the courthouse square, Gracie's Diner, and Woolworth's five-and-dime — about which certain people were fond of saying, "They sell everything you need and nothing you really want." There was also an Oldsmobile Automobile dealership.

Up the hill past the red light, maybe a half-mile away, stood a regal-looking redbrick elementary school. After Mrs. Kellogg passed through downtown, she saw a rusted out Massey Ferguson tractor with no tires and turned left on to another two-lane road.

They traveled nearly three more miles before she finally pulled into a driveway in front of a two-story frame house. Painted white, the house sat fairly close to the road; the driveway was a lot shorter than the Couzen's or the Bushkin's driveways — only about fifty yards from the road to the front steps of the house.

•   •   •   •   •

The property was surrounded by ancient oaks, maples and elms that stretched their mighty skeletal-looking limbs skyward. The surrounding land was white, flat and silent. In the back, beyond more trees, was an open field which appeared to run for an eighth of a mile and disappeared over a small hill. The acreage was surrounded by more snow-covered woods in the distance.

A wire fence bordered one side of the house; another house was on the far side of a separating pasture, where a pony wandered in the snow. A 1945 Chevrolet Fleetmaster sedan was parked off to the side of the driveway.

"Well, here we are, boys," said Mrs. Kellogg. She pulled the emergency brake and turned off the engine. "This is the Matthews' place; I'm sure they're inside waiting for us." She turned in her seat to look at Brian and the twins. Joey didn't cry or break into her thoughts; he had enough of his own. He was nervous, and he shivered.

"Boys, I want you to sit tight for just a minute while I let them know we've arrived." She turned back around just in time to see Mr. and Mrs. Matthews stepping down from the front porch. "Oh! Hold on, here they come now." She smiled and buttoned her coat before she got out.

Herb Matthews was a tall man with melancholy, deep-set dark eyes under overgrown eyebrows and dark hair that needed cutting. His hands were hard and weathered-looking, and he had an unshaved look. Wearing a soiled-looking baseball cap, with a Chevrolet emblem barely visible on the front, he lit a cigarette and tossed the match aside.

"Mr. Matthews is a mechanic, Joey. He fixes cars," Mrs. Kellogg half- whispered.

Joey had never seen a man as tall and skinny before. He wore a dark blue uniform with splotchy grease stains on the pants and coat. A smear of grease was evident on the side of his neck. The name "Herb" was embroidered in red above a top pocket holding his pack of Lucky Strike cigarettes.

His wife, Myrt, was a thirty-something woman with small, prim features. She had a warm smile, and her auburn hair was swept up on top of her head in an old-fashioned bun. She was short and looked even shorter standing next to the lanky Mr. Matthews. At five-three she probably didn't weigh more than ninety pounds. She wore a green cardigan sweater with baggy pockets and tan slacks. Joey had never seen pants on a woman before.

"Well, hello again, Mr. and Mrs. Matthews," chirped Mrs. Kellogg. Myrt seemed to pause for a moment, then, smiled at everyone.

"Hi, Judy. Remember, I said don't be so formal... my goodness. Herb and Myrt is just fine."

Mrs. Kellogg smiled and nodded. "Yes, that's right—sorry. Well, as you can see, I have brought some boys for you today." She opened the rear door of the sedan as she spoke to the twins. "Go ahead, boys—you can get out. Brian, you can get out, too, stretch those legs; we still have some driving to do." She paused and waited. The boys didn't move.

"Come on now, boys—hop out. It's cold out here. Go ahead, Joey, you can get out and come around here, too."

"Yes, ma'am," said Joey. He got out and slowly walked around the front of the car. Mrs. Kellogg slid his hat off and ran her fingers through his unruly hair in an attempt to get it to lie down.

"This young man is Joseph. He's the oldest and, as I told you, he's eight years old."

Mrs. Matthews put her hand out. "Hello, Joey. You can call me Myrt." She slipped her arm around her husband's waist. "This is my husband, Herb, and you can call him that, if you like." Joey first shook Myrt's hand, then Herb's. He heard a dog barking, but didn't see one anywhere. The twins got out and crossed over to stand behind Joey. So did Brian, who had settled into a stubborn silence.

"And these two young men are Joseph's brothers, Mitchell and Merrill—they're twins of course."

Myrt squatted and looked closely at the twins. She gently pulled them into her arms and hugged them. "Oh, my! You were so right, Judy, they are darling. Look, Herb—aren't they darling? They are four, you say?"

"Yes. Just turned four," said Mrs. Kellogg.

Herb tossed his lit cigarette in a snow bank and stuffed his hands in his pants pockets. "Yes. Nice looking boys, all of them." He bent his skinny body over and rubbed each of their heads. "Who's that fella' behind you?" He stared at Brian.

Mrs. Kellogg scooted Brian up front. "This young fellow is their brother, Brian. He will be going on with me to Messina."

Herb extended his hand. "How do ya' do, Brian?"

Brian hesitated and slowly backed up. He began to chew on his hand.

Herb rubbed his hands together briskly and blew on them. "What say, we all go inside where it's warm, folks?"

Myrt straightened up. "Well, yes, good idea, my heavens!" She took Mitchell's hand, and Mrs. Kellogg held Merrill's. "You boys come on... Brian — Joey, come along now."

"Yes, Ma'am," said Joey. Brian hesitated, then drifted along behind Joey.

Myrt stopped at the door, and held it open. "Joey — please... none of that 'ma'am' stuff here — call me Myrt, okay?"

"Yes, Ma'a... I mean Myrt." He felt his face turn red.

"And same goes for me," said Herb. "Call me Herb, son- please."

"Yes, sir." Herb studied Joey for a moment, then, smiled.

Joey smelled food the moment he entered the house. Something was cooking, and the teasing aroma reminded him of just how hungry he was.

"Here — give me your coats, boys," said Herb. "Judy — would you like me to hang yours up?"

"No, thanks, Herb — I'll just keep mine, if you don't mind."

The inside of Matthew's house was smaller than it looked on the outside — almost the same size as Gram and Gramps' house. Two easy chairs and a small sofa occupied most of the space in the living room. A console, Zenith radio sat underneath the window in the front room. Photographs of Herb and Myrt were situated at angles on top of it. A small hutch, containing various knick-knacks sat against a wall.

Piles of newspapers as well as *Look* and *Life* magazines were stacked in the corner of the room. The adjacent dining room table was covered with clothes. Most of them appeared to be Herb's work uniforms. Two baskets of ironing sat under the table, and an iron sat nearby on an ironing board.

An uneasy silence took hold as the boys surveyed the area around them. A dog barked, but still could not be seen. However, the barking sounded like it was coming from somewhere inside of the house.

Herb slid a pack of Luckies from his shirt pocket. He struck a match on his pant leg, lit up, then blew a heavy cloud of smoke toward the low, nicotine-stained ceiling. Tossing the matchstick in an ashtray on the kitchen table, he waved.

"Come right on in, everybody. Don't be bashful."

They walked down a short hallway that led to a kitchen, which was extremely small. Pots and dishes were stacked on the draining board of the soapstone sink. An enameled-steel bowl and pitcher sat next to an orange-and-blue box of *Oxydol* soap. A can of *Old Dutch Cleanser* was on a small shelf, just above the sink. A hand-operated water pump was located at one end of the sink.

The kitchen table was covered with oil cloth, which sort of matched the pattern of the linoleum floor. A small radio sat on the edge of the kitchen table. Against the far wall sat an iron stove and the room reeked of kerosene heat. Boxes of corn flakes, and canned foods, including Campbell's soup were stacked on top of the icebox, next to a can of *Spry* cooking lard.

"You boys hungry? Did you eat lunch yet?" Myrt asked. She looked at Mrs. Kellogg as she posed the question.

"Well, we didn't have time to stop on the way, I'm afraid," said Mrs. Kellogg. She didn't try to hide how she felt about admitting that. Two lines evolved around her mouth like parentheses.

Joey was holding Brian's hand and at the mention of food, he squeezed it, he squeezed it.

"I'm hungry, yes, Maaa... I'm sorry—I mean, Myrt. I'm hungry, so is Brian," said Joey.

"And, I'm sure the twins are also. Good—let's eat, then. I've got some leftover meatloaf heating on the stove. Have a seat; you're just in time. We were just getting ready to eat before you came and there's plenty. We'll have meatloaf sandwiches for lunch." She looked at Joey and winked. "I'll make some cocoa, too." She looked at Mrs. Kellogg, again. "Would you like a cup of coffee, Judy?"

"Why, yes, if it's not too much trouble." She looked at the boys. "Isn't this nice of these folks, boys?"

"Yes, Ma'am," said Joey.

Mitchell scrambled to climb up on a chair, and Merrill did the same. There was one chair left and Brian started to sit down.

"No, Brian, let's be a gentleman, and let Mrs. Matthews sit there," said Mrs. Kellogg.

"That's okay, hold on a minute, Brian," said Myrt. She went to the back porch and brought in two wooden milk crates. Herb followed her and brought in two more. "I think these will do nicely for now," said Myrt. "So sorry, my dining room table is covered up with ironing and what-not, but we should be alright here."

"Go ahead and have a seat, Brian," said Herb. He handed him one of the crates. He leaned back on the sink, tilted his hat back on his head and puffed on his cigarette and looked at Mrs. Kellogg. "Didn't you say there was a girl, too?"

"Yes — she's the oldest, ten-year-old, Elizabeth, "said Mrs. Kellogg. "I took her to her grandmother's house yesterday, as a matter of fact. The grandmother, poor dear, has that arthritis so bad in her hands. She seems to think her granddaughter will be a big help, so that works out real well. Her husband is not well either, actually. He's had heart problems recently. I think I mentioned that when we first talked."

The dog barked again and this time it began to scratch the other side of a door in the hallway. Myrt laid her hand on Joey's shoulder.

"Pay no attention to the barkingt, Joey. It's our dog, Tippy. She's just upset, because I haven't let her come in from the cellar to meet you."

"Cellar?" Joey felt himself flush.

"Yes, she gets excited when company comes," said Herb.

"I don't like cellars," said Joey.

"Well, we have one... just a lot of junk down there — that and my canning — and Tippy, right now." Myrt laughed.

"Do I have to go down there if I'm bad?"

"What? You... go down there?" Myrt pointed. "In the cellar? Joey — why in the world would you think such a thing? No! As a matter of fact, I don't want you in the cellar. Too many things to get into," she giggled. "And it doesn't smell very nice. Heavens no, but why did you ask?"

"Just because," said Joey. He lowered his head. Myrt looked at Mrs. Kellogg, who shook her head.

"I believe that Joseph has some concerns about the dark," said Mrs. Kellogg. You know how that can be when you're small-fry — being afraid of the dark?" She said it with a frothy, condescending laugh. Myrt and Herb exchanged glances and shrugged.

"Yes, of course," said Myrt. She continued making the sandwiches. Smearing oleo and ketchup on pieces of *Wonder* bread, she continued to talk with Mrs. Kellogg about some things she needed to know and handed out the sandwiches one by one.

"So, I'm to go through their clothes and let you know what they need — is that right?"

"Yes. You'll get a subsistence allowance for each of them — and if, after you go through their things, you believe they are in need of something, just call. We want to work with you in any way we can. That goes for their medical and dental needs also."

"Good," said Myrt.

"I never been to a dentist before," said Joey. "None of us have."

"Oh... is that right?" She finished making the meatloaf sandwiches and started the cocoa in a saucepan of milk. Her eyes caught her husband's who had finished his cigarette.

"Watch the cocoa, Herb — would you?"

The twins kept trying to get down from the table to check on the dog, but Mrs. Kellogg kept pushing them back onto their chairs. "You boys go ahead and eat those sandwiches, now," she said. "Don't worry about that dog."

Tippy stopped barking, but she whined and continued to scratch at the door. When the boys were nearly finished with the sandwiches, Myrt stood and smiled. "Well, I suppose I'd better let Tip in now. I know you boys are anxious to meet her." She went to the door and slid the bolt that kept the door closed.

Tippy came bounding out, and threw her front paws on Brian's lap, then Joey's. She was excited and panting. Mrs. Kellogg acted shocked; the smile dropped from her face like a mask.

The dog was black-and-gray-colored — not as big as the Bushkin's

Daisy who was fat and fluffy; Tippy was a skinny female with short hair. Her bushy tail wagged wildly. One of her back legs stayed up in the air and shook violently. The dog never seemed to put it down. It was as though it was permanently bent. She licked Joey's face, and made him giggle. Then, she jumped up and put her paws on Merrill. The boys all giggled and tried to pet her.

"Tippy! Get down!" Myrt shook her finger. "You just settle down." She grabbed her collar, but the animal kept trying to pull away and sounded like she was choking.

"Sit!" Myrt commanded and yanked on the collar until Tippy finally settled down. The dog continued to pant, and her slobber dripped on the floor while Brian continued to pat her head.

"My goodness, see how she's making a mess on your floor?" said Mrs. Kellogg. "I'm sorry. I never did have much stock in dogs. By the way, what's wrong with that leg?"

"Oh, Tippy got hit by a car out here on the road when she was a pup. That's why we can't just let her run. We put her on a chain out back when we let her out to do her business. Her leg is such a shame, but at least we still have her. She's very gentle and protective; the boys will love her."

"She's a real good watchdog," said Herb.

"Yes. I see, She's a very friendly dog, too, isn't she."

Soon after the boys finished their cocoa, Mrs. Kellogg began to put her coat on. "Well, I'd better be going, folks. It's still quite a ways to Messina, and I told Margie Vanderbarg I'd be there before dark."

She looked at all of them and smiled as she bent down to hug the twins and Joey. "Goodbye, boys. I know you are going to mind what these folks tell you. Be good boys, right? I want good reports from Mr. and Mrs. Matthews. I'm sure I'll see you before Christmas."

"Yes, ma'am," said Joey. He couldn't bring himself to look at her face. Brian and the twins had gotten down on the floor to play with Tippy. There was an awkward silence for a long moment until Mrs. Kellogg finally spoke:

"Come now, Brian. Tell your brothers good-bye—we really have to go."

"No!" Brian said as he wrapped his arms around Joey's legs. Joey wasn't sure what to do. He felt his neck burn, and his tongue turn to chalk. He knew it was futile to beg Mrs. Kellogg; Brian couldn't stay there."

"It will be okay, Brian. Go with her, alright?" He pulled him up on his feet, while Brian wailed and shook with anger. "No, I don't want to go." He sobbed loudly. Tears dripped off his chin and his nose was running.

Mrs. Kellogg reddened. "Now, now, Brian. We simply must go. Say goodbye to your brothers now, like a good boy." The last words caught in her throat; there was actually the shine of tears in her eyes.

"Nooooo! I don't want to!" "Nooooo!" Brian screamed.

Joey felt like a big liar. He felt terrible-sick to his stomach. "It will be okay, Brian—you'll see," he said. He draped his arm around his brother's shoulders. "Maybe Mommy and Daddy will be okay in time for Christmas, and we'll all be together at our own house—alright?" He felt helpless as he wiped tears from his own eyes.

"Go with her Brian, please."

"No! I want to stay with you!" He slid down and sat on the floor, screaming.

Mrs. Kellogg struggled to get Brian's coat on and pulled him by the arm. She slowly eased him out the front door, but had to drag him to the car.

"Goodbye, Judy. Bye-bye, Brian," said Myrt. She waved and called after them. "Oh, my," she muttered as she hugged herself. "That's terrible."

Herb strode out onto the snow-covered porch. Joey walked up behind him and they all watched while Mrs. Kellogg opened the car door and pushed Brian inside. Joey waved. He wanted to say goodbye again, hug his brother at the car, but he just couldn't stand to go through any more. Brian didn't wave back.

Mrs. Kellogg opened her own door and Brian could still be heard, screaming. She started the car, and after some cars passed by, she backed out onto the road... and Brian was gone.

The twins watched it all but said nothing as they continued to pet

Tippy. Joey finally came back and sat at the kitchen table. He lay his head down on folded arms and sobbed. No Beth, and now Brian was gone.

An uneasy silence dominated the air, such as that between husband and wife who have just had words. Myrt came in and sagged against the door with exaggerated relief.

"Well... let's see here . . ." She quickly cleaned off the couch, then smiled and kneeled to hug the twins. She let them continue to pet Tippy.

Herb sat on a straight chair, turned around so he could rest his forearms on the chair back. He studied Mitchell and Merrill and smiled.

"Nice looking boys," he said, as he lit a cigarette. "How do we tell which one is which?"

"That's easy," said Myrt. Judy told me. Merrill has a birthmark on his neck. It's real small, but you can see it." She pointed as Herb leaned in for a closer look.

"Ahhhh — I see."

Myrt pulled a red and white package of Lucky Strike cigarettes out of her sweater pocket. Joey had seen his Gramps smoke his pipe a lot, and his mommy and Gram smoked cigarettes too, but, when he saw Myrt smoke, he was surprised.

The Matthews puffed their cigarettes and studied the boys. Herb poked the smoke-filled air with a slender finger.

"So, Joey... tell me — do you like to go fishing?"

Chapter Twenty-Four

A fter Mrs. Kellogg left with Brian, everybody gathered in the living room and got further acquainted. Herb sat in his favorite easy chair and managed a slight grin as he rubbed his chin. Myrt was on the couch between Mitchell and Merrill. Joey sat on the floor in front of Herb and petted Tippy. They looked at one another and sat in silence for a few minutes.

"We have to get the twins some outfits that match," said Myrt.

"Oh, we will," said Herb. He winked at Joey and bent down to pat Tippy on the head. "What do you think of the dog, Joey?"

"I like him, sir. Does he bite people?"

"What, Tippy bite? Nah! Not that I recall... do you, Myrt?"

Myrt blew a thick cloud of smoke out of her mouth and nostrils at the same time.

"Uuuuh, uuh. No... he never did. Herb, I want to go to Montgomery Ward's tomorrow and pick out something for these boys to wear. Will you be able to take me into Watertown?"

"Maybe in the afternoon. I know I'll be real busy in the morning— it being Friday and all. I can come home early again, though, I imagine."

"That will be fine. I'm just so anxious to show our boys off, you know what I mean—our own boys." She grinned. "I never thought I'd see the day. Joey—you will come along, too. Maybe I can find new pants and shirts for you while I'm there. I have to go through your things and see what you need."

An uneasy silence took hold, and Myrt studied Joey for a moment.

"Come over here." She crushed her cigarette in the ashtray and wiggled it back and forth until it stopped smoking. Joey got up and eased over to her side. Myrt ran her fingers through his hair. "My goodness, we need to do something about this wild hair. Isn't it hard to comb?"

Joey shrugged.

"I noticed you all seem to have this curly hair, but yours is much, much too long. I'm going to cut it for you after supper."

Herb finished his cigarette and took a long swig from his coffee cup. "That hair *is* a bit of a mess alright."

"I try to comb it with water sometimes, but it just goes all over like this as soon as it gets dry. My sister, Beth, used to fix it real good sometimes when Mrs. Kellogg was coming to visit, though. It looked okay for a while."

"Well, no matter, I'll cut it and it will be lots easier to manage. When was the last time you had it cut?"

"I don't remember, ma'am. I don't think I ever got it cut." He fidgeted before he said, "I have to go to the outhouse, but I don't know where it is."

Herb and Myrt both laughed as Herb pointed to a door leading off of the living room. "We don't use an outhouse, Joey. The toilet is in the bathroom over there — right through that door."

"Just like in school — a real toilet?"

"Yes," said Myrt. "A toilet, a sink and a tub — we have them all in there." She giggled. "Be sure to lift the seat when you pee, okay?"

"Yes, ma'am." Joey went to the bathroom and closed the door behind him.

"Well — I've got to get back to the shop," said Herb.

"Okay, well, I'm going to get these boys settled in their rooms and whatnot. What time will you be home?"

"Around five-thirty, I imagine." He took another pack of Luckies from the carton on the dining room table. "See ya' then." He stuffed the pack in his shirt pocket and sauntered out the door.

"Come on, boys." Myrt guided the twins to the bathroom when Joey came out. "Let's see if we can go potty."

Myrt began to show the boys around after the twins finished in the bathroom. All of the bedrooms were up a small flight of stairs off of the living room.

There weren't very many steps going up, and they creaked under the weight of each step. The rooms were very small with enough space for a bed and a small dresser in Joey's room.

Doors were missing, except for at Herb and Myrt's room. The twins' bedroom was a bit bigger, with two beds and a dresser. Clothes were piled everywhere — on the beds, on the floor, and on top of the dressers. Small windows faced the driveway and road out front.

Joey took off his coat and looked outside. He saw the road as well as the far-reaching landscape of pure white. The change of scenery felt odd. There was no barn — no tractor or cows to be seen. The pony was still out there wandering the perimeter of the field next door.

Mitchell yanked Joey's hand.

"I want to see!"

"Me too," said Merrill.

Joey took turns lifting both of them up to look out while Myrt started emptying their bags. She put some clothes away in their dresser, then lit another cigarette. The twins immediately tired of looking outside and began to bounce up and down on their beds.

"I hope you like your room, Joey." Myrt sat on one of the beds and studied the boys in silence as she sorted through their bags of clothes. Her cigarette residue settled across the room.

"Yes, ma'am, it looks nice. It's small like the one I had at my Gramps' house, except there's a window here. I didn't have one at Gramps'."

When she was done putting clothes in the dressers, she told them they could go outside and play in the snow.

"Where's your snow pants? I don't see any in your bags."

Joey shook his head. "We don't have no snow pants, ma'am."

"Myrt, Joey... It's Myrt, remember. You mean you never got any snow pants at your last place? Are you sure you didn't forget them?"

"No, Ma...I mean Myrt. We never got any."

Myrt shook her head in disgust. "We'll have to do something about that tomorrow, for sure."

•   •   •   •   •

Before Herb came home, Myrt told Joey to wash up for supper. When they were both done she helped Mitchell and Merrill up on a milk box so they could wash their hands too. Herb smiled as he toweled his hands and watched. "I think you'll have to remind me which one is Mitchell and which is Merrill," he said.

Myrt cleaned the dining room table off, and everyone sat there for supper. Joey was surprised that nobody said grace, and Herb didn't read from the Bible before they ate either. They had hot dogs, fried potatoes, and green peas for supper, and it was all good, Joey thought. The boys drank cherry Kool-Aid while Myrt and Herb had coffee. When Joey wanted another hot dog, Myrt said there was only enough to go around, so Joey had more potatoes.

During the meal there was a good deal of silence, a good and acceptable kind of silence — nothing nervous or uncomfortable about it.

After supper, Herb lit a cigarette and eased into the living room. He turned on the radio, tuned in to *Gabriel Heatter and the News*, then stretched out on the couch with a copy of *The Watertown Times*. Joey wanted to listen to the radio too.

"You can go ahead and listen until I finish giving your brothers a bath, Joey... then it's your turn. Don't forget, I'm going to cut your hair first too, young man."

Joey wanted to listen to *Amos n' Andy*, but that wasn't on until eight o'clock according to Herb. However, he was happy just being there on the floor, by the radio, no matter what was on.

Herb was snoring under the newspaper, by the time Myrt was ready to cut Joey's hair. Joey sat on a kitchen chair, and Myrt draped a towel over his shoulders. She put old newspapers on the floor under the chair and used a big pair of scissors. The twins were in their pajamas on the other side of the table pointing and giggling while Myrt took off most of Joey's hair. It lay scattered in curly, brown clumps all over the papers.

"There," said Myrt. "You have had your ears lowered, Joey. How does it feel?"

Joey rubbed his head; it felt strange, but he said, "Good, ma'am."

"Here... come with me, you can look in my bedroom mirror."

Joey was shocked when he saw himself in the mirror. "Wow! I do look a lot different." He turned his head from side to side. "What do you mean, my ears are lower?"

The bath was overdue and the water was cold, but Joey welcomed it in an odd sort of way. It was better than that steel tub on the porch at Bushkin's place.

The twins had gone to bed without any fuss. Myrt was happy about that but found it unusual considering the changes they had been through that day. She was very satisfied with herself. Sitting in the living room with Herb, listening to Lux Radio Theatre, she puffed her Lucky Strike and rested her feet on a cloth-covered hassock. Cigarette smoke clung to everything in the house like cellophane.

Joey quit swishing the bath-water around for a moment and tried to hear what was on the radio, but it was too far away. When he finished his bath, he put on his pajamas, went upstairs and crawled into bed in his new room.

"Goodnight, Joey!" Both of the Matthews called up after him. It felt strange; it had been an awful long time since anyone offered a "goodnight", but he answered in a loud voice, "Goodnight."

The bed felt warm; there were plenty of covers. His head felt bare and cold with his hair gone. He heard the twins in their room. They were giggling. Somehow that made Joey happy... they weren't crying.

He stared at the ceiling and thought about everything. Beth? He wondered what she was doing right that minute.

I can't cry, but I feel like it – I miss her so bad. I wonder if she's thinking about me and the twins. She doesn't even know that Brian isn't with us. I miss her but I won't cry... I can't cry.

I wonder how far it is to Gram and Gramps' from here. Where is Brian? How long before he stopped crying? Maybe he's still crying. I hope he's okay. I wonder if these people will change and be like the Bushkins and Couzen's? It don't look like it. They seem nice. I hope they will like me. They sure like Mitchell and Merrill a lot. I wish I was a twin.

•   •   •   •   •

There were no schools in Ellisburg. His new school wasn't too far away, but Joey still rode the bus. It was in a town called Bellville, eight miles away, where he was in the fourth grade. Mitchell and Merrill weren't old enough for school and Myrt let them sleep as long as possible. Usually until just after Joey got off to school. He sat at the kitchen table eating his cereal and toast by himself until Myrt joined him.

It felt strange not to have a pot to carry outside. It was a good feeling to have a real toilet and there were no chores before school either.

Three weeks after he started school, Myrt sat and talked to Joey after she got done feeding Tippy. She struck a match on the table, lit her cigarette and sipped her coffee. Herb had left for work at the garage much earlier.

"So, how's everything going in school now?"

"Fine."

"You making any new friends there, yet?"

"No, ma'am."

"You mean, 'No, Myrt.'"

They held each other's eyes for a long moment. "No, Myrt," said Joey.

"None at all?"

"Well, there's this one boy, Carl. He sits next to me on the bus, but some kids tease him, because he doesn't talk right."

"What do you mean—talk right? What's his name again?"

"Carl—Carl Kyer." Joey watched her blow smoke through her nostrils. "He stutters when he talks."

"I see," said Myrt. She got up to get more coffee.

"Me and him talk a lot. He can talk real good sometimes when he sits with me. He laughs too, but, when he's in school, he hardly ever says anything, and he doesn't smile much, either."

"Well, that sounds like a good friend to have if you can talk to each other like that, I think. Tell me, how are you getting along at school? Behaving, aren't you?" Her face expressed the need for an answer to an important question.

"Yes," he said. He had decided not to tell her about the trouble he got into for fighting with Billy Wesleene at recess the previous week.

Myrt tied fifteen cents in the corner of a handkerchief so he wouldn't lose his lunch money.

"Well, you'd better finish your cereal and run along now; the bus will be here any minute." She stabbed her cigarette out in the ashtray.

"Yes, ma'am," He ran for the front door, and just in time, because he saw the flashing red lights from the bus; it was stopped down the road, at Carl's house.

"Oh! and, Joey . . ."

"Yes, ma'am?"

"You're still calling me 'ma'am'?" She stood with her arms folded and smiled.

"Yes, ma... Myrt."

Joey liked riding to school with Carl. It was fun talking about everything. Carl had a daddy and a mommy. He invited Joey to come over to his house sometime, but he lived too far down the road and Joey wasn't allowed to walk that far by himself. Besides he had to watch out for the twins, when they were outside.

"Any playing to be done, you can do it with your brothers," said Myrt.

Carl couldn't believe Joey didn't have a real mother and father.

"How co... come?" was a question Joey didn't know how to answer.

Carl stuttered but he constantly related to Joey all the things he and his father did together, like fishing, and shopping at Sears and Roebucks for clothes and tools. It made Joey feel strange... sometimes it made him angry and he wanted to cry. And, even though they were friends, there were times he wanted to hit Carl just because he was so happy. He knew it was a bad thing to feel like that, but he couldn't help it. He told Carl he would always stick up for him any time kids picked on him, because he wanted to be his best friend.

Joey's teacher was Mrs. Paige. She was an attractive, middle-aged woman who wore very little jewelry, except for a wedding ring, and her makeup was understated but expert. Especially expert around the eyes. She had big eyes and a warm and cordial personality. She was nice to everybody, it seemed. She reminded Joey of a movie star. She always wore pretty dresses and her long blonde hair tied up on her head like Ginger Rogers. It seemed to shine like gold in the sunshine that poured in through the classroom window. She had nice teeth, and a wide smile like Betty Grable's.

Joey felt his face burn red when she got angry at him for fighting on the playground. She embarrassed him when she scolded him in front of the other kids. He hated himself for getting in trouble and disappointing her.

His desk had been all the way in the back of the room, when he first attended Bellville, but after the first week, Mrs. Paige moved him up front, because he talked so much when she was teaching.

They said Pledge of Allegiance every morning, first thing. Some days, Joey was so proud because he got to hold the flag while the rest of the class recited the pledge.

Mrs. Paige assigned different jobs to the kids and most of the time Joey's responsibility was to take the erasers down to the janitor's room and clap the chalk out of them. Then, for some reason one day, she asked Charles Smithfield to perform the task.

Joey couldn't understand. Wasn't he doing the job the right way? Why was she taking the job away from him, he wondered? Why did she ask somebody else to do *his* job?

Charles took the erasers from her, and when she turned her back, he stuck his tongue out at Joey before leaving the room. Joey didn't want to get into trouble again, so he pretended he didn't see Charles teasing. The other kids laughed, but Mrs. Paige was unaware of the festering situation.

During book time Mrs. Paige read from Charles Dickens' *A Christmas Carol.* The students took turns reading paragraphs. Then, after a shortened arithmetic lesson, Mrs. Paige announced a special project to prepare for Christmas:

They would use Glasswax and decorate the small windows that faced the street. Each student was assigned three windows and could finger-paint Christmas trees, candy-canes or wreaths of holly. It was very close to lunch time when Mrs. Paige had everyone clean up. She walked to the door and opening it wide, she put a black flat-iron weight against the door to hold it open.

"Whew! I think it's warm in here, don't you class?"

They all answered at the same time. "Yes, Mrs. Paige."

The smells from the cafeteria oozed in through the door. Joey loved those smells; they made his mouth water. They ate at eleven-thirty and there seemed to be enough, so he didn't have to steal anyone's lunch bag.

Everybody lined up outside the classroom door before Mrs. Paige led them down the hall to the lunchroom. Suddenly, Charles shoved Joey from behind, and made him stumble. Joey turned and glared but kept moving along. His body shook with anger; he wanted so badly, to punch the other boy in the face.

Stacks of milk cases containing little glass bottles of white and chocolate milk sat by the door. Mrs. Paige shushed the kids to stop their chattering. Everything suddenly became quiet, as another class lined up behind them. They had spaghetti that day, with green Jello for dessert.

Charles Smithfield sat at the other end of Joey's table and they were no sooner seated when he stuck his tongue out again. Joey felt himself redden as he looked around for the teacher. His face turned hot and adrenaline raced through his veins. He made up his mind... Charles was going to get it when they got outside.

With lunch over, the kids lined up to go outside. It was slushy around the swings, but Joey ran to them, sat on one, and watched Charles getting on the teeter-totters. Billy West got on the opposite end from Charles and they began to ride.

"Hey, Joey, who gets to do the erasers now? It's gonna be my job always and forever. I'm going to do them every day from now on — Mrs. Paige said so. Nah! Nah!"

Joey hated that. He felt his neck turn hot again. He needed to retaliate — had to punch Charles — shut him up. He sidled over to the teeter totters slowly and waited until Billy's end of the teeter-totter was down on the ground, then he yanked him off the seat. When he did that, Charles dropped like a lead weight and hit the ground hard.

Baaang! It jarred Charles's teeth and made him scream. He bawled like a baby and everybody stared at him because he was suffering so loud. Then, all eyes were trained on Joey.

Mrs. Paige rushed up behind him. "Joseph! What did you do?" She held him by the shoulders and shook him for a moment as she eyed Charles. "What in the world did you do that for?" She screamed, then ran over to Charles to help him up. Most of the kids stood still as statues while Joey sort of drifted along behind her.

"Charles was teasing me, Ma'am."

"Is that any reason for you to hurt him like this?" Her words were slow and scornful. "You get inside and report to Mr. Westmore's office, right now, young man. Hurry up — right this minute! I'll be right along behind you. My goodness! Are you all right, Charles?"

Charles continued to cry, as all his classmates crowded around him and Mrs. Paige. "There, there," Joey heard her say as he ran for the gymnasium doors.

Mrs. Bowden was the assistant who sat at the desk outside Principal Westmore's office. Her hair was long and pulled back — tied with a clip except for a tightly braided bunch that poked out on the right side of her head. Her eyes were big, in a rather small head and her lips were thin and cracked.

Dominating the wall behind her was an enormous regulator clock nearly as long as a grandfather clock, with a carved dark-wood case, elegant Roman numerals, and a pair of gleaming brass pendulums.

Mrs. Bowden looked strangely at Joey when he came in.

"Joseph? What brings you in here?"

"Mrs. Paige told me to come here. She's coming, too."

"I see. What is this about?"

"Charles was teasing me at recess, ma'am, and I . . ."

Mrs. Paige rushed through the door.

"Emily. Is Mr. Westmore free? I have a problem with this young man, if he has a moment." She was obviously very upset.

"Yes, of course, Janet. He just got back from lunch. I'm sure it will be all right. Let me check though."

Joey shook inside and out. He was terrified of the unknown. He knew they would call Myrt. The thought came over him like a shroud. She would be mad for sure. He had no idea what the principal would do. He wondered if he whipped kids with a belt. Joey just wanted to get it over with.

Mrs. Paige came back out of Mr. Westmore's office.

"Come in here, Joseph."

Joey's knees wobbled as he walked into the office and stood in front of the principal's desk. Mr. Westmore slowly peeled off his glasses with an air of exasperation. A short, rotund man, his ripe, florid cheeks glistened damply; his chin was virtually non-existent.

"Now then, Joseph, Mrs. Paige tells me this isn't the first ruckus you've caused at recess. Is that right?"

"Yes, sir, but I didn't start it this time."

Mr. Westmore drummed his fingers on the edge of his desk as he contemplated what he would say. He stood and leaned over the desk and pressed his mouth into a tight line. Staring at Joey for a long moment, he finally said, "Young man, I don't really care who started this. My concern here is the safety of my students. You're a troublemaker. Is that it? You like to start trouble?"

Joey didn't answer.

"Well, do you? Answer me, son."

"No, sir. It's just that Charles has been sticking his tongue out at me all morning, and I wanted him to stop it, and I . . ."

"Stop! Hold it right there, Mister. I just told you, I don't care who started the fight. I need safety on the school premises. Is that perfectly clear, Joseph?"

"Yes, sir."

"It had better be! You can be sure of one thing—we will be calling your folks about this. We'll let them deal with you at home. But I warn you, any further trouble from you, and I will make you stay out of this school for two weeks... maybe more."

"Yes, sir."

His eyes drifted to the teacher. He shook his head again. "Thank you for bringing this to my attention, Mrs. Paige. Hopefully there will be no further incident from this young man."

"Joseph, you must learn to get along with your classmates," said Mrs. Paige. She walked a brisk pace on the way back to her room. "I want you to apologize to Charles and yes—your entire class." She suddenly stopped walking and eyed him with determination. "Most importantly, I need your promise that you will not cause any more trouble."

"Yes, Ma'am. I won't do it again."

"Do what again?"

Joey looked at her and shrugged. "Hurt nobody."

When they arrived back at the classroom, Joey stood up in front of the room. He felt sick to his stomach as he apologized. He felt as though he was going to throw up, and his knees shook again. His face burned and he couldn't wait for school to be over for the day.

Carl told him on the way home that his father spanked him with his belt if he did something wrong at school.

"I... I only... only got into troub... trouble one time, and... that... was for steal... steal... stealing a libary book," he stammered.

"I don't know what's going to happen to me," said Joey.

He was scared. Not because he was worried about getting a whipping, but because he didn't know what Herb would do. He had never been punished by either him or Myrt for anything up to that day.

Maybe he will have to work at the garage late tonight, and I'll be in bed when he gets home.

When Joey walked in the house, his brothers were taking a nap upstairs, and Myrt was ironing. Listening to the radio, she was there but not there. Her eyes were fixed on a distance that was far beyond the room they were in.

The Romance of Helen Trent was on. Myrt listened to all of her soap operas, as she called them, five days a week. *Young Doctor Malone, Ma Perkins, Our Gal Sunday* and *Portia Faces Life* were her favorites, and she didn't like to be disturbed. Joey wondered if the school had called her yet.

"Hi," said Joey. He started to sneak up to his room, but she waved at him, signaling him to stay downstairs.

"Over there." Myrt puffed on her cigarette and pointed to the couch.

Although she had been in a fairly good mood before school that morning, now she was obviously angry about something and Joey just knew the school had called.

When Helen Trent was over, Myrt sashayed over and turned the radio off.

"Well, young man, what have you got to say for yourself?"

Joey felt himself redden. "About what, Myrt?" *There — I called her Myrt; maybe she won't be so mad now.*

"You know very well what, Joey." She sat at the opposite end of the couch and lit another Lucky. She tossed the match in the ashtray and folded her arms. "Mrs. Paige called me about an hour ago. Does that refresh your memory?"

"Yes, ma'am." His head hung low.

"I don't like this. Tell me what happened... the truth, mind you — because I already know. I just want to hear your side of it."

When Joey finished telling her about Charles sticking his tongue out, she just stared. The silence was so loud, Joey could hear his heart rattling around in his ribs.

"Go on. What else?"

"That's all."

"No. That's not all, Joey, and you know it. What about the fight you had on the playground last week? You didn't tell me about that one, did you?"

Joey turned pale; his body sagged. "No, ma'am, I didn't."

"Well, just this morning, I asked you if you were behaving in school, didn't I?"

"Yes."

"And didn't you tell me that you were behaving yourself?"

"Yes." Joey felt sick to his stomach. The room felt like it was raising up under him.

"Well, then you lied to me, didn't you, Joey?" Myrt reddened.

He shook his head glumly. "Yes, I guess — sort of."

"No guesses about it! You lied to me!" She raised her hands in a calming gesture.

"This wasn't the first time, according to your teacher. All I can say is you have hurt yourself, young man, because I'm sure Herb will not like this either, and you will need to be punished. Understand?"

"Yes, ma'am." The twins came thumping downstairs, one after the other and Myrt's eyes lit up as she tracked them coming down.

"Well, my little darlings, did you have a nice nappy-bye?" They ran to her, and she hugged them tight.

Myrt likes them more than me. I can tell. I know Herb does, too. It's because they're smaller, and they're twins. I wish I was a twin

The twins' hair was all messed up from sleeping. Merrill stared at Joey.

"Joey... Go to your room," said Myrt. "We'll discuss this some more when Herb gets home."

Chapter Twenty-Six

J oey stretched out on his bed and waited for Herb to come home. Nearly two hours had gone by since Myrt sent him to his room to ponder his fate, and the remainder of the afternoon creaked by in slow motion.

He lay on his back with his fingers laced together behind his head. The tears had dried on his cheeks. Scary thoughts continued to ramble through his troubled brain as he awaited his fate. There was no clock in the room but the late afternoon sun was gone and the sky had turned from purple to dark blue.

What will Herb do to me? He has never whipped me with a belt yet; he doesn't even wear one on his pants. Myrt still didn't put me in the cellar either... so, what will happen when she tells Herb about the trouble in school? Maybe I won't get anything to eat for three days... just bread and water like at the Couzens' farm.

He rolled over onto his side and stared at the wall. *Things are sure different here. I'm not scared to eat stuff like I was at the Bushkins'. I haven't seen a Bible in this house, either.*

He heard the laughter of his brothers coming from the dining room. They were having fun playing. *I wish they would make Mitchell and Merrill behave, though. Myrt thinks everything is always my fault when they cry. I get blamed no matter what. They want to play, but they cry if they can't have their own way about stuff. I wish Beth was here. She would know what to do. I wish Myrt would hug me the way she does Mitchell and Merrill sometimes.*

It would be supper time soon, and the smell of cooking teased Joey's stomach. He was hungry and wondered what they were having—maybe fried chicken. Myrt always made good chicken and mashed potatoes. His mouth watered as he tried to think of something besides food and Herb coming home.

Christmas is coming pretty soon. I probably won't get anything from Santa Claus this year, especially after my trouble in school. I hope I get to go home for Christmastime. Maybe I'll get to see Mommy and Daddy — Gram and Gramps and Sis, too. I'll ask Myrt to call Mrs. Kellogg and find out, no matter what happens tonight. Herb said he was getting a Christmas tree on Friday, but now I probably won't be allowed to help decorate it.

He heard the sound of a car outside. Herb was home.

Joey scooted to the end of the bed and waited to hear Herb's voice, then crept to the top of the stairs in order to hear what was being said. Herb sounded like he was in a good mood.

"You know what I was thinking, Myrt? I was thinking we should all pile in the car after supper and go to the movies. *The Wizard Of Oz* is back at the Strand for the holidays. It would be a treat for all of us — get us in the mood for the holidays, ya' know?"

Myrt smiled in acceptance as she began to set the table for supper. "The movie is a good idea. I don't know about going tonight, though," she muttered.

He shrugged. "Why not? It's Friday night — no school tomorrow,-right?"

"I know, but you and I need to talk before supper." She guided the twins toward their Tinker Toys on the dining room floor and edged away towards the kitchen where Herb sat down and lit a cigarette. Tippy jumped up and down, and Herb patted her on the head.

"What's going on?"

"It's Joey."

"Yeah... what about Joey? What's wrong? What did he do?"

Myrt lit a cigarette and drew on it, the ash reddening. She inhaled and leaned forward on the table. "Well, he's been fighting in school, starting fights on the playground, and today the principal's office called."

"What?" Herb leaned back in his chair, crossed his legs and exhaled. "Well, what did you do about it?"

"Nothing yet. I sent him to his room and told him we'd wait until you got home."

"Okay... so, what do you want me to do about it?" He paused a long moment and studied her face. "Did you get Joey's side of it?"

"Yes. He said he didn't start it of course, but I caught him in a lie, too. It seems there have been other problems at school he wasn't owning up to."

"So — there we are. What now?"

"Well, at the very least, I think he should go to bed without supper — that and no playing outside for a week or so. You have any other ideas? You need to talk to him about this, Herb."

Joey hurried back to bed.

Herb exhaled a plume of smoke and kept the cigarette riding in the corner of his mouth as he went to the sink to wash up for supper. "Well, let's go ahead and get him down here then."

Myrt went to the stairs and called. "Joey! You come down here now, Herb wants you."

Joey slowly edged down the stairs and stopped to pet Tippy. He stood in the center of the kitchen, his head hanging low, his eyes unable to meet theirs. He could feel Herb's angry stare burning into him as he finished washing up and returned to sit at the table. Rubbing his palms on his knees, he said, "Well, what's the story, Joey?"

Joey didn't answer. He wasn't sure what to say. He knew Myrt must have told her husband everything already.

"Well? What about it? Answer me, Son." He reached over and patted Joey on the cheek. "What did you do in school that had the principal calling here?"

"I... I got in trouble for fighting with kids on the playground." His voice quivered as he spoke and the two stared at each other for a few seconds.

"That's putting it mildly," injected Myrt. She gave Joey a pitying look.

"And — you know of course that it was wrong?" said Herb.

"Yes, Sir. I'm sorry."

"But, you still went ahead and broke the rules, didn't you?"

"Yes, Sir." Joey looked the other way.

"So, what's your problem?" He paused a moment. "We won't put up with bad behavior, Son. You'll do without supper tonight. Now, go back to your room. We'll talk more about this and some other things later."

Joey hesitated for a moment. What other things, he wondered?

Herb held up both hands, palms facing Joey. He shook his head and eyed him with the kind of disgust usually reserved for spoiled food. "Go on, Son, I'm very disappointed in you."

"Yes, Sir." Joey whirled around and ran back upstairs. He put his back to the wall and slid down to the floor. He hugged his knees and buried his face, wishing he had never been born.

Although he was very hungry, he was grateful that this might be his only punishment. He stared at the floor. *What other things? What else did I do wrong? I didn't do anything bad.* He got up and dropped onto the bed. *I don't know what they're eating, but it smells like fried chicken.* His stomach growled.

As he lay listening to silverware clinking on plates and the family chatter, Joey felt guilty, alone and left out.

After supper Herb called, "Joey! Come down here!"

"Yes, Sir!" Joey yelled as he jumped. *Maybe they're going to let me eat after all. Maybe they changed their minds.* He clambered down the stairs and found Herb waiting by the last step.

"Joey, Myrt and I have discussed the school situation and your attitude around here lately. We want you to start treating your brothers much nicer." He paused. "Quit picking on them the way you do. There's no need in getting them so upset and making them cry."

Joey wasn't sure what Herb was talking about with Mitchell and Merrill, but he knew it wasn't a good time to deny anything. He stared at him for a moment, speechless, or knowing the wisdom of holding his tongue. "Yes, Sir," he murmured.

"What did you say? Speak up."

"I said, Yes, Sir!"

"All right, and we want it understood that there will be no more problems at school — ever." He paused once again. "Do you understand me, Son?"

Joey nodded. He had never seen such a look on Herb's face before. His eyes were so wide and mean-looking.

"Very well," said Myrt. "Now then, we're all going to the movies tonight, but you're going to stay here at home. I want you to take one of those chairs and set it over there facing that wall." She pointed.

Joey wasn't sure what she meant and hesitated.

"Here, Joey!" Herb snapped his fingers. "Bring a chair over here."

Joey picked up the chair and carried it over to where Herb stood by an outside wall.

"Now, turn it to face the wall."

Joey turned it around.

. "Now, while we're gone, you will sit on this chair and think about what you've been doing wrong. Think about your poor attitude and the way you treat your brothers. You'll have plenty of time to think about how important it is to behave at school. Also, lying will always cause you trouble. Understand?"

"Yes, Sir."

Mitchell jumped up on the chair before Joey could sit down.

"No, no, Mitchell," said Myrt. "Joey has to sit there." She scooped him up. "Come on, get down, now. We're going bye-bye."

Myrt slid into her coat then put a cigarette between her lips and lit it. It dangled from the corner of her mouth while she buttoned Mitchell's and Merrill's coats.

Herb collared Tippy and put her in the cellar. "We're putting Tippy downstairs," said Herb. "She's to stay there while we're gone. I do not want her up here in the house. Is that clear?"

"Yes, Sir."

"Remember what Herb said, Joey. You are not to move off of that chair. We'll be able to tell if you do, so please don't disappoint us," said Myrt.

Mitchell and Merrill stared at Joey sitting on the chair. Merrill tried to climb up on to his lap. "I can sit, too," he said.

"No, no, Merrill. Just Joey," said Myrt. Come on. We're going bye-bye."

When the door closed behind them, Joey was immediately overcome with a feeling of abandonment and fear. This was the worst punishment of all. Loneliness started with the door closing behind all of them. It continued to fester as Herb's car fired up. Joey cried when the sound of the car's engine faded away into nothingness.

It was getting to that moody time of day, twilight, when the long shadows make a familiar world look different. It all seemed to splinter his mind. Fear and anxiety had been building inside of him all day long, and his body desperately begged for emotional release. He sobbed out loud. For a long time, he simply allowed the tears to flow – recede - and flow again until it seemed he could cry no more. He rubbed his hands over his face and looked up at the ceiling.

The house was quiet and still. Joey sat and listened. His uneasiness was a physical thing that seemed to magnify sounds. He tapped the seat of the chair and the tapping echoed like thunder. When he exhaled, it sounded like a rush of cold wind wailing across the playground at school.

The dark was closing in.

He thought about Beth as he always did when he was troubled and alone. Why couldn't she be here now? He desperately tried to make himself think about other things - good things, but there just didn't seem to be any.

Then, somewhere in the flowers on the wallpaper, he saw candy canes. He visualized the ones he painted on the windows in Mrs. Paige's room for Christmas. Yes. Christmas at Gramps' house, with the new bubble lights on the tree. He wondered what Christmas would mean living here if he couldn't go home. Would Santa Claus come?

The silence was fractured when Tippy began to whine. Joey realized how alone the dog must feel locked in the cellar. He knew how lucky he was that he didn't have to stay down there too. He didn't dare let the dog out, but he wanted to. She would be good company.

Joey tried to ignore the whines and yelps and started counting lines and circles on the wall paper again. He let his mind make things — drawing them every way and any way he wanted. He saw a boy with a smiling face, but his teeth were missing for some reason. He conjured up a short giraffe and a lion, too.

The sun was completely gone and it was dark everywhere he looked.

The only illumination came from the single street light on the other side of the road. Joey could barely see the wall anymore. He turned in the chair and became aware that they hadn't left any lights on anywhere in the house. No lights in the kitchen, none shining down from upstairs, none in the living room and none from the bathroom.

His butt was starting to sting and he dared to stand just for a moment. Tippy must have heard, because she barked two times. It startled Joey and he sat back down.

He was afraid of the dark and yet there was nothing he could do. It was closing in on him like a black monster. It was scary to sit in utter silence - just like the dark in the cellar at the Couzens' farm. He became terrified wondering how long he would be left like that. His insides shook. He knew he could get up and turn on a light, but he was worried that Herb and Myrt would catch him somehow. He squirmed.

Myrt said they would know if I got off the chair. I don't dare turn a light on. I wonder if I could just sneak over to look out the front window. At least I could see headlights from cars going back and forth down the road.

He craned his neck. *There's a street light up on a pole that's shining from across the road. It isn't very much light - but at least there's some. I can always run and sit back down if they pull in the driveway. I bet they'll be gone a long time to the movie.*

He sat still. *It's so quiet. I can hear water dripping in the kitchen sink. Myrt's favorite clock is tick-tocking over in the living room. I hear cars swooshing by on the road, too. I wish there was more of them.*

Joey's body shook all over and he began to sob again.

I'm afraid of the dark; don't they know that? The cellar! The cellar! I didn't tell them about it, but they should know kids don't like the dark anyway. Beth! Please, Beth! I wish you could hear me. Look what they're doing to me again. I know you can't hear me, but I need to talk to somebody. Somebody has to come and help me.

When are they coming home? Please come home now, Herb. Myrt? Somebody? Please! I won't be bad any more, I promise. Just come home.

Tippy barked.

Herb opened the door and flicked the living room light on nearly two hours later. The switch was right there by the door. Joey was still facing the wall just like they told him to when they left. He looked up into the light and blinked then turned and saw Herb carrying Merrill. His head was on Herb's shoulder; he was asleep. Herb took him right upstairs and Joey watched as other lights went on.

Myrt carried Mitchell, who was barely awake. She followed Herb upstairs. When Herb came back down, he looked at Joey and lit a cigarette before he tossed his cap on the dining room table. Tippy had started barking the second they pulled in the driveway and wouldn't stop until Herb let her out.

"Joey, you stayed put right there, did you?" he said as he stroked Tippy's neck.

"Yes, Sir."

"Good. Well, you go ahead up to bed now, all right?"

"Yes, Sir."

Joey nearly ran into Myrt who was coming down the stairs. She grabbed his arm and looked him in the eye.

"Did you stay in that chair the whole time, Joey?"

"Yes, Myrt."

"You did?" She stared as though she could see inside his head. Joey nodded but didn't look in her eye.

"Well, go ahead and get to bed. We'll talk in the morning. Maybe we'll go get the Christmas tree tomorrow. Won't that be nice?" She smiled as though she had neutralized the huge gulf that lay between them.

"Really? Gee, that would be swell, Myrt. Can I help decorate it too?"

220

"We'll have to see. You need to learn to be more sociable and get along with other kids. I need you to promise me you'll be a good boy from now on, okay?"

"I promise, Myrt."

"Okay. Goodnight, Joey."

"Goodnight, Myrt."

.   .   .   .   .

It snowed that Friday night and it was a blustery Saturday afternoon when the 1943 Dodge coupe pulled in Matthews' driveway. The sky was gray and the air icy cold. It had snowed heavily all over St. Lawrence County for several days and, judging by the piles of snow thrown up by the plows, the road crews had been out in full force in the area. The roads were lined with snow banks nearly six feet high.

Apart from the shoveled path to the porch, there were about two feet of snow covering the landscape.

Herb and Myrt seldom had company, so it was odd seeing the car sitting in the exact spot where Herb always parked his '45 Chevy.

"Somebody's here!" Joey yelled to Myrt, who was mopping the kitchen floor. He rubbed more steam off of the living room window and pressed his nose against the glass.

"Really?" said Myrt as she slipped in behind him. "Well now, I can't imagine who it would be." She parted the curtains. Mitchell and Merrill crowded in and were up on their tiptoes trying to see.

They watched as a man in a dark overcoat struggled to keep the Fedora from blowing off his head. He looked lost in the white emptiness. The snow blew and swirled all around, practically blinding him. He managed to open the passenger door and help a woman get out.

She was heavy-set and wore a wool overcoat much like the color of the man's. She wore no hat or scarf and her hair was in complete disarray from the gusting wind. A cocoa-colored dress hung low-many inches below her coat.

As the man helped her out, she clung to his arm. They stood side by side for a moment in the chilly air and talked. Moving as slow as a glacier, she held on with both hands as they moved forward. She appeared to be having difficulty walking as they made their way to the front porch.

Joey stood as still as a statue. He suddenly recognized the woman. "Mommy!" he screamed and ran for the door.

Chapter Twenty-Seven

Joey's mother edged forward at a slow pace. She almost fell two times before she and Fred reached Myrt's porch. Their breath billowed out in rolling clouds of steam and the snow squeaked beneath their feet in the icy stillness of the afternoon. Fred had a good-sized box under one arm and appeared to be struggling somewhat to keep Alice upright.

Joey ran for the front door.

"Wait, Joey! Let them get on the porch first, okay?" said Myrt. She grabbed his arm and held him back. "Jumpin' Jiminy!"

She patted her brown hair that was gathered up and pinned. A few strands hung free and she pushed them in place as she held Joey back from the door.

Joey's excitement wasn't reflected by Mitchell and Merrill, who peeked out the window but didn't react in any way. They didn't recognize or remember their mother or the man with her. Joey didn't recognize him either, but he knew the man wasn't his father.

Myrt opened the door and smiled. "Hello, folks." Looking at the woman, she said, "You must be Joey's mother." She extended her hand. "I'm Myrt Matthews." She glanced at the man and nodded.

"Yes, I'm Alice Harrison and this is my friend Fred Simms." They all shook hands. Then Alice bent down and gathered Joey in her arms. She pulled him into her body as her eyes overflowed with tears and she fell to her knees, sobbing uncontrollably.

Fred stood silent. He had one of those faces you instinctively don't like — pinched and perpetually frowning, with high prominent cheekbones. He backed off to the side a bit then removed his hat — a gray fedora with a dark band that matched his coat. He seemed to be put out and annoyed by the commotion that had erupted.

Mitchell and Merrill ran over and took refuge behind Myrt's legs. Merrill dared to peek at the two visitors.

"Oh, Joey! Joey, my Joey!" Alice cried as she hugged him and planted kisses over his entire face. Grasping him by the shoulders, she shook him just a little and said, "Look at you! Look at you!" She held him tight against herself and continued to cry. "You've grown so big! Oh, I love you so much, Joey." Looking at him through watery eyes, her voice dropped when she said, "Mommy loves you, Son."

She reached over to gather in Mitchell and Merrill, but they quickly pulled back and clung to Myrt's legs. Alice crumpled like a broken doll. She blew out a long breath.

"Oh, my God, Fred. These poor babies don't even know me!" Still on her knees, she looked up at him as if to blame him for the situation. "For God's sake, Fred - please help me up." Her hand trembled and her body shook as she put her hand out. Fred quickly put the box he'd been carrying down on a dining room chair and used both of his arms to lift Alice.

Joey blurted, "Mommy, I know you! I do! I know you. I missed you so much, too, Mommy! I knew you would come for us someday. I just knew it." He sobbed and wrapped his arms around her inflated body.

After Fred helped her up, Alice fluffed her fingers through Joey's hair with one hand. With her other hand, she pulled a handkerchief from her coat pocket and dabbed at her eyes. "My God! How you've grown, Joey. You're so tall," she moaned between sobs. "What a big boy you are. Oh, Joey." She cupped his head and pulled him to her breast. Myrt watched with a smile on her face.

"Please forgive me for being so anxious," said Alice. "It's just—it's just been so long and I... well. I'm so glad to meet you, Myrt. I've heard so much about you. She stepped forward and half-hugged Myrt, then wavered slightly as she drifted back. Wiping her eyes, she then combed her wind-blown hair with her fingers and said, "It's so nasty out there. I must look a mess. I'm sorry." Her eyes seemed to well with sadness and despair.

Myrt smelled alcohol. It was definitely there, and she noticed

Alice's mis-steps.

"Yes," said Myrt. "It's good to meet you, too." She fumbled around in her sweater pockets for her cigarettes. "I'm a bit surprised, but then again, I'm not," she continued. "We were told you might be stopping by during the holidays. But since it wasn't definite, according to Judith Kellogg, we figured it was best to wait and see — if you know what I mean." She smiled and glanced at Fred who seemed unable to contemplate the entire situation.

"Yes, well, it was rough driving in this mess, but it wasn't that bad when we left Gouverneur," he said. Fred had sandy hair and pale, thin lips that needed blood. Wiry and gaunt, he appeared to be in his mid-thirties with a brownish complexion that could probably be explained by caffeine, nicotine and bourbon. His shady eyes confessed many hangovers.

"I know that wind must be causing a lot of drifting on the highway. My husband, Herb, should be along shortly," said Myrt. "He went to town for a few things. Please, let me take your coats. It's terribly cold out there, I know. You must be chilled clear through."

"Yes, the roads were getting bad," said Fred. He removed his coat and helped Alice out of hers. Under the coat, he wore a blue, double-breasted suit, white shirt and maroon tie.

Myrt noticed that removing her coat was somewhat of a problem for Alice; even with Fred's help she managed to get one arm tangled in a sleeve. "Darn. I seem to be all thumbs today," she groused. "Thank you, Fred."

Alice wore a flowered dress that resembled faded curtains. It ballooned over her body like a tent. A silver, heart-shaped pendant dangled from her neck. She wore no rings. With a large fleshy face, she had heavy makeup with blue eye shadow and bright red lipstick. Her crying made a mess of her mascara and her hair was awry, like thread caught in a comb.

"Please have a seat," said Myrt. "How about a cup of coffee?" She draped their coats over a dining room chair then scrambled to remove groceries that sat in the middle of the table with a pile of unfinished ironing. Again, she noticed Alice's gait as she wobbled to a chair and sat down with a heavy sigh. "No coffee for me, thank you, Myrt. Might I have a glass of water instead?"

"Of course. How about you, Fred?" Myrt asked. At the same time she tapped a cigarette out of her pack of Luckies, struck a match and lit the cigarette. She inhaled deeply before blowing a cloud of smoke toward the ceiling.

"Yes, water will be fine for me, too," he said. He sat down and fumbled in a pocket for his pipe.

"Certainly. We've got plenty of water." Myrt laughed and looked at Joey. "Joey, would you mind getting your mother and Mr. Simms some water? Use the glasses in the china cabinet."

"Okay," said Joey. He began to run.

"Slow down, Boy," Fred growled, in a take-charge way. He grinned sheepishly. "No sense in running." He lit his pipe and blew the smoke in the general direction of Alice who had a smile of contentment on her face as she watched Mitchell and Merrill. A rancid haze of old and new smoke hung in layers in the room.

Myrt took a seat. Her posture seemed somewhat defensive - shoulders hunched-knees tight together, hands in her lap. The three adults fell silent for a moment until she finally spoke to Alice in a secretive tone. "Have you heard from Joey's father, by any chance?"

Alice shook her head and gazed out the window. "No, I have not, unfortunately."

Joey returned with a glass of water in each hand. He carefully handed them to Fred and Alice then said, "Where's Beth, Mommy? How come she didn't come, too?"

"Well, Joey, I . . ."

Myrt said, "Joey, settle down now. Give your mother a moment to catch her breath for goodness sake."

Alice wrapped her arms around him. "Nobody else is with us today, Sweetie." The words seemed to catch in her throat. She bowed her head and looked away before she clasped his head between her hands and stared into his eyes. "Beth is helping Gram take care of your Gramps. He's not walking too well on his own anymore. They all send their love and hope to see you soon though."

She glanced at Myrt. "My father was badly wounded in the First World War, you know. He still has a lot of trouble with one of his legs." Her eyes drifted back to Joey who was sulking. "Oh, I'm so sorry, Joey. Beth wanted to come. Believe me." She dabbed at her eyes with the handkerchief as she spoke. She studied the twins for a long time. Mitchell and Merrill still shied away from her and continued to stare. They seemed alarmed that Alice was crying.

Myrt patted their heads. "It's okay, boys."

Alice leaned forward in an effort to reach out and touch them, but nearly slid off her chair. "Goodness! Look how much these boys have grown. Oh, dear." She began to cry again. "They were just babies. I want to hug them so badly. May I?" She looked at Myrt.

"Certainly, Alice. Go right ahead."

Alice reached out again. "Boys, I'm your mommy. Do you remember Mommy?" The twins stood by Myrt and continued to stare at the woman they didn't recognize.

Getting no response, Alice froze as if all the muscles in her body contracted at one time. Then she broke down. "Oh, sweet God. Fred, are you seeing this?" She looked in his eyes. "This is more than I can bear."

Myrt noted a slur in Alice's speech, confirming that Alice had been drinking.

Fred expelled a heavy sigh. "Honey, please don't get yourself all upset. They'll come around eventually." He sipped his water and set the glass down to re-light his pipe.

"I remember you, Mommy," said Joey. He tried to climb onto her lap, and at the same time keep his arms wrapped around her. He was both downhearted and exhilarated.

Myrt's brow creased with concern but she remained calm. Her shoulders, which had been raised, seemed to relax as she watched Alice's eyes. She gently massaged her temples. "The boys are really happy to see you, Alice." She waved a hand dismissively. "They just need to adjust a bit."

"Mommy! We're going home with you today, right?" Joey pleaded. "I mean... Mitchell, Merrill and me... all of us?" He smiled and studied her eyes, waiting for her to say yes. "You're gonna take us with you, okay?"

Alice hugged him. "Not today, Joey. Some day soon, but not today."

Joey pulled away and whined. "But why not, Mommy? Beth is with Gram and Gramps. Why can't we come too?" Nausea swirled through him like water sucking down a drain. "It's not fair." His body shook as he cried.

"Oh, no. Don't cry, Son. Please don't," Alice begged. "Guess what? We brought all of you boys some early Christmas presents."

Joey continued to sob loudly and fell at his mother's feet.

"I don't want no Christmas present. I want to leave here and go home with you. I want to see Beth and Gramps and stay there. Where's Daddy?"

"Shhhhh! Shhhhh, now. Here, come up here to Mommy." She tugged on his arms.

"Come, come Joey. Straighten up now," said Fred. "You're upsetting your mother." He paused a moment, his eyes intense under dark brows.

Alice glared at him and reached inside her pocketbook while Joey scowled and looked out the window.

"I hope you don't mind if we give each of them a box of candy, Myrt."

"No, of course not."

"Here, Joey. Take a look. Remember how much you love Sno-Caps? There's a box for each of you. Come on... take yours, Honey."

Joey shook his head and rubbed his eyes with his fists. "I don't want none."

Fred looked uncomfortable and gazed in the direction of the front door. The smile that twisted his mouth was mocking and bitter.

"Oh, Joey, take a box. Please? Mommy brought these special for you. Take them now." She held out the boxes to each of the twins.

"Go ahead, Mitchell. Merrill, go ahead. It's okay," said Myrt. "Take the box of candy your mother brought for you."

The twins hesitated but took the candy and began to struggle getting the boxes open.

Alice took a sip of her water then set it aside. "Can Mommy have a hug now?" She pleaded with outstretched arms.

"Go ahead, boys. Give her a big hug," said Myrt. "Isn't that nice of her?"

Mitchell and Merrill edged up closer to Alice and she gathered them into her arms. Tears poured down her cheeks as she squeezed them. "Oh, Oh—Oh. You feel so good. I love you so much, boys. God knows, Mommy loves you so much!" She held them as long as she could before they pulled away and continued to wrestle with their boxes of Sno-Caps.

Joey sulked but held the box of candy in his hand. He sniffled and watched his brothers for a bit, then attempted to scoot back onto Alice's lap but stopped to help Mitchell with his box of candy before opening his own.

Fred glanced at Myrt. "Can we give them their gifts now, Mrs. Matthews?" He reached for the box he'd brought in.

Myrt cleared her throat and extinguished her cigarette. "Well... I'm not sure... I mean I don't know if it's a good idea to let them open them before Christmas. I think . . ." She paused a moment, then held her hands up in surrender. "You know what... if you want them to see the things while you're here... yes, I suppose it will be all right. Go ahead."

There were two gifts for each of the boys. Everything was wrapped in red and green Christmas paper - no ribbons—no bows. Fred pulled the presents out one by one and read the names that were written on each gift. For Joey, there was a box of Lincoln Logs and a brightly colored spinning top. The twins each got different colored toy trucks. Their names were also on packages containing crayons and Peter Rabbit coloring books.

Myrt smiled and cleared her throat. "That's very thoughtful of you, folks. They will certainly have lots of fun with those gifts."

"Well, it was difficult to choose what to get them," said Fred. "Then, we figured we couldn't go wrong with those things."

Mitchell pushed his truck across the floor, while Merrill set his truck on the dining room table and shoved it back and forth until it flew off and crashed onto the floor.

"No, no, Mitchell! Not on the table," Fred said as Myrt picked it up and handed it back to him. "You don't want to scratch the table."

Myrt's face telegraphed surprise at Fred's involvement, but realized that he *was* Mitchell and Merrill's real father. Alice had been instructed by Mrs. Kellogg prior to the visit, saying, "Don't confuse the boys during the visit by indicating that Mr. Simms is the twins' biological father. Joseph would be confused for sure."

Joey had calmed down a bit and was experimenting with the new top.

"How are my boys doing, Myrt?" said Alice. "I'll bet they can be a handful at times."

"Oh, yes, but nothing unheard of for boys, you know. Joey tends to be a bit rambunctious at times, but other than that, we're fine."

Alice's speech quavered as she lowered her voice so the boys wouldn't hear. "I would give anything to be tucking them in at night and seeing them off to school each day." Tears streamed down her pudgy cheeks once again. "I'm so sorry that I can't. I want you to know how much I really appreciate you taking care of them. I'm glad to see they are in a nice home with caring folks."

"Well, we try to make things work as well as we can. You have some good boys, Alice. I must be honest with you. We were told very little as to the circumstances surrounding you and your family. It can make things a bit awkward, if you know what I mean."

"Yes. I understand," said Alice.

"Sure thing," said Fred. He tapped his pipe on the ashtray as he spoke. "I believe they purposely keep us all in the dark to some degree."

"There have to be reasons, I suppose," said Myrt.

Alice said, "It's my understanding that the people at the last home were somewhat cruel. I've been losing sleep ever since we found out about it. Their sister, Beth, told us some terrible things. I've been so afraid for my boys since then."

"I'll vouch for that," said Fred. His eyebrows crawled up his forehead. He leaned forward in his chair. "Sometimes, I'd swear this poor woman is ready for the asylum."

"I'm sorry. Well, I may be talking out of school here," said Myrt. She paused and glanced at the boys at play on the floor and paused as she lit another cigarette and looked at Alice. "I mean—I would keep it strictly to myself, mind you, but - how does it look for reconciliation of some sort between you and your husband?" She quickly glanced at the boys again, then back to Alice.

Fred winced and cleared his throat. He stuck a pinky finger in his ear, wiggled it around, then said, "Not likely."

Alice dabbed at her eyes with the handkerchief and shook her head. She sighed and spoke in a quiet and weary voice. "Not good—not good at all. Nothing good actually, I'm afraid." Her mouth was set in a stern line.

"What? What's not good, Mommy?" Joey asked as he got up from the floor and stood at Alice's side with the top in his hand. "What did you say, Mommy? Did you see Brian?"

"Nothing that concerns you, Joey. We're just talking about the war. No, Honey, I haven't visited Brian yet. But I am going to next week."

Joey hugged her arm and said, "Are you going to take Brian home with you?"

Alice patted his head and feigned a smile. "No, Joey," she whispered, her lips barely moving, her tear-filled eyes brimming with desperation.

•   •   •   •   •

Another half hour had passed when Fred stood up. "Well, Alice, we have a long trip back and I'm not sure what the roads will be like." He hitched up his trousers. "We'd best be on our way here shortly."

"No! Not yet," Joey screamed.

Alice drew him in to her and hugged him. She squeezed and rubbed his back in loving circles. "Yes, Joey, I'm afraid Fred is right. We have to be going."

"Why? You just came. Let me come with you. I have to. Please, Mommy?"

Myrt handed Fred their coats. "I think she's right, Joey. They have a long trip back and the snow might get very deep. We want her to get home safe. Isn't that right?" She looked at Fred. "I'm sorry Herb hasn't gotten back yet. I know he would have liked to meet you."

"Maybe next time," said Fred. He glanced off in the direction of the front door. "We'll be back again soon, Joey. We have to go."

"But not yet. My mommy doesn't have to leave yet. Why?" Tears began to form in his eyes to match the sadness in his voice.

The twins continued to play with their trucks until Myrt took them away. They still had chocolate smeared on their hands and lips and she started cleaning them up with a tissue. "A little clean-up here," she said. "Come, boys. It's time to say goodbye to your mother."

Alice's fingers fumbled with the buttons on her coat as she watched their lack of interest. She covered her face in a feeble effort to hide her anguish and disappointment.

Leaning over, she held each of them, kissing their faces, drawing them in to her. She sobbed her goodbyes. Fred kissed each of the twins on the forehead when Alice was done.

"Mommy loves you, Mitchell." She hugged him harder, then turned to Merrill and hugged him. "Mommy loves you, Merrill." She wrapped her arms around Joey and held him, but he was not consolable and would not stop crying.

"Joey, I'll see if we can have Beth and Gramps call you... okay?"

"Please don't go yet, Mommy. You don't have to go. Please?" Joey trembled and his heart raced as he stood in the doorway and watched them leave.

It had stopped snowing, but about two additional inches of snow had accumulated on the porch. The fair-weather clouds were showing orange crinkles from the setting sun. Fred took Alice's arm and guided her down the steps and to the car.

Tears continued to stream down her face as she looked back at the house and shook her head. When Fred helped her into the passenger seat she murmured, "I just know I'll never see them again."

Chapter Twenty-Eight

J oey and the twins remained with Herb and Myrt in foster care through Thanksgiving and Christmas of 1948. The holidays came and went without Joey hearing from his brother, Brian. Beth called on Christmas Day, but he hadn't heard from her since. The twins were content because they had no knowledge of their biological status and the Matthews had a tendency to spoil them. To Mitchell and Merrill, Myrt was their mommy and Herb, their daddy.

It was a cold morning in March with temperatures below thirty degrees, but the time for reawakening was on the way. The region had serious snowstorms all winter and it had snowed moderately during March. It was steady and dense. Although the flakes were light, there still were enough to cover the compacted dirty remains of the snow that came before them.

One Saturday morning, the boys were in the living room playing with their Christmas toys while Herb was at work and Myrt, who had been playing solitaire at the kitchen table, went upstairs with a broom in hand.

Joey played with his Lincoln Logs. The fort he worked on was already three tiers high and he was hoping he had enough pieces for another. Mitchell and Merrill stood close by, arguing over a yellow dump truck. Merrill tried to yank the truck out of Mitchell's hands.

"Gimmee that. It's mine!" Merrill whined.

Another truck just like it sat on the floor behind Mitchell. It wasn't quite as big, and it wasn't yellow, but it was a new truck. Merrill could play with that one if he wasn't such a brat, Joey thought.

"Let go of it, Merrill! You can have it after Mitchell gets done!" Joey said.

"No, I had it first!" said Merrill at the same time yanking on the truck. Mitchell hung on. They both screamed, and Joey knew Myrt could be there any second. She was upstairs, but it wouldn't take her long. Joey grabbed the truck away from both of them and Merrill kicked him in the leg.

"Owww! You kicked me!" he yelled. "I'm telling Myrt if you don't stop it." Merrill kicked him again with more force behind it. Joey was shaken. He pushed on Merrill's chest, and he fell back against the wall, crying as if Joey had slugged him.

He was sorry he reacted so quickly and tried to help his brother up. His heart pounded in his chest as he reached to help, but Merrill jerked away and ran for the stairs. He was still screaming when he fell to his knees on the stairs. Myrt was on her way down. She looked at Joey with undisguised coldness.

"Joey! What did you do to him?" She hugged Merrill and wiped his hair away from his tear-stained face. He wasn't hurt, but he wouldn't stop crying.

Joey's eyes widened. "It wasn't my fault this time. He kicked me two times; he kept kicking me in the leg." He pointed to Mitchell. "Ask Mitchell."

Myrt shot him a skeptical look. Her mouth was pinched tight as she bit down on her temper. Her voice was very clear, her speech precise. "I don't have to ask Mitchell anything, young man. I have eyes; I can see. I'm sure he didn't hurt you. Look how small he is, you big bully. Shame on you! Go to your room—now! Stay there until Herb gets home."

Joey ran up to his room and dropped on his bed. He crammed his face into the pillow. It was all he could do to keep from yelling back at Myrt. He had never needed to talk with his father or Gramps as badly as he needed to that day.

She never listens to me. It doesn't matter if they do something really wrong; she still always blames me. They're both brats, and I hate them. I hate her. The Matthews think they're so special, and everybody thinks I'm bad. I hate it here.

When Herb came home, Myrt gave her report, and Joey went to bed without supper again.

•　　•　　•　　•　　•

In April, Joey sat on the steps of the front porch and watched his brothers play, just as Myrt had instructed. It was his job. He admired the red and yellow tulips that poked through the ground. They were sprouting on both sides of the front steps. Out by the road, the uncut weeds of the previous summer stuck up through the diminishing snow. The cloudless sky was pastel blue, and a cool wind riffled in from the west. It was one of those breezy days—the kind where people could feel summer around the corner, even though it was still jacket weather. Mitchell and Merrill screamed and giggled as they chased each other around the front yard.

Easter vacation was underway when Mrs. Kellogg pulled her black sedan into the driveway and the twins ran for the front porch.

Three months had passed since the caseworker's last visit and Joey was anxious to hear some news from his family. How is Brian? Is he all right? Is Gramps still sick? When will Mommy come to see us again? He had so many questions.

Mrs. Kellogg took her time easing out of the car. She dropped her keys in her purse then smoothed out the back of her dress before walking to the front door. She feigned an odd smile as she approached Joey and waved with just the tips of her fingers.

Myrt came out of the house and stood behind Joey on the porch. He stood up and dusted off the seat of his pants. Myrt rested her hands on his shoulders.

"Hello, Myrt. How have you been?" Mrs. Kellogg asked as she approached the steps.

"Fine, Judith—just fine." She shaded her eyes and looked out towards Mrs. Kellogg's car. "Beautiful day, isn't it? Good to feel spring in the air at long last."

"Yes, it certainly is, thank goodness. I believe winter is gone for a while." She bent down and hugged Mitchell, Merrill and then Joey. "For six months anyway," she added. "Good to see you boys again. My, but they're growing like weeds, aren't they?"

"That's for sure." Myrt lit a cigarette. "Of course, we don't notice it as much as you do because we're with them every day. The twins have gone up another whole size since the last time you were out. They'll need more new clothes soon, I'd say."

"Really?"

Myrt nodded and opened the door. She glanced at Joey. "You boys stay out here on the porch for a while. I need to speak with Mrs. Kellogg. Come in, Judith. Can I get you a cup of coffee?"

"Yes. That would hit the spot; it's been another hectic day."

Joey wanted to ask Mrs. Kellogg about Beth and the rest of the family but he knew it would have to wait until the time was right. A half hour passed before Myrt called him.

"Joey! Will you please come in here now?"

Joey ran inside and found both women sitting at the dining room table. The twins tried to follow him in, but Myrt got up and held them back. "No, no, boys. You just stay outside. Joey will be right out." Her voice was strained as if she was being choked. The twins hesitated but ran back out on the porch to play with their Tinker Toys.

"Have you seen Brian, Ma'am?" Joey asked. "Can I go see him?"

"Whoa! Easy now, Joseph." Mrs. Kellogg fidgeted with her scarf. She shook her head slightly, as if there was something in her ear. She smiled and said, "Yes, I've seen Brian—not too long after I was here, as a matter of fact. He is fine—just fine. He told me to tell you he misses you and will try to get permission to call on the telephone."

"Oh," said a dejected Joey. "Well, when can I see Beth and my Gramps?"

An uneasy silence took hold as he noticed three brown sacks sitting on the dining room table. His heart skipped a beat. Myrt had evidently packed them while he was outside with the twins.

Mrs. Kellogg studied him for another long moment, then looked away, seemingly very unsure of herself, an expression of complete uncertainty on her face. As she rubbed her jaw, her brow furrowed. She cleared her throat before she spoke in a hushed voice.

"Joseph... we have to make some changes again." She made a sympathetic face. "I'll be taking you with me today. We have a new home for you."

Joey stared—first at her-then at Myrt. The information was like a winter wind blowing on his face. His heart seemed to explode and he began to tremble inside and out. He felt strange, not really believing what was just said. There seemed to be an echo inside his head, over and over. "*New home. New Home. New Home.*"

"You mean you're taking me away from here? Why?" Saying those words made him sick to his stomach. Tears rolled down his cheeks and he wanted to throw up. "Why can't I just go home? If I can't go home I want to stay here with my brothers." His eyes darted to Myrt. "Why can't I do that?"

Mrs. Kellogg held up her hand. "No, Joseph, I'm sorry. We have decided that you need to be around boys your own age. Lord knows, there will be plenty of them where I'm taking you." She gave him her pretend smile and looked at Myrt, who nodded.

"But why?" said Joey. He leaned back against the dining room wall and glared at them. His arms felt like lead weights, his legs, like they were suddenly missing. He continued to whimper as his body slowly slid down the wall. "No! I won't go! Why should I? No!"

"Well, let's just say it's time for you to move on, Joseph. No need in getting so upset, now. After all, you're almost ten years old. Be a big boy." Her chair creaked as she leaned forward and tenderly brushed a tear from his cheek with the pad of her thumb. "You need to be around older lads—boys your own age, fellas to pal around with and so on."

"I don't want to be around any other boys. I don't need to. I want to be with Mommy and Beth and Gram and Gramps."

"Oh, it will be okay. You'll see. It will be fine." She stood to leave. "I think you'll like it in Watertown." She paused and let her words hover in the air.

Myrt shifted a little in her chair and gazed out the window for a moment. "This will be the best thing for you, Joey. It really will."

"I don't want to go, Myrt. Where's Herb? Does he know?" Joey sobbed.

Myrt made a sound like a horse blowing air through its lips. She reached out, fluffed his hair and tenderly brushed some tears away. "Yes, Joey. Herb knows you'll be leaving. He would have been here to see you off but the shop needed him this morning." She glanced at Mrs. Kellogg who had circled her arms around one of the three bags.

"Come on now. Let's go say goodbye to your brothers. We have a long trip ahead, Joseph," said Mrs. Kellogg. She looked at Myrt again. "I trust all of his things are here."

"Yes. I packed everything." She handed one bag to Joey and carried one herself.

Draping an arm around Joey's shoulders, she said, "It's the best thing for everyone concerned, Joey."

Joey stopped. He was still sniffling when he looked up into Myrt's eyes and said, "What do you mean?"

"Oh, well - ahh-I just mean you are becoming a big boy. You need to be with boys your age as Mrs. Kellogg said."

They walked past the twins and Mrs. Kellogg opened the back door of the sedan and put her bag inside. She held it open and took the other bags from Myrt and Joey.

"Well, I guess that's about it. Myrt, I'll be calling you before I come back out. Tell Herb I was sorry I missed him. I trust you will have a wonderful Easter with the boys."

Standing alongside the car, Myrt had misty eyes as she hugged Joey and kissed him on the cheek. "Please be a good boy, Joey. We'll all miss you."

Joey hugged his brothers. He squeezed them one at a time and broke into tears again. His mind raced back to the day Beth left him behind, when she left for Gram and Gramps' house. He remembered how Brian cried the day he left. "Bye, bye, Mitchell. I wish I could stay here with you."

"Why are you going away, Joey? I like you to stay here," said Merrill.

Joey held Mitchell tighter. "I don't want to go, honest I don't." He turned and hugged Merrill. "Bye, bye, Merrill. I'm going to miss you and Mitchell really bad." He looked up at Mrs. Kellogg whose big concern was getting on the road.

Joey tried one last time. "Please... please don't make me go, Myrt."
She squeezed his shoulder. "You'll be fine, Joey. Goodbye, Son."

The twins started crying. It was as if the realization of their
brother's leaving was just getting through in their four-year-old
minds. "Can we go with Joey?" Mitchell asked.

"I want to go too," said Merrill.

"No, not today, boys. Joey's going by himself this time," said
Myrt.

Mrs. Kellogg jiggled her keys in her hand. "Well, we'd best be on
our way. Go ahead and get in the front seat, Joseph."

Joey jammed his hands in his coat pockets and continued over to
the passenger side without sparing her so much as a glance before he
hesitated, but got in.

Myrt lowered her voice. "I certainly don't envy you your job,
Judith. This must be especially hard." Tears glistened in her eyes as
they shook hands. "Goodbye, and thank you again."

"It can be difficult, but I'm just doing my job, as you know.
Someone has to do it. I will most likely see you before July. Goodbye,
Myrt."

Myrt took the twins by the hand and walked back to the porch.
They were still crying when the sedan backed out and drove away.
Joey waved but they must not have seen it because they didn't wave
back.

•   •   •   •   •

Joey's crying subsided after several miles had gone by. He was
reduced to sniffles before Mrs. Kellogg spoke.

"Now, Joseph, this new home is a lot different than the others.
There are lots of boys and girls just like you who are temporarily
separated from their families. They only stay until their moms and
dads get things straightened out—like I said, just like you. I think
you'll like the Children's Home. Most all the kids I've placed there are
quite happy."

Questions chased each other around and around in his brain.

"But, I liked it at the Matthews'. Why did I have to leave there?" He waited for what seemed like a long time before Mrs. Kellogg responded.

"Well... I imagine I should be honest with you, Joseph." She paused. "It appears you were having a lot of problems adjusting. You and your brothers were always at odds-fighting and what not. You must learn to get along with others, Son." She paused. "You need to learn control of your temper too."

"Myrt told you that stuff, didn't she?"

"Well, it really doesn't matter, does it? We know it's true, don't we?"

Joey kept his eyes on her but didn't answer.

"I don't understand why you would be so mean to the twins. My goodness, they *are your brothers*, you know. You should love and respect each other—be grateful you have them. Some children have none at all."

"Yes, Ma'am. It wasn't really like that though. Sometimes they just... "

Mrs. Kellogg raised her hand in a stop mode. "No, no. I really don't want to discuss it further, Joseph. Okay?"

Joey's head dropped forward. His chin touched his chest. "Yes, Ma'am."

They rode in silence for some time. Joey stared out the window thinking about how this move had all been Myrt's fault.

The journey to Watertown was spattered with dairy farms and small hamlets that never quite flowered into towns or villages. The road constantly curved and stands of trees curved with them. Somewhere behind those trees was the dark course of Black River, not far from Watertown. Intermittent clouds drifted across the sun and Joey watched the changes in the color of the grass. He turned sideways and asked, "Did you know Mommy came to see us?"

Mrs. Kellogg cleared her throat. "Yes, I knew that—just before Christmas wasn't it?"

"Yes. Did you know she came with a man?"

"Really?" There was a long pause before she said, "What was the man's name?"

"Fred somebody."

Mrs. Kellogg looked in her rear view mirror and said, "I'm not sure who that might have been."

"Did you talk to Mommy or Daddy about moving me again?"

"Yes, Joseph. I always make your mother aware of your whereabouts. I was over to see your sister the other day, though, and your mother wasn't there. Beth's happy. She's doing fine. She's such a big help to your grandma and grandpa, you know."

"Did she ask about me?"

"Why yes, of course she asked about you. I told her you were fine." She gave Joey a sidelong glance. "That was before Myrt called me again though, but it's just as well your sister believes all is well. Gramps is much better, but he had to retire from the railroad."

"Really? Well, can I just go see them?"

"No - not just now." She waved his question away. "I have to get you settled in at this new home for a bit, and then we'll see. Okay?"

Joey sat back and stared out the window. "Yes, Ma'am."

Mrs. Kellogg drove for another half hour before they reached Watertown. It looked like a big city to Joey, much bigger than Gouvernuer and Ellisburg. It was located less than forty miles from the mighty St. Lawrence River and Lake Ontario. The Canadian border was less than a hundred miles away.

Joey remembered that Watertown was where Uncle Glenn and Aunt Betty took them for ice cream that wonderful day that seemed so long ago. Lots of cars were parked on angles all along the main street.

Downtown looked like a movie set for the all-American town, the town square in the center, with its quaint old band shell and statues to history's heroes. There were old- fashioned brick shops and the courthouse built of native limestone. The Strand Movie Theatre had a vintage marquee jutting out heralding the showing at 7 P.M. and 9:30 of *The Ghost and Mrs. Muir*. It was right next door to the grand old Watertown Hotel in its Victorian splendor.

A giant, splashing water fountain was situated right in the middle of the square. Mrs. Kellogg circled around in order to get through to the other side of town. Everything looked different with the piles of snow gone. Joey looked for the ice cream parlor but missed it because Mrs. Kellogg was driving too fast.

His lip quivered and his eyes watered. "What's their name?" he asked.

"Whose name, Joseph?"

"The people's name where you're taking me."

"This is not a real house or farm like you are familiar with. It's a home for boys and girls. There's a superintendent by the name of Mr. Neagle. He and his wife are in charge there."

She smiled and went silent while Joey wondered.

Chapter Twenty-Nine

A lice awoke with a start from a dreamless sleep with the sun shining through a gap in the curtains. She didn't have to turn her head to know that Fred had already left for work two hours earlier. His scent still lingered in the stuffy air of the bedroom. She lay back on the bed, closed her eyes and placed the back of her wrist on her forehead. She had a vague headache and felt sick to her stomach.

Rubbing her fingertips on the sore area around her eye, she tried to focus on the argument the night before that left her with the painful, throbbing cheek. The entire area on the left side of her face was extremely sore and she sensed it must be black and blue. She didn't remember getting back to the apartment or getting in bed for that matter. Sitting upright, she covered herself with the sheets and tried to remember what she had done so wrong last night to stir Fred's ire.

Crawling out of bed, she slipped on her robe and shuffled over to the window, where, shading her eyes, she peered into the morning sky. The previous night's rain had passed and some sunlight had broken through a lingering cloud cover. The air was cool, but oddly heavy. She stood at the window a long time until the urge to throw up suddenly consumed her. She quickly ran to the bathroom, dropped to her knees by the side of the toilet and puked. It was a while before she finally stood and looked in the mirror. Yes—he had left his stamp of disapproval once again.

She hated confronting herself in the mirror. Aside from the damage induced by Fred, she looked tired and hollow-eyed and had developed a network of tiny wrinkles and lines around her eyes and mouth. Tears rolled down her cheeks. Just thirty years old, yet she looked old and haggard. The hardest thing for her was to be naked in front of Fred. She was convinced that her plump body was repulsive. She no longer had much to offer.

She shuddered as she traced her fingers over her cheek and left eye where he had smacked her. The entire area was black and purple and once again her mind raced ahead thinking about leaving Fred and moving back in with her parents. "It's wrong," she whispered. It's like I'm on a train that's jumped the tracks and nobody can stop it. I want to make it stop." Deep inside, however, she knew she would never leave... she couldn't because she loved him; he was all she had left and Fred knew it.

$$\bullet \qquad \bullet \qquad \bullet \qquad \bullet \qquad \bullet$$

As she dressed, her mind continued to recall the events of the night before. Their original plan was to stop for a quick one at the Feather Merchant tavern in Felts Mills and from there go on to the Watertown Steak House for a relaxing dinner. It was Fred's favorite eatery. They both liked the Merchant; it was one of their favorite watering holes. Arriving there, they found that it wasn't as busy as it could be. Only a half a dozen cars were parked at odd attitudes around the bar's tiny parking lot.

Even so, it was noisy inside with the warm, low hubbub and hoo-hah of a half-empty late evening joint in full swing. A Wurlitzer juke box provided the music. The bar ran front to back on the right, and there were tables and chairs on the left. The decoration scheme was really no scheme at all: wooden tables, ladder-back chairs, bar stools, board floor.

Fred and Alice sat on stools at the farthest end of the bar — as far away from the front door as possible. Those were their favorite seats. In fact, on occasion, Fred had asked customers to move so they could have their 'regular spots.'

The argument started off slow, as they always did after the two of them had consumed plenty of alcohol. Alice sniffled and wiped her eyes when she mentioned the twins being unable to recognize her on their visit last winter. Fred had a hair-trigger temper and a penchant for violence. Talking to him about the kids could be a bit like walking through cobwebs or accidentally raking your hand across a hornet's nest.

"Alice, why is it that we can never go anywhere but what you don't start yammering on about those kids?" He waved a hand back and forth in her face to punctuate his displeasure. "It's bad enough you go on and on at home, but good God, we are out to have a good time, aren't we?"

"Yes," Alice murmured. "But I just . . ."

Fred patted her hand. "Well then - why don't you dry up those wet doe eyes and relax. Have another drink, for Christ's sake." He yelled out, "Hey, Frankie! Give us another round over here, will ya'?"

Frank was at the till ringing up a sale. He poked a finger in the air to indicate he heard Fred and would be there shortly. A very patient man, Frank wore a decades-old faded sweater, his shirt collar secured all the way to his fleshy neck, thick with wattles. He had a massive head circled by a rim of grizzled gray hair that had not seen a barber's shears in months. His face was unshaven and his second chin lapped against his thick neck.

Alice said, "I'm sorry, Honey. I just can't forget." She exhaled a long hard breath of air. "Those babies didn't even know me."

"Ahhhh—to hell with that. Let it lay, will you? You saw for yourself." He glared at her, his face a rigid mask of hard planes and sharp angles. "They're just fine." He waved a hand dismissively. "Quit worrying over them. Would you do that for me?"

An hour later the juke box played Margaret Whiting's *Moonlight In Vermont,* while Alice did her best to veer away from the subject of the kids. However, two drinks later, she took a deep breath and tried again to get through to Fred when she mentioned Brian. "We never did see Brian like we were going to. You promised too. Will you take me out there?"

Fred frowned as he moved an ashtray aside to make room for his drink. He clenched his teeth and his jaw muscles bulged and shook as he scrutinized Alice with searching eyes and shook his head. "I said no!"

The color drained from Alice's face; she knew she had overstepped her boundaries but couldn't help herself. She seethed inside. She feigned calm when everything inside her was trembling at the fury she saw in his face. When he touched her arm she jumped as if she had an electric shock and stared at him with such anger in her eyes that he took a step back.

"What? You pissed off at me, are you?" He waited for an answer as Alice swallowed more wine and lowered her head.

"Hey!" Fred raised his voice as he placed his fingers under her chin and lifted. "Answer me, dammit!"

Alice was afraid and said nothing. The tension was so thick one could smell it. She waited until he moved his fingers away, pulled a pack of Chesterfields out of her pocketbook and lit one with shaky hands.

"Don't you clam up on me." He squeezed her arm so hard she felt his nails bite into her flesh. "You've got a rusty nail sideways in your head, Alice. Let it go. Quit feeding it," he growled.

Alice shrugged. She fondled a paper napkin, then tore it into tiny pieces.

Two men wearing hard hats sat a few stools away and watched everything. They sipped their beers and tried to act nonchalant as they took in the show. Fred glared at them. Then his eyes traveled back to Alice.

"Look, I don't really need any more of this. Let's get out of here. I've got to work in the morning anyway." He slammed his empty glass down on the bar and headed for the door without her. Alice quickly swallowed the rest of her drink and hurried after him. The two men followed them with their eyes and grinned at each other.

Fred rambled on as he stomped his way to the car. "It's getting so we can't do a damned thing without you turning it into a crying circus." He leaned against the car and tipped his head back to look at the sky. Alice stood on her side of the car and said nothing.

"I swear, the next time you pull that shit, I'm leaving you there. I'll go somewhere I can have a good time without your ass. Get in the car," he said through clenched teeth. Alice was obviously drunk and beyond caring about his threats. Without any warning a stiff breeze swept over them along with a spatter of over-sized raindrops. The wind died for a moment and then the rain lashed them with windy sheets of water. They got in and Fred started the car. The windshield wipers slapped back and forth removing the mud and insect collection.

Traffic on the outskirts of Watertown was somewhat heavy but moved well, like choreographed chaos yet Fred drove much too fast. Zipping in and out between cars, he weaved back and forth and crossed the center line more than once.

Tears still blurred her eyes when Alice said, "Fred — I wish you would slow down a little."

"Don't you tell me how to drive, dammit! How many times do I have to tell you that?"

Alice fell silent for a moment but Fred's stubbornness continued.

Panic closed her throat but she managed to say, "I just don't want you to kill us is all. I…"

As fast as a striking viper, Fred swung his arm around and backhanded her.

"*Owwwww!*" She shrieked in pain and grabbed for her eye. Doubling over, she braced herself on the dash with one hand and rubbed her cheek with the other.

"I told you, don't talk to me like that. I'm driving. You just shut the hell up."

•   •   •   •   •

Alice decided it would be best to move back in with her mother and father. Her heart pounded so hard it was almost unbearable. The rain was no more than a mist in the air, but it was thundering again when the cab pulled up outside her parents' house. The sunglasses she wore looked ridiculous on a rainy day. It wouldn't matter. They would be upset with her whether she had a black eye or not. Her eyes had dried, and she sat in silence for five minutes. There was no choice — she dreaded the situation but had to tell them.

Her father, Carl, was outside. He clasped his hands behind his back and stared moodily at the cultivated ground that would be his garden in the back yard — provided he had help. His face revealed lines of strain and old memories that etched deep into his face. His eyes took on a faraway look and all color seemed to have drained from his face since his stroke.

In days gone by, and indeed for most of his fifty-four years, Carl had the habit of humming the whole day through. He walked — he hummed; he worked — he hummed. After his stroke, however, Carl appeared to give up humming. He talked to himself a bit, then remained silent for a few moments before sighing deeply, then turned back to the house. He didn't see his daughter getting out of the cab. He ambled inside and went directly to his rocking chair where he sat with a loud moan.

The smell of brewing coffee and bacon and eggs drifted out from the kitchen as Alice closed the back door softly behind her. Lillian was washing dishes.

"Hi, Ma!"

"Oh, hi, Honey." Her mother turned from the stove and wrapped her spindly arms around Alice. Taking a step back, she stared at her daughter's black eye. "I don't suppose I need to ask you where you got that eye do I?" Her tone was that of a disappointed mother to a misbehaving child. Tears immediately coated her eyes. "Your pa ain't going to like that one little bit, you know."

"Is that Alice, Lillian?" Carl called from the living room.

"Yes, Pa. It's just me," said Alice.

"Yes, it is, Old Man," Lillian added. "Keep your shirt on — let her get in the door for Pete's sake." She gave Alice a cursory smile.

"Well, let her go for a minute and she just might come in here." He puffed his pipe to life and a pungent cloud of smoke rose above his head.

"Come on in here, Daughter. Give your daddy a hug."

Alice set her pocketbook on the dining room table and slowly walked in to see him. She immediately leaned down to hug and kiss him. "Hi, Pa. I love you and I've missed you."

"I love you too, Honey. Hey!" His smile disappeared. "What's going on with that again?" He tapped a finger on his cheek. There was a brief silence before he added. "Never mind—I can figure that out for myself." He paused and shook his head. "Damn him!"

She didn't answer him, but the weight of truth pressed down on her just the same. "How have you been feeling?" she said, trying to change the subject.

Carl puffed on his pipe. "Oh—I'm getting around a bit better now. A lot better than I was when I first came home, you know." His head jerked and he stared into her eyes. "Why do you stay with that lout, Honey?"

"Come on out here and sit, Alice," Lillian called. "Have you had breakfast yet? She wiped her hands on her apron. "I just finished feeding your father. I can fry some eggs for you."

Carl squeezed Alice's hand and studied her with a sad look in his eyes. She didn't answer him, but the weight of truth pressed down on her just the same. She saw the tear in his eye and patted his cheek. "I'll be okay, Pa."

"Why don't you move back in here with us?" he murmured. "Beth is at school right now. She's a blessing here. We can take care of you, too." He paused. "Keep you out of trouble—know what I mean?"

"Yes, Pa. I've been thinking about it—I really have."

"Come on out here and sit awhile," said Lillian.

Alice kissed her father on the forehead and went back out to the dining room.

Lillian pulled out two chairs. She smiled, walked to the pantry and brought back a gallon bottle of Gallo. She shoved a deck of blue Bicycle playing cards in front of Alice. "Sit down, Honey. Relax. We haven't played Rummy in ages. Have a drink with me." She leaned back in her chair and craned her neck in order to catch Carl's reaction.

"Well, all right, Ma. I guess it won't hurt. What time is it, anyway?"

Lillian looked at the clock on the wall behind her daughter. "Aaaah—it's just about eleven-thirty. Why?"

Alice shook her head. "Just wondering, how's Beth doing in

school?"

"Oh, she's just fine - mostly straight A's. She's a good girl, Honey. So much help around here — I don't know what we'd do without her." She paused a moment and gazed away toward the kitchen. "She misses you and her brothers. She frets a lot about Joey. That Mrs. Kellogg doesn't tell us anything worthwhile about them, you know."

"I know. God, but I miss them so much, Ma." Tears welled up in Alice's eyes. She pulled a tissue out of the pocket in her dress and dabbed them. Not able to meet her mother's gaze, she stared down at her feet. "I can't get over the way Joey cried when we left there." She took a long swallow from her glass.

Lillian studied the backs of her wrinkled hands and let out a heavy sigh. It was a long moment before she spoke again.

"Don't get yourself riled up now, Honey." She shuffled the cards. "I don't know why you don't just sic the police on that man. He belongs in jail!"

Alice shook her head from side to side. Her stomach churned. "No, Ma, I just can't do that. I probably deserved it. Besides Fred really is a good guy." She blew her nose and watched her mother deal. "I love him and I don't want to rock the boat. He could lose his job."

"Rock what boat? I'm sorry, Daughter, but you really are blind." She took a big swallow of her wine. "Fred is a selfish good-for-nothing, I tell you."

"You two are starting a bit early today, aren't you?" Carl chided from his rocker.

"Hush, Old Man. If I want to have a glass of wine with my daughter, I will. Just settle down. We're not bothering anybody, so hush." Lillian lit a Chesterfield and coughed as she exhaled a plume of smoke.

"Well, you're bothering me!" said Carl.

"Oh stop it now, Carl." said Lillian as she played a card and stared at Alice. "Are you going to stay a while today, Honey?"

"Yes, I am, Ma - a little while longer anyway." She played her card while Lillian poured more wine for both of them.

They had played Rummy for better than an hour when Alice decided it was time. She took a deep breath and said, "I need to tell you both something before this day gets much longer."

"Oh, really? Well — go ahead then."

"Yes. I might as well come right out with it. Ma... I'm pregnant again."

Chapter Thirty

I t was less than a half-hour drive from Ellisburg to the Children's Home of Jefferson County in Watertown. The grass was already green from the rainy April, and the trees with new buds now arched elegantly along route 193. Mrs. Kellogg and her passenger, Joey, had little to say to one another for the first ten minutes of the trip. He had begged to no avail and now the fight had run out of him.

Raindrops the size of dimes began splattering off the road and the windshield, bringing with them the fresh air smell of an incoming storm. And then, the rain was coming hard in sheets, the lightning almost constant. A long ragged bolt of lightning split the clouds. Thunder banged on the roof of the car like a bass drum.

Mrs. Kellogg drove the black sedan in complete silence.

"Ma'am, is Brian coming to this house too?"

"No, Joey. Brian is settled in very nicely where he is for now. There is no need in moving him again. You'll have plenty of friends at the Children's Home to play with though."

Her excuses bounced through his head, all of them true, none of them the truth. "I didn't mean to play with. I just wanted my brother to be with me."

"I understand and as I said, you will all be together when your mother and father get things straightened out with a new house and all.

"But when will that be?"

"Oh, Joseph, we've talked about this many times." She regarded him with a cool look, one brow sketching upward. She cleared her throat. "I'm not sure when that will be, but it won't be long."

Joey settled back for the rest of the drive and watched the scenery. He could hear nothing but the voice in his mind and the pounding of his pulse in his ears. *It won't be long. It won't be long.*

The thunderstorms were over. There were only traces of rain that were the kind one could actually enjoy. When the sky cleared and turned a soft blue again, the clouds to the west were like strips of fire.

As they approached Watertown twenty minutes later, the landscape was residential with a smattering of small businesses and factories. Downtown was a myriad of small stores side by side on both sides of the street. The Jefferson County Courthouse sat in the middle of a lovely and well-kept lawn in the center of what was known as Watertown Square. Around it were fountains, ancient oaks, park benches, war memorials and two gazebos. One could almost hear the parade on the Fourth of July and stump speeches during elections.

After they passed through town, Mrs. Kellogg turned left at a sign that said State Street. From there on, it was strictly residential, having block after block of ornate houses with big wrap-around porches reflecting an era long since passed. They sat side by side all the way along State Street and out of the business district.

A few minutes later, Joey saw a row of red brick buildings located on the right side. The grass in front of them was bright green and manicured. The premises appeared to stretch for nearly a city block. A sign centered on the front lawn said Jefferson County Children's Home.

Mrs. Kellogg turned in to a long gravel-covered drive and stopped in front of the brick building located in the center, separating the other four with two on each side. It was bigger than the rest of them and a tall brick chimney towered up in the rear. A sign over the front door said Administration.

"Here we are, Joseph. You can leave your bags in here for now and come in with me. They're expecting us." She let herself out of the car and sucked in the air that smelled of damp earth and green grass.

Joey was scared. When he got out he felt sick to his stomach, and his knees were wobbly. He hated those feelings; it was the same way every time he moved to a new place. His hands shook, and it was hard to breathe. *I wonder if these people know I got in trouble at school.*

What if they don't like me either? I'll just run away, that's all.

They walked on a sidewalk to the front of the main building which had round, cement pillars on each side of the entrance. Two big doors with shiny handles greeted them. A welcome mat was there.

Just past the vestibule was a room that resembled the one outside the principal's office at school. A wooden bench sat against one wall, and a tall grandfather clock sat across from it. Its gold-colored pendulum snicked back and forth. On the other side of the hall, a woman sat in a room using a sewing machine like Myrt's.

She had mousy brown hair laced with streaks of gray. Wire-rimmed glasses rested on the end of her nose. She appeared to be a solid capable woman, about sixty years old. Despite the fact that she was probably an excellent seamstress, she wore a dowdy five-and-dime housedress that swallowed her up and made her look older than her years. A yellow pencil was wedged between her teeth, and one foot jiggled up and down on a treadle under the machine.

Directly across from her was another room that resembled principal Westmore's office. The top part of the door was glass. It was closed, but a bald-headed man could be seen sitting behind a big desk. He wore a white shirt with short sleeves and a light blue bowtie. A phone receiver was sandwiched between his shoulder and ear, and he was scribbling something on a legal pad.

The woman in the other room took the pencil out of her mouth. "Hi there, Judy!" Studying Joey, she stood and ambled out into the hallway to greet them. "Who have we got here?" She smiled as she looked him over.

"Hi, Minnie. This young man is Joey Harrison, and he's come to stay with you folks for awhile." Mrs. Kellogg's chuckled and rubbed the top of Joey's head. Her laugh was less than convincing.

The woman extended her hand and he shook it. "Hello, young man. I know you probably feel a bit anxious right about now, but there's no need to be, is there, Mrs. Kellogg?"

"That's what I told him, Minnie—he's just a little shy, that's all." She glanced at the closed door across the hall.

"Mr. Neagle is on the phone," said Minnie, but he should be done shortly. Meanwhile, can I get you a cup of coffee, Judy?"

"No, thanks. I had too much coffee already, but I would like to use your washroom if you don't mind."

"Certainly." She pointed to her sewing room. "You know where it is, in the back. You go ahead. I'll just wait right here with Joey."

"I'll leave my pocketbook and briefcase here if that's all right," said Mrs. Kellogg as she laid it on the bench where Joey sat with his hands clenched between his thighs, his face downcast as though he had wet his pants.

"Well, Joey—what grade are you in school?" said Minnie. When she smiled, Joey saw that some teeth were missing. Her fingers nervously touched her earlobe.

"Fifth grade, Ma'am."

"Fifth grade, eh? Good. Lots of our kids are in the fifth grade. You'll like the school here. My, you certainly have curly hair, don't you?" She ran her hand through it and giggled. Hard to get a comb through it, I'll bet."

"Yes, Ma'am."

The office door opened and a man stood there. With a cigar sticking from the corner of his mouth. Joey thought he looked like a movie star named Edward G. Robinson. Joey had seen his picture in a *Look* magazine. Joey had never smelled a cigar before and he didn't like it. He glanced at the smoke as it billowed toward the plaster ceiling.

"And this is the young man we were expecting?"

"Yes." Minnie smiled. "Joseph Harrison, meet Mr. Neagle." They shook hands.

"Glad to meet you, Son."

Mr. Neagle was stocky with a pronounced belly, thick shoulders and chest and a huge, perfectly round face that smiled with practiced acceptance. He had removed his bowtie and his white dress shirt was mercifully unbuttoned at the collar, allowing his bulging neck to sag unrestricted. It looked like the buttons might pop off his shirt if he breathed too hard. A rain slicker hung on the coat rack together with a badly worn blazer. Joey noticed he wore a thick-looking, black belt with a silver buckle.

"Come in, Minnie. Come in." He stood behind his desk and removed the cigar from his mouth then smiled as he studied Joey. He nodded as though confirming something for himself.

"Mrs. Kellogg just went to the washroom," said Minnie. She put her hand on Joey's shoulder and looked at him. "Joey, Mr. Neagle and his wife, Emily, manage the home. You'll meet her later on. She put her hand out. "I'm Minnie Palmer, but the kids call me the sewing lady." She folded her hands and paused. "We'll take a good look at your things when you bring them in — see what you need."

Mrs. Kellogg came in. "Mr. Neagle, good to see you again," she said. "This is the young man we spoke about last week."

"Yes, name's Joey. We just met. Can we get you a cup of coffee, Judy?"

Mrs. Kellogg smiled. "No, thanks Minnie just offered. I'm fine."

Mr. Neagle sat in the shiny, wooden chair behind the desk. He put the cigar back in his mouth, leaned back and folded his hands over his belly. "Well, Joey, you'll be in cottage number four. Mrs. Alexander is the housemother down there. The boys call her 'Ma'. They think the world of her, and I'm sure you will, too." He made a steeple of his fingers. "I'll take you down there after Mrs. Kellogg leaves. You go ahead and have a seat out in the other room while she and I take care of some paperwork."

"Yes, Sir."

Joey followed Minnie out into the hallway and closed the door. "Go ahead and have a seat on the bench." She smiled and pointed.

A few moments later, the front door swung open, and a tall boy rushed in. He huffed and puffed like he had just finished running, stopped and stared at Joey.

"What do you need, Clarence?" Minnie asked.

"Uuhhh, Mrs. Campbell sent me to pick up the clothes for our cottage."

"Oh, yes. Just give me a minute." She disappeared in the back of the room, then brought out a small pile of clothes and handed them to Clarence.

"Tell Mrs. Campbell I said that's it for now. Okay, Clarence?"

"Okay." Clarence continued to stare at Joey as he ran out the door.

Minnie had Joey go out to Mrs. Kellogg's car, get his bags and bring them inside. Moments later, Mrs. Kellogg came out of Mr. Neagle's office.

Mrs. Kellogg hugged Joey. "Well, Joey, you're all set. I'll be in touch and see how you're doing. Meanwhile, you'll be in good hands here, I'm sure. I'll get back to the office." She turned. "Mr. Neagle, it's good seeing you again. You and your staff are so helpful at times like this."

"That's what we're here for," he said as they shook hands.

Mrs. Kellogg leaned forward and lowered her voice to a confidential whisper.

"Be a good boy, Joseph." She backed away. "Bye-bye." She gave him a wry smile and waved goodbye with her fingers.

After she was gone, Joey was more worried than before they had arrived. He felt his knees shake and his stomach whirled. Minnie patted him on the back. "You will be fine, Joey." She winked.

Mr. Neagle lit his cigar and blew a cloud of smoke. "Well, come along, Joey. We'll head down to your cottage."

A long winding sidewalk guided them. As they passed one cottage, Mr. Neagle said, "That's cottage number three, Joey. There's two more on the opposite end for the girls—numbers one and two. Like I said, you'll be living in number four, straight ahead."

Joey noticed a bunch of boys out in back of the cottages. They were running around yelling and laughing, having lots of fun. Some were crawling all over a giant Jungle Gym, and others were playing catch with a softball.

Joey followed Mr. Neagle up a few cement steps at cottage four. Mr. Neagle opened the door and stepped into a foyer without knocking.

A short, heavyset, sixty-ish lady greeted them. She was dressed like a spinster in a flowered dress, and her mousy gray hair was braided on top of her head. She wore tiny, wire-rimmed glasses and a broad, friendly smile. Her shoes were low and black, with tiny dots of holes in the toes. They looked like his Gram's dress-up shoes. She looked like somebody's grandmother.

"Mrs. Alexander, this is Joey Harrison, the lad we've been expecting. I've told him very little at this point, but he knows he'll be living with you and the boys in this cottage."

Mrs. Alexander smiled and folded her hands over her breast. "Hello, Joey." She had a soft, whispery voice. Even her eyes were smiley. "Welcome to your new home, young man," she said as she hugged him.

Chapter Thirty-One

T here was something about Mrs. Alexander that Joey immediately trusted. She just looked safe. As she studied him, her smile made crow's feet at the corners of her eyes; they were smiley eyes. Yet, so many different thoughts were churning around in Joey's head.

"Well, the rest of the boys are out back playing right now, Joey," she said. "I think I'll wait and introduce you when they come in for lunch, okay?"

"Yes, Ma'am."

Mr. Neagle still had a cigar tucked into the left side of his mouth. It gave the impression of having spent most of the day there. There was no smoke because it wasn't lit.

"Well, I'll be getting back up to the office," he said as he turned to leave. "Minnie is going through the rest of his clothes, and we'll send them along as soon as she's done. It'll be sometime today, though." Somehow the cigar stayed in place, bobbing up and down with his narrative.

"Yes, thank you, Mr. Neagle," said Mrs. Alexander.

Nagel looked at Joey. "You're all set, young man. I think you'll do just fine here." He paused and scratched the back of his neck. "Just pay attention to what Mrs. Alexander tells you. Go ahead and get settled in. We'll talk again later."

"Well, first of all, why not show you where you'll be sleeping?"

"Okay." He felt lost and somewhat numb as he followed her down a dark hallway.

As she went, she spoke over her shoulder. "There are 13 boys in this cottage, Joey – well 14 now, counting you."

The floor of the hallway was covered with a long, black runner made of rubber. At the end, there were dorms on both sides. The one on the left had single beds, whereas the dorm on the right contained a half a dozen bunk beds. All of the beds were uniformly covered with light blue bedspreads, decorated with off-white sailboats. Two big windows in each of the dorms had curtains that matched the spreads. The floors were maroon tiles that shone as though they had just been polished. Mrs. Alexander stepped into the dorm with the single beds.

"This is where you'll sleep. It's called the dormitory. The beds on this side of the hall are for younger boys like you, up to 11 years old. Our older boys, up to 16, sleep in the bunk beds on the other side of the hall. How old are you now, Joey?"

He paused for a long moment before he spoke. "I'll be 10 pretty soon."

"Oh—when is that?"

"June 15th, Ma'am."

"I see. Well, you're still quite a way away from 11, but you're getting there. We have to get past Christmas first, eh?" She laughed. Joey noticed that even when she wasn't smiling, she still had a nice, happy face like his Aunt Betty.

"This is your bed." She had moved over to one of the beds near the corner of the room. "You are expected to make it every morning— even on Sundays. We change sheets every other Saturday."

"Okay. I always make my bed."

"Good. Follow me now. I'll show you where everything else is." She led Joey to the bathroom, just a short way up the hall. There were six sinks, three toilets and two bathtubs. "Everyone takes a bath here on Wednesday and Saturday nights. Everything else is first come, first served so to speak. Everyone takes turns with the tubs. The older boys take theirs first."

A good-sized clothes storage room was right next door, where each boy had a small, open space to keep their clothes, including Sunday suits. Joey looked confused; he touched the sleeve of a suit. "I don't have one of these."

"Oh, don't worry—you'll be getting one. We go to church every Sunday. Minnie will take care of your suit and any other clothes you might need, Joey. Don't worry."

Mrs. Alexander led the way further up the hallway to the kitchen and dining room. They seemed huge to Joey. A very long table surrounded by straight-back chairs was in the dining room. A large hutch held dishes, glass and silverware.

To the left of that was the kitchen. It appeared to be the biggest room. One big cooking stove stood against a wall; kitchen cabinets and sinks occupied the rest of the room. The floor was square brick-colored tiles.

"You'll find that all the boys have jobs to do each day, and sometimes you will help out here in the kitchen when it's your turn."

Joey followed her into the adjoining living room where there was one big couch and two easy chairs, plus a rocking chair that sat a few feet away from a console Zenith radio. The wooden floor was covered with three circular rugs. The living room extended from the edge of the dining room all the way back to the front vestibule and door where Joey had come in with Mr. Neagle.

Mrs. Alexander sat in the rocking chair and pointed at a chair for Joey. She took out a tissue and began to clean her eyeglasses with neat, circular swipes.

"Things will all seem strange to you until you get settled in and meet the other boys, Joey, but—you'll be just fine, I promise. Now, then, we're having toasted cheese sandwiches and tomato soup for lunch today. Do you like tomato soup?"

"I don't know, Ma'am. I never had that, I don't think. My Gramps used to grow tomatoes in his garden, though, so I like tomatoes."

"It's a bit early, but my kitchen help will be in here soon to help me get things ready." She used her toes to shove her shoes off.

"You mean there's more people like you that live here, Ma'am?"

Mrs. Alexander laughed. "Heavens, no! I was talking about two of our boys. Like I said, everybody has certain jobs to do each day for a week at a time. This week, the two Houser brothers, Jimmy and Clark, have to help me in the kitchen." She paused and studied him. "I think I'll just put you on dusting to start with tomorrow until I make the schedule up for next week. You'll get your turn in the kitchen too, though."

"Yes, Ma'am. It's like some chores, you mean?"

"Yes, I guess you could call them that. You'll find we have a schedule here that we go by. We have a time to get up, times to eat, clean up time, homework time, bath time twice a week and bed time, of course. Every boy knows the routine. You will get used to it, don't worry."

"Yes, Ma'am."

"If you have any questions, be sure to ask, okay?"

"Yes, Ma'am." Joey thought for a moment, realizing he had a lot of questions. "Do you have a cellar?"

"A cellar? Why, yes, of course. I'll let you see it later, but there's nothing down there except canned food and stored things that belong to the boys. Why do you ask, Joey?"

"Nothing. I just wondered."

"You may have to go down there from time to time to fetch something for the kitchen when I ask you to, but that's the only reason. The washing machine is down there too. That's important to remember, Joey. Everybody shares the work here. We get along and help each other. The boys take turns with everything, the jobs, baths — everything, including picking their favorite radio shows. They take turns with those in order to be fair about it for all."

"Yes, Ma'am."

"We generally do some things together as a group too, though. For instance, all the children, boys *and* girls from all four cottages, walk to school together. Nobody leaves the home ahead of anyone else."

"You mean we don't ride the bus to school?"

"No. As I said they . . ."

Two boys ran inside and stumbled into the living room. "Whew!" said one.

"There they are! Hey slow down, you two!" said Mrs. Alexander. "Jimmy and Clark Houser — I want you to meet the new boy, Joey Harrison."

The two stepped up and shook hands with Joey.

"Hi!" said Clark and Jimmy.

"Hi," said Joey.

Both boys had orange hair, and freckles covered their faces and arms. Clark's top teeth stuck out with a pronounced overbite; he repeatedly licked them. Jimmy's hair grew over his ears. He wore horn-rimmed glasses and a mocking smile at the corner of his mouth. They both had rather big ears that stuck out quite a way from their heads.

"Okay," said Mrs. Alexander, "you two go ahead and set the table. Just bowls and spoons today, okay?"

"Yes, Ma," said Jimmy.

"How come he calls you 'Ma'?" Joey asked.

She smiled. "That's just what the boys have called me for years. I don't mind; in fact, I've grown used to it and I kind of like it. I feel like their moms for the most part. You'll find that even the kids from the other cottages call me 'Ma' when they see me. You can call me that if you wish. You'll probably like that better than saying Mrs. Alexander all the time, anyway." She smiled again.

"Yes, Ma'am."

"Well, we'd best be getting those sandwiches ready." She slid her feet back into her shoes and pushed her plump body up and out of the rocker.

"You come with me and watch, Joey. We can talk some more after lunch."

"Okay," Joey hopped up and followed her into the kitchen.

"Jimmy, you can open a new loaf of that Wonder Bread and lay out a bunch of slices on the kitchen table. Be sure to put the balloon on the window sill—not in your pocket. Clark, I want you to make up some butter before we get too far ahead of ourselves here."

"Ok, Ma," they answered together.

Ma eyed Joey who was staring at the balloon.

"Joey, the Wonder Bread comes with a red, white or blue balloon inside each loaf. The boys take turns keeping one when we open new loaves."

"Oh, I never heard of that before."

She gave Clark a big wooden bowl and four bricks of lard plus four packs of orange powdered coloring to mix and make oleo.

Joey remembered Beth doing the same thing for Mrs. Bushkin. He watched Clark open the packs of orange powder, empty them on top of the lard, then use a fork to smoosh it all together. It looked like butter when he finished. Clark licked his fingers when Mrs. Alexander wasn't watching.

They smeared the butter on a whole bunch of bread slices while Ma poured two huge cans of Campbell's tomato soup into a pot on the stove. She sliced pieces of cheese from a long brick she got from the icebox and placed the slices on the bread. Then she grilled them on the stove while Jimmy and Clark set the table. Aromas mixed pleasantly across the kitchen.

Ma glanced up at Joey. "You just stand there and look pretty," she said. "You'll get your turn soon enough—isn't that right, boys?"

"Yeah." The boys looked at Joey, giggled and nodded.

More boys suddenly raced in the back door all at one time and zoomed to the bathroom to wash their hands. They gawked at Joey and whispered as they shuffled down the hallway.

They all came to the table and stood behind their chairs. Ma had Joey stand next to her near the end of the table.

"Boys, I want you to meet Joey Harrison. We'll start with you, Alex, and go around the table. Tell your name; then you may sit down."

When they were done with introductions, Joey couldn't remember all the new names except for brothers, Alex and Hollis Baster. Alex was tall and thin. He had a very long neck and his Adam's apple bounced up and down when he talked. Hollis was shorter, but he was also thin and wearing glasses with thick, black frames.

Ma smiled. "Good. Now, let's say grace. Wayne, I believe it's your turn."

Wayne bowed his head and everyone did the same.

"Bless this food we are about to receive from our Lord. Amen."

In addition to the tomato soup and grilled cheese sandwiches, each boy had a tall glass of milk. Joey held his glass with both hands at his chin like a mouse nibbling on a morsel.

At first, they ate quietly. Talking was permitted at the table, but only one boy at a time was allowed to speak. Everyone else was to listen until the speaker was done.

"Summer vacation is almost over. School will start again," said Tommy Stockton.

"Yeah, but it will be time for football again, too," said Clark.

"Next week, Minnie Palmer is going to take you boys, three at a time, to get new school clothes," said Ma.

"Yaaaay!" Everyone cheered.

After lunch, it was Paul Bastar's turn to wash dishes, and Billy Borus dried. Everybody else took off for the back door to get outside and play.

"Joey, let's go back in the living room; we need to talk some more," said Ma. She sat in her rocker, nudged her shoes off and turned the radio on. Joey sat on the floor by her feet and waited. *The Romance of Helen Trent* was on. Joey recognized it from his stay with Myrt.

The end of the day was approaching, and the sky to the east was hazy with smoke the color of bone.

"I generally listen to this one every day." She turned down the volume.

"Joey, everyone in this cottage has responsibilities to both themselves and the group as a whole. We care for each other. There are certain rules to be obeyed. We won't tolerate stealing, swearing or fighting. I want to make that clear. And, like I was saying earlier, this cottage is your home, and you're all brothers here. Just treat everybody with respect. You know what that is — right?"

"Yes, Ma'am. I've got three brothers, but I don't know, where they are right now. I think my twin brothers, Mitchell and Merrill, live at the Matthews' house — but I'm not sure. Then there's Brian. Plus I've got a sister too; her name is Beth."

Ma looked at him with concern. "Well, I'm sure they'll be all right, wherever they are. You've met all of the boys in this cottage except for Jimmy Richmond."

"I just met Jimmy, I thought."

Ma Alexander giggled. "Yes, but we have two Jimmy's. You met Jimmy Houser, Clark's brother. The other Jimmy, Jimmy Richmond, just got back about an hour ago; he was away visiting his folks in Syracuse."

"Wow! He got to do that?"

"Yes. Some of our boys do get to visit relatives from time to time. Jimmy's down in the dorm unpacking right now. I noticed you had that one small bag you brought with you. The sewing lady, Minnie, has your other bags, doesn't she?"

"Yes, Ma'am."

"Well, you can go to the dorm and meet Jimmy. Put your things away and chat." She smiled. "He can tell you all about the woods out back and the football team the boys have here. Do you have any questions for me yet?"

"No, ma'am—not right now I don't."

"Well, after you put your things away, maybe you'll want to go outside and play. We have nearly twelve acres to roam on, out back. The boys are probably playing on the hills near the woods. Would you like to go out there with them for the afternoon? Good way to get acquainted, don't you think?"

"No, Ma'am, I don't really want to."

•   •   •   •   •

Joey found Jimmy stretched out on his bed. He was a short and bony boy with curly brown hair. His face was tear-stained and he sniffled when Joey sat down on the bed across from him.

"What's wrong?" said Joey.

"Nothin'," Jimmy said curtly. He bit his lower lip, then flipped over and looked the other way.

Joey thought about it for a moment, then went to the clothing room and put the few things he had away. He went back into the dorm and stretched out on his bed. A moment later, Jimmy spoke in a hushed voice.

"My mom and dad got mad at each other since I was there at Christmastime, and now Dad is moving away to California. I think they're getting a divorce."

"Gee! That's awful," said Joey.

"Yeah, I know, and now I'll never see him again. He says I will— but I know I won't."

"Well, I never see my mom or dad. I only got to see my Uncle Glenn and Aunt Betty one time and my mommy once since I've been in the foster places. My sister was with me for a long time, but they took her away too."

"So? Big deal!" said Jimmy. "Who cares about your old sister?"

There was an oppressive silence in the room.

"I do," said Joey.

Chapter Thirty-Two

Joey became friends with Alex Baster. Both Alex, and his brother Hollis, had been in The Home for over three years. Alex's background was similar to Joey's in that he had been in two other foster homes before being placed at The Children's Home. Neither of them had heard from their fathers in over four years. The Baster brother's mother died two years earlier in a car accident near Buffalo, New York.

On school days, all the children living at The Home, both boys and girls, met at 7:30 in the morning behind Mr. and Mrs. Neagle's living quarters, located at the west end of the complex. Mrs. Neagle came out on the back porch and surveyed the crowd with her eyes in an inspection of sorts, and then waved. The wave was the signal that she was satisfied with the count and their appearance. From there, no matter what the weather was like, the children walked as a group to Franklin Elementary school nearly six blocks away.

In school, Alex stayed as close as possible and guided Joey around. He introduced him to some of his friends who were outsiders—meaning, they didn't live at The Home. Alex warned Joey about a boy named Hank Jurgess right away, confiding that Hank was the biggest bully in the school, a powerful brute with the brains of a stump, who seldom passed up an opportunity to call names and throw punches in the hallway.

The boys both had the same homeroom teacher, Mr. Thompson, and Joey was impressed with him from the very first day. He was a thirty-five-year-old of medium height, with a thick neck and broad shoulders like a gymnast's. His nose looked as though it'd been hit once or twice too often. He had strong features: piercing eyes, wide mouth, a square jaw and a crown of curly brown hair. Teachers called him Max and some referred to him as The Gyrene.

Mr. Thompson made Joey feel accepted from the very first day.

"Joey Harrison, eh? Welcome to my class, Son." His right hand shot out like a boxing punch bound for Joey's stomach, but he stopped short of course, and grinned from ear-to-ear. "Gotcha," he said and Joey was smiling as he edged over to his desk and took a seat.

A decorated United States Marine, Maxwell Thompson's expertise was English, but he also supervised gym classes. An expert acrobat, he had some experience in the entertainment field and worked with *Fuller Brothers Traveling Circus* during summer vacation and as Joey would soon learn, he was admired by the students and teachers alike.

The kids had never seen him perform but they'd seen snapshots that Mr. Thompson brought in one day. The pictures showed him perched on a trapeze, walking a wire, and posing under a big top tent with sideshow people and clowns. Joey was very impressed.

Blocked, gold lettering on the opaque window of Mr. Thompson's classroom door said "Semper Fidelis."

"What do those words mean?" Joey asked Alex who stood by his side one day in the hall as the other kids were shuffling into the room. Mr. Thompson overheard.

"Ahh... you mean Semper Fidelis?" said Mr. Thompson. He pointed to the door.

"Yes, Sir."

"That is the Marine Corps motto, my boy. It's Latin and it means, "Always Faithful." It's pretty important to be faithful, wouldn't you say, Joe?" He grinned as he ushered the boys into his room. Over his shoulder, he said, "Do you know what faithful means, boys?"

"Ummm. I think so, Sir." said Joey. "I think it means to be good to people."

"No. I think it means that people can trust you, right?" said Alex.

Mr. Thompson chuckled. "Well, I guess that's close, boys. But it actually means you're dependable... you'll always be there for your buddies—for the ones you care about."

"Oh," said Joey. "Gee, that's swell." The boys stared at the writing a moment longer before they took their seats.

•　　•　　•　　•　　•

As the days slipped by, Joey grew to admire Mr. Thompson and looked forward to seeing him each day. He managed to maintain average grades and stayed out of any sort of trouble that was serious enough to warrant a visit to the principal's office. He also found life in general much easier to deal with than he had in a very long time. Although he still missed his family, he began to fit in thanks in large part to Ma Alexander's kindness and understanding. Mr. Thompson's strong personality and solid image meant so much to him. Joey thought about how great it would be to have a father just like Mr. Thompson.

One morning Mr. Thompson was standing by his door and grabbed Joey by circling one arm around his neck in a wrestler's hold and then he fluffed his hair. "Good morning, hotshot!" he said as he quickly released Joey, stepped back and grinned. He patted Joey on the back. "Come on in, Joe... the water's fine."

After the Pledge of Allegiance, Mr. Thompson always told the class a joke to get the class started on the right foot and wake up the sleepyheads. Sitting back in his chair, he twiddled a pencil between his fingers as he selected a different student each day.

"Charles! Knock! Knock!"

"Who's there?" said Charles.

"Boo!" said Mr. Thompson.

"Boo, who?" said Charles.

Mr. Thompson waved his hand at Charles. "Ah, never mind if you're gonna cry about it, Charles," said Mr. Thompson. The kids loved it.

In gym class, after jumping jacks and dodge ball, Mr. Thompson had the kids lay out mats and taught them tumbling and acrobatics. They learned how to build human pyramids, do headstands, back-flips and cartwheels. They also learned how to shimmy up a fifteen-foot rope and come back down again, using hand over hand techniques. Mr. Thompson was practicing his own skills also, both after school and on weekends at the gym.

•　　•　　•　　•　　•

One day in early May, Mr. Thompson announced that students would be putting on a program showing everything they had learned in acrobatics. The entire student body and their parents would be invited. In the case of the kids from the orphanage, Mr. and Mrs. Neagle would be asked to attend.

Teachers passed out fliers for each student to take home. It explained that the fifth and sixth grade boys would be putting on an exhibition at the school. It announced the date and time of the show. In addition, it said that Mr. Thompson would be performing some of his trapeze and rope skills as a special treat for the community. Everyone was excited, especially Joey.

•　　　•　　　•　　　•　　　•

At The Home all homework had to be finished before the boys were allowed to go out back and play. The kitchen helpers were kept inside to help Ma prepare for supper.

The girls living at The Home had the same responsibilities. They were also allowed to play in back of the cottages but were not to venture past the administration building which separated the boys and girls cottages. The building was the known "line in the sand" that separated the two.

At the supper table, Ma Alexander sometimes said she would be reading a story before bedtime, when everybody was washed up and in their pajamas. It was a favorite time for the boys. Most nights they gathered around the radio and listened to shows like *Little Orphan Annie, Captain Midnight, Amos n' Andy, Fibber Magee and Molly* or *Edgar Bergen and Charley McCarthy.* But when Ma said she would read a story everybody got excited, preferring storytelling over the radio.

The boys jostled for position at her feet for the readings which could last up to an hour. Ma sat in her rocker and read chapters from thick books with hard covers. It was not uncommon to see one boy jab another with his elbow if that boy was falling asleep during the reading because Ma might start thinking everyone was sleepy and stop reading.

The first time Joey got to listen to the reading Ma was on chapter 26 of a novel called *"Old Shep."* Alex had prepped Joey ahead of time, telling him it was a sad story about a dog named Shep who lived on a farm with a cruel master.

The week before the school show, the boys were clustered around the radio in their pajamas, listening to *The Green Hornet.* Ma Alexander sat in her rocker, crocheting. She pushed her glasses up on her nose with a forefinger against the bridge.

The telephone rang. It was located in Ma's bedroom which was situated at the far end of the living room. It rang four times, when Ma put her needlework down and got up.

"Move boys — shoo! Let me get by," she said and threaded her way through to head for her room. As usual, she closed the door when she talked on the phone.

A few moments passed before she came out and moved rather slowly back to her rocker. She removed her glasses and wiped her eyes with a tissue, then bent down and turned the radio off.

"Oooooh!" said Clark. "How come you. . . ."

Ma Alexander raised her hands as if to ward off a blow. "Shhhhhh! Please hush, Clark. Boys, I have something important to tell you." She paused and went silent. The boys endured another long moment before she sighed and said, "That was Mr. Neagle. It's about Mr. Thompson . . ."

Tears tumbled over the rim of her gray eyes and slid down her cheeks. "Mister Thompson has died."

Complete silence fell on the room. Ma paused, then held her hand to her breast, and struggled to continue. "He passed away around five o'clock at the school gymnasium."

Obviously shaken, the housemother tried to continue. She sniffed and swiped at her dripping nose with a disintegrating tissue.

"There was an accident... he fell off a rope while he was practicing for the gymnastics program."

A collective gasp went up from all the boys still gathered on the floor by the radio. Everyone was silent for a moment before the crying began from some, while others simply stared at Ma, in disbelief.

Joey slowly got to his feet and shook his head. He felt the color drain out of his face. A lump of cement formed in his stomach. His gaze slid away from Ma Alexander, his mouth turning down at the corners. He suddenly felt like he was inside of a bubble, and if he dared to move again, the bubble would burst and all sorts of feelings would wash over him and he would drown. His body shook uncontrollably and his knees began to give way, but he ran to the dorm and sprawled face-down on his bed and sobbed.

It was all so unbelievable. How could this be? Joey wondered. Wiping his nose on the sleeve of his pajamas, he settled onto his back and squeezed his eyes shut.

Alex and Jimmy quietly came into the dorm and sat on their beds. Both of them were crying. Nobody spoke.

Ma Alexander came down the hall and stood in the doorway. The remainder of the boys followed behind her. Some sat on their beds—others wandered about their dorms aimlessly.

"Boys, I know this is very difficult to understand and it hurts our hearts so terribly, but we must honor Mr. Thompson by letting our sadness give way." She paused again. "Let the joy of knowing such a wonderful man keep you going forward." She paused and scanned the room, noting each boy's reaction. "I want each of you to kneel and say a special prayer for Mr. Thompson before you get into bed."

She understood how impressed Joey had been with Mr. Thompson and saw that he was taking the news very hard. However, she felt it best not to single him out in front of the other boys by showing extra attention.

"It will be alright, you'll see." She paused a moment before turning off the light. "Goodnight boys."

Joey couldn't stop crying and trembling. After he kneeled and said his prayers, he lay awake in the dark and stared at the ceiling. His thoughts were scrambled. Tears filled his eyes over and over again. Pressing his body into the bed, he wrapped his arms around his pillow, pretending his sister, Beth, was holding him tight... telling him everything would be all right—that he didn't have to be afraid.

He simply could not fathom that Mr. Thompson was gone... really gone forever. He thought about the days ahead... days without his hero. Much later, he flipped over onto his back and pulled the covers up around his chin and tried to sleep.

His day to day existence had been so orderly and scheduled. Up at seven, breakfast at seven fifteen, to school by eight twenty. Then, he always saw the man who had become so important in his life standing there by the door to his room. *Semper Fidelis,* he thought. He was sure Mr. Thompson considered him special and perhaps loved him like a son. But, Mr. Thompson was gone.

School would never be the same... nor would Joey.

Chapter Thirty-Three

When winds gusted and red and yellow leaves tumbled from the trees, it was September in upper New York State and school resumed. Franklin Elementary School's name was changed to M. L. Thompson Elementary School. Joey felt warm inside on hearing about the change, but he cried when he was alone.

Christmas was right around the corner and a new year was in sight.

From time to time, one or more of the boys left the cottage for a visit with relatives. Generally they'd be gone for the entire weekend — perhaps longer for holidays. At times like that, Joey became withdrawn. He felt as though everyone had deserted him and he found it difficult to sleep. His real family occupied his mind day and night. He couldn't understand why Mrs. Kellogg had not come by to see him. He was told she had visited Mr. Neagle, but had a "tight schedule" that day and left without seeing Joey.

Hollis Bastar and his brother Paul went home with their mother during the Thanksgiving holiday. Jimmy Richmond left for Carthage to be with his grandmother and Charles Faddnish went to visit with his family in nearby Messina. When Joey heard this, his heart ached. With that many boys gone during the holiday, he felt left out and all alone. There were worse things than being alone. But as he sat there on his bed after school that day, he had a hard time thinking what they were.

Why hasn't Mommy or Daddy or Beth called or me? Christmas is coming pretty soon. Why hasn't Mrs. Kellogg come back? Is Brian all right now? What about Mitchell and Merrill? Joey's stomach churned when he dwelled on his situation. He was happy for the other boys, but envious. Two days after Thanksgiving, the kids returned to school, but Joey found it difficult to work on the Christmas projects in class as he worried about Christmas without his family again.

In early December, Ma Alexander met him at the door when he got home from school. She had been working in the kitchen and wiped her hands on a dish towel as she spoke. "Joey, I have something important to tell you." She smiled with a thousand watts of unconditional love, as she ran her fingers through his tousled hair.

"Tell me what, Ma."

She took a half step back, her face carefully blank. "Your caseworker came by today."

"Mrs. Kellogg? Really?" He bit his lip against a threatening smile.

"Yes, she said she was sorry she missed you, Joey. She did leave us with some good news though. You're going to your aunt and uncle's for Christmas."

"What? Wow! Really?" Joey jumped up and down. "No kidding... for sure?"

"Yes," she nodded. "It's for sure. They'll pick you up the day Christmas vacation starts. You'll be there for a little over a week. What do you think of that?"

Joey had tears in his eyes. His mind was spinning out of control as he wrapped his arms around Ma's waist. "Wow! I'm so happy, Ma. I wanted to go home for so long!

"Yes, I know that, Son. I'm so happy for you."

Joey paused for a second or two. "Did she say whether Beth and the other kids would be there too?"

Ma wrapped her arm around his shoulders and smiled. "No, she didn't mention your sister or brothers, but I think it's just wonderful for you. Maybe they will be there too. You never know." Her eyes glistened as she looked into his smiling face. I am so happy for you, Joey."

•   •   •   •   •

Uncle Glenn and Aunt Betty were there to pick him up at 9:00 a.m. on December twentieth. The morning had dawned rudely with a blast of air sweeping down from the Artic bringing below zero temperatures.

Mrs. Neagle waited with Joey at the administration building. It was icy cold, but a beautiful day with sunshine and a pastel blue sky. They could have waited in the warm vestibule, but at 8:55 Joey told Mrs. Neagle he wanted to wait out front. She understood Joey's anxiety and went out there with him. Folding her arms around herself to ward off the cold, she alternated a little toe-tapping from one foot to the other in order to keep her feet warm. The cold seemed to seep through skin to her bones.

"Brrrr!" she said. "You're awfully excited, aren't you?" Her breath came out of her mouth and went up around her head like smoke from a chimney.

"Yes, Ma'am, I am." He grinned. "I can't help it."

She smiled. "Do your aunt and uncle have a big house?"

Joey's hands were shoved deep inside his coat pockets as he tapped his boots together back and forth repeatedly. "No, Ma'am. They live in a trailer next to Uncle Glenn's gas station. It's not awful big. That's why I can't stay there while my mommy and daddy get things worked out."

"I see."

"I'll probably stay with Gramps, anyways though. Mrs. Kellogg told me last time I saw her that my Gramps was getting better. He was sick for a long time because of his bad heart. Did you know that already, Ma'am?"

"Oh no, I didn't know that. Well, I'm sure everybody's looking forward to your visit, especially this time of year." Her long skirt whirled around her legs like a matador's cape. "Listen, Joey, I think we should go back inside until they get here. It's very cold out here."

Joey looked disappointed. "Yes, Ma'am.

As if by magic at that very moment, a dark blue sedan turned in the drive coming in from State Street.

"Here they come! Here they come!" Joey yelled. He began to edge down the driveway and slipped on some ice, nearly tumbling over.

"Hold on! Hold on, Joey! Wait!" Mrs. Neagle waved her arm in windmill fashion, beckoning him back. "You don't want to get run over; they'll park right here. Just hold up and come back here, young man."

Joey shuffled back and stood next to her but continued to jump up and down. He shielded his eyes from the morning sun and attempted to peer inside the car. He saw Aunt Betty in the passenger side and spotted Beth waving from the back seat.

"Yup! It's them!" Joey couldn't stop waving before the car stopped right in front of them. Aunt Betty was the first to climb out. Reaching for Joey, she hugged him tight and squeezed.

"Oh, Sonny!" She looked into his face like she was searching for something. "Oh! God in heaven, Sonny, we missed you so much."

Beth was right behind her, followed by Uncle Glenn. "Hey, Sport!" Uncle Glenn reached for him, and after a brief hug, Joey edged past him to get to his sister.

"Sis!" Joey exclaimed as he hugged her. They both cried and hugged and kissed each other on the face. "Sis, I can't believe it's really you!"

"Joey! Joey! At last!" Beth yelled. Her eyes were intense and wet with tears. "You're right here in front of me. I'm touching you! I can't believe it!" She reached up and brushed a tear from her cheek. "Hey! You've changed — you're so tall." She drew him in and squeezed him. She sniffed and wiped her nose on the back of her hand. "Oh, I missed you so much!"

"I missed you, too — awful, awful bad."

"You're looking good, Sport." Uncle Glenn's arm circled Joey's shoulders and tugged.

"Beth is right. You have grown so tall," Aunt Betty added. She looked at Mrs. Neagle and smiled. "I'm sorry. We didn't mean to ignore you, Ma'am. You must be Mrs. Neagle."

"Yes, I'm Emily Neagle, the superintendent's wife. Jeff will be along shortly, and believe me, I don't feel the least bit slighted. It warms my heart to see these reunions. Why don't we all go inside and warm up?"

"Good idea," said Aunt Betty. "I'm Betty Powest — Joey's aunt, and this is my husband, Glenn." They all shook hands and followed

Emily to the front door.

Mrs. Neagle glanced at Beth. "And you must be Joey's sister, Elizabeth."

"Yes, Ma'am," said Beth, as she looked at Joey and smiled. "I'm Beth."

Aunt Betty fluffed Joey's hair. "You and that mop of curly hair, Sonny." She paused. "Just like your father's."

"Mr. Neagle gives us haircuts all the time. It's still hard for me to comb, though."

"We should only stay for a few minutes, Betty," said Uncle Glenn. He opened the trunk of the car and put Joey's suitcase inside.

Joey held Beth's hand. He looked at her and made an impatient face, rolling his eyes. "I just want to leave," he whispered.

"Mr. Neagle is taking care of another matter at cottage three," said Mrs. Neagle as she led them into her husband's office. "He should be along shortly. Of course, he wants to meet all of you if you don't mind."

"Yes. That will be fine," said Uncle Glenn.

"Have a seat, Betty." said Mrs. Neagle. "Can I get you folks a cup of coffee?"

"No, that's all right," said Aunt Betty. "We can't stay long. It's quite a drive back and the radio is predicting more snow. You know how that is."

Mrs. Neagle nodded. "I understand. I don't think we have to worry about having a white Christmas." She giggled. "So, Mr. Powest, Joey was telling us you own a business. A gas station, I believe?"

"Yes, it's the Mobil, over in Gouvernuer. There's only one other station around there besides mine. Joey told you all about that, eh?" He smiled and glanced at Joey.

"Oh, yes. He's talked about you folks a lot since he's been here. We're just so delighted that you can take him for the holiday. As you can imagine, the children need family so badly, but many of them don't get that opportunity, unfortunately."

"Yes," said Aunt Betty. "We wish we could have taken their

brothers for Christmas too, but there's only so much we can do, you know. I guess they're doing fine where they are, though, so at least we know they're in good hands."

Joey heard Aunt Betty and guilt nipped him immediately. He said, "Is Gramps okay?"

"Yes, Joey." She had a half smile on her face. "He's doing fine right now, and he's so excited that you're coming home."

"Yeah," said Uncle Glenn. "They told me I'd better not come back home without you, Sport."

Everyone laughed just as the outside door banged and Mr. Neagle entered. He stomped snow off of his boots and removed his steam-covered glasses. The end of his nose was red from the cold. The stub of a cigar was stuck in the corner of his mouth. He smiled at the visitors.

"Hi, I'm Jeff Neagle." He laid his glasses on his desk and shook hands with Uncle Glenn, Aunt Betty and Beth as his wife made the introductions. He scratched a match on his pant leg and lit his cigar. They all stood in silence for a moment as the smoke drifted above his head like a wreath. Yanking a white handkerchief from his rear pocket, he wiped his glasses, then sat down behind the desk, winked and grinned at Joey.

"Ahh, yes—Joey." He smiled at Aunt Betty and Uncle Glenn. "This young man has been on pins and needles ever since we told him you were coming, folks."

Beth smiled. "He couldn't be much more excited than I am," she said. "I still can't believe I'm seeing my brother. It's been such a long time."

"Well, I think Joey will be the first to tell you folks, The Home is a pretty decent place to live," said Mrs. Neagle. "But of course, there's nothing like real family."

"We've heard nothing but good things about The Home. That's for sure, Emily. Judy Kellogg says there's none better. She wishes she could place more children here."

Mr. Neagle put his cigar in an ashtray, then rose from the chair and walked back and forth behind the desk with his hands in his pockets. "That's very kind of her. Mrs. Kellogg is a fine caseworker."

A brief lull in the conversation prefaced Aunt Betty's next words.

"Yes, well, I think we'd best be going, Glenn. We still have a long drive home, and God only knows how the roads are going to be, you know." She smiled at Mr. and Mrs. Neagle... "Thank goodness for chains, eh?"

"Of course, Mrs. Powest, we understand," said Mrs. Neagle.

Beth and Joey were on their way out the door when Uncle Glenn stopped. "What day does Joey have to be back again?"

Mr. Neagle leaned back in his chair and took a deep breath. "Well, as long as he's back at least one day before school starts again, you can have him as long as you want. We like at least one day to get the children settled in before they go back. So, that would mean you'd have him back here fairly early on the second of January."

"Yes, they'll be going back to school on the third," added Mrs. Neagle.

"We'll have him back in time, and thanks for everything," said Uncle Glenn as he continued to walk out.

"Yes, thanks to both of you folks. We appreciate everything you've been doing to help Joey," said Aunt Betty.

All the adults shook hands again at the outside door. "Have a Merry Christmas, folks," said Mr. Neagle.

"Happy Holidays to you both," said Aunt Betty.

"Merry Christmas!" said Joey. He ran out to the car and climbed in the back seat with Beth. Aunt Betty sat in the front with Uncle Glenn. As they pulled out, Joey turned to wave goodbye, but Mr. and Mrs. Neagle had already disappeared.

Joey and Beth burst out laughing and hugging one another. "I can't believe this!" Joey shouted. "I'm going home — really going home. We're all going to be together again. I'll get to see Mommy and Daddy too maybe. I'm so happy right now. I don't ever want to go back, Uncle Glenn. I want to stay happy just like this forever."

Chapter Thirty-Four

I t was thirty-five miles from Watertown to Gram and Gramps' house in Gouverneur. Route Eleven was snow-covered and Uncle Glenn had to drive slower than usual. It had begun to snow less than ten minutes after they left the Children's Home and Joey was getting anxious. Everyone in the car had so much to talk about while Uncle Glenn concentrated on driving, but still managed to inject his thoughts from time to time.

"You think you remember where Aunt Betty and I live, Sport?"

"I'm not sure, Uncle Glenn, but I'll bet I can tell pretty soon, when we get into town, I mean."

There was a brief gap in the conversation as they approached Main Street in Gouverneur. The windshield wipers slapped back and forth and the tire chains *thump-thump-thumped* inside the fenders.

Aunt Betty breathed a noticeable sigh of relief. "Thank goodness, we're almost home. I hate driving in this stuff, kids. Uncle Glenn will tell you."

"She hates driving in this stuff," said Uncle Glenn.

Everyone laughed except Aunt Betty.

Christmas decorations were everywhere. Huge green wreaths with red ribbon adorned light poles and Christmas lights of red, blue, green and orange could be seen in every store window as well as silver and red garland. Last minute Christmas shoppers zipped in and out of stores, and with school out, the sidewalks were sprinkled with children running every which way in the falling snow.

Snow was piled between the sidewalk and the road, rising up like a miniature mountain range through which passes had been cut at thirty foot intervals. Joey spotted Uncle Glenn's Mobil gas station just beyond the blinking stop light in the center of town.

"There it is!" He pointed. "There's the flying red horse sign and that's your house, right next to the gas station, just like it always was — right, Uncle Glenn?"

"Yes, you're right, Sonny. That's it all right. Okay, I'm going to drop Aunt Betty off here at home, so she can get some supper ready. You and me and Beth are going to Gram and Gramps' house. They're probably worried sick about us. They're so anxious to see you — aren't they, Beth?"

"They sure are. Gram cried when Uncle Glenn told them we were driving to Watertown to get you."

"I missed them a lot, too," said Joey. "I missed all of you so bad. It was awful not seeing you for so long."

The snowfall grew heavier, with bigger flakes by the time Uncle Glenn pulled up to Gram and Gramps' house on Depot Street. Joey could hardly contain himself. His insides shook and it was difficult to breathe. Beth squeezed his hand and smiled.

"Look! They've got the Christmas tree right in the front window where they always put it," said Joey. "Wow!" He flung his door open and sprinted to the back door of the little house.

Alice was in the kitchen helping Gram with supper. When Joey opened the door she rushed to him with tears in her eyes. Wrapping her arms around him, she pulled him into herself, and sobbed. "Joey! Oh, my God, Joey! I'm so glad you're here, Son. Mommy loves you." She held him tight. "I've missed you so much!" She stepped back and kissed him repeatedly all over his face and pulled him back into her arms. "My heart has ached for you," she murmured.

Joey nodded. He believed the pain in her eyes was real and he cried with her. "I love you too, Mommy." They lingered in the embrace for a moment before Joey finally said, "Where's Daddy?"

"Oh, Joey. I just knew you would be disappointed, but your Daddy is in New York City for Christmas. It couldn't be helped. It's for the company he works for and he couldn't make it home for the holidays. I'm so sorry, Son."

Joey studied her eyes. "Gosh, I really wanted to see Daddy. I missed him just like I missed you and everybody else. When is he coming home?"

A few heartbeats went by before Alice spoke again. The room went still.

"We're not sure, Son." She looked away, avoiding his eyes. "God help me, I'm not sure. I wish I could give you a better answer, but I just can't."

Gram watched and waited her turn with tears in her eyes. She swiped a fresh tissue under her nose and crunched it into the shape of a carnation. She sobbed loudly the second she got her arms around Joey. Squeezing him hard, she giggled a bit—then cried some more. Her arms felt so good to Joey-warm, soft and secure. As she planted kisses all over his face, the smell of wine on her breath brought back memories of old for him.

"Sonny, you're really here! You're home! Let me look at you. Are you okay?" After a quick check, Gram drew him back into her arms and hugged some more before Alice took over and trembled as she hugged him again. "Oh, Joey, my big boy, I'm so glad you're home."

Gramps sat in his rocker next to the Christmas tree, the smell of his pipe drifted through the air. "What's all the commotion out there, Lillian?" he called from the front room. He got up and pretended not to recognize Joey as he edged into the kitchen. He was using a cane, and his gait was very slow as he approached Joey. He had lost a great amount of weight, and although his belly was still rather big, his face and arms were much thinner than Joey remembered. His hands were frail-looking—the color of skim milk.

Gramps grinned. "And, who's this stranger you brought with you, Glenn?" He winked and quickly turned his attention to Joey. "Oh, good Lord, it's Sonny!" He chuckled. "You've grown some, Boy!" He circled his free arm around Joey's shoulders and squeezed. With his classic Gramps smile he said, "It's sure good to have you home, Sonny." His eyes glistened with tears of happiness.

"He's shot up since we last saw him, hasn't he Pa?"

"Yes indeed. What a big lad. He sure looks like big Joe even more now. Don't you think, Lillian?"

"Yes, he's Joe Harrison's boy, all right." Gram spoke with a distinct air of disappointment while Alice stood off to the side blowing her nose into a handkerchief.

Joey clung to Gramps. "I missed you awful bad, Gramps. I thought about you a whole bunch, especially when I heard trains at night."

"Well, we thought about you all the time too, Sonny. I think the railroad misses us both." He grinned and gave Joey's shoulder another squeeze.

Joey sniffed at the air. "It sure smells good in here, Gram. What are you makin'?"

"Now, wouldn't you just like to know, big boy?" She tugged on the bottom of his ear. "I've got pies in the oven for the big Christmas dinner tomorrow, but the rest is for supper, and it's a surprise." She smiled. "You'll see soon enough, I promise."

Joey thought Gram looked older. Her hair, that used to be streaked with gray, was all gray now. Her face had become more wrinkled and was even more drawn and withered; the pouches of skin under her eyes seemed to be inflated.

Glenn said, "You might not want to count on me for supper, Ma. I didn't know you expected me to stay. Betty is already cooking supper for me and Eric. Eric was staying over at his friend, Chuck's house, but he should be home by now."

"Now, Glenn, don't be talking any such thing," said Gram. "This is special, and I promised Beth I'd make it for Joey's first night home. So, you just go have a seat in the other room with your pa. Things will be ready shortly, and I'm sure Betty won't mind. Go on now."

Gramps shrugged. "You should know better than to argue with your mother, Glenn." He ruffled Joey's hair absently as he slowly made his way back to the living room.

Joey followed and sat cross-legged on the floor by the tree and stared at the bubble lights. Gramps tapped his pipe on the ashtray. "Come on in here and sit, Beth. Leave your grandma be with the cooking for now. You can do that anytime... your brother's home."

"Okay, Gramps," said Beth. She rushed into the front room and sat next to Joey to admire the tree for a few minutes. Glenn leaned back on the couch and crossed his ankles.

"Doesn't this feel good, Sis?" said Joey. He squeezed her arm and grinned. "I mean here we are all sitting by the tree together again? I thought about this a lot—didn't you?"

"Yes, I really love this house and missed you last Christmas. Mom said she went to Ellisburg to see you. I was so mad I cried because I didn't get to go with her. And there was no phone here, so I couldn't even call. You must know I would have if I could."

Alice was in the kitchen, keeping her mother company, as she scurried back and forth from ice box to stove, banging pans and muttering under her breath. Gram refused to let Alice help, but they shared jelly glasses of wine from the gallon jug of Gallo that sat on the kitchen table. Gram paused from time to time to sip from her glass and puff on a Chesterfield that burned away in an ashtray nearby.

Joey couldn't take his eyes off his grandfather who was busy chatting with Uncle Glenn. He saw how thin Gramps' face looked. His huge muscular arms were no more. Mrs. Kellogg had said that he was getting better, but to Joey, he looked sick. There was a strange calm in his eyes and he spoke with more reserve. He leaned back in his chair and appeared to be looking off into the past. At one point, he shook his head, started to speak, but then puffed on his pipe and lowered his eyes. He stared at the floor and let his hands dangle uselessly off to the sides of his rocker.

"Well, you know, Truman won't put up with that nonsense," said Uncle Glenn.

"No, I don't imagine he will, even though MacArthur is right, as far as I'm concerned," he said on a cloud of smoke. He hesitated longer than he should have then continued. "What a doggone mess. First we had Germany, then Japan, and now Korea." He shook his head and paused. "Say, before I forget, did Charley Fedders get a hold of you? He stopped by here and said your station was closed up. He needed a fuel pump for his tractor."

"Yeah, he came by Thursday," said Uncle Glenn. "He always gets so durn jumpy, you know. I can't be there every minute, but some people like him expect me to sleep there, I guess."

"Yeah—Charley is a Nervous Nelly, all right. He always was. Anyway, it wouldn't surprise me a bit to see old Harry give MacArthur the boot pretty quick."

"You might be right," said Gramps. "But, I can't say as I blame the General for his stand either, you know? He's a good man, that one."

Soon, Gram called from the dining room. "Come on, everybody, soup's on." She quickly finished swallowing a glass of wine as everyone took their seats. Alice brought a bowl of canned corn and a platter of biscuits to the table and finished her drink before she sat next to Gramps.

"We're having Sonny's favorite tonight, everybody," said Gram. "Boiled macaroni, potatoes and onions, fried in bacon grease."

Joey grinned. "Yaaaay! Thank you, Gram! I haven't had this since we left here." An obvious silence fell over the room for a moment after that.

Gram managed a smile. "Well, it's simple enough to make, you know. I just fry the macaroni and potatoes with the grease until they're nice and shiny. Some of it even gets burned just a tad—same as the onions, but that's the way Joey likes it." She glanced at him and winked. "And I don't think anybody minds, Sonny."

"And thick brown gravy too," said Gramps, as he poured some over his potatoes. "Plus your Gram's canned corn. You couldn't ask for better than this, my boy."

"Well, we've got apple pie for dessert, too, Old Man... so you'd best leave room," said Gram.

"I just love your cooking, Gramma," said Joey. "This is so good. I missed this stuff. I remember you called it potato goulash."

Alice patted his arm. "I'm so glad you're home, Joey. We love you." She smiled. "And you'll have fun with Eric for a few days. I know you will."

"Well, what's the plan now, Glenn?" Gramps asked. He sipped his coffee, his eyes straight ahead as the steam fogged over his glasses. "How long is our boy going to be staying?"

Glenn took a sip of his coffee. "Well, Pa, Alice and I talked and we figured Sonny could stay with us a couple of nights first. Him and

Eric can catch up and play together. Then, if you don't mind, I thought he could spend Christmas Eve and Christmas morning with us then we'll all drive over here for dinner on Christmas Day, like we always do. I hadn't really planned anything beyond that. He's all yours for the rest of the time.

"Sounds good to me," said Gram.

Alice kissed Joey on the cheek. "I'll miss you, but I'll be right here when you get back, Son. Have fun at Uncle Glenn's."

Joey looked torn. He shifted in his chair, his expression, half scowl, half pout, like a petulant student trying to act tough in the principal's office. "But that way, I won't get to be with Beth on Christmas morning, like we used to."

"Well no — not first thing in the morning," said Uncle Glenn. "But, we just figured you'd be here with your mother and Gram and Gramps most of the time and Aunt Betty wants you at our place for a bit. Santa Claus will come to both places anyway, you know." He winked.

Joey looked at his mother. "Why can't Brian and Mitchell and Merrill be here too, Mommy?"

Alice sank back in her chair and cleared her throat. She was obviously holding back tears when she said, "The caseworker said it wouldn't be a good idea to do that, Honey. You must believe I wanted all of you to be together for Christmas, but Mrs. Kellogg denied my request." She hesitated for a moment. "I wasn't going to tell you this, but I've been sick too, Joey." Tears trickled down her cheeks. "I'm so sorry."

Joey got up and hugged his mother around the neck. "It's okay, Mommy. I still get to spend lots of time here with you and everybody. When Daddy gets back we can get our own house and be all together. Isn't that right?" A long pause followed.

"Mrs. Kellogg said so," Joey added, as he waited for an answer.

Alice nodded and wiped her eyes with her handkerchief.

"Sure we will, Joey," said Beth.

Joey's face suddenly looked drawn. "I don't even want to think about going back," he said.

•   •   •   •   •

It snowed Christmas Eve. Big flakes drifted down and buried Uncle Glenn's car, parked by the gas station. Glenn shoved his hands into his pockets and hunched his shoulders against the cold. The cold air sliced at his lungs, each ragged breath like a thousand knives. He sniffed and spit a glob of mucus in the snow.

The wind skimmed over the snow, lifting a fine powder into the air so that, from the end of the driveway, the trailer appeared shrouded in a mist. The gas station was closed, and he had begun to busy himself, shoveling the walkway leading up to the front door of the trailer.

Aunt Betty listened to Bob Hope emceeing the USO show on the radio, as she bustled about the kitchen preparing her specialty fruitcake for Christmas day. She hummed along with The Andrews Sisters who were Bob's guests and sang *Silver Bells*.

Joey and Eric played with a big wooden box full of Army toys. There were jeeps, tanks, guns and soldiers. German soldiers were different than American Army guys. Each soldier was identified by the shape of their helmets. Eric had the German guys. The boys had been playing war most of the evening, but every so often, Joey left the trenches specifically to admire the Christmas tree. It nearly touched the ceiling and shimmered with a plethora of lights, garland and excess icicles. The bubble lights still fascinated Joey as their bubbling action reflected off the foil icicles.

"Aunt Betty, you have the same kind of bubble lights as Gram and Gramps have on their tree."

"Yes, Honey. Uncle Glenn bought those the same day your Gramps got his from Woolworth's. Aren't they beautiful?" She patted Joey on the head.

"Yeah, I think they're swell. I remember that day I went with Uncle Glenn and Gramps to get our trees and the lights."

"Well, it's getting close to bedtime boys. How would you like me to make some hot cocoa before you go to bed?"

"Yaaaay! I'd like that a lot," said Joey.

"Me too, Ma," said Eric. "Ahhhh, why do we have to go to bed so early?" He groaned and stuck his lower lip out.

"Stop, Eric! If you don't go to bed, Santa Claus won't come, isn't that right, Sonny?"

"Yeah, everybody knows that, Eric." Joey said it with the air of a Santa Claus expert. Eric stuck his tongue out at him, but both boys enjoyed the hot cocoa before finally going to bed.

They lay awake and talked for a long time and Eric asked a lot of questions:

"Did Santa Claus come to that place where you're staying, Joey?"

"I was only there for one Christmas, but some people from a place called the Elks Club and another one called Masons had parties for us. They each gave us two presents."

"What did you get?"

"Some skis and ski boots, a sled and some new gloves and scarf. The Elks Club gave us a big bag of candy and fruit too."

"Gee! That's pretty neat for not even being at your own house for Christmas."

Joey frowned in the dark.

"You two had better go to sleep in there," shouted Uncle Glenn. His voice rumbled deep like thunder and it got quiet for a while until Eric dared to whisper:

"So, how long before you got to go back there?"

Joey didn't answer and soon, both boys were sound asleep.

•   •   •   •   •

When they woke up early Christmas morning; it was still dark outside. The clock in the kitchen showed it was just past six o'clock. The boys quietly slid out of their beds and tiptoed into the living room. The light from a small table lamp, near the tree allowed them to see the presents stacked underneath. Eric screamed as he ran to Aunt Betty and Uncle Glenn's bedroom.

"Daddy! Santa Claus came! There's presents under the tree!

Mommy! Santa Claus was here. Come, look!"

Joey watched Eric go and stayed sitting on the floor. He studied the presents and waited for a bit before he crawled on his hands and knees, searching for a present with his name on it.

With everyone awake, Aunt Betty percolated some coffee, and Uncle Glenn handed out presents. A small present with red paper and gold ribbon was tagged:

"Merry Christmas, Joey, from Santa Claus."

Joey wondered at how small the gift was. He couldn't imagine what it could be. He knew that most good things came in bigger packages. Ripping it open, he screamed his excitement.

"It's a Roy Rogers wrist watch! Wow!" His eyes were bright with excitement for all life had to offer him. "A real watch!" Eric crowded in to see as Joey pointed. "See? It's my favorite cowboy right here with his horse, Trigger, leaning back on his legs. Look at that! Wow! Look Uncle Glenn! I got a watch!" He ran to Aunt Betty and Uncle Glenn, in order to show them. They hugged him and helped to enjoy the balm of the moment.

"Gee, Sonny, Santa must have thought you were a good boy this year, huh?" said Aunt Betty.

"Real good boy," added Uncle Glen.

Eric opened a present the same size as Joey's. "Gene Autry! I got a watch, too, Joey!" He waved it above his head. "Look, it's Gene Autry and his horse, Champ!"

The boys compared their watches. Both had black leather wrist bands. Uncle Glenn showed them how to set and wind them then fastened them on their wrists. Joey held his up to his ear to listen to the ticking. Eric did the same. Uncle Glenn told the boys the watches would glow in the dark. Eric started jumping up and down. Both boys ran into Eric's room, closed the door and turned off the overhead light. The longer they stayed in the dark, the more the numbers on the watches seemed to glow.

"Wow! Ain't this swell?" said Joey.

"Yeah," Eric agreed.

"You know Gene Autry could beat Roy Rogers if they had a

fight," said Eric.

"Nope! Roy is King of the Cowboys. He could beat Gene at everything," said Joey.

"I bet not," Eric said. "He can't sing "Rudolph" like Gene does, so there."

"Well, that ain't nothing. Roy could sing that, too, if he wanted to."

They ran back out to the living room and watched Uncle Glenn and Aunt Betty open presents. Uncle Glenn got a new red and black checkered flannel shirt and some wool socks.

"Hey! How did Santa know I needed a new work shirt?" exclaimed Uncle Glenn.

Aunt Betty got a black patent leather pocketbook and a sweater.

The boys each opened another gift. Joey got a magic black ball. Aunt Betty showed him how to ask it a question, then shake it up, and watch, as the answer appeared in little white letters on the bottom. Joey wondered how it knew everything.

He quietly asked it if Daddy would be coming home soon. It answered by saying "not likely."

Chapter Thirty-Five

On Christmas Day, Aunt Betty and Alice helped Gram in the kitchen and it wasn't long before everyone sat down to a family dinner. There weren't enough chairs so Eric and Joey sat on the linoleum floor.

Uncle Glenn said grace and Joey thought about Brian and the twins. He missed them and wondered if they were having a nice Christmas, too.

Dinner was turkey with Gram's special stuffing, mashed potatoes, gravy, sweet potatoes, cranberry sauce and succotash. Aunt Betty's mince meat pie and Gram's pumpkin pie were served shortly thereafter. The adults drank coffee while the kids had cocoa. The fruitcake sat untouched on the end of the table.

The special day flew by way too fast for Joey. The sun was already sagging in the winter-white sky and it was turning dark outside when Uncle Glenn, Aunt Betty and Eric left for home. Beth and Joey stood outside by the old oak tree and admired the Christmas tree in the front window. Beth put her arm around Joey.

"I'm so glad you're here for Christmas, Joey. It wouldn't be the same without you."

"I'm really happy too, Sis. I just wish Brian and the twins could be here too — don't you?"

"Yes, Joey."

They stood outside the house for quite a while.

There was no traffic anywhere, nor anyone on the sidewalks or front porches or even in representation on a window shade, as though the earth had been vacuumed of humanity and turned into a winter stage set. Everything was so still they could hear snowflakes dropping all around them. It was truly a silent night.

Joey reached down and scooped up a handful of snow. When he began to smile and pack it with his hands, Beth backed away.

"Don't you dare, Joey!"

"Awwww, don't worry. I wouldn't throw it at you, scaredy cat. I was just teasing." He whipped the snowball at a snow-covered car parked in front of the house across the street.

Soon, the cold overtook them both and they ran to the back door where they brushed the snow off as well as could be expected and went inside.

"Leave those boots on the rug, you two," said Gram, who sat at the dining room table with Alice. They were playing Rummy, smoking cigarettes and sharing a jug of wine.

"We will!" Beth yelled. They finished hanging up their coats then went in and lay on the floor in the living room. They huddled as close as possible to the stove in order to get warm.

Gramps was reading his newspaper and listening to Lux Radio Theatre. He peeked around the corner of his paper and smiled. "You two should ask Gram for a cup of hot cocoa. I'll bet that would go good right about now, huh?"

•   •   •   •   •

The night before he was to leave and go back to The Home Joey couldn't sleep. He hated the fact that the morning would bring an end to his happiness. He didn't understand why things had be the way they were. His face went through a slow flurry of emotions — resistance, then be the way they were. His face went through a slow flurry of emotions — resistance, then consideration and finally, acceptance. His shoulders slumped.

Why couldn't Daddy be here? The one person who could save him from his fate was in New York City. *Why couldn't he be here with us? This is where a daddy belongs — with his family. If he was here I wouldn't have to go back to The Home. Don't they care that I have to leave again? Why should I have to go back, anyway? Beth doesn't.*

The way he saw it, there was room here at his Gram and Gramps' house. He had been sleeping in his old bed, after all. Of course, Beth had been sleeping on the couch since he came, but something surely could be done about that.

He didn't want to return to a life filled with a bunch of boys who didn't really know him or love him. They weren't his family. He knew Ma. Alexander loved him — but that was different, somehow.

When he shook his Magic Eight Ball before bed, he asked it why he had to go back. It said a dumb thing as far as Joey was concerned: *"Your future is in your hands."*

What did that mean? It was just stupid Joey thought, and deciding he didn't like the Eight Ball, tossed it in the bottom of his clothes bag and crawled under the covers.

·   ·   ·   ·   ·

The day Joey went back, the temperature rose and the sky fell. A ceiling of fat clouds the color of lead hung low above the wooded countryside. The snow had begun to fall, fine white flakes sifting down like flour from the sky.

Gram and Alice cried when they kissed and hugged Joey goodbye.

"I'll write a letter to you now and then. How would that be?" said Gram.

"And we'll tell you when we hear anything from Daddy, too," said Alice. "I promise." She put her hand to her mouth and tears welled in her eyes.

"You just keep being a good boy, Sonny," Gramps said. He squeezed Joey's shoulders while he looked him in the eye. "Everything will work out—you'll see." Gramps hugged him and rubbed a hand back and forth in Joey's hair. "Maybe we'll be able to finagle getting you back here for Easter if we don't hear from your father before then. That's just a few months away, you know."

Beth and Joey hugged really hard without letting go for a long time, even though she was going with Joey and Uncle Glenn for the trip back to Watertown.

Driving back to The Home didn't seem to take as long as it did to leave it nearly two weeks earlier. Several miles passed before Uncle Glenn broke the silence.

"Hey, Sport. I'm going to try real hard to get a hold of your father. And when I do, I'll have him call you—I promise. Okay?"

"Yes, Sir." Joey frowned as Beth squeezed his hand. "He means it, Joey. Uncle Glenn will try, just like he says. You know that."

"Yeah, sure."

When they arrived back at the orphanage, Joey didn't want to let go of his sister. He cried. They both did. Uncle Glenn looked at him with watery eyes.

Parting words had been building up inside Beth like water behind a dam. The last thing she said to her brother was, "Don't cry, Joey. Everything will be okay someday soon. You'll see." How many times Joey had heard those very same words, he thought. No one else could hear the pounding of his heart or the roaring of the blood in his veins as he got out of the car.

Beth stopped crying, then kissed and hugged him one last time. When they left him on the steps of the administration building and slammed the car doors, Joey desperately wanted to run and get back in, but Mrs. Neagle held his hand as his eyes followed the car out to State Street.

They stood there for a moment, the nerves in his Joey's stomach coming to life like a tangled pile of worms. Rubbing his eyes didn't stop the urge to cry. When he waved goodbye to Beth and saw her waving from the back window of the car, he was certain she was crying too, and he knew what he had to do.

Don't worry, Sis. I'm gonna run away from here as soon as I can.

•   •   •   •   •

Joey settled back in at The Home and running away became a bad idea. Instead, he anticipated letters from home. Beth wrote to him twice and Alice wrote to him one time but there was really no good news from anyone. Gramps was not getting any better and Joey's father wasn't mentioned at all.

The long, hard winter seemed to drag on.

Springtime reluctantly gave way to summer and vacation was set to begin. One afternoon just before school let out for the summer, Ma Alexander had company when the boys got home. The door to Ma's room was wide open as he began to pass, and Joey heard another woman's voice.

Ma called, "Joey! Come in here, please."

Stepping inside her room, he saw another woman sitting in a rocker across from Ma. He had never seen her before.

"Joey, this is Mrs. Marcetti. She's your new social worker, Son."

The portly woman stood and reached out to shake his hand. "Hello, Joey!"

Joey noticed right away that there was something amiss with one of the woman's eyes. It appeared to sag down and shut nearly all the way. A pile of mousy brown hair was tied in a no-nonsense bun on top of her head. She was dressed like one of his teachers, in a flowered dress with a small sash.

"Glad to meet you, Joey. I've heard so much about you." Both women studied his reaction and smiled.

Joey squirmed, feeling like a bug under a microscope. He felt his face become red. "Hello, Ma'am." Glancing at Ma Alexander, he said, "Where's Mrs. Kellogg, Ma?"

"Well, Mrs. Kellogg had to retire," Mrs. Marcetti injected.

Ma pulled her glasses off and set them aside. She said, "The doctor discovered that she has sugar diabetes, and her legs were going bad."

"Won't I do?" Mrs. Marcetti asked in a cheery voice. She had a notepad on her knee and rolled a pen around in her fingers while she talked. She looked at him, expectantly, so he nodded.

"Yes, Ma'am. Did you see my sister, yet?"

"No. Not yet, but I'll be over in Gouvernuer later this week, and I will be stopping by to see her then. I'll be seeing your brothers too, as soon as possible."

"Joey," said Ma, "give Mrs. Marcetti a chance to speak."

"That's all right," said Mrs. Marcetti. "We can't blame Joey for asking these things, Mrs. Alexander. Yes, as a matter of fact, Joey, I've even talked to your father."

"You did?" Joey felt a surge of adrenaline. His eyes lit up and his jaw dropped. For an instant, he thought his heart would explode from pounding so hard and so fast.

Mrs. Marcetti nodded. "Yes, I did," she said, but her lower lip twitched.

"Did you see my mother, too?

Mrs. Marcetti tugged at an earlobe and cleared her throat. "No. No, I'm afraid not. I'll see her when I see your sister."

"Well, is Daddy with Mommy at Gram and Gramps' house right now?" He studied Mrs. Marcetti for a moment, trying to read her — trying to anticipate a positive answer — something he wanted to hear.

"No. We can discuss that situation a little more in the future. But for now, the answer is no. Your parents will no longer be together, Joey. Your father is living on Long Island. That's down by New York City — a long ways from here, Joey. Your mother is ill. She will continue to live in Gouvernuer as far as we know right now."

Joey didn't know what else to say. Mrs. Alexander was silent for a moment. She reached out to gather Joey to her but he edged away. "What's wrong with my mother?"

"Well, that's why I'm here, Joey," said Mrs. Marcetti. Your father wants you to come and live with him." She looked directly in Joey's eyes and smiled. She glanced at Ma Alexander, then back at him. "Live with him for good, Joey. No foster home."

Ma Alexander stood. Tears leaked from her eyes and she swallowed against emotion. "What Mrs. Marcetti is telling you, Joey, is that your mother is too ill right now to have you all back, so you'll be going to live with your daddy. He really wants you with him. Right, Mrs. Marcetti?"

"Yes. Your father has a home for you," said Mrs. Marcetti. "He's requested, through our offices in Albany, that you come to live with him. You will be taking the train down to New York City about the first of July."

Joey beamed at Ma. "For real? I mean, really?" His legs felt like they would cave beneath him and a million butterflies took flight in his stomach. He felt numb and wasn't sure how to react as her words rang in his ears. "When did this happen? I don't understand."

"Your father will meet you at Grand Central Station in New York, Joey," added Ma. "Run along now. We'll talk some more later." Joey didn't move and Ma studied his face. "Go ahead now." She smiled. "Change clothes and go outside and play."

He stared at both of them. "Yes, Ma." He felt like his world had suddenly turned upside down, but he nodded at the woman, too. "Thank you, Ma'am."

Joey lay in his bed that night, staring at the ceiling and wondering why he wasn't happier knowing he would finally be with his father. The possibilities buzzed like flies in his brain. *I'll be leaving Mommy and Sis and everybody else, and I don't understand why. Why can't we all be together?* He closed his eyes and let out a shuddering breath. *How sick is Mommy?*

·   ·   ·   ·   ·

Several weeks later, Mrs. Marcetti took charge of seeing Joey off in Watertown. From there he would travel to Syracuse, then on to Albany where he would switch to the train that would take him to Grand Central Station in New York City to meet his father, Joe.

Joey was disappointed he hadn't gotten a chance to see Beth or any of the rest of his family before he had to leave. Everything happened so fast.

On the train ride, he thought about Mrs. Alexander and having to say goodbye to the woman he had grown to love. He knew he would miss her warm, caring ways.

"We will miss you, Joey," she had said. "I know you'll be happy with your father though. I do hope that someday you'll come back to see me. Goodness, what am I going to do without my favorite kitchen helper?" She held his hands in hers and smiled the smile that Joey had grown to love. She dabbed at her eyes but tears still trickled out.

Joey tried to wrap his arms around her plump body.

"I'll miss you too, Ma. I'll write letters to you if you let me," he mumbled into her apron.

"Well, of course, Son. Please make sure you do." She wrapped her arms around him and squeezed. "Yes. Please write to me."

•   •   •   •   •

Joey rode the train in silence with his suitcase between his legs and a brown-bag lunch in his lap. Ma Alexander had packed him four peanut butter and jelly sandwiches, four cookies and an apple for the trip.

An old man slid into the seat across from him. He had an angular face with sparse, bristly white hair and thick glasses perched on an impressive nose. His skin had the leathery look of a lifelong smoker. Joey studied the weathered old face. It was an impressive one that gave nothing away and at the same time hinted at many deeper truths than those on the surface.

Joey realized just how much he would miss his Gramps.

He watched as the old man opened a cotton pouch and stretched a line of tobacco down the crease in a small paper. He tightened the pouch string using his teeth, then rolled the paper and licked the edge in a movement that had been perfected over a great many years. He struck a match on the floor and cupped his hands around his smoke, creating a glowing ball of warm light. He blew smoke out his nose.

The train swayed back and forth with the rhythm and clickity-clack of the train. Joey's nose was pressed against the window as he watched the countryside fly by. Cow pastures on either side of the tracks were emerald green, dotted with buttercups pooled in shadows.

East of Black River, the hills finally yielded to the flatlands, and the highway cut through fields thick with cultivated green rows of corn and soybeans. Farmers on their John Deere's poked along the highway as if it had been built for tractors and not automobiles.

Joey could see for miles down the slope of the mountains to the broad valley that was carpeted in green. Pines stood shoulder to shoulder, ranks of them marching down the hillsides. Overhead, gray clouds drifted across the sky like bloated sponges, filling up the blue bowl, shutting out the sun. Every so often rain seemed to threaten.

The old man puffed his cigarette and stared at Joey. "How far are ya' going, young man?"

"New York City, Sir."

"Ah, yes! The big city. Big Apple, they call it." He smiled. "Ever been there before?"

"No, Sir. My Gramps used to work for the railroad until he got sick."

"Really? Good for him. Well you're in for quite a treat when you get to the city. I'm only going so far as Albany, myself."

"Yes, Sir. That's where I have to change trains. My father is meeting me in New York City, though."

"Oh, that's good. It's a big place, Grand Central. It's easy to get lost if you don't know your way around."

Joey sat back in his seat and continued to look out the window. He fumbled around trying to get one of the sandwiches out of the bag. The old man had closed his eyes and appeared to be asleep.

After he finished eating, Joey pulled out the picture Mrs. Marcetti had given him. It was a snapshot of his father. Joey had told her that he forgot what his father looked like. He wondered if his father would know what *he* looked like too. Mrs. Marcetti said she would be sure that Joe Harrison had a recent picture of his son.

Chapter Thirty-Six

Alice's pregnancy was not discussed openly during Joey's Christmas visit and she wasn't showing yet. She gave birth to her second daughter, Kathy, the morning of August 9, 1950. Despite her abuse of alcohol and diagnosed diabetes, the baby was healthy.

Fred Simms, the father, was somewhat supportive when the baby was born, but when Kathy was three months old, things changed. Just as with the twins, Fred decided that responsibilities such as changing diapers belonged to Alice. At his suggestion, their housecleaning, as well as washing diapers and preparing baby formula, became Beth's responsibility. She came on Friday after school, stayed over and returned to Gouverneur Sunday afternoon.

By late spring of the following year, she was riding the train from Gouverneur to her mother's rented house in Great Bend Township nearly thirty miles away. There was very little time for personal life with her friends as a result. Gram made sure Beth had the round-trip fare for the train.

When she left Gram and Gramps' house, Beth never knew when she would be returning, but Fred and Alice's habit of frequenting the bars and staying out all night usually meant she would not come back until late Sunday afternoon. Beth complained to Gram on occasion, but it did no good. Aunt Betty and Uncle Glenn were aware of the situation but didn't want to get involved.

"Your mother needs your help, Honey," said Gram, who approved of the arrangement. "She works hard at the restaurant, you know. The poor woman deserves to rest with her time off, not wash diapers and clean house. Besides, Kathy *is your* sister. She needs you. Your mother is sick." Any and all of this dialogue was followed by smiles and hugs from Gram. "Thank heavens she's got you to help her, Beth. I certainly can't leave your grandpa alone in order to go over there."

Gramps overheard the conversation from his rocker in the living room. He blew out a breath, his broad shoulders sagging under the weight of it all.

Adjacent to the southern part of the Fort Drum Army Base, Great Bend seemed an inappropriate name for a town so small that everybody knew each other by name. However, most of the residents were an old-fashioned bunch who took a lot of pride in their town. A khaki-painted World War I howitzer stood in the shadows of a giant oak on the courthouse lawn. A lonely Revolutionary War soldier in bronze stood atop a granite pedestal, gazing north and looking for the enemy while holding his rifle, reminding everyone of a glorious cause.

Kresge's five and dime, as old as the town, was a two-story brick building fronted with a wood portico. An old-fashioned hardware store sat across the street where shiny new spades, rakes and pitchforks leaned against weathered white clapboard. A sign in the window advertised a special on wheelbarrows.

A Sinclair gas station sat on the far end of Main Street next to the A&P store. The adjacent residential neighborhoods were lined with shade trees and bungalows.

Alice stayed with Fred in a small rented house on Dover Street that appeared to be empty. There wasn't enough paint left on the front to indicate what color it might once have been. Something that might have been curtains hung in tattered disarray in the front windows. The porch was ramshackle with a roof that sagged in the middle, and a cheap, unpainted plywood addition was stuck on the back like a cancerous growth. The driveway was more dirt than gravel and lined with disorderly hedges. There were a few neglected flowers in pots on the porch.

The interior was cozy but aging. The walls needed plaster and paint, and the floors were worn linoleum with spots that exposed gritty, bare floor throughout the entire house. The monthly rent was an expensive thirty dollars a month.

Beth always found the house a mess. The kitchen sink overflowed with dirty dishes, pots and pans. Baby bottles were scattered throughout the house; often they were found with sour contents inside. Dirty diapers could be found in many of the six rooms, and flies hovered over the garbage like tiny vultures.

At the end of their workdays on Friday, Alice and Fred usually hung out with friends in the neighboring bars until the wee hours of the morning. Many times there was very little food in the house and Beth was left to her own devices in order to eat. Often, there was not enough milk in the icebox for the baby. Sometimes Beth was left with the baby on Friday night and she wouldn't see her mother until Sunday morning. She never really knew when they would be home from their jaunts, and consequently, the milk supply that was expected to last a day had to be stretched over a two day period and the baby was hungry.

●   ●   ●   ●   ●

School was almost out for the summer and Beth was there for the weekend when Fred and Alice went out Friday night and got back at four Saturday morning. They slept the day away even though Saturday was a perfect day weather-wise. The sky was cloudless, the sun unyielding, but a merciful breeze kissed the skin and the humidity, which so often smothered the Adirondack region, had taken the day off. It was the kind of day tailor-made for picnics in the park. Beth wished with all her heart that she could go and enjoy the world outside—even if it was just a walk in the park, but she was forbidden from taking the baby out of the house. Other girls her age would be making a day of anything they wanted. Why not me? She thought.

She did her best to keep the baby quiet for the better part of the day, not wanting to raise the ire of Fred. However, Kathy started crying about three o'clock that afternoon and Beth could do nothing to satisfy her. She hesitated to wake her mother.

Alice finally woke up and looked at the alarm clock. It was five-thirty in the early evening. She heard the baby but sat on the edge of the bed for a moment before she tied on her robe and, leaning against the wall, brushed a strand of hair out of her eyes. Her thoughts were a jumble of faces and places and sounds, and she had a severe headache.

The bedroom door was closed. She turned to look at a snoring Fred who lay on his back, arms flung out, head turned to one side, mouth hanging open like a busted gate.

Edging over to the dresser, she studied herself in the mirror. The past and the present twined in her mind like vines attaching their sharp tendrils to her brain. Her pulse throbbed in her ears, pounded inside her forehead. She raked a hand through her hair and rubbed at the tension in the back of her neck. If only she weren't so powerless, so weak, she thought. She knew she was naive and foolish. *I can't be a real wife to a man who refuses to be a father, can I? I'm certainly not a mother. Look at me. What a failure I am. No wonder Joe left me. I'm not worth wanting. I don't really have anyone. I don't have anything—not even my kids.*

Such thoughts. Her moods and depressing images came and went on a more regular basis it seemed. She reached for her pack of Chesterfields and her hands trembled ever so slightly as she struck a match to light up before stumbling out of the bedroom. Rubbing her eyes, she yawned and slowly drifted over to where Beth was sitting with the fussing baby. She stood just inside the room, looking rumpled and ragged.

"Shhhh. Shhhh. Here—give her to me, Honey," she said. Beth breathed a short sigh of relief as her mother took the baby from her arms and patted her diaper. "She's not wet. She's probably just hungry, Beth. Why don't you get her a bottle?"

"There isn't any more milk, Mom."

Alice looked at her as though she were coming out of a trance. "Oh dear. That can't be. Are we out already? Have you been drinking a lot of it?"

"No. Kathy drinks all of it. She's always hungry."

"Okay. Well, of course we'll just have to get some more. I had no idea. Get my pocket book off the dresser. You'll have to walk to the A&P. Be quiet though I don't want to wake Fred right now. I want you to get two quarts. Your sister really goes through the milk, doesn't she?" She smiled as she jiggled the baby on her lap. "Shhhh. Shhhh, it's okay. Mommy's here now. Shhhh."

Beth tiptoed into their bedroom and came back with the pocketbook. "There's nothing to eat either, Mom. Can I get something at the store?"

"Why, yes, of course. Here, take this other dollar and get a jar of peanut butter and a loaf of Wonder Bread. Be sure and not lose the change, okay?"

"Okay, I won't."

Beth ran out, hearing the screen door slam behind her. Kathy's hungry cries made her want to cry too. She knew the baby would calm down as soon as she was fed, so she ran as fast as she could. She was so hungry herself that her stomach ached. When she got back, she hurried through to the kitchen and fixed a bottle while the air heaved in and out of her lungs in tremendous hot, ragged gasps.

Alice continued to cradle the baby for a few minutes while it loudly sucked on the bottle. Then she started to hand the baby off to Beth. "Beth, be a dear and finish feeding her, will you? Then you can change her for me."

"Okay, but first I wanted to make myself some sandwiches. All right?

"Oh, of course, Honey. Go right ahead." She continued to hold the baby and rock her with a smile on her face. Now, Fred and I will be going to a party, but don't think I didn't notice you tidied up a bit while we were gone last night. Thank you for that, Honey. You are such a good girl, helping Mom out the way you do."

"Yes, Mom."

When she finished making her sandwiches, Beth took the baby and watched as Alice went back toward her bedroom. She called after her. "Do you think there will be enough milk to last until tomorrow?"

"There certainly should be. We'll probably be back early tonight."

She stopped and edged back to where Beth sat on a kitchen chair. "My goodness, you needn't feed the baby every time she cries, you know." She placed her fingers under Beth's chin and smiled. "This is good training for you. Like I've said, someday you'll have kids of your own.

Beth swept a strand of hair behind her ear. "Yes, Mom. I don't think I want any for a long time though. I want to spend some time with my friends from school. I wish I could be with them sometimes on the weekends now."

The tension in the silence after Beth spoke was like a balloon filling and filling and filling with air until it was about to burst.

"Oh, sure you'll want kids of your own, Dear. You'll see when you get older; you'll change your mind." She paid little attention to Beth's expression while she lit another cigarette and inhaled deeply. She let the smoke ease out as if she regretted letting it go as she headed for the bedroom again.

"Why can't we get Joey and Brian and the twins back and get our own house? I miss them awful bad, don't you?"

Before Alice could respond, Fred stumbled into the kitchen. He smiled his minimalist smile, a slight widening of his narrow lips. His scalp and face were pulled tight with the beginnings of a hangover, the inside of his head still filled with the sounds of the highway bar they had been in the night before. Sitting on a kitchen chair, Fred turned it around so he could rest his forearms on the back. He waved his index finger like a windshield wiper.

"Don't you start about those brothers of yours again, Elizabeth. My headache won't take it today... or any other day from now on. You hear me?" He closed his eyes, let out a shuddering breath and stood. "It seems every time you come over here, you start that again." He waved his hand at the air as though swatting away insects. He coughed and hacked. His upper body swayed and bent and twisted as he spoke.

"Fred!" Alice shouted. "Stop it! Please don't be so hard on her. She's still just a child, and she only asked a question."

"Yeah, just the same one she's always asking—right? Trying to make you feel bad — that's all she's doing. Then I have to put up with your sulking all night."

Alice said nothing. She continued to stare at him, glassy-eyed and trembling

Fred eyed Beth and watched her face turn red.

He let the silence between them hang for a moment.

"And, your mother's right — this babysitting is good training for you."

Alice tapped the ash off her cigarette and raised it to her lips for a long drag. Then she crushed out the stub amid a dozen others in the ashtray and glanced at the kitchen clock. "Well, we'd better get dressed and get going, Fred, if you want to be there on time. You know Charlie is a stickler for everybody being on time."

"Yeah, you're right, I guess. I won't be long — just got to jump in the shower. You just worry about yourself, okay?"

I'll just be a few minutes," said Alice.

While Fred got ready, Alice washed her face and hands in the kitchen sink then dressed in a pair of blue slacks and a white blouse. She applied red lipstick but no other makeup.

It was dark and the crickets were in full chorus when they got in the car and pulled away.

Beth finished feeding the baby. She changed her diaper, rocked her and laid her in the baby bed. Much later, after Kathy fell asleep, Beth decided to go outside and sit on the front steps. She left the front door open with the screen door closed so the moths wouldn't get in. She would be able to hear if the baby cried.

She was still smarting from Fred's harsh words. Without thinking, she raised a hand to nibble at a thumbnail. She tried to understand why it bothered Fred for her to mention her brothers. *What does her Mom see in the man? He's not good-looking and he's mean. Why can't she find Daddy and stay with him? Why can't she get all of us kids back together again? Doesn't she care?* Beth pressed a hand to her mouth and blinked furiously at the tears that pooled in her eyes.

The night sky was a sheet of deep blue velvet studded with diamonds. The stars were like promises in the sky, bright and distant.

Well out of Beth's reach, they were too far off to chase away bad omens.

•   •   •   •   •

It was four o'clock in the morning when Brian finished dressing. He slipped into a long-sleeved shirt. It was late May but he knew there would still be a chill in the early-morning air. He wasn't anxious to get started, but his chores had to be done.

Living on a farm in Black River, which was less than forty miles from Great Bend, he had been there for nearly three years after Mrs. Kellogg removed him from the Bushkins' foster home. She had delivered him to the Vanderleest farm where he was given an abundance of responsibility. He had never realized the meaning of family and rarely pondered the somewhat skeletal memories of his brothers and sister. Now, nearly eight years old, he still lacked his own family and he learned the rigors of working on a farm early on.

As he tiptoed to the bedroom door, Brian tried to be as quiet as possible so he wouldn't wake the other six boys who shared the room. All of them were younger—ranging from five to seven in age. Since he was the oldest, more was expected of him. The others would be able to sleep in for an hour longer before it was time to eat and get ready for school.

Brian was three steps into the hallway when he suddenly stopped. He heard footsteps in the dark behind him. Fear swelled inside him like a balloon. His heart raced as he realized the only one up at that hour besides himself would be Ed, the thirty-two-year-old son of his foster parents, Charles and Florence Vanderleest. Ed was a sulky, hard-as-nails, slave-driving workhorse, who always managed to find something to nitpick in order to justify his penchant for both verbal and physical abuse. He must have been returning from the outhouse, Brian thought. *Maybe he'll leave me alone this morning.*

Edward Vanderleest was a slight, rather short man with salt-and-pepper hair that seemed premature, and a short, neatly trimmed beard. His face was weathered and his arms darkened by the sun. He had dry skin and a voice that rasped as if his larynx had been affected by cigarettes and whiskey or clotted with rust. His shoulders were rounded like the top of a question mark.

Brian stood still and held his breath. He listened closely but all he heard was the sound of his pulse pounding in his ears. As his eyes adjusted to the dark, he watched as Ed's silhouette seemed to wobble from side to side down the hallway until finally it disappeared into his own room. His door closed behind him with a loud snick.

Brian quietly skirted past the door and headed for the back porch where he slid his feet into his rubber work boots and eased out the back door. He sighed and stared straight ahead. His anxious breath expelled puffs of steam into the chilly air as he made his way to the pasture where it was his job to round up the herd of thirty-eight cows for milking. He would find them close by and coax them to the barn.

Rounding up the cows wouldn't take long, but it wasn't necessarily an easy task in the darkness. Brian had done it so many times that he knew the tricks of avoiding the rougher, uneven ground and piles of cow flop. Once he found the lead cow, the rest of the herd would follow with Brian's prodding.

Out of sight, above the farmhouse, the moon reflected the sun of a day not yet dawned, shining the pale light of tomorrow on the yard and on the paper birch trees. Screened by trees and swallowed by distance, the lights of the nearest neighbors could not be seen.

Brian was nearly done stabling the cows in their stanchions at the far end of the barn when he heard Ed's callous voice echoing across the barnyard.

"Brian! Where you at, Boy?" As if he didn't know, thought Brian.

Ed's voice sent a surge of anxiety coursing through Brian's body. Hair stood up on the back of his neck. *What will it be today? What did I do wrong? Did I forget something?* Those thoughts brought a host of past experiences bubbling to the surface and set Brian's stomach churning.

"Here! Here I am — in the barn!" he yelled.

Ed strolled into the barn with a cup of coffee in one hand, a cigarette in the other. He wore stained bib overalls and a red plaid bomber cap with flaps hanging down like hound's ears. He eyed Brian as he sipped the coffee and put the cigarette between his lips. He sucked on it as though he was deep underwater and it was a breathing tube. His breath came out of his mouth and went up around his head like smoke from a chimney. Squatting on his haunches, he stared into his own smoke with the concentration of a scientist, his hands draped over his knees like banana peels. He smirked as he stared at Brian.

"I'm right here, Sir." Brian continued to work with the cows while a chunk of silence passed between him and Ed.

"Ya' left that gate open again yesterday, Boy. Seems to me I've warned you about that enough times now. Thing is, this time I found the horses grazing up by the house and while you was goofing around in school, I had to round 'em up."

"Sorry, Sir." Brian quickly reflected back to yesterday. "I thought I closed it."

Ed stood, set his coffee cup on a ledge and strolled over to where Brian was. He struck like a cobra as he punched the boy in the shoulder. There was enough power behind it that Brian fell sideways and braced himself on the side of a cow to keep from falling.

"You been forgetting a lot around here lately, Boy. Pay closer attention and keep your mind on what you're doing. I had to have two of the other boys slop the hogs a few days back because you forgot. Maybe you need a special reminder to help you remember. Is that it?" He threw a hand out and clutched Brian by the shirt.

"No! No, Sir. I'll remember better. I promise."

"Well, you'd better. You'd best hustle extra fast this morning too. Get them gutters scraped. Then I need for you to give me a hand with the Old Man." He dropped his cigarette on the cement aisle and ground it out with the toe of his boot. "He wants to disc one of the fields today, so as quick as you get done out here we'll do that before your bus comes, hear?"

"Okay. Yes, Sir."

Ed's father, Charles Vanderleest, was wheelchair-bound. Nearly sixty-years old, he was the victim of a tractor accident that had crushed his legs eight years earlier. He was bitter, but refused to be left out of the running of the farm. He needed a lot of help with things, but generally managed to roll himself out of bed each day and into a special chair. His wife, Florence, helped him get dressed.

In her mid-forties, Florence, who was five-eight, had shoulder-length black hair with traces of gray that she held back with a clasp. By no means beautiful, she had a compact jaw, thin lips and a slender, wiry build, though her bare calves were muscled. She was gaunt, obviously overworked and overwhelmed by life.

Helping her husband get dressed was but one task among her many duties as a wife and caretaker for the man who could be very ornery from the moment his eyes opened in the morning until they closed at day's end.

Florence was a patient, loving soul who attempted to treat Brian and the other six boys in her foster home with a modest amount of understanding and respect. However, she dared not interfere with the say-so or discipline of her son, Ed.

A vague disquiet in the house arose in part from the perception that Florence and Ed were in a private conversation, one conducted without words, but rather furtive looks, nuanced gestures and subtle body language.

"Good morning, Charles." Florence smiled at him indulgently.

"Morning," he grunted. Charles insisted on wearing a long-sleeved shirt with a t-shirt underneath and suspenders every day. As she helped him with the shirt, Charles stretched and a joint snapped somewhere. He'd given up worrying where such sounds originated or what they meant. Suffering from congestive heart failure and a half a dozen other conditions that should have killed him, he was simply too mean to die.

When he felt like riding his John Deere to tend the fields, Charles needed arms to lift him out of the chair and up onto the seat of the tractor. Ed enlisted Brian's help whenever possible, although he did most of the actual lifting.

•   •   •   •   •

Brian ran to the house as soon as he finished shoveling out the gutters. He washed up, put on his school clothes and rushed to the table to gobble his bowl of oatmeal just before the other boys got to the table. Florence sidled up to his side. She patted his shoulder.

"Son, did you close the gate to the pasture?"

"Yes, Florence. I sure did."

"Good. Good. Edward was upset yesterday. I don't want you to have more trouble with him. Lord knows he can find enough. Oh – I need for you to weed my flower garden after school today if you don't mind?" She fluffed his hair with her fingers.

"Yes, Florence. Can I have a cookie when I get done?"

She smiled. "As a matter of fact, I plan on baking today." She paused and looked into his eyes. "Sure, you can have one or two. You'd best hurry now. The mister is riding the tractor today. Edward told you, I'm sure."

"Yes, Ma'am. Oooops! I almost forgot. I have to empty my pot, too." He ran.

There would be just enough time to help with Charles before the bus pulled up out front. Charles finished a cup of coffee. He would eat later as was his unusual habit. "I have to work some before I'm hungry," he noted.

Short and thin with thick white hair, he constantly worked a toothpick from side to side in his mouth as if it helped him think. His fingers were stained with nicotine, and he twitched a lot as though the absence of a cigarette made his life incomplete.

Tilting sideways in the wheelchair, his body had the sloping contours of a haystack. He leaned his head back as he waited to be lifted. Brian hustled up and stood beside him. Charles's fierce little eyes never left Brian's face, while Brian, tried not to return the stare.

Charles spat and moved the toothpick from one side to the other. His brow furrowed into burls of flesh as he spoke. "Boy, go see what's keeping Ed."

Just as he said that, they heard the tractor. Ed was driving toward them. "Never mind; here he comes," Charles croaked.

Brian held the wheelchair and kept it steady while Ed lifted his father up onto the seat of the tractor. Brian climbed up on the other side and helped strap Charles into the seat.

"There — you okay, Dad?" Ed asked.

"Yeah, I'm good. Get out of the way now." He tipped his head in Brian's direction. "That boy is gonna miss his bus" He pointed. "I can see the lights right down the road at Hecklers' place. The other boys are all out there already."

Brian quickly pushed the wheelchair back onto the porch, grabbed his books and ran fast and hard to the road.

A murder of crows clattered into the air above the elms and maples as Charles's eyes tracked him all the way to the mailbox as the bus pulled up.

"Well, it's a good thing he's able to run," the old man crabbed.

Chapter Thirty-Seven

Joey was tired, physically and mentally. He felt the stress of leaving and taking the trip. The Home had been a safe place. Everybody knew him there. Everyone knew what to expect from him and of him.

He gazed out the window of the train and reflected on Mr. Neagle's instructions at the train station before he left Gouvernuer. His questions and all the possible answers brought a flood of emotions. Fear, panic and grief, came all at once, like a rushing wave inside his head as the train rolled toward New York City.

"Now, Joey, listen to me very carefully. You'll take this train all the way down to Albany. When you get there, you'll change trains to this number right here—Number 357. See, I've got it circled. You'll be all right." He paused and pointed to the ticket. "You just have to switch trains that one time in Albany. Then, you'll take that 357 train all the way to Grand Central Station in New York. Don't get off-no matter where the train stops, until it gets to Albany and then in New York City. Understand?"

"Yes, Sir."

Joey's stomach was in a whirl. He was afraid, but not sure of exactly what. There was the trip itself, the possibility of getting lost and then meeting his father whom he could barely remember.

Mr. Neagle did his best at instilling confidence in the boy. "You're almost twelve years old now Son, and I think you can do this very easily. I'll have the conductor keep an eye out and help you if you have any questions on the way, okay?"

"Yes, Sir."

"He'll be wearing a blue uniform and a cap and will be walking through the train punching tickets. If you have any questions, ask him, and I'll alert him that you're by yourself too. He'll be glad to help, I'm sure. Okay?"

"Yes, Sir."

"You should be fine. Do you want to ask me anything, Joey?"

Panic and self-pity had clogged Joey's throat. "Yes, Sir. How will my father know me from all the other people at the train station?"

Mr. Neagle smiled and said, "Your father knows which train you'll be getting in on. He'll be watching for you."

"How will he know what I look like though?"

"Well, I was getting to that, Son." He reached in his jacket pocket and pulled out a gray tag. "See this tag? Read what it says."

Joey fixed his eyes on the tag. His name was printed in big black letters that said, "Joey."

"Yes, Sir. It says my name."

"Okay, I need you to pin this on just before you get off the train in New York City. Pin it right here, understand?" He tapped the place on the front of Joey's jacket, then shoved the tag down inside a pocket. Putting his arm around Joey's shoulders, he said, "Let's get in line, Son. Your train will be leaving pretty soon."

They stood in line until the conductor asked for Joey's ticket and smiled as he punched it. Mr. Neagle said something to him, and the conductor nodded his head and looked at Joey. Then he handed his ticket back.

Mr. Neagle shook Joey's hand and smiled. "Good luck, Son. Take good care of yourself. You'll be okay." He paused and patted Joey's shoulder. "Someday, when you're older, come on back to The Home and see us, will you?"

Joey felt like he wanted to hug Mr. Neagle, but for some reason, he was afraid to try. "Yes, I promise I will. Goodbye, Sir."

•   •   •   •   •

It was a seven-hour trip, and Joey would have plenty of time to think about things before the train arrived in New York City. He wondered if his father would like him. Would he want him-or would he send him back to The Home? What did his father look like? Did he live in a big house? He hoped it wasn't a farm like the Couzens' or the Bushkins' places. *I wonder if anybody lives with my father?*

He stayed seated and talked to the conductor from time to time when he passed by. The man's wide grin lit up a face that was a little bit rough and a bit lined—not exactly handsome, but utterly compelling. His name was George, and he gave Joey a *Look* magazine to read, noting that somebody had left it on the train the day before and wouldn't be back for it, so Joey could keep it.

George chatted with Joey when he had time and told him he had been working for the railroad for almost twenty years. He was married and had two grown-up girls. One was married. He seemed to be a nice guy and told Joey about things to see in New York with his father—like the Brooklyn Dodgers or New York Yankees baseball games. Joey didn't tell George that he hadn't seen his father in over six years.

He changed trains in Albany with no problem although he trembled through the entire process. Once he had become friends with a new conductor, named Jesse, everything was fine. Jesse was a heavyset man with a ruddy face left pitted by a long-over adolescent battle with acne. He had an engaging and warm smile and liked to talk.

An old man sitting across from Joey was sleeping. His head lolled to the side and moved to and fro ever so slightly with the sway of the train. Joey found his snoring both loud and funny.

After he ate his peanut butter and jelly sandwiches, Joey fell asleep. When he awoke, he was lying down on the seat, the magazine on the floor by his feet. He looked outside and saw millions of city lights dazzling in the night. Many were way up high in buildings built very close together. There were hundreds of apartment buildings and all kinds of stores with flashing neon lights. He had never seen skyscrapers before and was amazed. *How can they build something that high that won't tip over?*

The train whizzed past massive clusters of railroad tracks all side by side. Cars, trucks and buses zoomed like lightning bugs every which way. Papers cluttered the streets and sidewalks. Suddenly, the train was swallowed up by a tunnel. To Joey, it felt like they were riding down a slide — down, down, down into the ground; everything turned pitch black. He was scared and clutched his seat with both hands while the lights inside the train flickered off and on, then finally stayed on.

George was on the move. He hitched up his pants and glanced both ways then continued down the aisle. He steadied himself by holding onto the seats as he walked.

Joey began to worry. *What if nobody is here to meet me? Maybe my father changed his mind.*

"Graaaaand Central Staaaation next stop! Grand Central Station! Next!" Jesse announced. "Ladies and gentlemen, please check and be sure you take all of your belongings with you. Check around your seats at this time for any loose personal items. Thank you." When he approached Joey's seat, Jesse tilted his conductor's cap back on his head and smiled.

"Well, you made it, Tiger! You're here. This is New York City."

Joey remembered the tag and nervously fished it out of his pocket. He tried to pin it on his jacket, but his fingers wouldn't behave to accomplish the job because he was rushing.

"Need a hand with that, do you?" George asked.

"Thank you, Sir."

He helped Joey with the jacket. "You're quite welcome, young man — comes with the job." He winked and stuck out his hand. Joey shook it.

"So long, Son. Good luck!"

"Bye, Sir."

George said they were in New York, so Joey thought the train should stop, but it kept rolling along very slowly for a long, long time before it finally came to a stop. Joey got up, grabbed his suitcase and followed the flow of people moving towards the door.

"Grand Central! Graaaand Central Staaaation!" George still barked as he strolled down the aisle. "Watch your step, please."

Joey walked down the steps from the train. When his feet touched solid ground he looked around. He tried to scan each and every thing around him and searched the face of every man he could. The buzzing of so many voices and other sounds around him was overpowering.

He moved off to the side and took out the picture of his father that Mrs. Mancetti had given him. He was afraid nobody would be there to meet him. *I just knew something would go wrong.* He clutched the suitcase with both hands and began to walk in a circle for a moment, then stopped. *He must be watching for me, like Mr. Neagle said.*

His eyes searched the crowd of people who zipped to and fro and felt tears welling up as he accidentally backed into somebody. "Oooops!" He quickly took a step forward. "I'm sorry, I didn't mean to . . ."

The handsome man looking down at him wore tinted glasses. He was about six feet tall, with a strong-looking build and black, curly hair. He smiled at Joey and pointed to the tag on his coat.

"You're Joey, right?" He pointed to the tag.

The pressure of uncertainty railed inside Joey- it was like a clenched fist and he couldn't seem to prevent the words from pouring out. "Yes, Sir. I'm Joey." He quickly searched the man's face. "Are you my father?"

The man smiled. "Yes, Son... I'm your dad."

They stood looking at each other for an awkward moment.

His father was a strong-looking man with a tanned face. He wore a brown sports coat, white shirt, opened at the neck and no tie. The toes of his tan shoes were shined.

He appeared to be by himself when he reached out for Joey and hugged him. His strong arms felt good to Joey. The suitcase sitting by Joey's feet, blocked the way, but it didn't faze either of them. Joe put his hands on Joey's shoulders and smiled. The corners of his mouth curved subtly in a gentle smile of relief and understanding.

"Well, at long last, Joey. My own boy-right here in front of me. Hard to believe, isn't it?" He patted the top of Joey's head. "You sure are a big lad, Joey."

"Yes, Sir."

"We're so happy that you're here."

We're happy? Joey glanced around briefly and wondered who was with his father that made him say "we."

"Did you have any trouble on the train?"

"No, Sir."

"Never got lost—even when you changed trains in Albany, or anything, eh?"

"No, Sir."

"Sir, you say?" He chuckled. "Please don't call me sir, okay? Call me Dad or Daddy, Joey. 'Sir' isn't for me. My captain in the Army was a Sir."

"Yes, Sir," Joey repeated, then shook his head. "I mean, okay," he managed to say.

Joe stared at his son for a moment then smiled as he fished a pack of Lucky Strikes out of his shirt pocket. He lit up with a Zippo lighter, then closed it with a loud click before grabbing Joey's suitcase.

"Come on, Son. I've got somebody who's dying to meet you."

A mob of people were buzzing around like spring bees, but Joe seemed to ease through them and led Joey into a kiosk where there were stools and a lunch counter. A juice machine sat on the counter; it splashed orange-colored juice all around on the inside of a glass reservoir. Scripted lettering on the side of the machine said Nedicks.

The strong smell of onions, grilled hot dogs and coffee permeated the air. Squared orange tables with black chairs occupied limited space and most of the seats were taken. Joey eyed the hot dogs rotating round and round on rotisserie tongs in a machine behind the counter. His nervous stomach still churned, but the hot dogs looked so juicy, and he was hungry.

A man's voice suddenly boomed through the public address system:

"May I have your attention please? Your attention please. Now boarding at Gate 42, coach number 331 for Buffalo. Buffalo now boarding at Gate 42. Please have your tickets ready for boarding.

Thank you."

Joe took Joey by the hand and led him to the back of the kiosk where a woman was sitting by herself. She stood and smiled when Joey and his father approached.

"Look who I've got here, Honey." Joe looked back and forth between the two. "Joey, this is your step-mother, Connie. Honey, this young man is Joey."

Chapter Thirty-Eight

Joey sat next to the woman his father had introduced as his step mother. His father took a seat on her other side and draped his arm around her shoulders. Joey was taken aback by the news of another mother and sensed he was staring. He felt his face redden with embarrassment.

Connie tucked a lock of hair behind her ear and fiddled with the bauble that dangled from the lobe. She was fairly pretty with the exception of an unattractive dime-sized mole on her left cheek that resembled a large brown scab with fuzz. Her pale skin was complemented by brown shoulder-length hair, which she constantly brushed away from her forehead with a swipe of her hand. She appeared to be in her mid-thirties but had dark circles under her eyes — the kind a person gets from sleepless nights and problems with no solutions.

She extended a hand. "Well, hello, Joey! It's great to meet you."

"Hello, Ma'am." He shook her hand.

"Your father has told me so much about you, and we've both been looking forward to this day for so long." She hugged him. "Oh! Joe, he looks just like you!" She paused for a beat. "My goodness. Does he ever." She giggled, then plowed her fingers through Joey's hair. "Just look at this hair. It's not black like yours, but he's got your curls, Honey."

She wore bright red lipstick and had darkened red rouge spots on both of her cheeks. Everything about her seemed exaggerated and decorative. The cigarette between her sticky red lips, bounced rapidly up and down when she spoke. "What a nice-looking boy," she said as she took a deep drag and exhaled. She smelled of alcohol and it reminded Joey of the times when Gram and his mother drank from the jug in Gram's kitchen.

They all looked at one another and it was quiet for a moment.

Connie smiled and broke the awkward silence. "I know everything is so new to you, but if you like, you can call me Mom, Joey. It will take awhile for you to get comfortable, but you can call me that if you like. You're home now. Like I said, your father has been waiting an awful long time for this day." She tickled Joey in the ribs. "And so have I, young man." She paused to crush her cigarette out in an ashtray and smiled. "So, how was your trip?"

Anxiety stirred in Joey's belly. He felt uncomfortable about calling the woman mother or mom. *I don't want to do that. I don't even know what to call my father yet.* He fought down the lump in his throat and murmured an answer he hoped would satisfy her for now.

"It was fine, Ma'am."

Joe said, "That was your first train ride, wasn't it, Son? What did you think of it?"

"It was fun. There were two conductors. Both were nice. One guy's name was George, and he talked to me a lot. He told me about New York City." Joey paused. "He said maybe you would take me to see the Brooklyn Dodgers play, someday. Is Brooklyn very far from New York?"

Connie and Joe both laughed.

"A Dodger fan, eh? I hate to tell you, Joey, but I'm a die-hard Yankee fan. Now, that doesn't mean I won't take you to a game sometime — especially when those Brooklyn bums play the Yanks. Just don't count on too many games that way though. Coming in to the city is quite a haul from out on the Island. We listen to a lot of games on the radio though."

Connie took another L&M cigarette out of her pocketbook and leaned over so Joe could light it.

A young man with a bearded chin hustled back and forth behind the counter. He wore a white jacket and a tall, white hat. Both had the Nedicks emblem scripted on them in orange cursive. Flies buzzed around his head, but they didn't seem to bother him — or most customers for that matter. Connie kept waving them away as she spoke. "Are you hungry, Joey?"

"Yes I am, Ma'am. I ate the rest of my peanut butter sandwiches this afternoon but I'm hungry again." Connie squeezed his hand.

"Of course you are, dear. Well, your dad and I planned on taking you to a nice restaurant on 42nd Street, and you can have a big meal. We're going to a place called the Paramount Lounge." She glanced at Joe. "That reminds me, Joe, we'd better get going soon if we're going to get a table."

Joey stared at the hotdogs turning over and over on the rotisserie bars. His mouth watered.

"Can I have a hotdog?" he blurted out.

"Let's see- a hot dog." Connie repeated as she glanced behind her at the counter. "Well, yes, Joey. I don't see why not." She looked at big Joe as she patted Joey's hand. "Darling, let's get Joey a hot dog, okay? We have enough time, I think-don't you?"

Joe nodded. "Sure."

Connie turned to Joey. "You can eat it on the way, how's that?" She reached inside her pocketbook and gave Joe a dollar bill. "Would you get it for him?"

Joe checked his watch and grimaced. "Sure thing, Honey—but after that, I'd better go find a locker for this suitcase. I don't want to lug it around all night." He strolled over to the food counter, got a hot dog, and returned a moment later. "I hope you like mustard and ketchup," he said as he handed the hot dog to Joey. "I put both on it."

"Yes, Sir, thank you."

Joe drew a long breath and let go a longer sigh. "Son, you're going to drive me nuts with that 'Sir' stuff."

Connie wanted to fill the awkward silence that followed but quickly focused on Joe's eyes. "Oh, just give him a little time, Joe. Everything is new to him. He'll be fine." She looked at Joey and smiled reassuringly.

"Yeah, I guess you're right. I'll be right back." He stood and walked away with Joey's suitcase in hand to look for an empty locker. After it was locked up, he sidetracked into the men's room, ran cold water and splashed some on his face and dried off with a paper towel.

Standing with his hands braced on the sink, he stared in the mirror and checked himself over. *All those questions from the kid. I guess I should'a figured on that though. Hmmm.* He ran a comb through his hair. *Damn. The boy does look like me though.*

The public address system buzzed again and another announcement echoed just as Connie cleared her throat and began to speak. "Joey, the thing is . . ."

"Your attention, please. Mister Dennis Mosley- please report to the information desk. Dennis Mosley, please report to the information desk located on the main floor next to Traveler's Aid. Thank you."

Connie continued. "As I started to say, Joey, the thing is your father's just a little anxious for you to call him 'Dad,' that's all. Just bear with him - Don't worry about anything. It will all work out, you'll see." She smiled and patted his hand again.

"Yes, Ma'am."

"After we finish eating dinner, we figured to take in a movie before we go home. Would you like that?"

"Wow! Yeah, I sure would. I think that would be lots of fun. What's the name of the movie?"

"It's a comedy called *Born Yesterday*. It stars William Holden and Judy Holliday. You like funny movies, don't you? I know I sure do."

"Yes, Ma'am. Funny movies are great."

She tapped his hand. "Joey, stop that now. You're making me feel old. Please- at least call me Connie." She smiled. "I think you'll find that easier and I'd like it better, too. Okay?"

"Okay, sure."

"Dean Martin and Jerry Lewis have a new movie out too. It's called *Jumping Jacks,* but your father thinks this one's better for all of us."

"Wait 'til you meet your new brothers and sister, Joey. I know you'll get along with them. My son, Darren, is twelve - same as you, and... "

"You have kids too?" Joey's eyes widened. He stared at her as if she had just claimed to be from the moon.

She laughed. "Well, of course I do. There's Darren, Clifford,

Adam, and my only girl, Becky. She's the oldest... fifteen. Cliff's ten, and Adam is the baby-he's just six."

Joe came back and Connie and Joey stood and pushed in their chairs. Connie clutched Joey's hand in hers and followed Joe out of Nedicks. Joey finished the last of his hot dog as they walked up three long flights of stairs to the street level.

Joey saw daylight at the top of the stairs at the same time he heard car horns tooting and a myriad of street noises. The sun had dropped low in the west, throwing shadows through the streets. The sky was piled with clouds that looked like gold and purple fruit turning red around the edges. It would be dark before long.

Neon lights blinked and flashed everywhere Joey looked. Yellow, green and checkered taxis zoomed back and forth down a wide but traffic-loaded 42nd Street.

The excitement built and swelled up the back of Joey's throat as he held onto Connie's hand tightly. He looked up at the skyscrapers, and wondered if they could fall over. They were so tall and he felt so small in their shadows. *They look just like the pictures in the books at school.* He shaded his eyes and craned his neck to see as high as he could. *Wow. What would happen if those buildings fell down?*

They kept walking, dodging and zig-zagging around people, right and left, as they approached each corner and waited for the traffic lights to turn green. Joe rested his hand on Joey's shoulder and each time a light changed he steered Joey through the intersections. He tried to keep him from bumping into people.

Suddenly, there was a loud rumbling sound—like thunder. The ground vibrated under their feet. It was scary and Joey stopped in his tracks. The feeling quickly took him back to that day so long ago when he went to work with Gramps and felt the rumbling of approaching trains.

"Wow!" He looked up at his father. "What's that?"

"Oh—that's just the subway," said Joe.

"Subway?"

"Yes. That's just a different kind of train that travels underneath the streets in New York."

"Wow! Why do they do that?"

"Well, there's not enough room for all the cars and trucks to move people to where they want to go up here on the street." He shook his head. "There's just too many."

"New York is awful big, ain't it?"

"Yes, it is that, for sure, Son. We're in the heart of the city right now. It's called Manhattan. This part—42nd and Broadway is called Times Square."

With that, Joe let go of Joey's hand and edged over closer to the curb where he waved his arms up and down at whizzing cabs. None stopped. After a few minutes, Joe gave up. "Ah, that's okay," he said. "We can walk there just as fast. We don't need a cab right now, okay, Connie? This way you can see a bit more of the city too, Joey."

Sheets of newspaper, food wrappers and other trash littered the sidewalks. Cigarette butts were everywhere. Strange-looking people, dressed in filthy clothes, stood along the sidewalk hawking jewelry, books and religious verses. Big Joe ignored them and kept moving. "It's only a few blocks to the Paramount." He looked at the wonder reflected on Joey's face and grinned. "We'll be okay," he said.

"So says you!" Connie yelled over the noise. She continued to squeeze Joey's hand. "I don't care much for the city, Joey. Can you tell?"

"Ah! Nothing to it," said Joe. "One big circus, that's all. I would never want to live in the city, though. It takes some getting used to."

Some neon signs were as big as buildings. Joey's eyes focused on one in particular that was very high above the street. It advertised Camel cigarettes and showed a man with a cigarette between his fingers. A pack of Camels was next to his head and he was blowing perfect smoke rings out of his mouth.

Joey stared in amazement.

An equally huge blue and yellow billboard said "Chevrolet", with a picture of a new car. It showed a man, a woman, and a little girl sitting in a green 1952 Chevrolet. They were a happy-looking family, waving and smiling and a slogan underneath said: "See the USA in your Chevrolet."

A plethora of smells wafted through the air as they passed hot dog, pretzel and other food carts and kiosks. Vendors sold magazines, women carried baskets of apples, and others peddled fresh-roasted peanuts. A man with a cane wore sunglasses and had a sign hanging from his neck that said: "Blind." Another one sat on the sidewalk, strumming a guitar. The guitar case was open in front of him and both of his legs were missing.

When they got to the Paramount Lounge, there was what looked like a movie screen set up in the lobby. It was about eight foot long by eight-foot wide. Everything on the screen was in black and white. A man and woman were yelling and making faces at each other on the screen. Joe stopped in front of it.

"What's this?"

"That, my boy is a big screen television set," said his father. "You can bet there's not many TV screens that size anywhere else." He pointed. "And that's Sid Caesar and Imogene Coca doing their *Show of Shows.*

"You've never seen television before, Joey?" said Connie.

"Television? No. But I heard about it in school. We didn't have one at The Home, but some of the other kids told us they already had it at their houses. Can we watch for a minute, please?"

"Sure, take a look, but we have to move along shortly." said Joe.

"We have a television set at our apartment, too, Joey," said Connie. "It's brand new. Mind you, it's not nearly the size of that one, but we have one. You can watch it all you want."

Joey watched for a few minutes then the head waiter met them just inside the door to the restaurant and escorted them to a table in the corner. Another waiter, wearing a black bow tie, took over. He handed menus to all of them.

"Good evening, folks. Welcome to the Paramount - can I start you off with a cocktail?"

"Yes," said Joe. "Give the lady a glass of Burgundy, and I'll have a rye on the rocks. Would you like a soda, Joey?"

"Yes, please."

"My. Such a polite young man," said Connie. "What kind would you like?"

"Do they have Coca Cola?"

"Sure do," said the waiter. "I'll be right back with those and take your order."

Connie agreed and Joe ordered steak for all of them. It was the first time Joey had ever had steak. They each had two more drinks during dinner. Joey had another Coke. During the conversation that ensued, Joey learned that Grand Central Station was built underground nearly a hundred years earlier. "And it was remodeled sometime around 1915 or16," said Joe.

Joey cleared his throat. He paused and took a long swallow of Coke. "Have you talked to Beth? Will she be coming to live with us, too?"

Joe winced and Connie's eyes widened.

"No, I'm afraid not," said Joe as he worked on his steak. He didn't so much as glance at Joey. "We just don't have the room for everybody, Son." He took another swallow of his drink and stuck another piece of steak in his mouth.

"So where were we?" Connie asked, forking up some potatoes. "What do you think of the city, Joey?"

"It's awful big." He paused then looked at his father. "Where is your house, Dad?" It was the first time he had called his father, Dad and somehow it felt good. He felt the tension seep out of himself like air from a balloon.

"We live out on Long Island. We'll head out there right after the movie. We have another train ride to get out there. East Northport is the name of the town."

An uncomfortable moment of silence followed. Joey said, "Have you talked to Brian or Mitchell and Merrill?"

Joe made a face like he was passing gas. He paused mid-chew and shook his head. "No, Joey—I haven't." He picked up his glass and studied the rim. Joey sensed he was getting aggravated as he sipped his drink and lit a cigarette. After a few puffs, he ground it out in the ashtray. "Let's finish up here, okay?"

Connie reached over and squeezed Joey's hand. "Joey, your father and I have been together for six years. He hasn't spoken to Alice or the other kids since he got out of the Army."

Joey wanted to ask more questions but thought he should wait.

After the movies, they took a cab and went back to get Joey's suitcase. Then, taking another taxi to Pennsylvania Station, Joe bought tickets for the Long Island Railroad that would take them out to East Northport. They found seats and tucked Joey's suitcase underneath, on the floor. The train lurched forward and they were on their way.

A few moments slipped by and Joe said, "I see in the paper where your Dodgers are in first place already - and it's not even July, Joey. That should make you happy, eh? Those bums are finally doing something." He patted Joey's leg and laughed. "It's hard for everybody to believe, ya' know?"

"Yes, Sir." He was still pondering what his father had just said about Brian and the twins.

Joe said, "You know the Giants beat the Dodgers last year and knocked them out of the chance to play the Yanks in the World Series. Bobby Thompson's home run."

"Yes, Sir, I know that," said Joey. "But they won't this year because Jackie Robinson is helping us win."

Joe grinned. "Yeah, and the Yanks have got Joe DiMaggio too." They talked baseball for a while before Joe, laid his head back and closed his eyes. He dozed for the rest of the trip. Connie and Joey had very little to say to one another as the train rolled along in the dark.

Why doesn't Dad want to talk to anybody back home, Joey wondered? *I thought Mom said he was here on business?* The boy had so many questions, but the adrenaline slowly ebbed from his body, leaving the weight of exhaustion in its wake.

Nearly an hour later, when the train reached Huntington Station, Joe grabbed the suitcase and they walked to his car, parked near the station. It was a canary-yellow 1945 Dodge that showed its age. On the way to the highway, the engine died when Joe stopped for any reason at all, and there was a loud screeching noise whenever he applied the brakes.

From the station, Joe took Highway 25A, which was for the most part, residential except for a smattering of stores that were closed. Joey soon realized that Long Island didn't look anything like New York City. There were no skyscrapers, and the sidewalks were empty. Everything appeared to be cleaner, too. An Esso gas station sat on the far end of the main street next to an A&P store. The adjacent neighborhood was lined with huge shade trees and bungalows in East Northport.

It was almost midnight by the time Joe pulled in behind the apartment. From the back seat, Joey leaned up to see their headlights shine on a dirt driveway that wound around back of a store called Breem's Drugs and Notions.

The windows inside the apartment glowed weakly, like sleepy eyes. A barking dog was chained up at the back of the lot. Other than the dog and the hazy glow of a Television set somewhere inside, there was no sign of life.

"Well, this is it, Joey. This is where we live," said Connie. Everyone got out, and she fished around in her pocketbook for her keys while Joe opened the trunk and grabbed Joey's suitcase.

"Somebody's still up," Connie murmured.

"They can't be awake," said Joe, as they entered through the back door and into the living room. "See, the only thing on television is the test pattern."

"What's a test pattern?" said Joey.

Joe pointed. "See the big cross on the screen and you can hear that ungodly ringing noise. That means there is no more television until tomorrow morning. I'm not sure what they are testing, but that's what they call it - a test pattern."

"Every day?"

"Yeah - afraid so. Every day starting at midnight. No shows."

A girl was curled up on the couch. She was wrapped in a green-and-blue- checkered blanket that she peeled away when Connie leaned over and kissed her on the forehead.

"Wake up, sleepyhead." Connie sat down by the girl's feet.

Joe turned on a lamp. He pushed a button on the television and the screen went black. He scooted in and sat next to Connie on the couch.

"You fell asleep watching television, eh, honey?" said Connie.

"Uh huh," said the girl. She rubbed her eyes and stretched. "I was watching Lucy and Uncle Miltie with the boys - but I must've fallen asleep. They all went to bed, huh?"

Joey stood there, feeling out of place. The room was suddenly too small. Everything looked so strange. The walls closed in on him until he could barely breathe.

"Becky," said Connie, "Say hello to your brother, Joey. We were going to wait until morning, but since you're up - Joey this is my daughter, Becky."

Becky yawned. "Hi, Joey." She stood and hugged him then glanced at her mother. "Gosh... he looks just like Dad."

Connie stood up. "Yes, that's exactly what I thought," she said as she draped her arm around Joey's shoulders and squeezed. "Big boy, isn't he?"

Joey sensed movement behind him and turned. A boy as tall as himself stood there. He wore jeans, and had a major case of bed head. Barefooted and naked from the waist up, he folded his arms across his very thin frame. He had a narrow face and obvious bucked teeth.

"Joey... this is your brother, Darren," said Joe.

"Hello," said Darren, as he rubbed his eyes and reached out to shake hands.

"Hello," said Joey very sheepishly. He didn't know what else to say to the strangers.

Another boy entered the room and joined them.

"Oh, boy. Well... you're all up," said Connie. "It's just as well, I guess." She giggled. "Cliff, this is Joey."

"Hi." Cliff yawned and stretched. "I wanted to stay up for you guys. Sorry—I just fell asleep a little while ago." He put out his hand and Joey shook it. He appeared to be thinking of a private joke because his eyes lit up and a smile flickered at the corner of his mouth.

"Hello," said Joey. Cliff was considerably shorter than Darren and Joey, but also on the slim side. He sat on the easy chair and leaned slightly forward, his forearms resting on his thighs.

"Well, now. That makes everybody, except for Adam, our youngest," said Connie. "But, let's not wake him, okay? Morning will be soon enough."

"That's for sure," said Joe. He stood and stretched his arms out to the side. Yawning, he said, "I have to get up in five hours for work, so I'm going to bed. I'll catch up with you tomorrow, Son. Goodnight. Night, everybody." He disappeared down a short hallway - went through a door and closed it softly behind him.

"You kids get back to bed, too... school in the morning," said Connie. "Come on, Joey, I'll get you situated so you can get some sleep, too. You're probably dog-tired by now. It's been a long day, hasn't it?"

"Yes, Ma'am."

Becky giggled.

"What's so funny, Beck?" asked Connie.

"Nothing. It's just that he called you 'Ma'am'." She giggled again.

Connie looked at her for a long moment as she processed the thought. "Well, I happen to think that's nice. A little respect never hurt anybody." She put an arm around Joey and squeezed. "Give him time, for Pete's sake, Becky. How would you feel coming into this clan for the first time?"

"I know, All right, Mom. Geez! I'm going to go to bed now, too. Good night, Joey — see you in the morning. Goodnight, Mom."

"Good night, Honey."

Connie turned and smiled. She studied Joey in the complete silence that followed. Joey didn't know what to say. He felt his face turn red.

"I can't get over how much you look like your daddy, Joey." She moved her head from side to side. "It's really amazing." She paused ever so slightly and said, "Well now, as far as school goes - you won't start tomorrow. I've arranged to take off work Thursday morning. We'll get you signed up then."

"Yes, Ma'am."

Her mouth twisted in a sad parody of a smile. "Try, 'yes, Connie,' would you, Joey? I'd sure appreciate it." She smiled.

"Okay," said Joey.

"Follow me, Son." She led him down the hallway to a set of stairs. "The boys all sleep upstairs." She pulled a string that turned on a light. Darren and Cliff were still awake; they pulled the covers over their heads when the light came on. There were two bunk beds in the room, and the two boys had the top of each one. The other boy, Adam, was asleep in the bottom bunk, under Cliff. The room smelled like dirty feet.

"You can take that other bottom bunk, Joey. Do you need anything out of your suitcase before I turn the light off?"

"My pajamas, is all."

Darren and Cliff giggled.

"Don't mind them, Joey. They think it's funny to wear pajamas because they sleep in their underwear. They don't have any pajamas. There's nothing wrong with wearing pajamas, you two. You go right ahead and put yours on, Joey. Why don't you go to the bathroom and change, so you can see what you're doing, okay?" She hugged him and kissed him on the forehead.

"Good night, Ma'am."

Darren and Cliff giggled again.

When Joey slid into his bunk, the sheets were cold, but it felt good to lie down. It was so odd to not be sleeping in a dorm. He was exhausted, but he lay there thinking about his unusual day. He had finally found his father. And New York City- skyscrapers, the subway, the taxis, flashing neon lights — everything was so exciting.

He folded his arms behind his head and closed his eyes. His mind was a kaleidoscope of the memories he had seen in the hours since he'd left The Home. Now that he had opened those doors in his mind, he couldn't seem to close them. Faces, voices, feelings, sights sounds, all swirled around and around.

I miss Mom, Gram and Gramps - Sis too. What about this woman, Connie and all her kids? I know I have to stop calling her "ma'am," but I just can't call her "Mom." It was even hard for me to call Mrs. Alexander "Ma." I hope Connie doesn't get mad at me for not calling her "Mom." Dad doesn't look anything like I thought he would - except he's a big man – just like Sis said. I can't remember from that picture Mrs. Marcetti showed me before I left. I wonder... how Dad can be married to Mom and Connie too? How can I have two mothers at the same time?

It wasn't long before he forgot about the strange bed as sleep carried him away.

Chapter Thirty-Nine

Twelve-year-old Joey had been living on Long Island with his father for nearly eight months. During that time the family moved three times — from rental apartment to rental apartment and changed schools twice. Finally, they rented a three-bedroom house in Huntington. It had been built by Connie's father, Mike Machinaglo, a stone mason born and raised in Sicily. He had built the home, stone by stone, with his own hands right after World War two.

Joey adjusted to his new life fairly well, all things considered. He called his father, dad and became comfortable calling Connie, Mom. He never stopped thinking about his real mother, Alice, or Gram and Gramps. They exchanged occasional letters but they were rare. He never heard from Mitchell and Merrill or Brian, but Alice convinced Joey that they were all comfortable in their foster homes.

His father worked for Kissick's Coal and Oil Company in East Northport. They had no money in savings and lived from paycheck to paycheck. Joe shoveled coal and earned sixty dollars a week. Connie was a cleaning attendant at the Veteran's Hospital in nearby Northport. She rode to work with a black co-worker named Jake and helped with the gas money.

It didn't take long for Joey to learn that being part of a big family had its problems. Seven people, including five kids, sharing one small bathroom proved to be a daily adventure, especially during school days. Joey reminded himself that taking turns was still much better than emptying chamber pots and sitting in a sweltering or freezing outhouse

He took on a paper route delivering Newsday during his first summer on Long Island. Rolling 115 newspapers with string, he packed them like artillery rounds into the two bags hanging from his handlebars. Riding an old bicycle down the streets and sidewalks, he sailed newspapers with the accuracy of a marksman onto porches, whapping them solidly against front doors.

Darren and Cliff chose not to take paper routes and instead worked as caddies at the Cold Spring Harbor Golf Course.

Quarreling naturally broke out between the boys from time to time over most anything but usually the bickering involved whose turn it was to pick television shows. Joey liked *Captain Video* and *Roy Rogers,* while Darren and Cliff insisted on watching *The Cisco Kid* and *The Lone Ranger.* Adam still liked stuff for younger kids like *Howdy Doody and Kukla, Fran and Ollie.* Joe and Connie rarely watched television, but when they did, it was usually a news program, *Your Hit Parade* or *I love Lucy.* Becky was an avid reader and enjoyed doing homework. In addition, at fifteen, she was boy crazy, so television was not a big concern for her.

Once the excitement and novelty of living with his father wore thin, Joey realized his father was a very distant person. He was not a hands-on, affectionate man. Rarely, if ever, did he hug Joey or any of the other kids. In fact, there were never any extended father-and-son conversations.

He usually came home from work, drank a beer, smoked and studied the daily horse racing section of the newspaper. He ate supper by himself, showered and went to his room, closing the door behind him. There, he lived in his own private world. Sitting on the edge of his bed, he smoked Luckies and drank beer while he reading magazines and books. Louis Armstrong, Charlie Parker or some other Jazz music played on his Webcor phonograph. Nobody was allowed to disturb him except Connie who replenished his cans of beer from time to time.

The biggest adjustment for Joey was learning that the blessing of living with one's own family, rather than in foster homes, didn't guarantee security or happiness. He was living with his father less two weeks when he witnessed the outbreak of an argument between his father and Connie. It didn't take long to realize that conflict between the two could erupt with alarming frequency.

Joey had never heard such commotion between husband and wife in any of the foster homes. He remembered hearing Mr. And Mrs. Bushkin arguing in their bedroom from time to time, but with doors closed their voices sounded like little more than loud conversations. Gram and Gramps rarely argued either. There were some arguments when Alice and Gram drank their wine, but there was never name-calling or cursing like that between his father and Connie.

That first argument was loud and nasty, with a lot of shouting and name-calling by both Connie and Joey's father. The other kids, including Becky, didn't seem to be as bothered by the situation but Joey was confounded and hurried upstairs to his room in order to escape the riff. When he rushed into his bedroom, Darren sat on his bunk and laughed. "What's wrong, Joey? Haven't you ever seen people fight before?"

"No, I haven't. They act like they hate each other or something."

Cliff sat on his bed sifting through his baseball cards. He snickered. "Well, get used to it. They fight all the time don't they, Darren?"

Joey's eyes widened. "Really?" He cut Cliff a look then turned back to Darren.

"Yeah, really." said Darren. Boy, you sure are stupid. "Ask Becky if you don't believe us. You know her bedroom is just down the hall from theirs. She gets to hear it all."

"Yeah," said Cliff. He grinned. "You ain't even seen a really big fight yet."

•   •   •   •   •

A year later in 1953, Joey, who had once been overjoyed to be living with his father, was more determined than ever to stay in contact Beth, Brian and the twins. He yearned to see Gram and Gramps and his real mother, Alice, too. When he found a rare opportunity to ask his father about them, he was told not to worry about such things. "They have their lives — you have yours," said Joe. "Be happy about that, okay Son?"

The fighting often broke out in the dining room or kitchen, but more often than not, the skirmishes took place in Joe and Connie's bedroom, which was adjacent to the living room, where the kids watched television.

Sometimes, when Connie saw an explosion coming, she sent the boys upstairs to their room or herded them into the living room, where she turned up the volume on the television and closed the French doors.

Most of the altercations between Connie and Joe stemmed from Joe's drinking and betting on the horses. Friday night when he got paid, he cashed his check and stopped at Jerry's Bar and Grill to tip a few with his fellow workers. The bar was loud and very accessible — actually within walking distance of home and the coal yard where Joe worked. Sometimes, when he got home he was drunk. Connie would naturally be upset and a fight would likely ensue. Their voices started out low-toned, but anxious — then graduated in stages — from grumbling and snarling, to shouting — and ultimately ended in name-calling. A crescendo of full-blown rage could develop in a very few minutes. Eventually, a door was slammed and the fight might end then with abrupt silence.

Other arguments would sputter off and on all night long and into the next day, when the silent treatment went into effect by either one or both parents.

•   •   •   •   •

It had been blistering hot that day with popcorn clouds floating in the sky. The temperature remained in the eighties with humidity so high that everybody found it difficult to breathe. There was no air conditioning.

"Air conditioning is for the rich people," Connie had said.

The sun was disappearing behind the trees to the west, casting the back yard into long shadows and silhouettes. Joey and Darren sat in the living room watching *The Milton Berle Show*. Joey was sprawled on the couch while Darren slouched in his favorite chair, elbows on the arms, fingers steepled in front of him.

Outside, the blacktop was still steaming and the boys had raised the windows in order to get some relief. A stingy, sporadic breeze fluttered the skimpy curtains and it was quiet except for the laughter coming from the television. The French doors separating the hall from the living room were closed.

Sixteen-year-old Becky was out on a date with her boyfriend, Bart Windercrane. Cliff had walked to Heckscher Park with his friend, Billy Stanley, and seven-year-old Adam was upstairs in the boys' room, messing with an erector set.

It was a Friday, Joe's payday, and he hadn't come home in time for supper. The boys heard Connie's voice all too soon that night when Joe finally got home around eight. The fight erupted in their bedroom about ten minutes later.

"No! You're the one who starts this shit, Joe, when you plop your ass on that barstool instead of coming home!" Connie screamed. "I should have known, it being Friday night. You just can't be trusted with your paycheck, can you? You're like a kid."

"That's because you treat me like one, you bitch! I'm tired of having to fork over all my money to let you dole it out any way you see fit. It's not right, dammit. I'm a man!" He gave her a cold glare and turned away, throwing his hands up as if to signal he was finished with the conversation, conceding the fight to her.

"Well then, act like one." Connie stood up to him like an angry mouse taunting a lion. She was bright red in the face and looked as if she was about to have a stroke. "We tried giving you money for yourself, remember, Joe? How many times, huh? You always end up blowing it on the fuckin' horses. Who in the hell pays the bills around here? Not you—that's for damned sure. Nothing would get taken care of if it wasn't for me, and you know it."

Joey heard the whole thing and wished his father would just be quiet. He quietly opened the doors and skirted the wall leading to his father's bedroom. His ears were ringing as he pressed his head flush against the jam of their door. Every cell in his body was trembling. His fear was like a band around his chest. He couldn't seem to get a deep breath. He didn't want to get caught listening, but couldn't help himself.

"You know what your problem is, Connie? You need to get your nose out of Jake's ass. That's the real problem—isn't it? I think you've been giving that black bastard more than gas money, to tell the truth."

"That's a damned lie, and you know it, Joe! Jake has nothing to do with any of this."

"Yeah, you're fucking him, but he has nothing to do with any of our problems? I'm just supposed to sit back and take that shit, huh? Well, that just won't fly, Lady."

"Joe, I told you before, I'm not doing anything with Jake or anybody else." Her voice quivered as she spoke. "He's my ride to and from work at the hospital—that's it. You're just drunk, or you wouldn't be saying that."

"Awwww, bullshit! He's your ride all right! You think I was born yesterday? I'm sick of your treating me like a kid. We go through this shit all the time. I don't have to listen to this. I want out! The sooner the better, you hear?"

"Why does everything have to be so one-way with you, Joe? I know one thing; you've threatened me for the last time about leaving. You got it, you bastard! You don't care what happens to the kids, do you? You never did. You don't even care about your own kids. Well you can leave tomorrow—we don't need you. Get out!"

Connie sounded as if she was fighting back tears as she edged closer to the bedroom door. Joey tensed up as he watched the knob turn. He raced back to the French doors, into the living room, and jumped onto the couch with tears in his eyes. Darren stared at him and sniggered.

"Whoa! Why do you want to listen to that crap, anyway?"

Joey murmured, "Well, maybe you don't care, but I do. My dad is leaving, I just heard him say so." His shoulders sagged as his chin dropped.

"Oh, that's bull, too. They both have said that stuff before, but they never do it."

Connie rushed out of the bedroom. She stopped and looked

through the panes of glass on the French doors. Staring at the faces of the boys, she dabbed her eyes with Kleenex. Then, suddenly, she turned back to the bedroom door and flung it open.

She gritted her teeth and said, "I hope you know your son heard this whole thing, smart guy."

Joe didn't answer.

Connie slammed their door and rushed down the hall to the kitchen where she opened a bottle of beer and sat at the kitchen table.

Joey ran out and followed her. Meanwhile, Adam had come downstairs.

Connie sniffled and blew her nose then dabbed at her eyes before crushing the Kleenex in her hands. Joey hesitated then put a hand on her shoulder and rubbed. "It'll be okay, Mom."

Adam watched Joey attempting to comfort his mother and slid off his chair. Walking around the table, he stood on the other side of her. "Yeah, Mommy. It will be okay."

Suddenly, Joey's father was standing there. He seemed big and imposing as he took an aggressive step toward her. "Connie, I want the rest of my paycheck back, too."

Connie whirled around in the chair. "You're not getting squat, Mister! I need to pay the rent, one way or the other, to keep a roof over our heads. You're not getting anything!"

Joey eased away from all of them and stood with his back against the kitchen sink. He felt sick to his stomach and his knees were wobbly.

Joe's body dipped and swayed back and forth as he rammed a finger in Connie's face and tapped on her nose. His eyes narrowed and his jaws clenched as he growled, "Don't you go turning my kid against me either, you bitch!"

"What! Are you nuts, Joe? You've already scared him to death. Just look at him. You think these kids are stupid? They see what goes on around here. They'd have to be blind. Look at you! You can hardly stand up." She shook her head. "You drunk son of a bitch."

She paused a moment and turned. "Go in the other room, boys — right now! Go! In fact, go upstairs. This has been enough for one night." She reached for Joey's arm. "Go ahead, Joey. Go to bed now."

Adam sobbed as he ran upstairs. Joey chased after him and sat on his bed with him. He curled an arm around the boy much like a father would to console a son. "It'll be okay, Adam. Don't be scared. They'll stop fighting pretty soon."

"How come they have to fight, anyway?" Adam cried.

"I don't know. Didn't they fight before I came?"

"Yeah, sometimes, but not like now."

Darren slipped into the room and closed the door behind him. He jumped up onto his bunk letting his long legs dangle over the edge.

"Well, your dad thinks our mom is messing around with some guy at the hospital, Joey."

"What do you mean? What are you talking about, Darren?"

"Just what I said. Jake is this colored guy that works on the same floor with Mom. She rides to work with him because our car is junk. Dad thinks Mom and Jake are doing stuff. Didn't you hear him while you were sneaking around outside their door?"

"I wasn't sneaking! And I heard something, but I don't know what he meant."

Darren rolled his eyes. "Well, now you know, Joey. See? It's all your father's fault."

"Well—is it true? Is Dad right?"

Darren waved the question away like it was a fly. "Mom told me it wasn't true the last time he said it to her—and I believe her. I don't care what your father says."

"When was that? I wasn't here yet—right?"

"Nope. That was way before you came."

"Your daddy gets mad about everything," said Adam.

"Well, so does your mom, Adam," Joey quickly countered.

"Not like he does."

Cliff came into the room and tossed his baseball cap on his bunk. He flopped down on his bed.

"Your dad's drunk again, huh?"

An awkward moment of silence prevailed for a moment—then they heard it.

Craaaaash! "Damn you!" The noise came from downstairs. The boys gawked at each another.

"Oh, oh. What was that?" said Darren. He jumped down off his bunk and they all bumped into each other, clamoring to get downstairs.

Yellow glass was scattered all over the floor. Two big chunks glistened on the table.

Joe was standing by the kitchen window, leaning on a chair. There was tightness around his mouth, a grim, angry look in his eyes.

Connie stood on the other side of the table, face flushed and hands planted firmly on her hips. Her hair was damp on her forehead, and her eyes darted feverishly around the room.

"You're lucky I didn't smash it over that thick head of yours, you bastard!" Her eyes were wild and her lower lip jutted out.

Becky suddenly appeared from somewhere down the hallway. Her jaw dropped and her eyes widened. "Stop this, Mom! Stop, now — both of you! Are you crazy? Stop!" she screamed.

Both combatants turned their focus on Becky and it was deathly quiet for a moment.

"What happened?" Becky stared hard at her mother. Her face was a mask of concern. "How did Grandma's platter get broken?" She waited while the silence stretched taut between them.

"She did it." Joe pointed. "It's such bullshit!" he said, as he stumbled and nearly fell as he brushed past everybody on his way to his room. His body swayed from side to side and he bumped the wall as he stalked off down the hall. "Fuck you, bitch!" he mumbled just before slamming his bedroom door.

Connie sat on a kitchen chair and sobbed. All her life she thought she needed a man. She had the idea she was a flashlight and men were batteries. She couldn't shine without one in her life. She wondered how it had all come to this. Joe seemed so right when first they met, but everything had changed. She tucked a tumble of wild hair behind her ear and sipped her second beer.

"I threw the platter at that son of a bitch; that's what happened. He's goddamned lucky it wasn't over his head. The next one will be."

"Mom, stop! You don't mean that, and you know it." Becky struggled to find words. Tears sprang to her eyes. It was as though, for the first time, the seriousness of the situation was finally sinking in. Her lower lip trembled. She studied her mother's face.

"You've been drinking too, haven't you?" She wrapped her arm around Connie's shoulders and looked at the boys. "Get out of here, you guys. Go outside—or go watch television—do something... just go, please!"

The boys all headed down the hall except for Joey.

Connie grabbed her pocketbook and cigarettes and stood up. "I'll be back when I feel like it," she snarled on her way out the back door.

For Joey, the sense of panic was and huge, like an explosion. "Are my Dad and Connie really going to split up?"

Becky patted the top of his head. "I don't really know, Joey." She hung her head and sighed. "I don't know anything anymore. They have said stuff like that before. Just go to your room for now, okay?"

"But... what will happen to me if they do that, Becky? Where will I go?"

A tear slid out of his eye and rolled down his cheek.

Chapter Forty

Joey couldn't sleep the night of the horrendous fight between his father and Connie. Thoughts of the Buskin farm rushed back in Technicolor and the thought of going to another foster home made his insides quiver. He stared at the ceiling in the dark bedroom wondering if there was a way to turn off his mind. The waiting and wondering was the worst part. Every minute was like a bubble that grew and grew, filling with anticipation only to burst so that another might begin to form and grow and grow.

Joe got home from work before Connie the next day. He had the small Philco radio in the kitchen tuned to the horse racing results while perusing his newspaper. He jotted notes on a piece of paper until all of the racing results were announced then took a shower and hustled to his room with a towel wrapped around his waist. The kids didn't see him the rest of the night.

It was as if nothing had occurred the night before, but Joey's mind was in a whirl wondering what would happen next. *Have Dad and Connie made up? Is everything okay, again.* He had been lying on the floor in the living room watching *The Lone Ranger* with Darren when he suddenly got up and walked out.

"Hey, where are you going?" Darren asked.

Joey didn't answer but stepped out and sidled up to his father's bedroom door. He heard Louis Armstrong trumpet music and knocked on the door.

"Who is it?"

"It's me, Dad—Joey."

Silence followed for a moment before Joe asked, "What do you want?"

"Can I come in for a minute?"

Another brief pause followed. "Sure. Come on."

Joey eased into the room, where billowing cigarette smoke clouded the air.

"Close that door behind you, Son."

Joey hesitated a moment, then skirted around to the other side of the bed where his father sat in his boxer shorts with a book in one hand, and a cigarette in the other. His dirty work clothes lay in a pile on the floor at the foot of the bed. He glanced at Joey and exhaled smoke through his nostrils. He ground the cigarette out in the ashtray.

"Dad?"

"What is it, Joey?"

"Can... can I sit down?"

"Sure." His father scooted over but kept his eyes focused on the open book. Finally glancing at Joey, he said, "Well?"

Joey cleared his throat. "Dad, are you and Connie really going to break up?"

A long pause followed. "I don't know, Son." His eyes bore into Joey briefly as he flipped a page. "Maybe. We'll see," he said as he hung a fresh cigarette from his lip and lit up.

Joey decided it might be best to change the subject and ask about something else. "What's the name of that book, Dad?"

Joe turned the cover up to show him. "It's *God's Little Acre*, by Erskine Caldwell. It's a good one. You should read it someday when you're older."

"Okay, I will." He hesitated for just a moment. "Dad?"

"Yes?" Joe appeared to be impatient. The book dangled loosely between his legs as he took a deep drag on his cigarette and started coughing. "What is it, Joey

"Well, I just wondered... before Connie gets home, will you tell me about you and Mom?"

Joe appeared to be stunned as he slid away from Joey. He blinked at the thought of Alice, as if an invisible hand had slapped his face. His eyes widened and a red scald rose up his neck into his cheeks. He ground the cigarette out in the ashtray and slowly closed the book.

Laying it on the nightstand next to his pack of Luckies, he shook his head and breathed a heavy sigh. He leaned forward and placed his elbows on his knees, making their conversation more intimate. "Why? What do you want to know?"

"Anything, Dad, like—well—when was the last time you saw her? Was she sick? How come you guys didn't stay together? How can you be married to Connie if you and Mom are still married?

Joe studied his son for a moment then lit another cigarette and blew a plume of smoke. His eyes and mouth creased in a rare smile. His eyes took on a faraway look as he stared straight ahead out the window.

Joey could see that his mouth had tightened and his expression had become fiercely angry. He rubbed his fingertips along his jaw, idly contemplating his answer.

"Your mother was a beautiful woman, Joey. She even won a beauty contest early on when we lived in Washington. She was very intelligent too, Son." He paused and blew another puff of smoke. "But anyway—I haven't seen her since I came home from the war." He paused again for what seemed like a long time. "You would know more about her than me. I thought she was living with your grandpa and grandma in Gouvernuer. Isn't that right?"

"Yes. Most of the time, she did. Sometimes she stayed with a friend of hers though."

Joe murmured, "Yeah, so I heard. He quickly changed the subject. "So, how is the old man?" He smiled. "I liked Carl a lot. Is he okay?"

"No. Gramps had a stroke and he has trouble walking now." Joey paused. "What happened between you and Mom?

Joe brought the book back up in front of him and absentmindedly flipped a page back and forth. "Things just happen, Joey." Staring out the window again, he said, They happen, sometimes for the best."

A long pause followed before either of them spoke again.

"Dad, did you know that all those foster people were really mean to us kids? Me, Beth and Brian—even Mitchell and Merrill?

"No, I didn't. But, I didn't have any contact with anybody up north for lots of reasons and I was never aware of that, Joey. I'm sorry." He shook his head. In fact, Connie was the one who looked into getting you to come and live here."

"Well, can you just tell me . . ."

The door swung open and Connie rushed in and Joey cringed wondering if he was in trouble for being in the room.

With her hands on her hips, she said, "Joey, you need to get out of here now; me and your father need to talk!" she snapped.

Joey hesitated as he stood. "You're not going to fight again, are you?"

"No. I don't think so, Joey. Go ahead now, Son. Go out in the living room with Darren."

• • • • •

There were no more fights for over a week. Joey did his Newsday route every afternoon after school, and by the time he got home, he was generally too tired to do homework, so he ate whatever was left over from supper and went right to bed. When he got back from his route on Wednesday night, Connie sat in the dining room with a beer in her hand.

"There he is." She flashed him a bright smile and patted the top of his head. "How's the paper business?"

"Oh, okay. I'm hungry. Something smells good."

"You just wash your hands and have a seat. We had meatloaf. I kept a plate warm just for you."

When he was ready, she slid a plate overloaded with meatloaf and mashed potatoes in front of him and sat next to him. The eyes she turned on him were filled with sadness. Joey barely noticed as he shoveled the food into his mouth.

"Joey, we have to talk before you go to bed."

He set his fork down and stared at her. "Oh no, what did I do wrong now?"

Connie took a long swallow of the beer and folded her hands in her lap. She couldn't seem to fix her eyes on him and gazed at the floor. There was a long pause before she finally looked up. She rubbed his arm and feigned a weak smile. "Nothing, Joey. You haven't done a thing—I'm proud of you. You're really a good boy." She patted his arm. "But, we have to move."

"Move? You mean to another new house?"

"Yes. We fell behind on the payments for five months and my father won't put up with it anymore."

"But, I don't want to move." He turned to face her, his eyes meeting hers. "I like this place. I like my school and all my friends are here in Huntington—and what about my paper route?"

"Well, that's not all—there's something else." She'd stopped looking at him and stared at her feet instead. Her eyes reflected regret, sympathy, empathy.

"What?"

She looked around as if in a daze, her chin trembling and said, "Your father and I have decided that we need to separate for a while—not a divorce. We may get back together someday, but we need time apart." Her eyes were wet and red, and her voice soft and weak.

Joey's chest felt strange, as if there were pins and needles jabbing at it. He felt the tears welling up and shook his head. "No! Why?" He jumped up and looked down at her, his face a map of shock. "Why are you doing this?" She reached out and squeezed his wrist.

"I just told you, Son. We aren't getting along. You know that don't you? Of course you do. I know you do. Remember that big fight last week?" She tucked a loose strand of hair beneath her ear, always a sign that she was nervous.

"But you guys aren't fighting now. I thought everything was going to be okay."

"I'm sorry, Joey. I really am. We both wanted to make a home for you." She began to run her fingers along his arm. Joey winced and jerked away from her touch as if she had burned him.

There was a very long pause of silence while waves of nausea crashed through his stomach. He felt he might vomit. "Where will I go?" He nearly choked on the question. "Where will Dad go? What about everybody else?"

"Well, Becky is going to stay with her girlfriend, Shelly and her family. The boys are going to stay with me at my mom and dad's place in Huntington Station. You will be going to live with foster parents in Greenlawn." She took a long swallow from the bottle of beer and said, "I'm really sorry, Son." Now there were tears flowing from Connie's eyes.

Joey ran to his room and dropped face down on his bed. He didn't take his clothes off. Clutching the pillow, he held it over his head and sobbed. He cried until his stomach ached. He wrapped his arms around himself and clamped his teeth together.

It's not fair. I hate her for this... I hate both of them. I need to talk to somebody. Gramps? Uncle Glenn? Sis? Yes, that's it. I need to talk to Sis.

•   •   •   •   •

Joey awoke early from a restless sleep. He felt relieved to have the previous night behind him. Soft yellow sunlight and a fresh breeze spilled in the through his bedroom window as he lay there thinking.

Connie had told him that the new social worker, Mrs. Ballanger, would be there at ten to pick him up. He jumped up and clambered downstairs to see his father before he left for work. Joe was finishing a cup of coffee when Joey came in. He sat down across from his father. Connie conveniently stayed in the bathroom and everyone else was still in bed.

Joey said, "Don't send me away, Dad. Please?" He swallowed at the combination of disappointment and uneasiness that crowded the back of his throat.

Joe shook his head and lit a cigarette.

"The split will only be for a little while, Son. One way or the other, you'll eventually be coming to live with me — with or without Connie. I just need to get settled in someplace so they'll let you live with me. You understand?" He paused and looked the other way.

Joey shook his head in frustration. "No. I don't want to go to a foster home again."

Joe stood and faced him, hands jammed down in his pockets, his right shoulder pressed against the wall. He tucked a pack of Luckies in his shirt pocket. "Sorry, Son. I have to get going." He fluffed Joey's hair and grinned. "Don't worry; I'll stop by and see you once you're settled in Greenlawn."

Joey wanted to believe what he said. He felt like he had to have hope or he wouldn't have anything to look forward to despite the feelings he harbored deep inside. He followed Joe out the door and watched him as he got into the car and backed out of the driveway then he sat on the patio and stared at the car until he could no longer see it.

I don't think he cares... I don't think he ever did care about any of us. Here I go again — moving farther and farther away from everybody. I wonder what Beth is doing. What about Brian and the twins? I always think about them. I miss her so bad — especially when things like this happen. I wonder what she would tell me right now. I feel like I've lost her for good. It feels so wrong, leaving here. I wish something could have changed their minds. I wonder if this is the way Dad left Mom.

At ten minutes before ten the caseworker pulled in the driveway. Mrs. Ballanger was a tall woman. She wore wire-rimmed glasses and had long, red hair that hung well below her shoulders. A black book was tucked under her arm as she walked toward the patio. Spotting Joey, she stopped in front of him.

"You must be Joey?"

"Yes, I am." Anxiety grew like an air bubble in the center of his chest.

She extended her hand and smiled. "I'm Gloria Ballanger. Pleased to meet you, Joey."

Connie suddenly came out the back door and addressed her. "Good morning. You must be Gloria?"

"Yes, and you're Joey's mother, Connie."

"Yes. That's right. They shook hands. "Joey's dad had to leave for work earlier. Won't you come inside? I have some coffee ready if you'd like."

"Yes, thank you."

Connie looked at Joey's suitcase sitting by the table. "Joey, please take your suitcase out and set it by Mrs. Ballanger's car."

Joey hesitated at first then said, "Okay."

Connie poured two cups of coffee while Mrs. Ballanger opened her black book and pulled out some papers. She had tears in her eyes and wadded the Kleenex in her hands.

Mrs. Ballanger said, "He appears to be a nice, healthy-looking young man, Mrs. Shussler."

"Yes. Joey is a good boy. I hope to get him back as soon as possible." She dabbed at her eyes. "Of course, I don't blame you. I know this is difficult, Mrs. Shussler." She sipped her coffee. "I see so many heartbreaking situations in this job, you know." She sighed. "Now if you'll just sign on the lines I've marked here... and here — we'll be all set."

Joey came back inside just as Connie finished signing and soon after that, Mrs. Ballanger was ready to leave. She checked her watch. "I've got a very busy day ahead of me, so I'd best be going," she said. "I wish I could stay and chat a while, but you know how it is."

Sobbing, Connie threw her arms around Joey and squeezed so hard Joey thought he might suffocate. She kissed him on both cheeks. "Be a good boy, Son. We won't be apart long. You'll see."

Tears rolled down Joey's cheeks. "Goodbye, Connie."

After Mrs. Ballanger backed out of the driveway, she said: "Well — we're on our way, young man. Won't be long and you'll be settled in at your new home."

Joey had nothing to say for a long time. *I wonder where Dad is going to live? I'm all mixed up. I wish Beth was here right now.*

"Ma'am?"

"Yes, Dear?"

"Where is my dad is going to live?"

She shrugged. "Well, I believe he'll be staying someplace right there in East Northport, close to his job. He'll have to let our department know his address right away though. We must be able to contact him at all times."

They rode in silence for quite some time before Mrs. Ballanger spoke.

"You'll like these people you'll be staying with, Joey. They're very nice. They like children and have had others live with them."

Joey wanted to scream at her. *Doesn't she know I've heard all that stuff before? I wonder what Mr. Neagle and Ma Alexander would say if they knew I had to move again already. My father isn't keeping me with him like he promised when I left. I wonder if that welfare place would let me go back to The Home. I miss Ma.*

Chapter Forty-One

T he gray morning darkened when they left for Greenlawn, which was only four miles from Huntington. Joey gazed out the window but saw very little. His mind was filled once again with fear and anxiety.

He wondered what the new foster home would be like. *Will the people be mean like the Bushkins or the Couzens? How long will I be away from my father? Will I be able to call Beth and tell her what has happened?*

Mrs. Ballanger had very little to say during the short trip and Joey was glad about that. He was tired of hearing the same old lies from caseworkers. He looked at her nervously as the miles passed in silence. She said his new foster parents' name was Comstock and that was all he needed.

Their driveway was difficult to see from the road, because huge trees and lilac bushes sheltered it on both sides of the entrance. Flowering pink rosebuds clung to a wire fence that extended from the mailbox, all the way back two hundred yards or so, to a one car garage. The clapboard house was painted light green with chocolate-brown shutters and wasn't very big, but the front and back lawns were huge.

Mrs. Ballanger parked the car as close to the garage as possible and Joey got out. He grabbed his suitcase and they walked to the front door where an elderly couple was waiting to greet them.

The man said, "Good morning, Gloria." He looked at Joey then backed up a bit and said, "I see you've brought a young man to us. He is a big lad, isn't he, Mary?"

His wife smiled and said, "Yes, he certainly is." She quickly extended her hand to Mrs. Ballanger. "Good to see you again, Gloria. Please come in."

The home appeared neat and cozy inside. The foyer was carpeted and a vase of flowers decorated a small table by the door. Mrs. Ballanger and Joey followed the couple into the living room. A strong smell of fresh coffee and fried bacon permeated the air.

Otto Comstock was bald except for some fuzzy brown hair that resembled a halo circling the outside of his rather large head. The left side of his face drooped dramatically and his mouth appeared to be lopsided. He had a gray mustache and wore black-rimmed glasses. He was a tall man. His pants were held up by suspenders but appeared to be too short. Consequently his white work socks were exposed like the stockings of a horse.

He blew out a heavy breath and jammed his hands at the waist of his pants. "Well now, good morning, Joseph." He offered his hand and Joey shook it.

"Good morning, Sir."

Comstock's wife, Mary, was a short, big-boned woman wearing a dark blue dress with white polka dots. She had a round, friendly-looking face, and her gray hair was covered with a hair net. Her elbows were dimpled and her tan nylon stockings were rolled up to her knees and looked like doughnuts.

"Good morning, Joseph," she chirped as she studied Joey. Her lips were pressed together tightly and her head tipped slightly as she looked closely at his acne. "My, he has a rough skin condition, doesn't he?"

"Yes — well, he's at that age, you know," said Mrs. Ballanger.

"Yes, of course," said Otto. "But he'll outgrow that soon enough. We all remember those adolescent days, don't we?" He chuckled. "Won't you have a seat in the dining room? We've got some coffee ready if you'd like a cup, Gloria? Mary will show Joey where his bedroom is and he can put his suitcase in there."

"Yes, coffee sounds good, Otto. It sure smells wonderful." She giggled. "And I must confess, I haven't had my three cup quota for the day yet."

Mary took Joey's hand. "Come on, Joseph. I'll show you your room. We're so glad to have you staying with us. You can consider yourself part of the family now."

On the way down the hall, Joey barely noticed a birdcage that dangled from a long chain on the ceiling. He ducked just in time to avoid bumping his head. He looked back in awe of the yellow canary perched in the cage.

"Oh, be careful there, Joseph. Don't bump your head on Sweetie's cage," said Mary. "Here we are. This will be your room. I think you'll like it."

The room was small but tidy. A twin-sized bed sat on one side of the room with a two-drawer dresser against the opposite wall. The floor was shiny, polished wood and a colorful, braided rug covered the area by the bed. Lacy, white curtains covered the only window in the room. There were no pictures on the walls. In fact, there was nothing except a calendar with a picture of Jesus kneeling in prayer.

Joey set his suitcase on the floor at the foot of the bed.

"You can unpack and put your things in the dresser. Go ahead and make yourself to home while we finish up some business with Mrs. Ballanger," said Mary.

When she left, Joey sat on the bed and absorbed his surroundings. He felt empty, aching and hollow, as if everything inside himself had been yanked out and discarded. He studied the picture of Jesus for a moment and thought of Mr. Bushkin. He knew this place wasn't to be anything like sharing a dorm with other boys. And the room that he had shared with his stepbrothers was much larger.

He sat motionless, face impassive, as he pondered his future: *How long will I have to be here? What will my new school be like? Will I get enough to eat here, or will it be like living at the Bushkins' farm where I had to sneak food and get into trouble all the time? I won't have any other kids to play with here – or talk to. How can I get to call Sis?* His thoughts were interrupted about fifteen minutes later when Mrs. Ballanger called out, "Joey, come out here please."

He sighed heavily and hustled out to the dining room. He saw Mrs. Ballanger nodding as she closed her black folder. Preparing to leave, she stood and moved to the front door with her pocketbook draped over one arm and the folder tucked under the other.

"I'm leaving now, Joey." She looked at the Comstocks. "Thank you again, folks. If there are any questions, you know how to reach me." Back to Joey, she said, "You be a good boy for Mr. and

Mrs. Comstock, okay?"

"Yes, Ma'am." He feigned a smile and chewed on his lip.

"I'll be checking in with you from time to time until things with your parents get straightened around."

"Yes, Ma'am." He looked down at his feet. "When will you come back again?"

"Oh, in a few weeks, I suspect." She shifted her pocketbook and draped an arm around Joey's shoulders. She squeezed. "You'll be fine, Joey. Bye-bye now."

Joey wanted more assurance and opened his mouth—but no words came out.

After she left, Otto Comstock glanced at Joey and pointed to the couch. "Have a seat over there, Joseph. We need to talk a bit." He sat in an oversized armchair facing the couch, his hands dangling between his knees.

"Yes, Sir." Joey sat in the middle of the couch and Mary sat next to him. He fidgeted as though he was trying to find a comfortable spot.

"We have some rules we might as well spell out right off the get-go, so we don't have any misunderstandings." His grimace was unmistakable. "Your homework must be done before bedtime which is always nine o'clock—except Friday and Saturday nights when you will be allowed to stay up until ten."

Mary faced Joey with her arms folded and looked him directly in the eye. "The school bus will pick you up right in front of the house at five minutes after seven in the morning. You must see to it that you are never late," she said.

Joey nodded. "Yes, Ma'am."

Otto said, "You can never turn the television on without permission and then only if your homework is all done. You are to stay out of the basement, and you cannot go into the refrigerator for anything without permission. And you can never drink my ginger ale."

Mary added, "Make your bed every morning before you leave for school, and never leave your clothes lying around. Clean up after yourself everywhere, especially in the bathroom."

"Yes Ma'am."

"You'll be at the table with your hands washed for supper at six, or you will not be allowed to eat," said Mr. Comstock. "You're allowed to walk around the yard in front and back, but you are to stay out of the garage and my tools." He studied Joey for a moment. "Is that clear?"

"Yes, Sir."

"And, one more thing—you are not allowed to walk into town like some of those other teenage yahoos in the neighborhood. It's near a half mile away anyway, but still, I'm telling you, so we're clear."

Joey swallowed past the lump in his throat. "Yes, Sir."

Mary said, "You are not allowed to use the telephone, and that means don't let friends call here either. When we have company, you are to stay in your room unless we tell you otherwise."

Their words echoed in Joey's mind as he walked back to his room.

After that day, very little conversation took place between the Comstocks and Joey. Good morning and goodnight was practically all there ever was. Each time the Comstocks did speak to him, it concerned emphasis on things he forgot to do. It was as though Joey didn't actually live there or have a voice.

Mrs. Comstock always said grace before meals, but she didn't read from the Bible the way Mr. Bushkin had. Joey was glad she was an excellent cook, and there was always enough for seconds. Very little talking took place at the table, and when it did, it was only between Otto and his wife.

•   •   •   •   •

It was a balmy spring morning, and summer vacation was not far away. Joey had been at the Comstocks' for over five months and would be graduating from the eighth grade at Greenlawn Elementary School. During that time there were no visits from his father, no telephone calls. His only respite came from the new friends he made in school.

He was running late that morning and had to scramble in order to catch the bus on time. In his haste, he accidentally smacked his forehead on a sharp corner of the birdcage that hung in the hall. The pointed edge of the cage caught him hard and it left a trace of blood smeared on his forehead.

Mrs. Comstock stopped him at the door and inspected the bump that was obviously redder than the rest of his pale complexion. "What did you do here?" she asked as she touched the spot.

"I hit my head on the birdcage, Ma'am." He scrunched up his face and rubbed it.

"Well—it will be okay," she said. "There's just a tiny little cut there. Wait right here." She went into the bathroom and came back with a Band-Aid which she applied and said, "There—go ahead. Run along or you'll miss your bus." She shook her head. "You've got to be more careful."

During the day, the bump became more sensitive and Joey kept rubbing it from time to time. The swelling was becoming much more pronounced by day's end.

Three days later, he attempted to show it to Mrs. Comstock when he got home from school. She was busy rolling pie dough on the counter in the kitchen.

Gently rubbing his forehead he said, "This still hurts a lot, Ma'am."

She slammed her rolling pin on the counter before she said, "Oh, for goodness sakes! Let me see." After a quick inspection, she said, "It's a bit swollen, but it's bound to swell up when you crack your head on something like the corner of a birdcage. My goodness."

Otto had just come in from the garage. He heard his wife and glanced at Joey's forehead. "Yeah, it takes time for the swelling to go down on things like that—sort of like a black eye." He waved a hand dismissively. "Don't worry about it." He lit up a Camel and blew out a thick cloud of smoke and watched it rise and fade away. "Keep an eye on it."

Joey found it hard to sleep that night because of the throbbing pain. His forehead continued to swell ever so slightly with each hour, and it was hot to the touch. He felt tears burning his eyes.

When he left for school in the morning he felt as though his entire body was on fire. Classmate, Maxine Idone, lived across the street. She was 13 and rode the bus with him every day. He usually sat next to her, and they talked about everything.

"Gosh, Joey. that's really swollen up a lot just since yesterday. Doesn't it hurt?" She reached out and touched it with her fingertips. Joey pulled away from her touch. "Ouch! Yeah, it hurts a lot."

"Oh, I'm sorry," said Maxine. "It feels awful hot too. Did you know that?"

Joey answered with a shrug and a frown. "Yeah, it does hurt, but Mrs. Comstock says it will be okay."

When he got home from school that afternoon, he told Mrs. Comstock once again. "My head hurts real bad, Ma'am."

She squinted as she looked at the bump as if his head had gone out of focus. She went to the refrigerator, got an ice tray and spilled some ice in the sink. "Here." She handed him a kitchen towel wrapped around ice cubes. "This should help to bring that swelling down."

Joey wasn't hungry and didn't eat supper. He couldn't sleep at all that night. Tossing and turning, he heard himself moaning.

The following morning he tried to eat his Cheerios, but didn't finish.

Mrs. Comstock said his forehead looked better despite the way he was feeling. "If that still hurts tomorrow, we might have to get you in to see the doctor."

"Yeah, that's quite a lump you've got there," said Otto, as he sipped his cup of coffee. He spoke in a tone that was almost businesslike.

Joey was sweating when he took his seat in homeroom that morning. Mrs. Kowalski stared at him with concern on her face. She appeared to be squinting. Before the Pledge of Allegiance was recited, she went to Joey's desk. With an awkward smile, she said, "Joey, do you not feel good today? You don't look well—you're sweating and your forehead looks terrible."

She leaned over and scrutinized the bump. "I think you should go down to the nurse's office right now. My goodness—look at you! You're sweating." She shook her head in amazement.

Joey felt small and out of place as the whole class watched. He stared at her for a long moment as the burn of embarrassment colored his face and he headed to the nurse's office.

The school nurse, Mrs. Baskins, was a sweet, caring lady. She studied the bump closely under a lamp. "What happened here, Joseph?"

Joey felt a catch in his breath as he explained everything that had happened from the time he ran into the birdcage. When he was done, Mrs. Baskins called Mrs. Comstock to inform her that she felt it was her duty to take Joey to the doctor's office immediately. Mrs. Comstock agreed and said she would meet them there.

Eight people were in the doctor's waiting room. Mrs. Baskins and Joey were waiting for Mrs. Comstock when the nurse came out. Noticing Joey's condition, she turned around and went back inside. A few moments later, Doctor Bradburn came back out with her. He was a rather short man with hair as white as cotton and with all the symmetry of meringue. His nose and cheeks were threaded with tiny blue and red capillaries, and his stomach and hips protruded over the narrow hand-tooled western belt he wore.

"Young man, come on back," he said as he placed his hand on Joey's shoulder and smiled wryly. "You should come too, Mrs. Baskins. Evidently the boy's parents are on their way, is that right?"

"Yes, his foster mother has been notified."

The nurse guided them into a small room and helped Joey up onto a paper-covered table. "Just lay back," she said as she produced a small pillow for his head.

The doctor examined Joey's eyes with a small light. Then he checked his ears, nose and throat. He checked his temperature and listened to his heart with a stethoscope. Blowing out a gust of air, he said, "His temp is elevated for sure." He touched the bump on Joey's forehead and pushed just a little. "Yes, we need to take care of this immediately."

"*Owwww!*" Joey yelled.

"Easy, Son. Easy. You'll have to lay still for me now. You have a bad infection, and I have to get it out of there right now. Understand?"

Joey groaned. "Yes, Sir."

"I know you've been in lots of pain, haven't you?" said the doctor. "Trouble sleeping and so on?"

"Yes, Sir," Joey whimpered.

"It's the infection. Once I remove it, you'll feel a whole lot better, I promise. Just lay still."

A trembling Joey said, "How... how are you going to do that?"

"Well, you just lay back, Son. We have to apply pressure in order to push the infection out. It will be done before you know it." He let the pause linger then smiled as the nurse handed him two large squares of gauze. Joey felt the nurse hold one of his arms, while Mrs. Baskins held the other. He clenched his fists at his sides.

The doctor applied a slow, steady pressure on the swollen area. Joey groaned and tears ran down his cheeks. The doctor's knuckles pressed down on his forehead and Joey yelled. "Owwww!" as an unmistakable swooshing sound was heard.

"Got it!" said the doctor. "My goodness, look at this!" He showed the two women the gauze that held a three-inch glob of yellow pus. The nurse set it aside as the doctor used two more patches of gauze and continued to apply pressure.

"Easy now, Son — we're almost done here. Just hold still."

The doctor continued to push on the area, and Joey continued to moan and groan. He looked up at him through a wavy sheen of tears as the doctor extracted another glob of pus.

When he was satisfied that he had all that he could get, Dr. Bradburn said, "Miss Baker, put a warm compress on here, please. Does your head feel better, Son?"

"I think so," Joey muttered.

There was a knock at the door.

"Yes?" said Miss Baker.

Another nurse leaned just inside the door. "Doctor, Mrs. Comstock is here. She's upset and wants to come in."

Without hesitation he said, "Good, let her in — by all means."

"I can't believe this," said a flustered Mrs. Comstock as she rushed in. "Is it infected? How bad is it?"

He stared at her. "It certainly is. See for yourself, Madam. Look at the volume of pus I extracted from the boy's forehead." He gave his head a small disbelieving shake as the nurse handed him the gauze. He paused for a moment. "We're very fortunate we got this when we did. It would have very likely traveled to his brain within another 24 hours."

Mrs. Comstock stared with her mouth agape. She demonstrated a pang of guilt as she covered her mouth with both hands. "Oh, my goodness! We had no idea it was that bad."

"Well, he'll be okay now. I want to see him back here in three days. I must follow up, Ma'am. Meanwhile, give him a teaspoon of this antibiotic three times a day. It will help to clear up any remaining infection. If there's any change in the appearance of the affected area, I want to see him back here, immediately. Miss Baker will give you our twenty-four hour number. Be sure to call if need be."

"Yes. Oh, thank you, Doctor. Good God! I just had no idea," she said as she rubbed Joey's back in small circles. "Are you feeling better now, Joseph?"

"Yes, Ma'am," Joey murmured.

•　　　•　　　•　　　•　　　•

School had been out for nearly a month when Mrs. Comstock made a cake for Joey for his fourteenth birthday. A few days later he was on his knees out front, weeding her bed of iris and impatiens when she called him inside.

In the middle of baking chocolate-chip cookies, she wiped her hands on her apron and poured herself a glass of lemonade. Her graying hair was formed into a bun, and sweat glistened on her upper lip.

"Sit down, Joseph." She pointed to a dinette chair and sipped her lemonade. "Would you like some lemonade?"

"Yes, Ma'am. I sure would."

"I just got a call from Mrs. Ballanger. I have some good news for you. Your mother and father have reconciled and decided they are ready to get back together."

"Really! You mean my dad and my real mother?"

"No—no. I'm sorry. I should say your dad and your stepmother, Constance, are getting back together."

"Really? How? I mean when?"

"Yes, it's true. Mrs. Ballanger was adamant. She'll be here to pick you up day after tomorrow. You need to be ready as she tells me she has other appointments that day also."

Joey could barely contain his excitement. The hours of waiting dragged by. Thoughts of the future overloaded his brain night and day. He could barely sleep.

Will things work this time? Yeah, maybe Dad has changed. Maybe he doesn't drink anymore. I wonder if Connie still does. Maybe they don't fight anymore. I wish I could talk to Beth, just once. Just for a little while. I miss her so much — Gram and Gramps too. I wonder how my real Mom is feeling?

Chapter Forty-Two

Joey found that his father and Connie were living in the same house he had left when they separated and sent him to live in Greenlawn with the Comstocks. All of Connie's kids had been staying there all along while Joey was in foster care. They hadn't ever been separated from their mother.

There were some notable changes. Becky had a steady boyfriend named Bart, who was allowed to spend time in her bedroom during his frequent visits. "Becky is seventeen now and deserves privacy away from her brothers when she has company," Connie explained.

Connie still had her job at the Veteran's Hospital in Northport, but Joe had switched to a new job at the Grange League Federation where he loaded and unloaded trucks of fertilizer. It was a dirty job and required a lot of lifting. He wasn't happy with it but had been there for over three months by the time Joey came back. He no longer spent Friday nights in the bar, but Connie usually managed to have a six pack of Rheingold in the fridge for them.

Life in general seemed to be much better for Joey. After the stiff restrictions at the Comstocks' foster home, he appreciated his freedom to come and go as he pleased much more than his siblings who had never had such restraints.

There were no violent arguments occurring between Connie and Joe for quite some time. Evidently the two of them had learned to compromise and rarely had disagreements of any kind. However, as the weeks went by, the harmony gradually eroded and they could be heard talking loudly from time to time from the confines of their bedroom.

Joey took a job setting pins at the Striking Lanes Bowling Alley a few nights a week and during the day joined his brothers caddying at the Cold Spring Harbor Country Club for the rest of the summer of 1954.

Being a caddy entailed carrying two golf bags, one slung over each shoulder, for eighteen holes in the blistering sun. It paid twelve dollars a loop—six dollars for each bag plus tips. However, the boys were not allowed to keep all of their money. For each twelve dollars earned, the boys had to give ten to Connie. "School will be starting pretty soon. You boys need to help pay for new school clothes. We can't afford to buy them without some extra money," Connie claimed. "You're old enough to help out."

When they weren't needed at the golf course, the boys rode their bikes to Sunken Meadow State Park and spent the day lolling in the sun and watching girls frolic on the beach. Other days were spent fishing for flounder.

In September, Joey went back to Huntington High School for his sophomore year. He still had not heard anything from Beth or his brothers up north. He wondered how Gramps, Gram and his mother, Alice were doing. He had no idea what the telephone number was for his grandparents' house, so no contact was ever made.

The holidays were pleasant enough. Somehow, Connie managed to buy new English Racer bicycles for all three of the older boys that Christmas. They were a gift from Joe and Connie, but she was sure to let the boys know it was she who had finagled a way to afford the bikes. The boys were thrilled even though they couldn't ride them very much until spring. The bikes were stored in the cellar until April.

In May, Joe and Connie began to fall back into their pattern of arguing. Their confrontations had been carried out behind the door to their bedroom, but as the weeks passed, fights could break out most anywhere in the house. Usually they took place in the dining room— where they sat at the table smoking cigarettes and drinking beer.

When Connie and Joe had a fight, they always started out in low tones and gradually escalated into shouting matches. When things reached the nasty name-calling stage, the kids found a spot to hide.

Relationships between Joey and his step-brothers and sister became more and more strained as their parents' partnership soured.

Anger with each other festered day by day into vicious and hateful fighting.

Joey retreated to his room when loud talk became a volatile fight between his father and Connie. He turned his radio up loud so he wouldn't have to hear the cruel barbs thrown back and forth downstairs.

Joe had fallen back to his old habit of stopping at Jerry's Bar for drinks with his fellow workers. He would easily go through twenty dollars of his seventy-dollar paycheck in a few hours and come home drunk. Connie attempted to avoid any discussion with him in order to avoid a big battle. Sometimes it worked and Joe went directly to his room. Other times, it was as if he just wanted a reason to pick a fight with anybody who got in his way. He was surly and miserable with the fire of alcohol to embolden him.

When he failed to pick a fight, he slammed the door to his bedroom, where he smoked cigarettes, read books, listened to his jazz records and sulked. After a while, Connie would slide into the room very quietly and they would begin the makeup procedure. It was always the same. After some fairly quiet conversation, Connie ended up going to the liquor store for more beer and a fifth of rye whiskey.

One Friday night, following one of their big blowouts, Connie waited until Joe went into their room and slammed the door. Joey was still awake and had his ear pressed against his radio. He was listening to the new music called Rock and Roll. Alan Freed was the disc jockey on WINS in New York City. He called himself The Moondog and coined the term Rock and Roll. He actually began in Cleveland in 1951, but by 1954 he had become King of the Rock n' Roll in the minds of teens. While adults condemned the music as perverted, Freed was a god to his listeners. He promoted the music in every way possible, including emceeing sold-out stage shows at the Paramount Theatre in New York.

Joey found refuge in the music, but Joe had said on more than one occasion, "That crap is just a fad — it will be gone before you know it."

Connie went upstairs and told Joey to come down. "I need to talk to you." She lowered her voice and said, "Don't wake the other boys up. Just come down to the dining room."

Joey found her sitting alone. The portable radio was on and a Nat King Cole song called *A Blossom Fell* could barely be heard.

Her hair was a mess. She had let it dry on its own after her shower and it made a wild cloud of waves and tangles around her head, thick strands tumbling into her face. She smoked a cigarette and an empty beer bottle sat in front of her. She took a long swallow of another in her hand. She looked glassy-eyed, and Joey could tell by her flushed cheeks that she had been crying. He started to sit across from her.

"There's root beer soda in the fridge if you want some," she murmured.

"Okay, Mom. Thanks." He poured a glassful, put the bottle back in the fridge and took a seat. Connie stared at the bottle in her hand and said nothing for a moment.

"Your father is back to his same old tricks, you know. Friday night he stopped at the bar again."

Joey nodded but said nothing.

"Ha!" Connie said, mustering a brittle smile. "You should have seen him when we were split up, Joey. I visited him every weekend just to stay in touch and make sure he was all right." She glanced away. "He doesn't have the sense to take care of himself. He had an infected toe from an ingrown nail and wasn't taking care of it. If I hadn't caught it in time, he probably would have lost the whole damned foot. I bet you didn't know that, did you, Son?"

Joey shook his head. "No, I didn't."

Connie's head lolled back and forth as if it was on loose hinges in her neck. She took another swig of beer and waved her hands dismissively. Laying her elbows on the table, she leaned forward. "I know you didn't. Nobody did. He wouldn't let me tell anybody about it. He's too proud for his own good."

Joey nodded and sipped his soda.

"Yeah, I know. There's a lotta things you don't know, Joey." She leaned in so that her face was only inches away from his. Some of her words were slurred.

When she spoke again, the strong smell of stale cigarettes and beer on her breath caused Joey to pull back. "Thass what I want to talk about, young man." She looked at him with a lopsided grin and lazily stubbed out her cigarette in an ashtray. "We're not really married, you know."

Joey shrugged and nodded. "I thought so."

"That's right. Your father is still married to Alice. So, I'm not even your stepmother, Joey." She paused at that point to see Joey's reaction and her face paled as though she was the one who would be shocked. "What? You mean you knew that?"

"No. I mean I just wasn't sure — but I thought something must be wrong — that's all."

"Yup. Adam is your half-brother and he's a bastard. Do you know what that is?"

Joey shook his head.

"Well a bastard is not just a bad word. It's what they call a kid who is born without married parents." She paused and fumbled with her pack of Luckies. Tapping one out, she lit up and exhaled a huge cloud of smoke. "Thass your brother — Adam."

Joey didn't know how to respond to that and said nothing. He took another swallow of his root beer and stared at her.

"Your father and I have been living together like married people but we are not married. That means we don't need to get a divorce to split up anytime things aren't working out." She took another deep drag on the cigarette.

"But I thought everything was all right now."

Connie shook her head from side to side. "No, and God knows I've tried to make it look that way for the sake of you kids, but we just don't get along, Son." She squinted her eyes.

"But, I thought you were getting along okay, Mom."

Connie smiled and reached out to caress his arm. "I love hearing you call me Mom, Joey. I really do." Tears welled up in her eyes and trickled down her cheeks. She pulled a Kleenex out of her pocket and dabbed at her eyes.

"No. Your father promised me there wouldn't be any more bar hopping as long as he could have his beer at home and I tried to make sure he had his beer. But—well, you see how good his promises are, don't you? He still goes out drinking after work every Friday night, and then he gets mean. Stinking mean!" She shook her head back and forth again. "And, it's a wonder I can pay all the bills and still keep food in this house because he has to be a big shot and buy for his buddies."

She blew her nose and paused for a beat as she took a leisurely drag on her cigarette and exhaled. "Listen, Joey—if it wasn't for me, you'd still be in that orphanage in Watertown. Your father didn't care enough to do anything about getting you out. You can see he still doesn't care what happens to you. I'm the one that got us back together this time—not him. You didn't know that either, did you?"

Joey stared at her, feeling as if he'd just been hit in the chest with a hammer. "You mean it was you that got me out of The Home?"

"Yes. It's a long story, but when I met him after the war, your father told me that someday he wanted to have his only son live with him, but he never lifted a finger to talk to the right people and make it happen. Just like he promised to divorce your mother and marry me. That's never going to happen either." Her eyes took on a faraway look. "I should have known."

"But, I'm not his only son. What about Brian and Mitchell and Merrill?"

She leaned against the back of the chair and groaned, bringing a hand up to push her hair back, then squeezed his arm and shrugged. "Your father has never talked about any other kids 'cept you and your sister Elizabeth." She paused and studied his face. "He says he's going to do a lot of things when he's drinking."

Groaning, Joey sank back down on his chair and sat with his elbows on his thighs and his hands hanging down between his knees. "Then why do you bring beer home for him?"

That sharp jab punctured her momentum and deflated it. She seemed to shrink a little before his eyes, drawing inward on herself.

"Why? Okay, I'll tell you why." She heaved a heavy sigh. "I figure if I bought his beer, he wouldn't have to stop in the bars and spend money we can't afford. At least he'll be home where he belongs and I can control the money. See what I mean?"

"But you drink beer too. I mean—I see you drink it with him lots of times. You're drinking it right now."

"Yes, but... oh, Joey, you don't understand, do you?" She shook her head back and forth in disgust. Drawing on her cigarette, she let the smoke drift from her mouth and waved at it in a lazy gesture, then gave him a long searching look. "I'm so sorry. I really tried this time. I really thought we could make it work for all of us."

Joey took a deep breath. "I know, but everything is okay. I just wish both of you would stop fighting."

Connie shook her head and shrugged. "I won't take his being mean anymore, Joey. I can't. The arguing is about to drive me insane." She rubbed his arm. "We're going to go our separate ways again, Honey. I'm so sorry. It's not fair—I know that."

He scowled at her and pulled his arm away as if she had just told him she had leprosy. "If you know that, why do you two keep breaking up then?" Tears welled in his eyes and he blinked them back furiously. "I don't understand. I just want to stay here at home. I mean—even if you and Dad do argue sometimes—it's better than me having to move to another foster home." He looked down at his lap, then to Connie. "Doesn't he understand that?"

She stood and circled her arms around his neck. "Your father agrees it's for the best. He knows he's not a good father, Joey." Tears streamed down her cheeks as she said, "So, I got hold of Mrs. Ballanger last Thursday. You'll be going to a foster home by the end of next week."

Joey's face was like a stone mask, but tears had escaped down his cheek. He sat glued to the chair, telling himself it wasn't true. It wasn't really happening again. Without further comment, he shook his head and then angrily swiped the tears away with the back of his hand and ran back upstairs.

Chapter Forty-Three

Joey remained quiet as they took the car ride through the rolling Long Island countryside. Mrs. Ballanger's '52 Chevy hummed along and followed the asphalt ribbon of road as they skirted the north shore. Seagulls rode the breeze above them.

Dense evergreens as well as fragrant, shady pines and beautiful green meadows gave way to acres of scrub pines. Wildflowers hid in the grass, their heads bowed demurely in deference to the strong breeze.

"You'll like the Roddericks, Joey. They have a son of their own, but he's away at college. Mr. Rodderick is a big baseball fan too." She glanced at him and grinned. "How about that, Joey? Didn't you tell me you like baseball?"

Joey sighed heavily. He didn't say a word, but stared straight ahead like he'd been turned to stone. He was trying to reason away the shock of this latest move. Mixed up and depressed, he was missing his sister, Beth, more than ever. Maybe Connie was right when she said, "Your father doesn't care about you or anybody but himself."

Mrs. Ballanger looked out the window and absently fingered the gold crucifix around her neck, all the time keeping one hand on the wheel. The air was chilly and overhead, gray clouds were rumbling across the sky like bloated sponges, filling up the blue bowl and shutting out the sun.

"Looks like we may have some rain after all," she said.

Joey watched her squint, squeezing lines into her forehead. It was another one of her facial expressions. He learned she had three or four: deadpan, open mouth, this one and her gee-whiz grin. As far as Joey was concerned, she was just like Mrs. Kellogg used to be —

distant and too busy to listen.

"Will I be able to call my sister, Ma'am?"

"Well, yes. As a matter of fact, you can do that today. We could have done it earlier, but I thought we'd wait until we were away from your house. You know what I mean?" She glanced at him and smiled. "You'll have more freedom to talk that way." She gave him a crooked smile that held more humor than he would have expected.

Joey scooted up in his seat and searched her expression for truth. His stomach did somersaults and his heart thundered in his chest. "I've been wanting to call her for so long but never had a telephone number—and besides, it probably would have caused trouble with Dad if I tried to call. But you said I can today—right? I mean you're really gonna let me call?"

Mrs. Ballanger nodded. "Yes, you can call her. I'm sure your sister will be very happy to hear from you. From what I've been able to ascertain, you two have always been quite close."

"Yes Ma'am. I love my sister more than anything." He slumped back in the seat. "I haven't talked to her in almost three years."

"Oh my, that's really too bad." She clicked her teeth and shook her head in a show of sympathy.

Joey was pensive—still unsure. A fist of tension clenched in his chest. A long pause followed before he said, "So you will really let me talk to her now—today?"

"Yes, of course." She patted his arm. "Why wouldn't I? There should be no harm in that. My goodness. I would have let you call her the last time we moved you, but I just... well—I just didn't have enough information on her at the time. I think it would be a good idea for you to speak with your grandmother too. I need to stop by my office anyway. It's right on our way. You'll be able to use my telephone, okay?"

"Yes, Ma'am." He pondered what she had said. "Did you already talk to her?"

"Well, no. I actually talked to your grandmother, Lillian. Elizabeth wasn't home at the time. I was told she was babysitting for your mother at another location in Black River."

"What do you mean, Ma'am? Are you talking about my real mother, Alice?"

"Yes—of course—your real mother. She's in Gouvernuer. Well, that's not right either. Actually, she's living in Black River now but that's close to Gouvernuer as you know." She kept one hand on the wheel and tapped her pocketbook with the other. "I've got your grandmother's number right in here. Perhaps your sister will be there today."

Joey stared at her and thought, *What if she's not? Then what?* "Ma'am—how long has my mother been there?"

"In Black River? Oh, I'm not sure. I'm really not that familiar with her case. I do know she has been there for some time and she has two little ones now—a girl and a boy. Your sister will no doubt be able to answer a lot of those things for you. I'll see what I can find out from our Watertown office, too."

When they arrived at her office, Mrs. Ballanger unlocked the door, flipped on the light and immediately opened two windows. "Whew. We need to get some air circulating in here." She set her pocketbook on the small desk. "Have a seat, young man. We'll take care of that call right now."

She rummaged through the pocketbook a moment and retrieved a small green book. Thumbing through it, she found the number she was looking for and gave it to the long distance operator.

Excitement filled Joey's eyes and his heart raced.

Mrs. Ballanger covered the mouthpiece of the phone with her hand. "It's ringing. You can't stay on the line too long now, okay?"

Joey nodded. "Okay."

"Hello, Mrs. Powest?" She paused. "Well, good morning, Ma'am. This is Gloria Ballanger again from Social Services on Long Island, the caseworker down here for your grandson. How are you today?"

Joey frowned as he listened. There was a long empty space where nothing was said and he felt the electric mix of emotion traveling the phone line but could do nothing except wait.

"Yes. Fine, thank you. We spoke earlier in the week about Joseph. Yes... Yes." Mrs. Ballanger nodded her head and smiled. "That's right, from the Social Services office in Northport. Yes, well, I have that anxious young man sitting right here in front of me. Yes. I may speak with you more in a moment, but right now he's very eager to talk to you, so I'm going to put him on. Here he is."

She stretched the cord and handed the phone to Joey.

"Hello, Gramma." The words seemed to catch in his throat.

"Hello, Sonny! Oh, goodness, we have missed you! How are you, Son?" Joey heard her crying as she spoke. His heart jolted at the sound of her voice but he answered, "I'm okay, Gramma. Please don't cry."

"I'm trying not to, Honey, but it's so good to hear your voice again." Her words brought tears to his eyes.

"How are you and Gramps?"

"Oh, we're getting by okay, Sonny."

Joey could picture her dabbing at her eyes with a Kleenex. He could see her shoulders pulling forward—curling in on herself due to severe arthritis. She was probably sitting sat at her dining room table with a small glass of wine at her fingertips.

"Your Gramps doesn't work anymore, not since that stroke, you know. But we're okay. How about you, Sonny? My Lord, it's so good to hear your voice."

"I'm okay, Gram." Tears welled up in his eyes. "I just miss you a lot. Did you get a lot of snow?"

"Oh, yes. Last month we had two feet or more—now it's the rain. You sound like such a big boy, Sonny. I'll bet you are real tall now, aren't you? What's this that lady told me, you're not living with your daddy anymore? Is that right?"

"No, I'm not, Gram—not anymore. Dad broke up with his girlfriend."

"Girlfriend? Oh, my good God, Sonny. I am so sorry," she said fearfully. "Where in the world will you go now, Sonny? Oh my, not with more strangers? I wish so much we could have taken you with us. None of this would have happened. Oh, my heavens."

"I'm okay, Gramma. I think about you and Gramps all the time though. How's Mommy?"

There was a long pause before Lillian cleared her throat and said, "Well—not too good, Sonny. I don't want to worry you, mind you, but she hasn't been well since she had Johnny."

"Johnny? Who's Johnny?"

"Oh, good heavens. That's right, you haven't talked to any of us in so long." She breathed a heavy sigh.

"No, we haven't talked in an awful long time, Gram."

"Well, your mommy had another baby two years back. It was a boy and she named him Johnny."

"I've got another brother named Johnny?"

"Yes, Sonny." There was more hesitation in her voice. "Beth helps her out with babysitting Johnny and Kathy but it's hard on everybody. After she had Johnny, she began to have all sorts of problems. Her legs and ankles swelled up and she put on a lot of weight. Beside that, she had real bad itching all over her body. She takes pills for everything now."

"Oh, no. Is she okay now?"

"Well, not really. After two months of still feeling bad, she finally saw Doctor Baxter and he made her go in and get some tests done."

"What kind of tests?"

"Oh, blood tests and the like. The doctor said your mother has the symptoms of something called cirrhosis. It's a disease that generally affects the liver, Sonny. My Lord, she's only thirty-three, you know. I'm at my wits' end."

Joey heard her sniffling. "Please don't cry, Gramma." He wiped his eyes. "What are they doing to help her? Is she going into the hospital or something?"

"Take it easy, Honey, and listen to me." She coughed and cleared her throat. "The doctor told your mother she had to stop drinking. No more wine. He said alcohol was the worst thing for her, so she quit right away, of course."

"So, she's all right now?"

"Well she's been in and out of Good Samaritan Hospital getting things checked, but she's okay with the liver thing—for now at least. Doctor Baxter put her on a strict diet and he's having her take lots of multivitamins. She has been eating right again, so things are much better, Joey. Listen, I don't want you to worry a whole bunch now — okay? She'll be all right. I just knew I should tell you. Of course your father wouldn't tell you because he doesn't know. They don't speak to each other, Sonny."

"I know. Dad doesn't even talk to me very much. I'll try not to worry, Gram, but it's just... I don't know. I wish I could be there to see her and Sis and all of you. That's all."

"Well, please try to call us more often somehow, will you? You can call collect if you want."

"I'll try, Gram. I promise."

"I'll count on that — and please take care of yourself, Son. We do love you, and we think about you all the time. Bye now." Joey heard her sob before she handed the phone to Carl. "Here's your grampa."

"Hello, Sonny."

"Gramps? Hi, Gramps! How are you?"

Gramps chuckled. "Oh, fair to middlin', Sonny. How about you?"

"I'm okay, Gramps. I just wish I could be there with you right now."

"Well, we sure miss you, Sonny. You sound so grown up now."

"Yeah, I have gotten bigger, all right." He caught himself smiling. "Do you ever go by the railroad shack anymore?"

"Oh no, Son. Shucks — I haven't been by there for close to a couple of years now. I stay here at home pretty much. My old engineer friends toot the horn when they pass here every day, but I can't go out there to wave, you know. I've got other things to care about. The old ticker, you know. Besides, your gramma won't let me out of her sight, except to go to the outhouse." He chuckled.

Mrs. Ballanger kept her eye on Joey as she slowly paced the floor. He dodged her steady gaze and she finally eased her way out of the room and drifted outside to smoke a cigarette. Joey watched her every movement out of the corner of his eye.

"I wish I could come and see you, Gramps."

"Well, we'd sure like that a lot, Sonny. Maybe sometime soon, eh? I'll give you to Sissy now, but promise you'll stay in touch from now on, all right?"

"All right. I will, Gramps—I promise. Bye. I love you."

"I love you too, Sonny. Here's Sis. Goodbye now."

"Hi, Joey!"

The moment Joey heard Beth's voice, he had to choke back tears. "Hi, Sis!"

"Oh, Joey, it's so good just to hear your voice. I miss you and I want to hug you."

"I miss you, too, Sis—real bad."

"That caseworker, Mrs. Ballanger, said you weren't living with Dad anymore. Is that true? What happened? How was it living with him?"

"Not good. He has a girlfriend named Connie and they were fighting all the time. She has four kids of her own and now we don't get along either. When Dad and her broke up she kept her kids but I had to go to a foster home. I'm on my way to a new foster home right now. It's the second time, Sis."

"Oh, no! Geez! I wish you could get settled down back here. I'm so sorry, Joey. You know I love you, don't you? Maybe Dad and that Connie woman will work things out, and you can go back for good— at least until you're eighteen."

"No, Connie told me this time it was for keeps. She and Dad are done and besides, I don't think I want to go back to live with them. I love you, Beth, and I want to come back up there and be with you and everybody."

"Oh, I know—I want that too, Joey."

She cried. "Oh, God! Gram is all upset now; she's taking this awful hard. Gramps is trying to calm her down. Maybe we better hang up, Joey. You can call us again, can't you? I'll tell them that."

"No, please, Sis... not yet, wait."

Mrs. Ballanger returned as Joey was wiping his eyes with the heel of his hand. She handed him a tissue and sat across from him.

"Gram says Mom has been sick. She says you're over at her place a lot. How is she doing?"

"Well, she's still living with that Fred guy. We've got a half-sister and a half-brother now. Their names are Kathy and Johnny. I thought you knew about it. I babysit them over in Black River all the time."

"No. I didn't know anything about it before this morning."

"You remember that man that was with Mom when she came to see you that Christmas while you were living at Matthews' house with Mitchell and Merrill?"

"Yeah, I think so. But, I don't understand. Nobody ever tells me anything!"

"Dad should have told you, Joey. I thought he knew."

"Not Dad." Joey sighed. "You don't know him, Sis. He doesn't talk about things. I've tried to ask him stuff about Mom and he won't answer. He doesn't even talk about you or Brian or the twins either. Have you heard anything about them by the way?"

"No. Mom never talks about them. Fred won't let her. She tells me she misses them though. And she sure misses you too."

"I don't believe that, Sis. I just don't."

"Oh, Joey, please don't say that. She works a lot and she has been sick, too. What is this Connie like? Do you get along with her? How come they broke up two times?"

"She's all right, I guess. Sometimes she acts like she cares about me. They both drink beer and stuff though, and that's when they have real bad fights. I get scared, Sis."

"Oh, that's terrible, Joey." He could hear her stifling her tears. "Mom and Fred used to drink a lot of wine here, too. But Mom quit most of it because the doctor told her she had to. I'm so sorry, Joey. We sure have mixed up parents, but you can't help that—neither can I. I think things will get better someday. I just know they will. They have to."

Mrs. Ballanger was back and skirted behind her desk. "Joseph, I'm sorry, but we have to be going," she half-whispered.

He nodded. "Okay. Sis, I have to hang up now. I wish I could talk more, though."

"I know, I want to see you, Joey, but try to write to me, will you? Or call again if you can—soon okay?"

"Okay, I'll try. I promise."

"Goodbye, Joey."

"All right. Goodbye, Sis." Tears seemed to come against his will, but he didn't have the strength to stop them. They rolled like pearls down his cheeks.

"Joey! Wait! Wait!"

"What?"

"You must believe me. We all love you."

"I love you, too, Sis."

"Goodbye, Joey."

"Bye."

Joey's heart sank like a stone in a pond and his body shook as though he had just emerged from a pool of icy water. He covered his face and sobbed as Mrs. Ballanger led him back out to her car.

•   •   •   •   •

Upon their arrival in the early afternoon, Mrs. Ballanger introduced Joey to Mr. and Mrs. James Rodderick. They lived in a beautiful Colonial house with lush landscaping and a big spreading oak tree in the side yard.

Cora Rodderick greeted them at the front door. She was an unusually thin woman with bright blue eyes and a warm, inviting smile. Her salt-and-pepper-colored hair was pulled back in a French roll that was held in place by antique combs. She had pale skin, but it was healthy-looking with a few freckles. Her lipstick was pink and feathered out into the deep crevices that lined her mouth.

Her husband, Jim, was a tall, white-haired and studious-looking man with a reassuring smile and a strong handshake. He had a square jaw, deep blue probing eyes and a well-groomed handlebar mustache. Joey would learn that he was a broker who worked in a big office in New York City and commuted on the Long Island Railroad five days a week.

Everything was handled so quickly this time, Joey thought. After the introductions, Mrs. Ballanger had the couple sign some papers and she was ready to leave.

"Well, you should be all set, folks. You have my number. If you need anything at all, just give me a call." She faced Joey. "Joseph, I know you'll be on your best behavior for Mr. and Mrs. Rodderick, won't you?"

Joey nodded. "Yes, Ma'am. Will you let me know if you hear any more from my sister or grandmother?"

"Why yes, of course, Son. I'll be in touch." She shook hands with the Roddericks, hugged Joey and left .

Joey couldn't sleep that night. He hadn't tried. His stress went bone deep, but the fear went deeper. He was alone. It didn't seem to matter that a roof was over his head. He was alone.

•   •   •   •   •

After two weeks had passed, Joey realized the Roddericks were different from any foster parents he'd ever lived with. Jim had the pale, fragile look of a man whose most dangerous sport was chess. They were both kind and caring and treated Joey as if he were their biological son. Kindness and understanding seemed natural for them and they never argued. They had one son of their own. Roger was away at Farmingdale College and would be gone until Christmas vacation.

Cora proved to be a kind, practical woman with the patience of a saint. When Joey addressed them as Sir and Ma'am, she had immediately set things straight. "You needn't be so formal with us, Joey. You can call me Cora, and I don't think my husband minds if you address him as Jim."

Joey was a junior at Kings Park High School in March of 1955. He hated switching schools. Making friends all over again was tough, but nothing new for him. Once he was settled in, he realized there were good things to look forward to.

Spring was around the corner. He could ride his bike, plus spring training for baseball was underway. His Brooklyn Dodgers would be back at Ebbets Field before long. The smell of lilacs would be in the air again. They reminded him so much of Gram's back yard in

Gouvernuer. And, Cora agreed to let him use the phone once a month to call up north.

His life would change in unforeseen ways too. In math class, he noticed a beautiful girl named Deirdre Guillane and for the first time felt an attraction for the opposite sex. Everybody called her Dee. Joey was immediately smitten.

Dee had long, auburn hair that cascaded down her back. Her eyes were green. Joey had never seen anyone with green eyes before. She had dimples and her smile was contagious. When she took a seat in class that first day, Joey was befuddled. He wanted to talk to her but was afraid he'd say the wrong thing or say the right thing wrong.

He slouched down in his seat and stared into his notebook, pretending not to notice her. His eyes narrowed and his mouth puckered into a tight knot of concentration. Flipping to a fresh page in the notebook, he started scribbling, gripping his pen so hard his knuckles were white. He found himself staring at her as if she had just stepped out of a movie.

When he looked up one time, she was smiling at him. A week later, during study hall, he thought he caught her watching him again and he blushed. Dee smiled, and he wondered if she noticed that his face was red. No girl had ever looked at him and smiled like that before.

When study hall was over, Joey hurried down the corridor and headed to Mr. Dirksen's history class, wondering when he'd see her again. Lunchtime followed. He saw Dee getting something out of her locker and he felt his insides quake as he dared to walk up to her.

"Hi."

"Hi!" she said with a smile that made his heart swell. Her dimples reminded him of Debbie Reynolds.

"I'm Joe," he said with as much bass in his voice as he could muster.

"I know," she said and closed her locker. There was a beat of silence.

He smiled. "How did you know?"

"The teacher called attendance, remember?" She reached up and brushed back an errant strand of her hair and giggled. "I'm Dee."

"Oh yeah, that's right." His face felt like it was on fire. "Glad to meet you, Dee."

His stomach flipped. She seemed more beautiful up close—just a foot or so away. He couldn't believe she was talking to him. He nervously looked down at his feet.

"You're new, huh?" she said.

"Yeah, I just moved here from Huntington."

"Well, I just started here this year myself," said Joey. "Hey, what've you got next?"

"Oh, Mrs. Claypoole's English." She glanced at a paper in her hand then looked into his eyes. Joey felt as if she were looking right through him. "How about you?"

He blushed and shrugged. "I've got history with Mr. Dirksen, then I go to lunch."

"Well, I have lunch at 11:20, too." She slowly swayed her hips from side to side as they walked—not showing off—just real cute, Joey thought.

Joey asked, "Well, would you mind if I sit with you at lunchtime? We could talk some more or something."

They stopped and she faced him. "Sure, I'd like that. I'll wait for you in the cafeteria. I'll save two seats for us somewhere. If you get there first, you grab them, okay?"

"Sure thing—I'll see you then."

His heart skipped a beat.

Chapter Forty-Four

J oey still hadn't told Dee anything about his family background. As far as she was concerned, the Roddericks were his real parents. He was afraid of what she would think of the things he had endured, the cold blackness that surrounded his young life and crept into his mind constantly. He felt as though he had spent the past four months putting himself back together since living with Jim and Cora Rodderick.

He was reconstructing himself from the shambles his life had been for so long. With only a few months remaining of their junior year, Joey and Dee were seeing a lot of each other and it became more and more difficult to hide the truth from her.

Everything was definitely rolling in the right direction it seemed. The Roddericks were kind and continued to support him in his relationship with Dee. When he missed supper because he was at her house, he didn't suffer any consequences. The only rule was, during the week, he had to be home before ten. On weekends that was extended to eleven. Life was good, he thought.

He found himself spending most evenings riding his bike to and from Dee's house, a mile and a half away, to do their homework together. Dee's parents liked Joey. Her mother, Joyce, offered sandwiches and homemade cookies when Joey came over, and she always had lemonade and root beer on hand. Her husband, Gil, worked as an engineer for The Edison Company in Long Island City, and he consistently treated Joey like the son who was away at college.

Joey rode to Dee's house one evening in May, while the day still offered plenty of light, and neighbors worked in their yards tending their budding flower beds and vegetable gardens. The two lovebirds sat on the patio and listened to 45 RPM rock n' roll records on her portable phonograph. Joey had never learned how to dance and Dee was teaching him how to slow dance to a song called *In The Still of the Night* by The Five Satins.

She guided Joey's arm around her waist, very slowly. "Like this," she cooed. Her face seemed to turn softer in the shade, like a flower in late afternoon. She held his other hand and showed him how to make a square with his feet, by counting aloud—"one, two, three, four—one, two, three, four." Joey kept making squares, and before long he realized he was dancing, but his natural tendency was to stare at his feet.

"No, Joe," said Dee. She used her fingertips to gently lift his chin. "Up here. Look at my eyes, not your feet, Silly."

He found it difficult to concentrate because her pert breasts were rubbing ever so lightly against his chest and it sent tingles down his spine. With his cheek pressed against hers, he smelled the perfume of her hair and felt her hot breath on his neck. Everything about her brought out feelings he had never experienced and he did his best not to show embarrassment.

They continued to dance long after the needle started skipping at the end of the song. Finally, Dee eased away and went to the record player. She glanced up at the kitchen window to see if either of her parents was watching. Satisfied that they still had privacy, she started the same record over again.

Joe became emboldened. He slipped both arms around her waist, and they gazed into each other's eyes. There was no need for talking, nor whispering for that matter. The only communication was in the slow and easy swaying of their bodies to and fro with the rhythm of the song. She felt soft and sweet with her body melting into his.

His nerves jangled as he felt a stirring in his groin.

Leaning forward, he kissed her on the lips—soft and slow at first. *I don't want to mess this up—do it wrong. I want her to like me as much as I like her.*

Her lips were hot and wet and he pulled her closer. She moaned, and Joey heard himself moaning, too. He softened the kiss, making a sound of surrender in his throat as her lips parted beneath his invitation. The kiss deepened and Joey felt himself going under, losing himself. He pressed harder and felt her tongue go past his lips. It was unexpected, but it felt good and Joey matched her with his own tongue. Everything seemed to come so naturally.

Dee snaked her arms around his neck while the kissing continued and Joey felt himself getting hard. An unfamiliar rush of blood coursed through his body and he felt hot all over. He wondered what she must think. *Can she feel my hardness pressing against her? She must feel it — but what can I do? I can't just stop dancing, can I?*

The needle made a *ta-teesh, ta-teesh, ta-teesh* skipping noise when the record ended a second time. The two lovers slowly backed away from each other for a moment, then decided the skipping record didn't matter as Joey once again engulfed her in his arms.

The heat of her body was unlike anything he'd ever known and he didn't want to let go. He tentatively caressed a silky tendril of her hair, and the contact sent affection surging through his entire body. His fingertips followed the curve of her ear down to the line of her jaw, and there was another shot of desire. He was engaging in self-indulgent torture and enjoying every minute of it.

"Joe," she whispered as she brushed his cheek with her lips. "Oh, Joe."

They were still gazing into each other's eyes when the screen door suddenly creaked open and snapped shut, causing them to back away from each other.

"Dee, Honey, supper will be ready soon," said her mother as she moved across the porch. She picked up a potted plant and smiled. "Joe, you can stay and eat with us if you'd like." She took the plant with her and headed back inside. "This thing needs water," she muttered.

Dee bit down on her lower lip then giggled and drew Joe back in close to her. "Mom thinks she's so clever. She's just being nosy. You can stay if you want, though. I'd like that."

Joe didn't want to go; he wanted to keep holding and kissing her, but he had promised Jim he'd help him clean the garage before bedtime. "Dee, listen... I want to stay real bad, but I can't tonight. I feel bad but I told my folks I'd be home by six-thirty. I'd better go now, or they'll wonder why I'm not back yet."

Dee sighed.

Trying to keep a straight face, he said, "Well, I did promise."

She smiled and rolled her eyes. "Okay, I wish you could stay though." She paused and held his hand. "You want to call them and see if it's okay?"

"No, that's all right. I really have to go."

She kissed him on the cheek. Her kiss was hot and wet and just for a moment he thought about staying after all.

She caressed his forearm. "I hate to let you go, but I'll see you tomorrow, okay?"

"Yeah. I'll meet you out in front of school, same as always." He pulled away and headed for the side gate, but Dee reached out and tugged at his arm. "Hey, Joe."

"Yeah?"

She smiled. "You kiss real nice—ya' know that?"

He blushed. "You do too." He grinned and squeezed her hand before he turned and left.

In bed that night, it was the same as with so many frustrating nights since they had met. He ached and thought about making love to her. It was best to try and think about other stuff in his life and he tried. He wondered how Beth and his brothers were. How was his mother? Was she still sick? But, in spite of everything, before he went to sleep, Dee was the one who always oozed into his mind, like smoke under a closed door.

•   •   •   •   •

On a hot, humid summer evening in June, Joey took Dee to the movies. It was a Saturday and they found seats in the very back row to watch *Blackboard Jungle* starring Glenn Ford and Sidney Poitier. It was the first time they heard *Rock Around the Clock* by Bill Haley and the Comets. They saw very little of the movie because they kissed and petted heavily during the entire show. Both of them were worked up to a fever pitch by the time the movie was over and barely noticed when the house lights came on.

Joey walked her home, and it was almost ten o'clock when he got home and found Jim and Cora sitting in their living room watching the late news. Jim sat in his favorite armchair. His eyeglasses lay on the newspaper in his lap and Cora sat on the couch with her knitting. Joey strolled in and plopped down next to her.

"Hi," he said as he slumped back on the couch. "You two have a nice night?" There was no immediate answer and in the lamplight, Joey noticed that Cora's face looked splotchy. Her eyes were glassy and wet. It was obvious that she had been crying.

Jim said, "Joe, we have to talk, Son."

"Okay." He smiled and tilted forward. "Am I too late? Did I do something wrong?"

Jim shook his head and frowned. "No, my boy, you didn't do anything wrong. How was the movie?"

"Real good," said Joey. "Lots of cool music in it."

Jim picked up his glasses and folded his newspaper in half. Clearing his throat, he carefully made a steeple with his fingers and smiled. "You did a good job on the lawn yesterday, by the way. I appreciate that."

"Thank you," said Joey. He felt somewhat relieved but still sensed something was wrong.

"Joe, you know, even though you have been with us less than four months, Cora and I think the world of you."

Joey shrugged and nodded. "Yeah—sure. I feel the same way about both of you. Gosh! You're nice people." The red in his face kicked up a notch but he wasn't sure why.

Tears sprang into Cora's eyes and she suddenly jumped up and rushed from the room. At the same time, her husband's face took on a grave appearance.

"Well, we might as well get right to it, Joe. We've got some bad news. You won't be staying with us after school is out." There was a long pause before he said, "Mrs. Ballanger called today; your mother and father have reconciled again. They want you back to live with them before the new school year begins."

Joey felt the air stick in his lungs. He jumped to his feet and backed up.

"What? No! That can't be right! No! No!" He paced back and forth in front of the couch, his hands flying every which way. "Remember, Connie said this last time was for good. She told me that, Jim! Honest she did. She told me she would never get back together with my father! Never!"

Jim stared at the floor and nodded his head. "Yes, we know that too, Joe, but . . ."

"Please, Sir—don't let them do this to us. I can't go. No! I just won't go!" He dropped back onto the couch.

It was suddenly dead quiet except for the sound of Cora's sniffling coming from the kitchen. She came around the corner, and seeing the injury in Joey's face, sat next to him and clutched his hands in hers. Staring at him through a wavy sheen of tears, she said, "We are so sorry, Joey."

Her eyes closed, and tears squeezed onto her eyelashes. She was unable to control herself and letting go of Joey's hands she began hammering the tops of her thighs with her fists. "It seems so unfair. You must believe me. We don't want this. We love you, Son."

A long silence hung in the air before Joey responded. He dropped his head in his hands and blew a breath out, wishing he could just snap his fingers and make it all disappear.

"Where are they living now?" He formed a fist and punched one hand into the other. "No, it doesn't matter! I hate this! Please, Jim, can't you do something? I'm happy with everything just like it is."

Jim looked up and glanced at him, a frown eclipsed his normally calm features. Cora cried louder and Jim stood and walked over. He stood close to both of them and then, stroking his wife's shoulder remarked, "No. I wish I could, Joe. It's out of our hands, though. Mrs. Ballanger reminded us that their placements can be temporary, at best. You'll be living in Huntington and going to Huntington High to graduate next year. I'm so sorry."

Joey stared at the floor. Anger and frustration and fear rushed through him like a fire. His hands found the pockets of his jeans and slipped in, fingers knotting into tight fists. He shook his head and tears welled up in his eyes.

"I don't know what to do. What can I do? This just isn't fair." His heart thundered in his chest as he stood there with the air around him damp and suffocating. Standing motionless in the doorway, he studied their faces. When he didn't get the reassurance he sought, he shuffled away to his bedroom and softly closed the door.

•   •   •   •   •

In late July, Joey moved back in with his father, Connie and the kids. Becky was no longer living there. She was sharing an apartment with her girlfriend, Faith, in Huntington Station. Everything else was the same as before Joey had left. His father and Connie were getting along as if nothing bad had ever occurred in their relationship. Joey found out that Connie had never given up her parents' house or her kids, including Adam, during the separation. *It seems like every time Dad does something wrong, I get blamed too and we both have to leave. Everybody else gets to stay here.*

He had no choice; a few days before the move Joey told Dee everything. He took his time and told her about his life before he came to Long Island — the foster homes and the orphanage. He went on to tell her about the rest of his real family up north. Dee listened as tears formed in her eyes. She sat there like a little girl who had been given an unpleasant surprise — stunned, hurt, disillusioned.

When Joe finished, she hugged him. They held each other for a long time before she spoke. "Oh, Joe, I'm so sorry. It's all so terrible. But why didn't you tell me all of this a long time ago?"

He closed his eyes like a man in pain then shook his head and shrugged. "I don't know. I was embarrassed, I guess. I'm ashamed of so much. I was so excited to come and live with my father and look at how bad everything turned out. He is what they call an alcoholic and Connie is just as bad. They fight all the time. I'm sorry." He looked into her eyes and said, "Please don't cry." He wiped her tears away with his fingertips. "All I can say is, I love you. Please try to understand, okay?"

They continued to embrace and whispered, "I love you too, Joe. And I forgive you for not telling me sooner. I do understand. Just don't ever lie to me or be afraid to tell me anything again. Promise me."

He didn't answer her for a moment, then said, "I promise."

•   •   •   •   •

He went to work as a stock boy for Stan and Herb Metzger at a record store downtown. The Hall of Records was the only music store in the area and business was good. A new singer with a tune called *Heartbreak Hotel* had become very popular and there were extraordinary sales of singles and LPs. His name was Elvis Presley and his records sold out faster than the Metzgers could keep them in stock. Joey was constantly opening cases of records by Presley. All the girls, including Dee, were crazy about Elvis. Most boys were jealous and wouldn't admit they liked him too.

Joey earned a dollar an hour and Herb befriended him and listened to his problems with a fatherly ear. He became aware that Joey was unhappy at home and he knew how much he cared for Dee. As the summer wore on, Joey spent very little time at home. Between working and riding his bike back and forth to be with Dee he managed to miss altercations between his father and Connie. He missed the Rodderricks and his family up north too, but felt more stable with each passing day.

Every Friday, when he got his paycheck, Connie had her hand out. "You're making decent money, Son. You can certainly help us buy your school clothes this year." With that, she kept Joey's check and gave him five dollars for himself.

"What time will you be home?" she asked. "It's Friday night so I suppose you'll be late."

"Before eleven," said Joey on his way out the door.

"Huuuh. Why don't you just move in with Dee and her folks?"

Connie whined. "You spend more time over there than you do here."

He ignored her sarcasm and headed to Dee's house.

Saturday morning, Darren told Joey that his father and Connie had a big argument when Joe got home Friday night.

Joey's heart sank. He really believed there would be no more drinking or fighting when he came back. He heaved an impatient sigh and threw his hands up in exasperation. "So, what happened?"

"It was his payday and he came home drunk. Mom tried to stay out of his way, but your father was really being mean. They got into a big one, Joey. Both of them sat at the dining room table drinking and yelling at each other. You know how it goes. So, me and Cliff saw it coming and went out and rode our bikes to the park. We messed around down there for a long time. When we got back around nine-thirty, Mom had a black eye." He paused and lowered his voice. "He shouldn't do that, Joey."

Joey shot him a sideways glance—a flash of anger crossed his face. "Wait a minute, Darren. You don't know if he hit her or not." He threw his hands up like he was surrendering. "All I know for sure is I'm glad I missed the crap. I knew they would get into it again before long. You did too—you know you did, Darren." He paused and looked at the ceiling. "You know Adam told me he's going to run away the next time they fight. I know how he feels. I can't wait until I'm old enough to get out."

•   •   •   •   •

Labor Day Weekend was blistering hot. Saturday morning was muggy, the sky hazy. Joe and Connie had planned a barbeque and invited some friends. All the kids knew there would be trouble when the drinking got out of hand. Joey was invited to Dee's house that afternoon for a cookout. He was on his way downstairs when Cliff said, "Yeah, you're lucky. You've got somewhere else to go. Even Adam is staying over at Everett's house tonight, but we'll have to stay here and listen to all the drunks."

"What? No, you don't," said Joey. "Quit whining. Ride down to the beach and go swimming. Stay away until dark, that's all."

"Yeah, sure," said Darren.

"Well, I don't know what to tell you guys. Geez. Don't blame me. I've got nothing to do with it and I don't want to either."

He rode his bike up to Dee's and enjoyed the entire day. Dee's father cooked chicken, hamburgers and hot dogs on the grill and her mom made creamy potato and macaroni salads. There was plenty of Coke and cream soda on hand — plus strawberry shortcake and watermelon. Dee's parents had one other couple over, neighbors from next door who brought corn on the cob and a chocolate cake with creme filling. The adults drank beer but enjoyed themselves without fighting.

When the sun went down, the neighbors and Dee's parents went inside to play Rummy while Joey and Dee stayed out back by themselves. They talked, played records and danced.

"You know I really liked living at the Roddericks' place, but now I can't wait to be on my own," said Joey. He wrapped his arms around Dee. "As soon as I can, I'm gonna get a car and my own place. I need to get away from my house."

They sat together in the wooden swing and he draped his arm around her shoulders. She tucked a strand of hair behind her ear and said, "I agree. That does sound like the best thing for you to do."

"I know. In fact, I was thinking of moving back up north to be near my sister until — well — until I met you. Now... well, now, I love you and I don't want to leave Long Island."

They kissed and she laid her head on his chest. "I love you, too, Joe and I do understand. I don't care about your parents — I care about how crazy they act. I feel bad that they do that stuff around all you guys." She tilted her head up and searched his eyes. "My mom and dad love you. You do know that, don't you?"

"Yes. I sure hope so."

Joey left her house a little after ten o'clock that night. It was another hot one, a night with stars drifting through a hazy sky and humidity so thick you could almost drink the air. When he turned into his driveway he noticed the yard was empty. All the cars that had been starting to park every which way earlier were gone. Good. The party must be over, he thought. He parked his bike, put the kickstand down and approached the patio.

White smoke still drifted above the grill and empty beer bottles sat everywhere. Partial bowls of salad, pickle trays, ketchup and mustard bottles were on a small table and plastic silverware was scattered everywhere. Two brown grocery sacks were overflowing with garbage. An empty cake pan lay upside down under one of the folding chairs.

Joey heard Connie yell, "You sonofabitch! You're a liar. I caught you."

He trembled and wanted to sneak in the house and go to his room without being seen, but he would have to walk by the kitchen in order to get to the stairs.

They were in the kitchen all right. He saw Connie's head pass back and forth in the kitchen window as she paced in the heat of argument. Joey decided to sit on the patio until things calmed down.

All the good things that happened that day—all the wonderful images of time spent at Dee's—suddenly died like a match flame in a breeze.

Chapter Forty-Five

J oey stood still. He was afraid to go inside. He might end up in the middle of their argument somehow and he didn't want to be involved in any way. He wasn't sure what the fight was about, but it wouldn't matter. He did not want to be put in a position to have to take sides with either his father or Connie. He held his breath and continued to listen.

"You only see what you want to see, you bitch!" his father shouted. "I swear, I wish I'd stayed right where I was. Coming back here with your ass was the worst mistake I ever made. Talk about not being able to hold your booze. You've been plastered all fuckin' afternoon. You're the problem, Constance, not I. You make yourself look small—you don't need any help from me."

"Yeah. As if you could ever be embarrassed, you bastard! You've got a constipated mind. You had your head about eight inches up Norma Cassick's ass all afternoon, so how would you see what I did or didn't do? Oh, it's you all right, Joe. If it ain't the booze, it's your fuckin' ponies, and if it ain't that, it's some broad. You think I don't know why you sit in that room day after day? No time for the kids or anything else. You hide in there and dote on Alice."

Joe threw his hands in the air as if he were under arrest and rolled his eyes. "Here we go again—same old bullshit! You don't know a damned thing about what I think; that's the trouble, Connie! You don't know me. And I could care less anymore."

Joey's stomach twisted in knots. *Maybe I should go back to Dee's.* He turned to go then stopped. *No. I can't do that. It's too late. I'll just wait here until they get tired or take it in their bedroom. I wonder where the other guys are. Probably hiding upstairs.* He continued to listen.

Connie stood in the dining room with hands on her hips. "Yeah,

Joe, that makes two of us. I don't care either. I'm tired of your daydreams about Alice." Now her volume outmatched his. "You remember her Joe—the one you love so much—but left high and dry while you waltzed off to the Army? The mother of all the kids you saw fit to forget about so conveniently. I don't think you were hanging around when they passed out consciences. Now today, you were trying to get in that blonde's pants while I stood out there doing the grilling. Ha! Mr. Big Shot. You weren't fooling anybody, Joe. Everybody saw it." Tears filed her eyes. "I felt like a damned fool."

"You want to talk about screwing somebody else, Miss Innocence? How about good old Jake? He's probably still hanging in the shadows. You're probably still fuckin' him for all I know. I'm so sick of you. I wouldn't even be with your ass if you hadn't been knocked up with Adam."

Craaaaaash! Baaaaaang! The loud noise was jarring. Joey tripped and nearly fell as he rushed inside. He found Connie with a butcher knife in her hand. She jabbed it back and forth at Joe as they both circled the dining room table. The silverware drawer was upside down on the floor; knives, forks, spoons, and other junk was scattered everywhere.

Joey stood in the doorway with his hands over his ears. His legs shook as he attempted to move forward and yelled, "Mom! Put the knife down, okay?"

She ignored him. It was as if she was unaware of his presence as she staggered towards Joe. He continued to move around the table, staying as far away from her as possible in the small room.

"Dad! Tell her to put the knife down, please?" Joey shouted.

He watched Connie lean forward, slashing the knife back and forth across the table. "You told me you'd never throw that shit in my face again, Asshole. You promised me if I took you back things would be different. You're a liar! I'll cut your fuckin' heart out, you bastard."

Darren, Cliff, and Adam were suddenly behind Joey—bumping him forward.

"Mommy, stop it!" Adam screamed.

"Come on, Mom, put that down!" Darren yelled.

Joe smirked as he backed away, raising his hands in surrender and glanced at the boys. "There, you see what a crazy bitch your mother is, boys? Look at her. Did you ever see me pull that shit? Swinging a knife around? Hell no! I tell you, she's off her damned rocker!"

"I'm calling the cops," said Cliff. He whirled around and headed for the living room.

"Get back here, Cliff!" Connie yelled. "We don't need the cops. I won't go to jail for this sonofabitch! He ain't worth it." She flipped the knife into the sink, and it hit with a resounding *claaaaang!* She snatched her purse off the counter and staggered as she shoved the boys out of the way. Stumbling to the patio door, she turned and stared at Joe as if he were something she stepped in. "You're a pathetic excuse for a man, Joe."

A brief silence followed while she fished around in the purse for her keys then slammed the door behind her. Everybody heard her car start up and saw the headlights spray across the woods out back as she circled around and drove toward the road.

Joe shoved past the boys and staggered to his room. "Crazy bitch!" he mumbled and slammed his door. He could be heard talking to himself.

Joey felt himself sag with relief. The boys scurried to clean up the mess. Cliff picked up the silverware, while Joey and Darren cleaned the rest of the garbage off the patio. Adam was shaking and sobbing when he dropped down onto a chair at the table. "Where is Mommy going? She'll come back, won't she?"

"Yeah, Twerp. You know how this goes; she'll be back," said Joey as he fluffed the youngest boy's hair.

"Yeah, so why don't you go watch television before it goes off for the day?" said Darren. "The Late Movie is still on."

In the aftermath, the trembling stopped and Joey went to bed, but the panic remained, hollowing out his stomach, constricting his breathing. His throat closed up with misery, and scalding tears squeezed out of his tightly closed eyes. He was sick of the fights — tired of being scared. *Somebody is going to get hurt. I'm fed up with moving in and out of foster homes. I'm tired of seeing them drunk. I was so happy at the Roddericks'. Why couldn't they just leave me alone? I wish Cliff would have called the cops. Maybe they would have sent me back there.*

•　　　•　　　•　　　•　　　•

The first day back to school was a miserable one. Joey felt lousy. The events of the past few days had shadowed his every moment, plus Dee had stayed home. When Joey called, she said she would probably see him the next day. She wasn't feeling well — stomach cramps or something.

After school, Joey walked from there to work at the record store. Just as with every other day, he passed the military recruiting offices located next to the library. He had passed the small building many times, but never took time to look in the window or give the place much thought. Something made him do it that day. He stopped and looked at the posters showing men in uniforms. He was anxious to get to work, but held up long enough to take a closer look at the recruiting posters. There was the Navy with a sailor. The poster said "Join the Navy and see the world." But the uniform looked strange. It reminded him of Donald Duck clothes. The Army and Air Force signs didn't impress him much either.

He liked the Marine's uniform the best — all those gold buttons and emblems on a dark blue uniform, white hat and gloves, light blue trousers with a red stripe down the side. The poster said, "Join the Marines." The Marine looked so handsome, strong and brave with the United States flag in the background.

Joey heard about the Marines; they were tough. Everybody said they were the best. Even his father who had been in the Army said he admired the Marines. Joey had seen John Wayne in a Marine movie called *The Sands of Iwo Jima.* His mind suddenly drifted back to the orphanage and his teacher, Mr. Thompson. How upsetting it was when the former Marine died from a fall in the school gym. He studied the poster for a moment, then decided to take just a minute to go inside.

The Marine stood behind the olive-drab-colored desk when Joey entered. He was a young man—at least six foot tall—who had a corded neck and tightly muscled body that appeared very trim. Just above his wrist was a green and red tattoo of the Marine Corps globe and anchor emblem.

He wore a khaki shirt with two chevrons on each sleeve and matching tie. His light blue trousers had red stripes down the seams. A crimson-red block of wood with yellow lettering sat prominently on his desk. It said "Semper Fi."

Joey suddenly remembered the gold lettering Mr. Thompson's, classroom door. It said the same thing—Semper Fi. He had told Joey it was the United States Marine Corps motto, and it was Latin for "Always Faithful."

"Hello, young man." A smile curved the corners of his mouth when the Marine spoke.

"Hello, Sir" Joey hesitated before he said, "How old do you have to be to join the Marines?"

·　　·　　·　　·　　·

Joey made up his mind while he was at work that night. It was the answer he was looking for. He would join the Marines. Herb, his boss at the record store, was taken off guard and very surprised, but proud of his young charge. "Are you old enough, Joey?"

"Yes. The corporal said I only have to be seventeen with parent's permission."

"Well, I hope it works out for you, Son. Let me know what your folks say about it."

After work, Joey went right home and found his father sitting at the kitchen table reading his newspaper. Connie was in the bathroom. Everything was quiet—just as if the fight the night before had never occurred. Joey wondered where Connie had been all night. She had left in such a huff and he hadn't heard her come home.

The other boys were in the living room, watching TV. His father slid a cigarette from the pack of Luckies on the table and lit up. He dragged smoke into his lungs until there was a half inch of glowing ash at the end of it. Smoke curled from his nose and rolled out the side of his mouth. He squinted at Joey through the haze.

"Where've you been, Joey?"

"I just got off work," said Joey. I work every Monday, remember?" He paused and took a seat. "Is Connie all right? Where did she go last night?"

Joe shook his head and grinned. "She stayed at her mother's place. It's not the first time, you know."

"Yeah, you're right. I just wondered, that's all," said Joey. He did some mental knuckle cracking and tried not to look nervous.

Adam ran into the room just as Connie finished in the bathroom. He clung to her side as she pulled out a chair and sat down. Connie's hair was a distressed ball of frizz around her head. She wore a cotton housedress in a bright flowered print that was subdued somehow by her general aura of gloom.

"Hello, Son," she said, as she drew Joey to her side and hugged him. "How was work today?" She grabbed a section of Joe's newspaper and flipped through it. Neither she nor Joe spoke. Joey sensed the coolness between them. Even without words, body language told the story. It appeared to him that everything had been settled in some way and that thought encouraged him to get up and stand behind Connie's chair. His throat felt dry and the palms of his hands were sweaty.

"I want to join the Marines," he said. "I've got the papers right here." He carefully laid them on the table in front of them.

His father stopped studying the racing form. He took a last drag on the cigarette, stubbed it out in the ashtray and cleared his throat before he folded the paper and tossed it on the table.

Connie whirled around in her chair. "What?" She looked at Joey as if he was from another planet. Then she giggled. "Are you serious? You're not old enough to join anything, Joey—much less the Marines." Joey watched as she stood and went to the refrigerator. She bumped the door closed with her hip. She had a can of beer in each hand. Taking her seat again, she set one in front of Joe and took a long swallow of hers.

"You've got to finish school first," said his father. He put his elbows on the table and leaned forward.

"No, I don't, Dad. See, the recruiter said I can take what's called a GED after boot camp and get my diploma that way."

Connie pressed fingers to her temples and sighed heavily. Putting up her hand in a traffic cop gesture, she said, "You're not old enough. Why would you want to do such a thing anyway?"

"I only have to be seventeen, and my birthday just passed. I could leave for boot camp at Parris Island, South Carolina, in November."

Silence hung in the air for a moment. Joe stared at his son—nothing mean—just a hard stare. Connie, who had been looking up at Joey, turned around to face the opposite way. She shook her head in amazement. She was emphatic. "I say no!"

"Wait a minute here," said Joe. "Don't I get any say-so in this?" He reached for another cigarette. There was another block of silence.

"Adam—you go on now. Go watch television," said Connie. She lit a cigarette and took a leisurely drag.

"Awwww. Why do I have to leave?" said Adam. "Are you really gonna become a soldier, Joey?"

"A Marine, Adam. And I said go in the other room," Connie growled.

As he edged out of the room, he said, "What's the difference?"

Connie pointed. "In the other room—now!"

Joe leaned forward with his forearms on his thighs and his hands dangling down between his knees, as calm as if he were sitting over a fishing pole waiting for a bite. "You'll never make it in the Marines, Son. It's a hard road there—a lot tougher than the other branches. Hell, I read in the paper last week where one of the drill instructors at Parris Island drowned six recruits.... bet your Marine friend didn't tell you that?"

Joey hung his head for a moment. "No, he didn't... but I don't care. That's not going to happen to me. I'll be all right."

His father's expression turned to stone. Joey had his full attention, staring at him now like he was hypnotized. "Why in the hell do you want to go in the Marines of all things? Why not the Army or the Navy? Even the goddamned Air Force would be better."

Joey hesitated. "I don't know, Dad. I just do. Please, just sign for me?"

More silence. Connie glared at Joe. Her cheeks were scarlet from the exertion of controlling her temper. "Joe—don't let him do this. He's way too young. You know that."

Joey studied his father's face—especially his eyes and waited. The silence grew heavy, weighted down with the importance of his answer.

"Well, to tell the truth, I don't see the harm in his joining up. I wish he'd choose some other outfit, but yeah, he can go ahead as far as I'm concerned." He stared at Joey. "Maybe they'll make a man out of you." Then back to Connie, "It's probably the best thing for the boy."

Connie continued to glare at Joe. She seemed to shrink as the fight went out of her on a sigh. "You sound like your mind is made up, Joe. Are you absolutely sure about this?"

"Yeah. I'm sure. Here, let's look at those papers," he said, at the same time cleaning his glasses on his shirt-tail. He scooped up the papers and thumbed through them. He tossed aside the full-color brochures of Marines in dress blues. "Government propaganda," he said as he slid them over to Connie.

"Aaaah, here's the permission forms, right here. These are the important ones." He adjusted his glasses and began to read. After a few minutes he tossed the papers on the table, looked at Joey and said, "Says there, you've got to have your real mother and father sign." He snickered and stared at Connie as he shoved the papers over to her. "How about that?"

"What?" Joey picked up the papers and searched for the information. "I don't see why. What's she got to do with it?"

"Because she's your real mother, that's why," said Connie.

She slid a cigarette out of the pack of Old Golds on the table and lit up—for the moment resigned.

"Even if I sign these papers, Son, you'll have to go up north and see Alice and have her sign too."

"When you went to the Roddericks', Mrs. Ballanger told us where Alice was living. We'll have to get a hold of her on the phone and see if she's willing to sign. Maybe she'll say no," said Connie. "So, don't get all fired up just yet."

Chapter Forty-Six

A lice told Mrs. Ballanger she would sign for Joey to go in the Marines but only if he could bring the papers with him and visit her in Gouvernuer.

Connie stared at Joey. "I don't know where the money is going to come from to pay for all this. It's going to cost forty-four dollars round trip on the train. Greyhound is even more." She shook her head. "I suppose I could borrow it from Mom and Dad." She paused and paced back and forth in the dining room, shrugged and lit a cigarette. Anyway, since Alice is going to sign you can ride up there on the train and take the papers to her. It will be good for you to visit your real mother. I think you should." She pulled out a chair and looking at Joey's father said, "Don't you, Joe?"

Joe sneered and shrugged. "It doesn't matter what I think, does it? The boy's got his mind made up. He needs her to sign the papers. That's it. We'll see to it that you get up there, Son."

•   •   •   •   •

In late September, after school, Joey and Dee strolled across the street to Heckscher Park. The air was crisp and the sky pale blue. The pungent smell of fall was in the air. The grass was still a vibrant green, but shades of red and orange rippled through the trees. Daily visitors to the park were getting scarce. Jackets and sweaters were needed. Joey guided Dee to the bench under their special tree where other lovers had carved their names in a heart.

Joey worried about breaking the news to Dee regarding joining the Marines. Trudging along, kicking through the fallen leaves, he considered his situation. His thoughts chased each other around in his brain until he wanted to shake them all out. He didn't want to address his leaving with Dee yet because he wasn't certain his mother would really sign the permission papers. He knew Dee would be upset — probably even cry — and the last thing he wanted was to hurt her. Not wanting to hurt anybody, Joey simply wanted to get away from the situation at home once and for all. Taking off his jacket, he found a good spot and spread it on the ground. "Let's sit here for a while, okay?"

"Sure," said Dee. "It sure is nice out." She curtsied and giggled. "Thanks for being such a gentleman, putting down your jacket, Sir."

Not saying anything about joining the Marines would be okay; there was no lying involved. He decided all he needed to tell Dee right now was that he was going upstate to visit his real mother.

After he told her, Dee said, "I just love that, Joe. I mean, I'm so happy that you're going to see your real mom. I'll bet you can hardly wait, huh?"

"Yeah. It will be great! I haven't seen her in over six years."

"What about your Dad and Connie? Are they upset? How come they're letting you go?"

Joey shrugged. "I don't know. They just are, and I'm glad. I'm just hoping they don't change their minds."

"Oh, I'll miss you so much, Joe." She squeezed his hand, then tucked her hair behind her ear and gave him that beautiful little half smile that quickened his heartbeat. "How long will you be gone, do you know?"

He hated lying to her, but figured he could explain everything later on. He hesitated a bit and said, "I think for a week. Listen to me," he said as he tipped her chin up. "I'll miss you too; you must know that, don't you?"

"Yes, I know. It's just going to be hard, that's all." She kissed his cheek. "There's something I want you to do for us though." She grinned as she fished around inside her pocketbook until she retrieved a very small pocket knife and handed it to him.

"Go ahead — you do it. The guy is supposed to, I think."

"Huh? Do what?"

Dee smiled as she stood, turned slowly and edged over to the tree. She rubbed her fingers over the carved heart that said, "Billy and Judy" and giggled. "I wish you could see that look on your face right now. Come here, silly. Carve our names on the tree, right next to theirs. Won't that be cool?"

"Yeah, I like that." He ducked his head and grinned shyly. "Okay. Here, give me the knife."

By chipping, digging and scraping, it didn't take long before he had it done. Then they both stood back and studied his handiwork. He had made their heart a bit bigger than the other one and although it wasn't shaped like a perfect valentine heart, Dee loved it. It said: "Joe + Dee 1956," with an arrow slashed through the middle of it.

They stood beneath the tree, their arms encircling each another. Joey sucked in a startled breath as his heart vaulted into his throat. His pulse pounded in his ears. He closed his eyes and kissed her. It was a long, lingering kiss. She laid her head on his chest and faced the tree. "Just think, Joe. Our names will be there forever—just like our love."

•　　•　　•　　•　　•

The days seemed to drag by into October while Joey waited on final plans to go north. Then good news came one Friday afternoon after school.

"Mrs. Ballanger called today, Joey," said Connie.

His heart skipped a beat and he felt a surge of adrenaline race up his spine. "Really? What did she say? Is everything okay?"

"It's all set. Your mother will meet you in Watertown on the twentieth, one week from Friday. The recruiter told us if she signs, you will be reporting for induction on the 20th of November."

"Wow! That's great!" Joey shouted and clapped his hands. "Just great, ain't it, Dad?"

Joe appeared to be lost in watching his son's reaction. He grinned and said, "Yes, Joe. Good for you. Looks like a Marine you'll be. I'm proud of you."

Connie hugged him. "Well, you know, I still don't approve of you joining anything." She stepped back and searched his eyes. "I say you're too young." Pausing briefly, she put her arms around him again. "I'm proud of you, too, Joey."

Joey thought he saw tears in her eyes.

• • • • •

The morning Joey left for Watertown, his father had to work, so Connie drove him to meet Mrs. Ballanger in Syosset. She gave Joey his ticket and from there Mrs. Ballanger would take him to Grand Central Station in the city. When Connie kissed him goodbye, she slipped him eight dollars. "This is from me and your father. Put it in your pocket, and don't spend it all on junk."

"Thank you," said Joey. Connie hugged and kissed him again. "Goodbye, Son. Be careful, okay?" She wiped away a tear with the back of her hand.

"Goodbye, Mom. I'll be okay. Don't worry."

Passengers were still boarding the train when Mrs. Ballanger spoke. "Remember now, Joey, you'll change trains in Albany. Then your mother will be at the station in Watertown to pick you up. Your sister, Beth, will be with her and your mother has assured me that she will be able to spot you, so I wouldn't worry. Okay?"

"Yes, Ma'am."

After he was situated on the train, Joey thought about the night before with Dee. She had cried.

"It's only for a week," he told her, but guilt snapped at him.

"I know, but what am I going to do while you're gone? I'll miss you so much, Joe."

With the lulling clickety-clack and swaying of the train, Joey stared out the window and watched as the city eventually became country. His mind raced every which way contemplating who and what he would see when he got to his destination.

I'll finally see Sis – Gram, Gramps, Uncle Glenn, and Aunt Betty too. I wonder if their house looks the same. It's too early to put up the Christmas tree, but I wish they could. Put it up where Gramps always did — in the front window. I haven't seen those bubble lights since that one special Christmas. I'll never forget. I wonder what my mother looks like now. I hope she's not still sick.

Fourteen hours and many small towns later — plus a switch of trains in Albany, Joey's train arrived in Watertown. When he stood to get his suitcase from under the seat, his knees were shaking and he felt sick to his stomach. He felt excited but strange. It was as if he were taking some last step into the unknown. Beth came running up the moment his feet touched the platform. Their eyes locked on each other and Beth was in tears, her arms wide open and waiting. Alice appeared to be tagging along behind her.

"Joey! Joey! Joey!" Beth yelled. "Oh, thank God, you're here at last." They hugged and she said, "Let me look at you! Oh, you've grown so tall. Wow!"

Joey couldn't hold back his tears as the two of them hugged for a long time. Beth was just as he remembered her, only taller. She was beautiful even with tears streaming down her cheeks.

Joey looked over at his mother and smiled. He couldn't help feeling how strange this meeting seemed. Alice appeared so sad and lonely-looking as she stood off to the side, waiting her turn, while he and his sister joyously embraced. It was as if after so many years, she was afraid to come near her own son. She stared at the scene through wet eyes — a thirty-five-year-old woman wearing the ravages of alcohol and disenchantment with life.

Finally, Alice stepped forward and circled her arms around him. "Oh, Joey," she cried. Beth stepped back and gave them room but stayed close enough to rub her mother's back while she held Joey and sobbed.

"Oh, my boy, my boy. Let me look at you." Her hands trembled and tears tumbled down her cheeks. "It's really you, Joey. Oh my goodness. What a big boy, I mean young man." She managed a chuckle as she stood back and smothered his hands with her own.

His mother had gained an immense amount of weight from what he could recall. She had a striking pallor but wore bright red lipstick.

Her hair was brown but thin and frizzy. Something about her transported him to the distant past. The old-looking brown coat she wore was the heavy winter variety and it didn't fit well due to her bloated stomach. It seemed to stick out in front. Deep shadows were under her eyes and Joey couldn't tell what color they were because they were filled with tears.

Rubbing her hands briskly up and down the sleeves of his coat, she nearly dropped the pocketbook tucked under her arm. She managed a slight smile as she stared at him.

Joey moved in and hugged her and kissed her on the cheek. "Hi, Mom."

"Joey, how you've grown. You're so tall and handsome." Tears shimmered in her eyes, magnifying them, making them look like huge liquid jewels. She clutched his head between her hands and kissed him repeatedly on the face.

Joey smelled alcohol.

"You're the spitting image of your father." She smiled as she wiped the tears from her eyes with her fingers. "Beth, be a good girl and grab his suitcase, will you?" Joey draped his arm over his mother's shoulders as they slowly strolled to the car where Uncle Glenn was waiting.

"Hey, Sport!" Uncle Glenn grabbed Joey and hugged him. "By golly, it's great to see you!" He laughed. "I wouldn't recognize you if these two weren't with you. You have really sprouted up, young man. So durn tall."

Joey gave him a lopsided grin and shrugged. "Yeah, I guess so. I'm sure glad to see you again, Uncle Glenn. I missed you and Aunt Betty a lot." He was so overjoyed to see his uncle but couldn't help but notice how gray his hair had gotten.

Everybody loaded up in the car, with Alice in the front, while Glenn drove and headed for Gouvernuer. Autumn was in its advanced stages in northern New York. The leaves on the white birch trees fluttered like golden spangles as they passed through the countryside. Glenn looked at Joey in his rearview mirror. "So, how have you been, Sport? We haven't heard from you in ages. How's your dad these days?"

Alice immediately turned her head to gaze out the passenger side window. Color rose to mottle her face with polka dots.

Joey wasn't sure how to answer. "He's okay."

"Is he working?" Glenn asked.

"Yup, he works at the Grange League Federation. They sell feed for farm animals and stuff like that."

"I see," said Glenn. Silence permeated the car for a moment after that.

Joey asked, "Where's Aunt Betty?"

"Well, we wouldn't have room in here for her. She's got a bit of a cold anyway, so she stayed home. She'll be seeing you tomorrow, most likely."

Glenn dropped everybody off at Gramps' house on Depot Street. "We'll all see you tomorrow, Joey. Have fun at your gramma and grandpa's house tonight."

Gram and Gramps' house was filled with the sweet smell of freshly baked cookies and melted chocolate and fried food of some sort. The inside seemed much smaller to Joey—especially the kitchen. It was as if every room had shrunk since he had last been there five years earlier.

"Look at my oldest boy, Mom," said Alice. "Isn't he a good-lookin' devil?"

Gram was overjoyed. She came out of the kitchen raising her eyebrows as if totally surprised. She smiled while quickly drying her hands on her apron. "Oh, my goodness! Here he is—the man of the hour," she cried. Her eyes overflowed with tears.

Joey noticed that she had lost a lot of weight. Her bone structure looked like that of a praying mantis and she had a hump in her back. Her hands shook as she caressed Joey's face.

"Yes. Oh yes. He's Joe's blood all right—looks just like him. I can't believe he's so tall though. It's so good to see you again, Sonny. Please take off your coat and stay a while. Grandpa is upstairs taking a nap, but he'll be getting up soon. Alice, you move out of the way, so I can get some hugs. My goodness!" She wrapped her withering arms around Joey and held him tight. "Your Gram loves you so much. And just look—you're taller than I am now, Young Man."

Joey grinned. "Yeah, I guess I am." He stepped back and smiled at the difference in height. "Is Gramps okay?"

"He's fine—just takes a nap every day. You know how it is."

Joey watched his mother remove her coat. He noticed that her belly stuck way out in the baggy blue dress that buttoned down the front and had a white collar. Her nylons were rolled like doughnuts just below her knees.

"Go ahead, Joey. Make yourself at home," she said. "It's so good to have you here. I know I'm going to cry."

Even though it was all family, Joey felt awkward. He found himself watching his mother's every move. With her arms crossed over her chest, she paced nervously back and forth. Joey wanted to know her. He needed to get close to her. His eyes followed her from the living room to the kitchen and back. He wanted to know how she walked, how she talked—everything and anything about her in the short time he would be there. It became strangely quiet as everyone contemplated their own thoughts for a moment.

Alice looked downcast, as if it seemed to register that any answers she might have would be a testament to her failings as a mother.

Everyone took a seat at the dining room table and Gram set a gallon jug of Gallo wine on the table. Alice poured some into two tall glasses.

"You kids want some hot cocoa?" Gram asked as she lit a Chesterfield.

"Yes, I'd like that," said Beth. "How about you, Joey?"

"Yeah. That would be great! Just like old times."

Beth said, "I'll get it, Gram."

Alice studied her son's face. "So, you want to be a Marine?"

"Yes, Mom, I do."

She took a long swallow of wine and swiped at her lips with her fingers. "Why the Marines?"

The silence was deafening before he said, "I'm not sure. I just know the Marines are the best—that's all. I want to join the best there is."

"And the most dangerous, too," said Gram.

"You do realize that, don't you, Son?" said Alice. "The Marines are always the first to go when there's trouble." She slid one of Gram's Chesterfields out of the pack on the table and placed it between her lips, but quickly pulled it from her mouth and held it up like an exclamation point. Her look was clearly one of skepticism. "My God, Joey. You don't even shave yet, do you?"

"No—I don't shave yet. Why? Am I supposed to?"

"No, not really, Son." She giggled just as Gramps came down the stairs. He moved slowly and grunted with each step. The stairs creaked under the weight of his big, rotund frame. His chest had shrunk over the years but his belly seemed larger to Joey. He was forced to hike his pants up under his armpits. Blue-and-white-striped suspenders dangled from his hips as he shuffled over to hug Joey and slap him on the back.

"Hello, Sonny. Tarnation! It's good to see you home where you belong, Lad. I missed you. We all did."

Joey smiled. "It's so good to see you again, Gramps. I missed you, too."

He hugged Joey again, but his arms didn't feel as strong as Joey remembered.

Gram said, "Hasn't he grown a bunch, Old Man?"

"Yes, he's all grown up now! It does my heart good, I tell you. Listen, Alice, I heard you talking about him joining up. Leave the boy alone. If he wants to join the Marines, more power to him. I'm proud of you, Sonny."

"I am just as proud as you are, Pa. I just want to be sure he understands what he's getting into, that's all," said Alice.

"He'll make a great Marine," Beth chimed in from the kitchen.

Alice finished her glass of wine and took both glasses out to the kitchen as she continued to listen to the conversation between Gramps and Joey.

Gramps lit his pipe, and the aroma instantly took Joey back to days gone by when he was a little boy. He had forgotten that wonderful fragrance that reminded him of much better times so long ago.

With an audible grunt, Gramps dropped down into his rocking chair. "When do you report, Sonny?"

"November twentieth is when I'll leave for boot camp in South Carolina."

"It's hard to believe you're seventeen, Sonny. Time has skipped right on by me, I swear." He paused and ruminated a moment while he puffed on his pipe. "What's your father think?"

Alice attempted to catch every word from the kitchen.

"Uhhh... he's fine with it," said Joey.

Beth brought their cocoa in and sat beside Joey who sat cross-legged on the living room floor. The two of them commenced to talk about their experiences—both good and bad. When Joey casually mentioned the cruelty he'd suffered at the hands of Mr. Bushkin, a long pause ensued and nobody in the room spoke. It was as if they might choose the wrong thing to say—or hurt feelings at the very least.

Alice wrestled with her guilt. Drying her eyes, she took a puff on her cigarette, lifted her head and exhaled a cloud of smoke that swirled away in the dim light.

Gram cleared her throat. "It's so good to see you again, Sonny. I want you to enjoy yourself while you're visiting your gram and gramps. Goodness knows, it's been so awful long—so let's not talk about sad things, okay?"

"Sure, Gram. Okay," said Joey.

Gram fidgeted in her chair then blurted, "Well, I have to go about getting some supper on the table. Good Lord, Joey is probably starving. Alice, will you please give me a hand?"

"Sure, Ma." Alice still had tears in her eyes. She sniffed and glanced sideways at her mother who patted her on the shoulder. Joey's eyes followed them as they went to the kitchen. A few minutes later, the clatter of pots and pans broke the silence.

Joey stood and walked as far as the kitchen door. "Mom, can we talk after supper? We haven't done that in so long and I've got so many questions." He edged into the room and stood behind his mother, watching the little tremors that shook her shoulders. He could hear her catch a breath and knew she was trying valiantly not to cry.

Alice turned and gave him a slight smile. "Of course, Son. I want to do that, too. Don't forget, though, you're here for a whole week. We'll have plenty of time." She leaned on the table and ground her cigarette out in the ashtray. She bit her lip, but her face was otherwise expressionless.

After a meal of fried pork chops, mashed potatoes, corn on the cob, sliced fresh tomatoes and homemade bread, Joey sat back and said, "I always like your cooking, Gram. Nobody does it better and this was great. There wasn't much to eat on the train and I was hungry."

Gram smiled. "I'm glad you liked it, Sonny. I hope you left room for some of my blueberry pie."

"I sure did."

Gramps burped. "I just made room for my piece." He winked at Joey. "Well, we certainly missed hearing from you, Sonny." He leaned in a bit and lowered his voice. "I hope you'll stay in touch when you leave here this time."

"I promise I will, Gramps. I'll write to you all every chance I get."

Joey thought his mother was right. *We have six whole days before I go back home. I'll wait to ask questions.*

•   •   •   •   •

After the adults went to bed, Joey and Beth stayed up and talked. They slipped on their coats and sat out on the back steps so they wouldn't disturb anyone. The night was October chilly, clear and utterly silent. Overhead, the velvet-black sky was filled with winking stars.

The two young people talked about everything and anything. Beth told Joey about his new brother, Johnny, and sister, Kathy. "They're living over in Black River with Mom and Fred. I don't know if you know this, but Mom and Fred have never gotten married because she never got a divorce from Dad."

Joey shrugged. "I sort of figured that out, Sis."

Beth shivered and wrapped her arms around herself to keep warm. "Somebody wants to adopt Johnny and Kathy, I guess."

"What? Why?" His eyes widened.

"It's a long story. I'll tell you later, okay?" She squeezed his arm and whispered, "I've got to leave here, Joey."

"Huh? You mean, go away?"

"Yes. Oh, Joey, you just don't know what it's like here. I can't get a job because Mom has me baby-sit all the time. And she doesn't pay me anything either, so I have no money of my own. Nothing for myself. I need to start doing other things." She stood up and pulled on Joey's jacket, drawing him away from the back door—out deeper into the yard.

"I've got a boyfriend."

"Huh?" He smiled in the dark. "Well, great! So... what's wrong with that?"

"Nothing, but I have to sneak around. I've been seeing him, but nobody knows. I've actually been seeing him a lot." She stared at her feet. Anyway, His name is Walter, and he just got discharged from the Army." Excitement laced her words, and Joey saw her smile in the moonlight. "I met him downtown when I went to the movies during Easter vacation. I was with my girlfriend, Adele."

"Wow! I'm glad, Sis. There's nothing wrong with having a boyfriend though. Wait till I tell you about Dee. She's my girlfriend. Anyway, why do you want to leave here? Where would you go, anyway?"

"I just have to leave. Listen, Joey, I've got a secret I'll tell you, but you have to promise you won't tell anybody."

"Okay, I promise. Now come on—tell me this big secret."

She bit down on her lower lip to keep it from trembling. "Joey—I'm pregnant. I'm going to have a baby."

Chapter Forty-Seven

Joey was torn. On one hand, he wanted to get the papers signed by his mother so he could join the Marines. But now that he was back in Gouverneur with family, he realized he could be happy living right there close to his sister, Beth.

That first night, after Beth revealed her secret to him, Joey was speechless. His mouth was open and his eyes wide. It just didn't seem possible. Gouverneur was a tight-knit little community that ran on gossip and pot roast. Keeping her secret would be nearly impossible, he thought.

His mind still reeled with the thought that his sister was pregnant. "A baby? You're not old enough to have a baby, Sis."

She sighed. "Well, I'm going to. I just don't know how to tell Mom or Gram yet, Joey. You're the only one that knows now—except for Walter, of course."

"What does he think?"

"Walter's fine with it. He's a nice guy and he loves me. He wants to marry me. And that's what I want too." She studied her brother's face. "Please keep your promise, Joey. Don't tell anyone, okay?" She sighed. "I haven't been able to tell you any secrets for a long time, but I'm hoping I can still trust you."

"I promise I won't tell, but everybody is going to know sometime soon, right?"

"That's true, but I want to wait for a while. Believe me I'll know when the time is right." Beth put both hands on Joey's shoulders and searched his eyes. "I just don't want my dream to be over before it's even started." She pecked him on the cheek. "I love you, Joey. See you tomorrow. Goodnight now."

"I love you too, Sis. I hope you know what you're doing, that's all. Goodnight."

●   ●   ●   ●   ●

When Uncle Glenn and Aunt Betty arrived the next day, Gram and Alice were sitting at the dining room table playing Rummy and drinking wine. Alice was in a sour and restless mood. She realized that she had a lot of explaining to do for Joey's benefit and there was no getting around it. In addition, she and Gram had been bickering all morning.

Gramps sat in his rocker in the front room, away from the window. He puffed on his pipe and glared at Gram and Alice while tapping his fingers on the armrests of his chair as though trying to communicate something in Morse code.

Beth and Joey strolled out to the car to meet Uncle Glenn and Aunt Betty just as Gram got up and took the wine glasses to the kitchen. When the company came in, she was busy poking around in one of the kitchen drawers, feigning a search for something or other.

Aunt Betty charged up and hugged Joey and they all drifted back into the house. "My oh my, you have grown so much, Sonny!" Her eyes were filled with tears. "Lord, have mercy. Last time we saw you, you were half as tall, I swear." She stuck her arm out to demonstrate. "You were only ten or eleven years old, I think."

"Yup, I remember," said Joey. "I was eleven when I stayed with you and Uncle Glenn that Christmas when Santa brought me a Roy Rogers wristwatch."

"Yes. That's right. I will never forget that Christmas either. It was 1950, just before you went to the orphanage in Watertown. You were staying with that terrible family out there in Carthage. What was their name — Bucknells or something like that?"

"Bushkin," said Joey. He didn't bat an eye.

A momentary pall fell over the room.

Gram's face turned red. "We're not discussing any of that stuff from the past today, Betty." She cleared her throat and her body seemed to become erect. "Right, Joey?"

"Right. Sure—okay, Gram."

"Lord knows it's hard enough on Alice and these youngsters without all that terrible old craziness flying back and forth. I won't have it in my house today." She winked at Joey then looked at Betty. "How about a cup of coffee?"

"Okay, yeah, Ma—I'll have some."

"Me too. That would be great," said Glenn. He nudged Joey in the arm. "Hey, Sport, we brought a treat for you and Beth." He set a brown bag on the table and pointed to it. "Can you guess what's in there?"

Joey grinned from ear to ear. "No, I can't." He reached for the bag. "Can I peek?"

"Sure. Take a look."

Joey's hands shook as he fumbled to get the bag open. His eyes widened. "It's ice cream! Chocolate too, Beth. Wow!"

Beth wrapped her arms around Glenn's neck. "Thank you, Uncle Glenn."

She grinned. "It reminds me of the time you took us for ice cream in Watertown that day. Remember Pee Wee, Joey?"

They all laughed. "Yeah, I'll never forget Pee Wee," said Joey. His boyish smile made a half-hearted appearance, flickering and fading in the blink of an eye. "That was a swell day. Thanks so much, Uncle Glenn—you too, Aunt Betty."

Gram seemed to be a bit put out and said, "Well, I've got some sandwiches and macaroni salad made, everybody, so just you hold your horses, young man. Let's have the food first. Then you can dig in to the ice cream. Glenn—please put it in the ice box for now, okay?"

Everyone was in a good mood, enjoying lunch and the ice cream while they discussed the problems Uncle Glenn was having with his furnace. A couple of hours later, Uncle Glenn and Aunt Betty left for home and Joey saw what he hoped was a good opportunity to finally talk to his mother. Gramps had gone upstairs to take his nap while Gram and Alice continued to play Rummy. The glasses of wine were back in front of them. Beth and Joey sat next to each other. The house was quiet and calm; the tension appeared to be gone.

Joey took a long steadying breath. "Mom, do you want to see those papers now? I can show you where to sign and everything."

Alice rubbed the back of her neck as if it troubled her. It was pin-drop quiet for a moment before she sighed and answered. "Yes, Joey—I suppose so."

He watched as Alice stubbed her cigarette out in the ashtray, maybe giving herself time to think. "There's really no hurry, but if you want to let me to have a look now, it's okay."

Joey suddenly felt empty inside. It was as though there still remained so much distance between him and his mother, even though she was right there in front of him. He remembered how, at the orphanage, Ma Alexander was always full of smiles—and how she hugged and kissed him for practically no reason at all. That was what a mother should be like, he thought.

He went to his suitcase that lay in the front room and brought the papers back. "Here they are, Mom."

"Okay, Son. Just let us finish this hand first, okay? Like I said, there's really no rush is there?" she smiled and patted his hand.

"No, that's right." Noticeably nervous, his hands clenched, Joey settled in on the chair next to hers. There were a few more hands of cards before he said, "Mom, can we just talk while you keep playing cards?"

Beth frowned and nudged Joey's foot under the table. She rolled her eyes and made a face.

"Sure, Son," said Alice. She shook her head, took a big drag, and blew the smoke out through her nostrils. "What do you want to talk about?"

Hope surged like a geyser inside him as he realized she was ready.

"Why did you put us in foster homes? How come we ended up there?"

He could see Alice going over the story in her head, trying to come up with the good answer. She stared at her wine glass as if the answer might be contained in there. She picked up one card, discarded another and said, "I had no choice, Joey." She fanned her cards out face-down on the table and stared at him. "Your father left us. He lied about having dependents and joined the Army."

"What do you mean dependents?"

"Dependents, Joey. That's a wife and kids. That was me, Beth and you, at the time. And I was pregnant with Brian. Your father told the Army he had no wife and no children. He left us with no money, nothing — no way to support ourselves. He lied to everybody, Joey."

Joey stared at her with widened eyes. They sat in silence for a moment, neither of them able to put further feelings into words. Joey felt the weight of regret on his shoulders like a pair of hands pressing down, compressing the emotions into hard knots inside him.

Alice yanked a handkerchief out of her pocketbook and began to cry. "Mommy needed some help, kids." She pulled Joey closer. Tears trickled down her cheeks as she ran a hand through his hair.

Anger and frustration rushed through Joey like a fire. "I don't understand. Why did he do that?"

"Your father said it was his duty to join. All of his buddies were going in. The Army wanted men so badly they didn't bother checking things out as much as they should've back then," said Gram. "Your mother didn't know anything until it was too late. He was gone." She paused long enough to light another cigarette and handed the pack to Alice.

"At first, you kids stayed here, living with me and Gramps. She hoped your father would come back. None of us knew where he was at that time. We couldn't track him down."

Alice's attention swung back to her son: "When I figured out what was going on, I intended to keep you both here until I could get on my feet — get a job and so on. I hoped your father would send some money home to help us out, but of course he never did."

"That was another one of his lies. He wrote letters after a while. He said the Army was taking money from his check and an allotment check would start coming right to your mother," said Gram.

Alice stood and paced back and forth. "I had to find a job and I did work for a while at the Sunset Diner as a waitress and cook. But that didn't last long either because . . .," She sobbed loud and hard into her handkerchief, ". . . because I was pregnant and couldn't work." She puffed on her cigarette and turned her head slightly to exhale a slow stream.

"I know you can't possibly understand everything that was going on. You were both so young. And I'm sure your father didn't know I was pregnant when he left, but I don't think it would have made any difference, do you, Ma?"

"No!" Gram glared at Beth and Joey. "Joe Harrison was a selfish liar and didn't care about any of you. I'm sorry, kids, but it's the truth."

Joey hung his head and stared blankly at the cards on the table, unsure of what to say. Alice exhaled a full plume of smoke before she spoke again. He dropped his head in his hands and blew a breath out, wishing he could just snap his fingers and have it all disappear.

Alice continued. "As the days passed, things became too much for Gram and Gramps with all of us, including Brian on the way and all. There were simply too many mouths to feed. I had to get help from the Welfare Department. They were the ones who decided that foster homes would be the best thing until things got straightened around between me and your father. It was just supposed to be for a little while. God knows, I never wanted you kids to be hurt in any way. I felt terrible every day while you were gone. I love you and worried about you — all of you."

She turned to Beth. "Beth, you know that's true. How often did Mommy talk about the boys?" She patted Beth's arm and looked at Joey. "Do you understand now, Son?"

"You told me some of this before, Mom," said Beth. "But you never came to see us or any of the boys after I came back here. You never called us or anything, not even a letter. We didn't know where you were — where Dad really was."

"We were scared and we missed you," said Joey. "Mrs. Kellogg wouldn't tell us anything either. We wanted to hear from you awful bad. We didn't even know we had brothers until that day Mrs. Kellogg brought them to the farm."

"Well, hold on now," said Alice. Embarrassment and shame flooded her entire being as she broke into heavy sobs. "I wanted to see you. I always wanted to, but I couldn't bear leaving you behind if I saw you. I didn't know what to tell you. Your father wrote and promised when he got discharged we'd all get back together. I believed him. Lord knows, I wanted to believe him. Then he never wrote me another letter, and I never got any allotment like he promised—nothing. I just couldn't come and see your little faces and tell you I couldn't take you with me. Can you try to understand that?"

Alice's body shook as though she had just emerged from a pool of icy water. She looked pathetic. "Remember I did come to see you that one Christmas at the Matthews'. Fred brought me—don't you remember? Leaving you and the twins behind that day ripped the heart right out of me." She buried her face in her hands.

"But, where did the twins come from anyway?" Joey asked.

Beth squeezed his arm. "Joey—please don't."

Gram got up. "I think that's just about enough of this for now," she said. She patted Alice on the back. "You don't need to go on anymore, Honey." She smiled and quickly looked at Joey. "How about some more of that ice cream, kids?"

Joey shook his head. "Not me, Gram."

"Me neither," said Beth.

Gram lit a cigarette and moved her chair out of the way. In the kitchen, she poured more wine into glasses for both herself and Alice, then came back. She gathered up the cards into a deck and slid them into the box.

"I'll just say this. When your mother found out she was pregnant with Mitchell and Merrill, she didn't know which way to turn—what to do. She kept hoping that she and your father would get back together and round all you kids up to live as a family. I know that's what she wanted. So, that's enough for now, okay? Let's just change the subject for a while, kids."

Alice's sobs slowly subsided and she lit a cigarette then sipped her wine.

"The next thing I heard was your father was living with another woman on Long Island somewhere. And she was pregnant too. I couldn't believe it. I didn't want to believe it. He asked me for a divorce but I wouldn't give him up—I said no."

"Connie," said Joey. "Yes... I guess that was her."

"But you still never wrote to us. You never came to see us, Mom!" Joey's eyes filled with tears. He looked in his mother's eyes. "You just never did, that's all. Why couldn't you just write me a letter?"

Alice almost knocked over her glass as she suddenly stood and smothered Joey's head with her fleshy arms. A fresh wave of tears filled her eyes, and her mouth began to tremble. "Oh, Joey, I'm so sorry. Please forgive me? Please—both of you." She kissed the top of his head and squeezed his hands. "I tried. You have to believe me. I was so ashamed. I just didn't know what to tell you in a letter. And I couldn't face seeing you and having to explain things that I had no answers for. I don't know. I can't say anymore. There is no excuse. I'm so sorry. Your father—I mean, do you blame your father for any of this? Please try to realize it wasn't all my fault." She sobbed uncontrollably.

"What about Brian? Mitchell and Merrill—where are they now?" Joey asked. "When was the last time you saw them?" He let out a measured sigh between his teeth.

Beth put her finger up to her lips, trying to signal Joey. Nothing more needed to be said. Their mother was upset enough.

"The twins are still living with Myrt and Herb Matthews, and Brian is still living on that farm with the Vanderleest family. They are fine the last I heard." She sobbed even harder now. Her shoulders shook, and she appeared to have difficulty breathing.

Beth lay her hand on Alice's shoulder; Joey slowly put a hand on her other one.

"It's okay, Mom," said Beth. She nodded at Joey.

"Yes, Mom. It will be okay now," said Joey.

Alice continued to cry and Joey threw his arms around her neck and held her. Gramps came downstairs and plopped into his rocker. He yawned and tapped his pipe to empty it.

After she had calmed down, Joey asked, "What about this other man, Mom? Beth told me his name is Fred. And we have another brother and sister — is that right?"

"Yes, Joey. When all was said and done, Fred Simms was there for me during those years when your father wasn't. Yes, I had the twins and then two more babies by him — Kathy and Johnny. But Fred was mean and we split up recently. I can't even take care of Kathy and Johnny. I've been living on Welfare checks. The kids are staying in a foster home over in Black River." She paused for a moment and cleared her throat.

"My health is in bad shape, Joey. It's serious too. Didn't Beth tell you that? I've got what's called cirrhosis of the liver, and I've been in and out of Good Samaritan Hospital in Watertown for treatments." She pulled away from Joey and blew her nose even as she continued to cry.

"Fred never came to see me except that one time right after Welfare took Kathy and Johnny. I haven't heard from him since then. The State is looking for him to pay child support, but I also heard the people who have the kids are asking to adopt them, so he'll probably get away without paying once they find him."

"They should string him up when they find him," Gramps mumbled.

"All right, Old Man. That'll be enough out of you. We all know how you feel," Gram snapped.

Joey rubbed Alice's shoulder. "It'll be okay, Mom." Alice's tears dampened the side of his face. The smell of wine on her breath was overpowering.

This is my real mother no matter what, he thought.

"I'm sorry, Mom, but I'm still glad we got to do this. I want to ask more stuff, but I just can't — not now at least."

"It's good that Joey came when he did," said Beth. "We needed to have you explain some of these things, Mom."

"Yes, I know, and I don't blame you. It hurts so bad though, Beth." She looked at Joey. "No need to worry, Son. I'm going to sign the papers, but there is one thing you could do for your mom when you get in — that is, if you want to. It's entirely up to you. I need help,

Joey. I'm sick—I have no job and no money. I live off very little money the Welfare Department gives me each month. Gram and Gramps are doing all they can, but I just . . ."

"I'll do anything I can to help you, Mom. What is it?" Tears welled in his eyes and he blinked them back furiously.

Alice's eyes had dried and her voice returned to normal. "If you could request an allotment in my name, it would sure help out."

"Allotment? What is that again?"

"It's a small amount of money that you have the Marines take out of your paycheck every month, and it would come directly to me. It wouldn't have to be much. Can you do that for me, Son?"

Chapter Forty-Eight

Joey spent his last few days in Gouvernuer as close as he possibly could with his family. Old memories were discussed, while new ones were being created.

He had packed the night before and would be leaving for Long Island early next morning. The permission papers were signed by his mother and tucked away in his suitcase. Dinner was over and everybody sat outside on the front porch. Small talk had made the rounds three or four times when Joey nudged Beth with a gentle elbow to the ribs.

"Hey, Sis, want to go for a walk?"

"Yeah, sure, why not? We haven't done that in a long, long time, have we?"

"The last time I recall seeing you two head out towards town was when you went to the movies together, five or six years ago at Christmastime," said Gram.

"I think you're right," said Beth. "Anything you need from the market while we're down there, Gram?"

"Lillian, give Beth some change for some Prince Albert, since they're going," said Gramps.

"All right, Old Man." Gram went in the pocket of her dress and handed Beth some change. "And don't be gone too awful late, you two. Joey, you have to get up real early, you know."

"Uncle Glenn will be here at five to take you to Watertown," said Alice.

They took their time walking into town. Joey admired this and that along the way, things he had forgotten about. The sidewalks were tipped from tree roots and worn smooth from generations of baby buggy wheels, roller skates and leather-soled shoes. An old man sat on the front steps of the corner house, smoking a cigarette and drinking a beer. Joey waved and he waved back.

"It all seems so long ago," said Joey. "Nothing has really changed though, has it?"

"Nothing will ever change in this town, Joey. It's a real burg, in case you don't remember. Houses are small, streets are narrow, and television sets are rare." She giggled. "Are you thinking of coming back here after you get out of boot camp — or are you going back to Dad's place?"

"I don't know. I haven't really thought about that part. I guess it depends on a lot of stuff, but I definitely won't go back to Dad's place."

"Where then?"

"Well, gee, I don't know. Where will you be then? Are you leaving Gouvernuer?"

Beth shook her head. "I'm not sure."

"You'll be married. Where will you and Walter live?" He kicked a stone and slowed down a bit as he watched it land in a puddle of water.

"I'm not sure, Joey. It depends on a lot of stuff, like when Walt gets out of the Army and so on. He's close by over at Camp Drum right now, but that won't last forever."

"My boot camp is thirteen weeks long. I want to visit you, wherever you are when I get leave. You said you'll write to me, so tell me where you are and I'll come and see you."

"That's fair enough, Joey. I'll be sure to let you know."

He glanced sideways at her. "I don't know what to do right now. I mean, I told you I have a girlfriend, Dee. We love each other a lot. In fact, I didn't tell you before, but we are already talking about getting married."

"Married? Oh, Joey — you're much too young to get married."

"Me? How about you, Sis? You're going to have a baby already."

"Yes, but that's different. I'm older."

"I know, but if Mom is real sick, you might end up staying here after you get married, don't you think? And don't forget Gramps is not well either."

"They'll be all right, Joey. I can't do anything for Mom if she doesn't stop drinking that wine. The doctor told her that. Gram knows it too, but she keeps right on drinking with her. That's hard on Gramps too. Don't you know that? What am I supposed to do? I have to live my life just like you."

As they slowly approached the Strand Theatre, Joey stopped and stared up at the neon-lit marquee. *The Court Jester* with Danny Kaye was playing. "Do you remember the movie we saw the last time we were here, Beth?"

"Of course I do, Smarty. It was *The Day the Earth Stood Still* with that Michael Rennie guy."

"And Patricia Neal," said Joey.

"Yeah. Funny how we can remember that so well, isn't it?"

"It was a special treat, that's why. We were together again for a while. Just the two of us."

They continued to walk another block before Joey finally said, "I see what you mean about Mom's drinking. I don't know what we can do. It's just that everything is... everything in our family is so messed up. Dad drinks a lot too. It's not our fault though, is it, Sis?"

"Of course not, Joey. I made up my mind. I can't worry so much about it. Go ahead and go in the Marines. I'll write to you as soon as you let me know what your address is, okay?"

"Yeah, that will be great. You promise?"

"Yes, I promise."

·   ·   ·   ·   ·

The next morning Joey bid farewell to everybody.

"Goodbye, Gramps." They shook hands and hugged. "I'll miss you. Please take care of yourself. Don't try to do too much stuff that's bad for your heart, okay?"

"You take care too, Sonny. Show them Marines what you're made of. Your uncle was a fine soldier. He has five Purple Hearts. He sure did his share. You go and make your Uncle Glenn and all of us real proud of you, hear?"

"Yes, Gramps." He pointed to his grandfather's leg. "I know you did your share too. I'm going to do my best. I promise."

When he kissed his mother goodbye, Joey felt strange. It was as if they had just begun to know each other a little bit. He felt as though he should say more and maybe do something to comfort her. He hugged everybody, including Beth and then turned back to Alice.

"Mom, I want you to know that I do love you... and, I forgive you." They hugged again and Joey squeezed her hard. "I can't be mad at you. What good would that do? I even forgive Dad, even if it does sound like most of everything was his fault. I didn't tell you before, but he won't talk to me about anything from back then."

"I'm sorry, Son. I cannot explain your father; I never could. You just worry about yourself."

"I'll be back as soon as I can. Take care of yourself, please? And this time, keep your promise and write to me."

"I will, Joey. I'll do the best I can, Son. You've got your papers signed, so you're all set. Be careful you don't lose them on the way home. Make sure you take care of that allotment business, too — okay?" She kissed him, dried her eyes, then turned and left as quiet as smoke.

Uncle Glenn and Beth took Joey to the train depot. Joey hugged all of them and tried to ignore the tears in Beth's eyes when it was her turn. They held each other tight, not knowing when they would really see each other again.

"Please write to me, okay, Sis? I'll miss you so much. It seems like I just got here and now I'm leaving." He kissed her on the cheek. "Be sure to let me know how Kathy and our brothers are doing. Tell me about Mom, Gram and Gramps and you and Walter too. I want to know everything."

"I promise I will." Beth whispered.

Joey waved goodbye. While he boarded the train he read Beth's lips. As she waved she was mouthing, "I love you."

●　　　●　　　●　　　●　　　●

Connie picked Joey up at the train station about ten-thirty the night he got in at Grand Central. She hugged him and seemed happy to see him but wasted no time in fishing for all sorts of information as they drove home—especially regarding Alice. "What's she like? Was she nice to you?"

"Yeah, she was real nice," said Joey.

"Is she pretty?"

Joey glanced at her in the darkness of the car. "Yes... very pretty."

"Did she ask you about your father?"

"What do you mean?"

"Well, I mean, did she ask how your father was doing—if he was happy with me or not—that kind of thing?"

"Nope. Nothing like that, Mom. She didn't talk about either one of you. Why?"

Connie shook her head. "Just wondered, that's all. So tell me about your time up there. What did you do?"

•　　•　　•　　•　　•

Joey's nerves were all a-jangle anticipating seeing Dee. By the time he got home it was much too late to run over to her house, but he called to let her know he was home. They would meet at school in the morning. He decided he'd take her over to visit their special spot in the park.

What am I going to say? How can I tell her I've joined the Marines without making her cry? Maybe I should wait for a week or two. No... I better just do it right away and get it over with. But what will I do if she gets real mad about it?

His eyes closed that night, but he slept very little.

•　　•　　•　　•　　•

According to Connie, the days had been warm and sunny around Huntington while he was gone. It was a perfectly clear blue autumn sky with an October temperature in the high sixties that next day. The touch of wind was cool, but it seemed almost hot. Dee waited just inside the front doors at the school. She was dressed in a dark pleated skirt and boots and a burgundy sweater with a colorful scarf around her neck. Her hair was done, her makeup perfect.

Joey blushed as he slipped his arm around her waist. All he could manage was a whispery,

"Hi."

"Hi, yourself, stranger." Dee gushed.

Joey's palms were sweating and his heart was beating so fast he thought it might burst and send blood spewing everywhere. Lots of kids were walking by, so he couldn't chance kissing her, but they squeezed hands and gazed in each other's eyes for a moment.

Dee said, "I can hardly wait to talk. I want to ask you so many things. I'll bet you have all kinds of stuff to tell me too, huh?"

"Yes, I do, so like we said last night, meet me right here for lunch, okay?"

"I will." She said as she clung to his arm and smiled. "What's your mom like though? I'll bet she's nice. You have to tell me everything."

"Yeah, she's real nice, Listen, I've got lots to tell you, but let's wait 'til lunch, okay?"

The bell rang.

"Oops! Looks like I will have to wait, huh?" said Dee.

"See you at lunch. We can meet in front of school."

"Okay, but wait a second." She tugged on his jacket and pulled him around a corner holding another bank of lockers. She kissed him lightly on the lips and Joey kissed her full on the lips. He glanced around and pulled her in. His heart skipped a beat as he felt her softness in his arms once again. The special feeling he had missed for a few days, that seemed like months, was there again.

She quickly looked in his eyes and whispered, "Oh, I missed you so much, Joe."

"I know what you mean. I thought about you all the time, especially at night. I love you too, Dee. We better hurry. Let's go to the park at lunch time, okay?"

"Yeah, that will be great."

•   •   •   •   •

When lunch time rolled around, Joe put his arm around her waist and they strolled to the park. He steered her to their favorite spot under the maple tree that held their initials. They kissed again, and it was a long deep one. Joe eased her down onto the bench and sat next to her. "Dee, I felt awful bad when I left you to go upstate. You know that, don't you?"

"Of course, and I'm sure I felt twice as bad. But it was worth it. It was important for you to meet your mom. We both know that." She caressed his hand and gave him the smile he missed so much. "So, come on, tell me — what's she like?"

"Uh, well, she's nice, all right. She was real happy to see me and told me things about why her and my dad split up — stuff like that, you know."

"And... ?"

"And, what?"

"And, why did they break up? Tell me more — come on."

"Ah, it's a long story. Listen to me for a minute. I have something real important to tell you first, okay?" His face was inches away as he searched her eyes — eyes so happy and excited. He would give anything to have her keep smiling as she was at that very moment, but he knew it wasn't possible. He needed to hold her as tight as possible to ward off the inevitable.

"Okay — okay, Mr. Serious — go ahead. Geez! What is it?" She squeezed his hands and giggled.

There was a moment of silence while he wrestled with guilt. His heart dropped into his stomach. "Well... first of all... you know I love you — right?"

"Yes, of course." Her face suddenly turned to stone as she got up from the bench. "Oh, oh. I smell something coming that I won't like, Joe. Are you breaking up with me — is that what you want to tell me?" Tears glistened in her eyes and she began to shake.

"No! What? No, no!" He jumped to his feet. "Why would I do that? I just told you — I love you, Dee. I could never break up with you."

"So, what is it then? What is so important, Joe?" She looked so serious.

He placed his hands on her shoulders. "Listen—you know how bad I want to get out of my house, right? I told you what goes on there—you know all of that."

"Yes, Joe. So, what is it?"

He continued to search for the right words. "And, well, we both know that we're going to get married some day, right?"

Dee smiled at that. "Yes. I know, and it makes me so happy. Oh, did I tell you Mom gave me a complete set of dishes for my hope chest?"

"That's nice." He squeezed her hand and paused. "Dee, please listen, and try to understand." He sat back down.

She shook her head, making a rueful comic face. "Understand what?"

His eyes lowered to stare at his feet. "I'm joining the Marines."

She shot him a look of pained amusement and laughed. "You're kidding, right?"

Joey shook his head and his brows furrowed. He raised his eyes to her face and felt a strange shiver pass over himself from head to toe, making his scalp tighten and his fingers tingle. Bracing his hands on his knees as if to balance himself against the shifting of the world beneath him, he said, "No. I joined."

Dee's face settled into stubborn lines that slid into a sulk. "That's impossible. You can't do that." She appeared to be in shock—her features drawing tight. "You're not old enough."

He wanted to make himself very small and disappear. "Well, yes I am old enough if my parents sign their permission—and they did."

She turned her face into his shoulder and squeezed her eyes shut against the tears, forcing them past her lashes to roll down her cheek and soak into his black T-shirt.

"Please don't do this, Joe. You can't! Tell them you changed your mind, that's all."

He took a long breath and shook his head. "No, Dee. I can't do that. This is the best way for me. There'll be time for us to get married when I come home from boot camp." He reached out and brushed the tips of his fingers against her cheek, pushing a stray strand of auburn hair back behind her ear. "I love you."

Dee was sobbing when she surged to her feet. "No, Joe! You don't love me or you wouldn't do this to me. How could you?"

"That's not true. I do love you. I just have to do this. Why can't you understand?"

Dee was still crying when she whirled around and glared at him over her shoulder as she ran towards the school.

$$\bullet \qquad \bullet \qquad \bullet \qquad \bullet \qquad \bullet$$

They didn't talk for three days. Dee didn't come to school and wouldn't return his phone calls. Her mother was polite on the phone, but curt. Joe could tell that her parents were upset with him and that made things worse. He hurt inside but felt helpless. But there was plenty to occupy his time as he officially quit school and made preparations to leave for Parris Island and boot camp in late November of 1956.

During the weeks that followed, the atmosphere around his house was one of awkward apprehension, with the entire family making it crystal clear that he would be missed. Darren was jealous of Joey's escape and had been hounding Connie about letting him quit school to go into the Air Force. At one point, Connie had glared at Joey and said, "See what you've started here?"

Within a week, Dee and Joe had things patched up between them and saw each other almost every evening. Dee was never happy with having to wait, but agreed to put off marriage until the following year when Joey would be home on his first leave. Many hours were spent together. There was a lot of heavy petting, but they never had the opportunity to reach the stage of having sex.

Dee's parents appeared to understand Joey's decision to join the Marines and treated him as a future son-in-law.

On the day he left town, the first hint of morning turned the sky a pearly gray. That Thursday, November 20th, 1956 did not seem to bode well, weather-wise.

Neither Connie nor Joe was able to take off work without losing pay, so consequently hugs and goodbyes were handled the night before by everyone.

Dee's father picked Joey up at six-thirty in the morning. He dropped him off in New York City at the Armed Forces Induction Center. Dee didn't come along to see him off. She had sobbed the night before and said she couldn't face seeing him leave.

At eight-thirty that morning, in New York City Joey raised his right hand and was sworn into the United States Marine Corps.

It was goodbye to many things—New York State and his family, including both those living upstate as well as those on Long Island. He would leave behind four brothers, two sisters, three step-brothers, a step-sister, and the first love of his life.

It was the beginning of a new life for Joe Harrison Jr. —one that would be of his own making.

Epilogue

The Harrison family story is based on true events occurring between 1937 and 1998. The events that took shape after 1956 could be categorized as incredible to say the least.

On July 30th, 1961, the central character, Joe (Joey), was a twenty-two-year-old Marine stationed in California when his mother, Alice, died from cirrhosis of the liver. She was just forty years old.

From 1957 until Alice's passing in 1961, Joe Junior kept his word and arranged for government allotment checks to be mailed to her every month. He came home on emergency leave for her funeral held in Watertown, New York.

Beth, Gram, Aunt Betty, Uncle Glenn and two additional aunts named Evelyn and Mannie also attended Alice's services in Gouverneur, New York.

Before passing, Alice had signed legal papers for her two youngest children, Johnny and Kathy to be adopted by their foster parents who had been raising them from infancy. Both were under six years of age at the time, and none of the other five siblings would meet Johnny or Kathy for nearly thirty-five years.

Gramps passed away two years before Alice on June 2nd, 1959. He suffered a heart attack. Gram followed six years later on January 4th, 1965. She also died from natural causes (and probably a broken heart.) Aunt Betty died of heart failure in 1989 and Uncle Glenn passed away from cancer in 1995.

Fred Simms died in 1971 of heart failure. Although he fathered the twins as well as Kathy and Johnny, he had no contact with any of them for many years prior to his death. The subsequent histories of the foster parents, Bushkin, Couzens, and Roderick are unknown, as is that of the Children's Home supervisors, Jeff Neagle and his wife, also Joey's housemother, affectionately known as Ma Alexander.

In 1954 Beth married Walter and moved to Long Island with their firstborn, Lori. Two years later, her second child was born—a son—who they named Steven. Beth would give birth to two additional daughters in the years that followed and named them Alissa and Linda.

Walter was a full-time fireman when Beth went to school at night to study nursing. She finished her schooling and became a Registered Nurse. However, her marriage to Walter would end after twelve years and Beth would raise her children as a single mother. Walter left the area for parts unknown and never reappeared or paid child support.

Beth and her father lived less than twenty miles from each other, but unfortunately they rarely talked before his death in 1969.

Joe junior did not marry Dee. There was a lot of letter-writing back and forth, but within a year of his departure to Parris Island, the fire slowly went out and both she and Joe were in other relationships. Their paths would never cross again. However, twenty-two years later, in 1978, Joe would hear that Dee had married and bore two children before an eventual divorce.

Joe and sister, Beth, had stayed in touch and spoke by telephone frequently. In addition, they wrote to each other on a regular basis and he stayed with Beth and her family whenever he was home on leave—usually at Christmastime.

Joe served two consecutive four-year hitches in the Marines and then, after his discharge in 1964, went to Chicago, Illinois. He settled down in the windy city and attended Columbia College at night under the G.I. Bill and majored in journalism. Working during the day as a room clerk for the Ambassador and Drake hotels, he met his wife, Patricia, in 1965, and their son, Joe III, was born in 1967. The boy died in a freak accident in 1981 caused by blunt force trauma from a loose bowling ball inside a car.

·　　·　　·　　·　　·

As the years passed, Neither Joe nor Beth connected with their other siblings until July of 1969, when their father, Joe Senior, suffered a massive heart attack that took his life. He was fifty years old and working as a youth counselor for troubled teens in Suffolk County on Long Island at the time of his death. How or why he managed to acquire that position was never made clear by Connie who attended the funeral but did not associate with any of Joe's children. She and her children moved away and were never heard from again by any of the Harrison family.

Beth and Joe decided they should do everything possible to track down their siblings. Beth started making phone calls and found out that Myrt and Herb Matthews never did adopt Mitchell and Merrill. Both boys went to Ithaca State University in New York and majored in Journalism. Myrt, being in constant contact with the boys, gave Mitch's phone number to Beth. From there, Beth pressed forward, and with her brother joe, located brother Brian and made him aware of Joe his father's passing.

Mitchell, Merrill, Brian and Joe Junior were pall bearers for the funeral in that summer of '69. The twins were still unaware that Joe was not their biological father.

After the funeral a lot of catching up was done by all before the siblings separated again. Backgrounds were exchanged.

While attending high school, the twins had worked as disc jockeys for sock hops in the Watertown area under the name of "The Top Tune Twins." They took business and journalism courses at Ithaca State University then joined the Army. When they were discharged, Mitch, had attained the rank of Major and Merrill was an enlisted man.

After their discharge, Merrill worked at radio station WRVA, in Wheeling, West Virginia as a newsmen and later went to work for Associated Press's Washington Bureau. His job in the eighties was to shadow Ronald Reagan for newsworthy information. He has been at AP for almost forty years and announced his retirement in December of 2017. He lives with his wife, Terry, and has a daughter named Kelby

•   •   •   •   •

After his military service Mitch went to work for the government t Fort Lee Virginia. He worked for twenty-two years as Manager of Food Services for all of the armed forces. After retirement he developed his own company and still tours the country as a professor -giving lectures on food management for various corporations. He still resides in Virginia and has speaking engagements each year, around the country. He is married with a daughter, Amy, a son, Jimmy and two grandchildren.

Brian had been living at a foster home/ farm until he was eighteen. From there he worked various jobs and earned his tuition for college at Syracuse University. He graduated with honors and ultimately took a position as the Director for the New York State Water Authority. He was single at the time of Joe's death. Years later he would marry and have a son named Mark.

•   •   •   •   •

After the funeral a lot of catching up was done by all before the siblings separated again.

While attending high school, the twins had worked as disc jockeys for sock hops in the Watertown area under the name of *"The Top Tune Twins."* They took business and journalism courses at Ithaca State University then joined the Army. When they were discharged, Mitch, had attained the rank of Colonel and Merrill was enlisted man.

After his discharge, the twins worked at radio station WRVA, in Wheeling, West Virginia as a newsmen and Merrill later took a reporters position at Associated Press's Washington Bureau. His job in the eighties was to shadow Ronald Reagan for newsworthy information. He has been at AP for almost forty years and announced his retirement in December of 2017. He lives with his wife, daughter and granddaughter in The Washington D. C. area.

After his military service Mitch went to work for the government as a civilian at Fort Lee Virginia. He worked for twenty-two years as Manager of Food Services for all of the armed forces. After retirement he developed his own company and still tours the country as a professor -giving lectures on food management for various corporations. He still resides in Virginia and has speaking engagements each year around the country. He is married with a daughter, a son and two grandchildren.

Brian had lived on the Vanderleest farm until he was eighteen.

From there he worked various jobs and earned his tuition for college. He graduated with honors and ultimately took a position as the Director for the New York State Water Authority. He was not married at the time of Joe's death. Years later he would marry and have a son named Mark.

•   •   •   •   •

At their father's funeral service, phone numbers and addresses were exchanged and everyone agreed that someday it would be nice to have a family reunion.

From that day forward, everyone spoke on rare occasion on the phone, but nothing was done about a reunion.

Finally, on July 13th, 1992, nearly, twenty-five years after Joe's passing, a family reunion was held in Virginia Beach, Virginia. It was hosted by Uncle Glenn's daughter, Glenda and everybody was in attendance including Joe and his wife and son, Beth and her husband and three children, Mitchell, his wife and two children, Merrill, his wife and daughter, Brian and his wife and son, Aunt Betty had passed away a year earlier, but Uncle Glenn and son were there.

Also, in attendance were Aunt Evelyn and her children, Aunt Mannie and her family and many previously unknown cousins including Bill Savage and wife, Trish, as well as Sharon Card and family. Kathy and Johnny Gaines were not available at the time but would attend all future reunions.

Fantastic food as well as catching up were the order of the day for everyone in that summer of 1992. Tears were in many eyes before, during and after the reunion. Mitchell and his wife hosted that next reunion in Virginia.

He said a prayer then proposed this memorable toast:

"Here's to all of us — one big family, together at last. Kathy and Johnny are not with us, but we know they will be next year one way or the other."

Mitch paused and looked around the crowd. Everyone could see the tears in his eyes and hear them in his voice as he proudly stated, "Alice must be looking down on us right now and smiling."

Everyone cheered.

Before they parted company that glorious day, all agreed that it would not be the last reunion. And it wasn't. There have been Harrison family reunions every year for the past twenty-six years. Each year it is held in a different location. Every sibling takes their turn having it at their homes--- whether it be in Virginia, New York, Pennsylvania or Michigan.

View other Black Rose Writing titles at www.blackrosewriting.com/books and use

promo code **PRINT** to receive a **20% discount** when purchasing.

BLACK ROSE
writing™

CPSIA information can be obtained
at www.ICGtesting.com
Printed in the USA
BVHW03s1748010918
526221BV00001B/1/P

9 781684 331208